OTHER BOOKS BY
BRITTANY M. WILLOWS

THE CALYPSIS SAGA
The Calypsis Project
The Calypsis Project II: Rebirth
We Have Each Other (A TCP Short Story)

THE CARDPLAY DUOLOGY
Bloody Spade
Bleeding Heart

BLEEDING HEART

THE CARDPLAY DUOLOGY: BOOK TWO

By Brittany M. Willows

CONTENT ADVISORY

Please proceed at your own discretion. This book contains content that may be sensitive to some readers, such as . . .

- Coarse language
- Blood and violence, some gore
- Moments of graphic violence
- On-page character death
- Mild sexual content
- Body horror, eye trauma
- Vomiting
- Grief/bereavement
- Anxiety, PTSD, panic attacks
- Trauma related to kidnapping/physical abuse
- Parent death (mentioned)
- Car accident (mentioned)

ISBN 978-0-9936472-8-4 (ebook)
ISBN 978-0-9936472-9-1 (paperback)

Cover illustration by Brittany M. Willows

Proofread by E.M. Wright

For those still finding themselves

ACT I

BEHIND THE VEIL

CHAPTER ONE
NOVEMBER 22, 2027 | LILLIDALE PARK

FATE LED TO NO SINGULAR DESTINATION. One had many possible fates, a vast web of opportunity and misfortune traveled by way of decision. Some strings drew people together, others led them apart. Many stretched long, while many more were unfortunately cut short.

Generally, these strings would be left to weave the fabric of reality unseen and undisturbed. Once an eon, however, threads tended to run astray, and an earthbound individual would be granted *sight* in order to reweave this delicate tapestry through action. Through guidance and conversation, by being at the right place at the right time.

Not all strings were visible at all times, and it was impossible to discern the precise ends and crossroads to which they may lead. Pull too hard, and the whole thing could come unraveled. But with a delicate hand, wayward strings could be corrected. Balance restored.

One such string had led Hikaru Ritsuo to Lillidale Park. It stretched on ahead of him, shimmering faintly as the earliest hints of daybreak cast the world in monochrome. And waiting at the end was a portly man on a bench. His waxed cotton jacket had been dusted in snow, his bulbous nose reddened by the cold.

Hikaru halted under the cone of lamplight, leather driving glove scrunching around the lacquered handle of his cane—carved into the shape of a lion's bust. "Unusual for you to call on me in the small hours. Should I be worried, Clive?"

Clive Gardner, Chief of the Hildegrand Police Department. Their strings had become entwined over two decades prior, when Gardner had been assigned as his training officer. Together they'd weathered many a storm, the greatest of all being the Reemergence—the event that ended Hikaru's policing career, and set him on the path to become headmaster of the world's first magic academy and emergency response unit.

"This makes us even," grumbled the man, slugging back a dose of caffeine from his piping paper cup. Shy a full eight hours rest, no amount of coffee could remedy his mood. He indicated the drink tray between them as Hikaru lowered himself to the bench. "Got your tea. Sorry I couldn't get it in one of those tiny china cups you like so much."

There was a falter in his teasing remark that forewarned of grim tidings, and when Hikaru lifted his own cup from the tray, he noted an abnormal protrusion on the bottom. Hard, rectangular, crinkling at his touch.

A flash drive taped to the cup's concave underside.

He set it in his lap. "Clive, why have you asked me here?"

Gardner stared across the park. "We're being taken off the case. Got an order to relinquish all files to the National Guard. Evidence logs, victim statements, interrogation transcripts . . ." Those must've been the documents on the flash drive. "Do with that what you will. This is as far as I go."

The news settled heavily in Hikaru's chest. He couldn't blame Gardner for bowing out. If he were caught working a case he'd been ordered to drop, it would be more than his job on the line. He could be convicted, lose his pension. The people they were up against wielded too much power, too many contingency plans, and years of careful preparation behind them.

The board belonged to Charles Wiseman, and his subordinates were his pieces to play. Right now, his queen—Valerie Renard, president of the Wiseman Corporation—was fulfilling her role as scapegoat. She'd taken the fall for the founder's crimes while he played the bamboozled businessman, going so far as to emerge from his hermitage to publicly condemn her actions.

"This is obscene," he'd told the papers. *"Never in my wildest dreams,"* he'd told the news. *"Devastated,"* was how he described his reaction to learning of Valerie's betrayal.

As the story went, she'd approached Blackjack of her own accord and supplied the late Kane Kros with the tools for his inhumane experiments, the goal being to weaponize the dark magic of the Void. And who could refute her when every Blackjack operative arrested in the raid corroborated her story? There wasn't even an iota of DNA to place Wiseman at the complex. According to the city gatekeepers, he hadn't set foot in Hildegrand since the Reemergence.

With the evidence overwhelmingly in his favor, the Crown had been inclined to accept Valerie Renard's confession. Hikaru had to wonder whether they genuinely believed her or were too scared to confront the possibility that they had a monster in their midst.

If the public knew the man who gave them the technology to suppress and combat magic was the same who instigated its violent return, there would be outrage. But all they had to go on were the claims of three Empowered youth: a disgraced icon, a young woman who'd previously been roped into serving Blackjack herself, and the boy thief at the start of it all.

Taking care not to divulge their shared secret—that Wiseman had hunted them for their legendary power—each had provided a victim statement. Lacking the proof to reinforce them, however, those statements held little merit. And with the case now switching hands, the whole scandal would likely be swept under the rug.

Their faces flashed across Hikaru's mind: Alexander Jane, Kyani Oto, Iori Ryone. All made to recount their trauma for naught. "What am I supposed to tell them?"

"I don't know, Ritsuo. You're the wordsmith, not me." Gardner thumbed the tab on his cup's lid, freeing a wisp of steam. "I've gotta warn you, some of the footage we scraped from the Blackjack servers is distressing. They documented Oto's procedure from start to finish; sixteen videos over the span of a month. Your boy's, on the other hand . . ."

Recalling how Alexander had come out of that place, how long they'd held him there, Hikaru closed his eyes in anticipation of the blow. "How many?"

"You don't want to know."

"I have to watch them regardless, Clive. How many?"

Several long seconds ticked by.

"Sixty-seven."

The number squeezed Hikaru's heart.

"There are more," Gardner added gruffly. "Seems Kros kept a private collection for his personal entertainment. Sick bastard." He sipped his coffee, allowing Hikaru a moment to digest the information. To let it sink in and filter through so he could focus on a solution.

There'd been no indication that he had strayed onto the wrong path. If this was where he was meant to be, then the strings would soon lead him to another crossroads. Another decision to make.

"You've got that look in your eye," observed Gardner.

"I don't have a *look*."

"You do. It's the reason I gave you that flash drive." A solemn smile passed over his stubbled lips. "It's also why you would've made an excellent detective. If there's anything in those files that can connect Charles Wiseman to this mess, you'll be the one to find it. But proceed with caution. People like him don't hesitate to eliminate threats, and those Jane kids were orphaned once already. If things get too hot, I'd advise you leave well enough alone." Gardner rose from the bench, dusting the snow off his jacket. "Take care of yourself, Ritsuo. Give Elizabeth my best."

Hikaru gave a short nod. "Thank you. For all you've done."

With a final firm pat of Hikaru's shoulder, Gardner left the lamp's warm pool of color and lumbered off into the monochrome dawn.

In certain cases, yes, withdrawing to avoid further harm would be the wisest decision. That wasn't an option here. This case was bigger than abductions, bigger than human experimentation. Not even Hikaru could see the full picture yet, and the portion he'd unveiled for Cardplay was smaller still, but if he allowed the dark forces at play to have their way, this world would be doomed to a dismal fate.

Magic, Keepers, the Domain, and the Void . . . Much as he valued the opinion of his former superior, Chief Gardner didn't have the knowledge to counsel him on this.

What he knew barely scratched the surface.

CHAPTER TWO
NOVEMBER 22 | JANE RESIDENCE

NORMALCY. The word had gained popularity after the Reemergence. Everyone longed for it, tried to reclaim it as if lost. But their world was ever-evolving, and Ellen Amelia Jane was determined to prove that they could prosper in the new magical state of normal they found themselves in.

Today, that mission continued with a meeting.

Ellen drew the white locks from above her ears and tied them back with a silky black ribbon. Tugging the bow to secure it, she smoothed the pleats of her skirt, buttoned her beige sweater, and crossed the hall from bath to bedroom.

"Iori, if you don't get up soon, we're going to be late," she addressed the mound of blankets on the bed. A furry black tail poked out from the bottom, and a mop of curls the same shade from the top. Hoping the light would spur him into motion, she whipped open the balcony curtains and let the sun pour in.

A sugary layer of snow coated the balcony's wooden deck and railing. It was rare for snow to settle in the southernmost regions of Amethis, so to have two considerable snowfalls in the past week was a beautiful irregularity. Ellen chose to view it as a good omen.

"Looks like it's going to be a nice day, don't you think?"

A grunt emanated from the blankets. Rather than encourage wakefulness, the daylight had driven Iori further into hiding. He'd pulled his tail under the duvet and hauled it fully over his head. They'd been granted a few days off to recoup after raiding the Blackjack complex, but their period of rest and relaxation was over.

Ellen parted from the wintry vista to nudge the lazy lump. "We're leaving in an hour. If you want to shower and eat, you need to get moving."

The lump didn't budge.

Cheeks puffed in disapproval, she grabbed two fistfuls of duvet. "Rise and shine!" She ripped the covers off, and her playfulness receded when Iori curled into a tighter ball, ears flat and tail hugging his legs. Bundling the duvet in her lap, Ellen sat on the side of the mattress. From what she could see past the barrier of his arms, he looked ghostly pale. "That nightmare last night really shook you up, huh?"

She took his lack of response as confirmation.

"Do you wanna talk about it?"

"Not particularly."

He seldom did, but she always asked. She knew these terrors had plagued him for years, had witnessed him battling them in his sleep for as long as they'd shared this house. This bed. And in the months since discovering Charles Wiseman was alive, they'd worsened. She wasn't sure of the best method to dispel the lingering malaise; however, after the car accident that orphaned her and her brother, she'd learned that a hearty breakfast in good company worked wonders.

She leaned over, catching Iori's gaze. The black and deep crimson of his right eye had become a hollow pit in the shadowy crook of his arm. "Would pancakes cheer you up?" she asked, coaxing a soft huff of amusement out of him.

"I appreciate the effort. I'll pass." His tail's tense curve loosened somewhat, but still he made no move to rise.

"A shower could be refreshing," Ellen suggested.

"You're not going to stop until I'm up, are you?"

"Nope." She popped the P.

Iori drove a sluggish heel into her hip. One last act of defiance. "Alright, alright." He dragged himself from his pillow, its creases imprinted on his cheek. "I'm up. You can go."

Ellen rocked to her feet. "I'll see if Alexander can give us a ride. Spare us the walk." She placed the duvet in a heap by the footboard, then left Iori to get ready and headed for the neighboring bedroom.

The last thing she expected her brother to be doing the morning after being discharged from the infirmary was cleaning, but there he was, sorting through a mountain of papers on his desk. The rest of the room was in a similar state of upheaval. Clothes piled on his bed, furniture partially rearranged, computer monitors askew and unplugged.

"What're you doing?" asked Ellen, hovering in the doorway.

He dropped another wad of papers into an overflowing wastebasket. "Just some reorganizing."

Ellen retrieved one of the discarded pages. Instantly, she recognized the logo at the top. The shield, the crossed swords, the crown. The other documents in the bin were stamped with it, too. "This is all your Ulridge stuff . . . Are you throwing these out?"

Since childhood, Alexander had dreamed of enrolling at the prestigious military academy and becoming a soldier. Sure, those dreams had also been crushed by a rejection letter citing his Empowered status, but did that really warrant erasing such a significant phase of his life?

No remorse or resentment disturbed his expression. In fact, he looked more content than she'd seen him in ages. "You don't need to sound so sad."

"Ulridge was important to you. Getting rejected doesn't mean you have to give up on it. You can reapply in—"

"I'm not giving up," Alexander interrupted gently. His focus slid to the metallic foil logo on the large yellow envelope in his grasp. "The National Guard aren't what they used to be. The Reemergence transformed them into something ugly and hateful . . . Or maybe that's how they always were, and the Reemergence just brought it to the surface. Point is, I wanted to make a difference, and I will. But change has to happen on the inside first." Was he talking about them, or himself? "In the meantime, I'll do what I can here."

A tiny flourish of pyric magic set the envelope aflame, and Ellen let out a futile whimper as a wave of crackling orange devoured the paper. Whatever his reasoning, it saddened her to see things he used to hold dear reduced to ashes.

"It's okay, really," he assured her, firelight dancing in his golden eyes. "It's freeing, like burning your ex's stuff."

"Says the guy with zero exes."

"You get the idea." He snuffed his conjured flames before they triggered the smoke alarm and dropped the half-charred envelope into the trash. "Did you need me for something?"

Her brain buffered. "Oh, right." She knew she'd come here with a purpose. "I was wondering if you could give me and Iori a ride to headquarters?"

"Sure. I was gonna join you, actually. I want to ask Hikaru about getting reinstated."

Reinstated? Already? He was discharged *yesterday* after four days of rest, prior to which he'd been in captivity for nearly five months. It hadn't even been a full twenty-four hours since he got home.

"Don't you think that's a little . . . soon?"

Alexander moved to the clothes heaped on the bed, hair falling into his face as he bent to rifle through them. He swept it behind his ear. "Don't worry, I'm not planning on jumping straight into field work. Thinking I might help out in the arena." The strands he'd tucked away fell loose again. He combed them back. More fell forward, and he swore under his breath.

Ellen giggled. "How about I give you a trim so you don't go to Hikaru looking like a bum?"

With the bathroom occupied, the shower hissing in the background, Ellen set her brother up on a kitchen stool and broke out the hairdressing kit. The scissors' pointed tips glinted in the rays streaming in from the patio doors.

"So, what'll it be? Wanna go back to your old cut, or try something new?" Ellen ran her fingers through his hair. Where once it had been straightened and cropped to the nape of his neck, it now fell past his jawline in loose, shaggy waves.

"Let's just take a little off the ends. Tidy it up."

"You sure?"

"Yeah. That old cut required too much maintenance." He used to spend close to an hour washing and styling it each morning. "Besides," he said. "I kinda like it long. You could say it's *grown* on me."

Ellen cringed. "The comedy committee should revoke your joking privileges."

"Hey, come on, that was decent."

"In a circle of dads, maybe." Ellen took her scissors and comb and began to trim the excess fringe. "I like it this length, too. Makes you look distinguished."

Intermittent snips and cheerful humming filled the kitchen in lieu of conversation. Exciting as a life touched by mystical powers could be, these were the moments Ellen had come to appreciate most—tending to mundane tasks in the company of family and friends, where the purest magic was in the bonds they shared. No matter how topsy-turvy the world became, she could always rely on them to carry her through it.

The shower squeaked off upstairs. Fringe tidied, Ellen moved behind Alexander and spotted him twiddling his thumbs.

"Do you want to know why I decided to go back so soon?" he asked quietly. Well-acquainted with her curiosity, he didn't need to wait for a reply. "All I've done these past few months is *think*. About you, about Cardplay . . . I can't be cooped up with my thoughts anymore, Ellen. I need a distraction."

She'd figured as much. He'd always buried his troubles under work instead of dealing with them proactively, which was why his eagerness worried her. If he bottled up the hurt, the anger, and the trauma Blackjack had inflicted on him, it would inevitably lead to another blowup like at the charity ball.

But as he continued, her concern lessened.

"I'd also prefer to be around the people I care about. Part of the reason I'm simplifying my routine is so I can actually *be here* and don't miss out on more than I already have."

"You didn't miss much," said Ellen. Nothing he would have wanted to be present for. She took another white lock between her fingers.

"I did, though. It's small stuff, mostly, but it matters to me. There've been changes around HQ, there were interviews I was supposed to do. I also missed just being with you guys. Not to mention, my little sister getting her first boyfriend."

The scissors skipped upwards, chopping off a significantly larger chunk of hair than intended. Blushing furiously, Ellen did her best to amend the error as she sputtered out a hasty response. "W-what are you talking about?"

"You and Iori." Alexander twisted slightly. With her cheeks burning hot as they were, she was grateful he hadn't turned far enough to see. "Aren't you two together?"

"It's not like that," she insisted. "We're friends."

"Sorry, I shouldn't make assumptions. Seeing how you interacted at dinner just made me think something was going on there." After an awkward beat of silence, he added, "Even if you're not into him, he's pretty obviously into you."

Ellen frowned. "What makes you say that?"

"Because he looks at you the same way Aryel looks at Naomi. The same way Mom and Dad looked at each other." Now he twisted fully around to face her. "Have you seriously not noticed?"

She averted her gaze to the clippings on the floor, feeling awfully exposed. "No," she told him, and it tasted like a lie on her tongue—perhaps because he wasn't the first to point it out. Her memory rewound to the night of the ball, to her friends ambushing her at the banquet table and teasing her about sparks after she'd waltzed with Iori.

"There's no denying it; that boy's got a crush on you . . ."

How could she be so certain?

". . . and I bet you've got a crush on him too."

At the time, Ellen had shrugged it off as Tatiana being Tatiana and playing matchmaker. But for *Alexander* of all people to mention it . . .

What could everyone else see that Ellen couldn't?

Shaking her head to clear it, she forcibly turned her brother's away from her. "I don't know what you think you're seeing, but nothing else is there. Now keep still or you're going to end up with bald spots."

CHAPTER THREE
NOVEMBER 22 | CARDPLAY HEADQUARTERS

AFTER BREAKFAST, ELLEN THREW ON HER PEACOAT, boots, and a chunky knit scarf and hopped into the passenger seat of her brother's sedan, quietly obsessing over what he'd said whilst Iori hassled him about his choice of radio station from the rear.

The bad blood between the boys may have been settled, but it'd take time for them to properly warm up to each other.

When they arrived at Cardplay Headquarters, rolling to a stop at the curb, the yard was already packed. Between the day and nightshift Jokers and the regular staff, not a single parking spot had been left unfilled, and several more vehicles sat in stalled rotation in the circular drive.

Following Alexander's disappearance, Joker training had been put on an indefinite suspension. With his safe return and the dissolution of Blackjack, that suspension had been lifted, and the students, freed from school for the winter holidays, had come to resume their training.

Ellen emerged from the car's cozy interior. "*Brrr,*" she said through chattering teeth, the warmth she'd soaked up from the heated seats gone in an instant. "It's so cold."

Iori exited behind her, retrieving his duffel bag from the backseat. "Don't know what you expected." He stuffed his hands into the pockets of his thin leather jacket. "It's winter, and you decided to wear a skirt and tights."

"They're *leggings*, and they're fleecy!"

"Not fleecy enough, apparently."

"You're one to talk. Your jeans have holes in them!" Ellen gestured to the weathered rips across his knees.

Smirking, Iori stooped to her level and said in a purr of a voice, "I'm not the one complaining about the cold."

Ellen's mind blanked at the closeness of his face, and in a heinous act of treachery, her body saturated her cheeks with warmth.

Beep-beep.

Saved by the chirp of her brother's car locking. Dressed more appropriately for the weather than either of them in his fully intact pants and shearling jacket, he led them up the driveway, the wrought iron entry gates rattling open at the flash of his ID card.

Already, the snow was beginning to melt under the rising sun. Clumps slid off the mansion's mansard roof, plopping into the shrubs below, and a pitter-patter like rain filled the leafless cherry tree grove encircling the property.

The students were enjoying it while it lasted. The five of them scampered about the side yard, engaged in a snowball fight. A tall boy called Aziz ducked behind a tree as the Hein twins, Haden and Sem—identical in both appearance and magic type—pelted it with frozen projectiles. The other two, Xiaolin and Layla, exchanged blows on the run.

With no increase in Empowered since last autumn and their most recent enrollment being almost two years ago, these kids were predicted to be Cardplay's final class. While they could still receive new enrollments from previously-documented Empowered, it seemed magic was a gift bestowed upon a select few, and many had chosen to stifle it.

Fortunately, Cardplay had a small but brilliant percentage of the Empowered population on their roster, and all would be present for today's meeting. A few loitered in the yard and on the porch, the door guards an audience to their conversations but never taking part. Still as statues they remained, committed wholly to their duty.

Spotting the trio on approach, Alexander's friends and fellow First Classers departed from the porch, Ikkei Toi pausing to stamp out a cigarette. His dark attire had a splash of blue to match his dyed faux hawk, but black hair and black clothes almost made a silhouette of his sister Naomi. Even her arm sling was black. And in contrast to them both, her boyfriend Aryel Rizka wore pastel colors.

"Good morning," he sang. "And what a glorious morning it is!"

A fan of neither the cold nor the snow, Alexander responded flatly, "I beg to differ."

"Don't be a grouch," chided Ikkei. "Give us some love."

The group shared hugs and pleasantries, Iori retreating to the sidelines to avoid getting sucked into the throng. He hadn't quite spread his social butterfly wings yet, but Naomi made sure he wasn't excluded.

"*Osuri*," she greeted him cheerily in Jeidish.

He offered her a shallow dip of the head. "*Osuri te.*"

For safety's sake, Naomi and Aryel had driven Ellen and Iori to and from work while Alexander was away. Naomi had spent the commutes trying to wheedle Iori out of his shell by meeting him on common ground: their Jeidish roots, a topic he hesitated to speak on but was gradually opening up about. Another part of that past he'd been running from.

Ellen understood little of their discussions. A word here, a phrase there. Unlike her brother, languages never had been her strong suit. Even so, it was nice to see Iori socializing more, and she enjoyed listening to him converse in his native tongue.

"How's your shoulder?" Ellen asked Naomi.

She flapped her injured arm, which had been dislocated during the raid on the Blackjack complex. "Dr. Fornell says I can take the sling off tomorrow. Gonna be on part-time duties for a few weeks, though, and it'll be a while before I can use both of my whips again."

"As if you're not scary enough with one." Ikkei's comment earned him an elbow to the gut from his sister. He doubled over, wheezing. "It was a compliment. Why do you have to be such a bitch?"

"Living up to expectations."

Aryel scrutinized Alexander. "What're you doing back anyway?" He gasped suddenly, eyes a shining pair of saucers. "Could it be you missed us?"

"No," Alexander firmly denied, but the reddish tinge to his ears indicated otherwise. "I have business, that's—"

"ELLEN!" a wail cut him off.

Before Ellen had a chance to turn around, Tatiana crashed into her. She wobbled unsteadily as the girl's blubbering face rubbed against hers. "Wh-what's happening?"

"She's been inconsolable since you went on break," explained Soren on a more civil approach, thumbs tucked under the straps of his backpack. "She smothered me on the bus this morning, too."

"It's only been a few days."

"It felt like a lifetime! First we lost Soren, and then you *left* me." Tatiana squeezed Ellen so tight that it forced the air from her lungs. "How am I supposed to save the world without my best friends at my side? I'M NOTHING WITHOUT YOU."

The group watched in bewilderment as Ellen suffocated in her hold, then Soren came to the rescue. "Let her breathe, Tatiana."

"I'm also surprised to see you here," Aryel said. "We thought for sure your parents would terminate your contract."

Soren scratched his sandy-haired head. "It helped that they had time to process it. Didn't stop them from lecturing me on my way out the door, but I'm here, so. I can't really complain."

As a minor, his fate at Cardplay rested in his parents' hands. Considering the stunt he and Tatiana pulled, sneaking him onto a police boat to join the raid, it was a miracle the masters hadn't fired him themselves. But it was their battlemaster Elizabeth Howard who rose to his defense. She'd made the decision to let him fight, and he fought valiantly.

Ultimately, it was Soren rallying the guts to advocate for himself that convinced his parents to let him continue his working as a Joker—on the condition that, until he reached the age of majority, he would not be put in such peril again.

In fairness, it wasn't every day they raided the lair of evildoers who were attempting to build an army of monsters.

"Well, we're glad you're back," said Ellen.

With the meeting imminent, they followed the rest of the crowd into the warm, spice-scented air of the mansion. During the holiday season, it always smelled of gingerbread.

The cafeteria would soon be stocked with festive treats, too. Shortbread, roast buzzard, and fudgy coconut and custard bars. And on the eve of the solstice, the masters would host a traditional Amethistian feast, complete with honey-glazed ham and caramelized vegetables.

Drying their boots as best they could on the slush-soaked rug, they hung their coats on the rack and proceeded down the sloping corridor that would take them to the command centre. The command centre itself was reminiscent of a cinema, dimly lit with multi-tiered seating bisected by a carpeted walkway. A shallow, vacant stage lay at the bottom, backed by a massive projector screen.

Iori surveyed the room, tail waving with intrigue. "So this is where you devise all your top-secret plans."

It was also where student exams and magic history classes were conducted, and only authorized personnel were permitted entry. Prior to earning his stripes as an official member of Cardplay, Iori hadn't been allowed inside.

The group split, nightshift to the left and dayshift to the right. Alexander and his friends descended to the front row with the other First Classers, Second Class filtering into the middle, and Third Class joined the students in the upper row. Ellen slid into her usual seat, Iori on one side of her and Tatiana and Soren on the other.

A loud crinkling came from that other side. She shot a look at Tatiana, who was cramming a granola bar into her mouth.

"What?" she mumbled defensively around a chunk of oats and cranberries. "I was running late. Can't save the world on an empty stomach either."

The masters entered a minute later, and Tatiana scarfed down the last of her granola bar as they assumed their positions on the stage. At the click of Elizabeth's remote, the Cardplay insignia filled the projector screen, and Hikaru took the spotlight, bringing the ferrule of his cane to rest at the toe of his shoes.

"Good morning, everyone. We have a few orders of business to get to, but first, I would like to extend a very warm welcome to our returning students and Jokers." He motioned to them with a wide sweep of his arm. "I hope you're all ready to resume your duties."

Several nods passed through the audience, the students rather more hyped up than the rest.

"I see some of you are particularly eager," Hikaru observed, to which their heads bobbled again. "Excellent, because the five of you will be receiving your medallions this May alongside Iori Ryone, whose completion of the rehabilitation program and commendable performance in the field have placed him on the fast track to graduation."

The students cheered and high-fived whilst Iori sank into his seat to escape the congratulatory applause of his soon-to-be-fellow Jokers.

As the cheering waned, Hikaru relinquished the spotlight to his spouse. Year's end also marked promotion season. She began by addressing those advancing from Second to First Class. Among them was the electric-empowered Joker, Dax, who made extensive use of xyr hacking abilities in the raid; and the "shield-maiden" Sabine Brozak, nicknamed for her kinetic barrier which had proven invaluable during the spring influx.

"Lastly," said Elizabeth, posture straight as a board, "Tatiana Kosta and Ellen Amelia Jane will be advancing to Second Class."

The girls stared, dumbstruck, as their peers clapped. First year promotions had been rare since the bygone days when they were determining which qualities defined each class. With those parameters set, Ellen hardly thought herself worthy of a position in Second Class.

Second Classers were inspirational.

Second Classers displayed courage and conviction.

Second Classers put their lives on the line to save others.

However, when she caught the battlemaster's eye and saw the reflection of her efforts therein, polished by a pride awarded to few, she realized that when it came down to the wire, she could and had embodied all of those traits. And if Elizabeth believed her worthy, she had to believe it too.

"You two demonstrated exemplary teamwork in the midst of a high stress situation," added Elizabeth. "And your improvisation was undoubtedly the decisive factor in our rescue of Alexander Jane."

Ellen's gaze fell to her brother's head, which hung low as the attention shifted to him. Ikkei reached over and clasped the back of his neck, his whispered words nearly audible from the upper row in the sobered silence of the command centre.

Some victories were best celebrated without applause.

Elizabeth withdrew, pausing to speak to Hikaru. The way she held his arm—a comforting touch intended to be discreet—made Ellen uneasy, and when Hikaru retook the stage, a certain gravity appeared to drag at his heels.

"Before we move on to general updates, there is a development I must address." That gravity, too, weighed on his tone. "Effective immediately, Cardplay will no longer be participating in the investigation into Blackjack. Nor will the Hildegrand Police Department. By order of the Crown, the case shall henceforth be helmed by the National Guard.

In an instant, the announcement sucked all the oxygen out of the room. Not a breath was drawn or a word spoken . . . until Iori's seethed out like venom between his teeth.

"So you're saying the investigation is dead in the water."

Seated to his right, Ellen couldn't see his eye beneath its patch, but he wore his outrage plain in the curl of his lip and the glint of his fangs.

The headmaster regarded him with grave sympathy. "I am deeply sorry. I know this isn't what you wanted to hear, but the matter is beyond our control."

"What happens to Wiseman?"

"Without evidence to place him at the complex, it is unlikely that the National Guard will pursue him as a suspect. His alibis have been verified and the Crown is satisfied with Valerie Renard's confession. For all intents and purposes, this case is closed."

The sentencing of those arrested was guaranteed. Blackjack's Players had already been detained to the Hildegrand Correctional Institution for Empowered, and Valerie Renard was scheduled to be transferred to a federal prison outside the city. But without the kingpin in custody, those wins were a mere drop of justice in an ocean of turpitude.

Iori shifted forward, ears angled back. "He's *guilty*. I know it, Oto knows it, Alexander knows it. What was the point of those statements we gave? Doesn't the word of Cardplay's star Joker hold merit?"

"It doesn't. Not anymore." It was Alexander who responded, and no explanation was necessary. The drunken rage he'd flown into at the charity ball had recolored the public's view of him. The masters had done their best to smooth things over, and although the incident had been largely forgotten after news of his disappearance broke, it was clear the damage had been done.

Gone was the idol, the golden boy. The media were more interested in using him as an example of Cardplay's failings. Journalists who'd once clamored for interviews hadn't made a peep, and new ones were crawling out of the woodwork hoping to get the scoop on the *charity ball brawl.*

His reputation had been tarnished, and only time would tell if he could scrub it clean.

"So, what? We bow our heads in submission?" Iori's voice quavered as it rose. "Blackjack was the tip of an iceberg. All we did was postpone Wiseman's plan—which, by the way, continues to be a big, fat looming question mark."

"Ryone, lower your volume."

"Why should I?" he snapped at the battlemaster, white-knuckle gripping the arm of his chair. Ellen laid a hand on his, urging him to be calm, but if he'd taken notice, he took no heed. "Why should he get to walk free after what he did to me? That bastard shouldn't even be alive!"

Elizabeth leveled a reproachful look at him through her oval glasses. "This is not the time or the place, Ryone. I will not tell you again."

He stared her down, the chill of his Suit's corruption intensifying, invigorated by his rage, and the tingle Ellen always felt in his presence now raised goosebumps on her skin—her own magic alerting her to the beast caged inside, gnashing at its bars. Then he shoved to his feet, ripping his hand out from under hers, and snatched his duffel bag off the floor. "Screw this. I'm out."

"Where are you going?" Elizabeth demanded.

"To the arena."

"We're in the middle of a meeting. Get back in your seat!"

Ignoring the battlemaster's order, he continued up the aisle toward the exit, tail lashing behind him. She made a move to go after him, but Hikaru barred her path with his cane.

"Let him go," he said as the door clanged shut.

Ellen's fingers prickled from the friction of Iori's swift departure. Just like that, the promising day she'd envisioned evaporated into a fantasy.

They had hoped the next update would be to inform them that Charles Wiseman had been apprehended, or at least brought in for questioning. Now it seemed more likely his corporation would take a hit for Valerie's purported betrayal, and that would be the end of it.

The abuser would get a slap on the wrist.

And the victims would bear the bruise.

CHAPTER FOUR
NOVEMBER 22 | CARDPLAY HEADQUARTERS

UPON CONCLUSION OF THE MEETING, Ellen parted from the crowd and followed the sloping corridor deeper, to the arena situated under the backyard. The clap of her rubber soles bounced off the buffed concrete interior, washed in harsh white by a series of strip lights.

Like the infirmary's secure ward, the arena and tunnel were lined with magic-repellent mesh powered by the same electrical currents as the gear unempowered authorities wore. The very same that also coursed through the city's boundary fence and reinforced the walls of the Blackjack complex.

Wiseman Corporation tech, all of it.

It made her skin crawl, knowing that the invention of a man who'd orchestrated so much pain hummed around her now. And if it unsettled her this much, how must it affect Iori? While Alexander and Kyani were victims of his abuse too, their experience with him had been limited. It was Kane, mainly, who had made playthings of their minds and bodies.

But Iori had been Wiseman's, and Wiseman's alone.

Ellen shriveled at the memory of him on his dorm's bathroom floor, inconsolable as he told her about all of it. The isolation, the starvation, the bruises and welts—none of which quite compared to the seal-breaking voltage of the original Rending Machine, the device responsible for awakening his corrupted Suit and thereby triggering the Reemergence.

No one could blame him for being angry.

Having stalked off to the arena, she presumed he would be taking that anger our on target dummies. Catharsis in the form of pummeled burlap, straw, foam, and wood.

Instead, she heard music.

Tucking herself in by the doorframe, Ellen peered inside, and over the lip of the observation level, down in the sandy pit, she saw Iori like never before.

In the right hands, his hands, the ink of malice produced by the Void could be made malleable. During the honing process, he had utilized the Spade's acoustic prowess to fashion it into all sorts of shapes: a glassen treble clef, a spiked orb, a liquid infinity loop. On the battlefield, it could become armor or a weapon. Knife-sharp talons, whipping tendrils.

Here, they twined ribbon-like around him, molded by music and motions that evoked a sense of anguish—present in the cry of the violin and the toss of his head, in the crash of cymbals and the sweep of his legs. He didn't need acoustic levitation to defy gravity.

This fluid grace combined with the change of clothing, from jeans and long sleeves to billowy pants and a cropped turtleneck, made him look even more cat-like than usual.

"Puts on quite a show, doesn't he?"

The battlemaster sidled up beside Ellen. She must've come to check on Iori. In the pit, he dropped into a spinning crouch, ink whirling tighter and tighter around him as he pulled his arms inward. Then he flung them out, throwing the cyclone wide.

"It still resists him from time to time, but the progress he's made is nothing short of impressive. He'll downplay it, of course. The kid's a cocky little shit until you compliment him, then he goes all shy." She snorted. "You'd think he was allergic to praise."

To praise, to sympathy. To anything that put a focus on his behavior, his accomplishments, his flaws, his past. To the slightest indication that a version of himself other than the one he chose to display had been perceived.

Masks and shields were wise in the company of strangers and foes, but when would he realize he didn't need to hide from his allies?

At least he could drop his guard for Ellen most of the time.

"Was this your idea?" she asked in a hushed tone. Seeing how Iori had once detected the wind chime hum of her magic halfway across the building, it was surprising he hadn't heard her already. The music had to be drowning her out.

"No, this was all him," said Elizabeth. "Couple weeks before the raid, he requested off-hours access to the arena. Didn't say why. We'd been struggling, though, so I was willing to try anything at that point. Decided to poke my head in one day after his mood and control improved, and . . . well. He found an outlet." She folded her arms. "Drill instructors in the National Guard are expected to discipline, never accommodate. I carried that training with me to the HPD, and I brought it here. You kids have softened me up over the years, but working with him made me reevaluate my methods. Taught me that sometimes the best thing you can do for your student is take a step back." Her gaze lingered on Iori a moment longer, then flicked to Ellen. "Don't tell the others I said that. It'd ruin my image."

Ellen stifled a chuckle. "I won't."

The song gradually trailed off. Iori's movements slowed and his inky ribbons retracted, filtering through his shirt into the Void mark he'd summoned them from.

Elizabeth began her retreat. "If he asks if I was here, *no I wasn't.*" She doubled back up the corridor, and Ellen crossed the threshold into the arena.

Iori drew himself tall for the finishing pose, black-slippered toe pointed forward and arms extended in a circular formation. With no more music to overwhelm Ellen's hum, his ears and head snapped to her in quick succession.

"Uh, hi," he called to her, dropping clumsily into a casual stance. "When did—h-how long have you been there?"

"Not long," she said, a mite of guilt creeping in. The open door wasn't an invitation; the rules prohibited it from being shut while students and low-ranking Jokers were training unsupervised. Hoping to dispel the awkwardness, she produced a paper bag from her purse. "I packed you a sandwich. Thought you might get hungry since you skipped breakfast. You can have it now, if you want. I imagine all that exercise must've worked up an appetite." She shook the bag, as if to entice him. "It's tuna. I remembered to leave out the cucumbers this time."

Iori considered the bag, chest still heaving from the exertion. Then, combing his fringe off his sweat-slick brow, he accepted her offering.

They settled on the bleachers overlooking the pit. Iori propped his elbows on the bench behind him, granules of sand glittering on his light honey-toned skin.

Reclined as he was, crop top hiked up another inch or two, nearly the full length of his bullet wound scar was exposed. If not for his stubbornness leading to sepsis and surgery, it would've been a tiny pockmark. Instead, the incision line stretched from rib to hip, dipping into the shallows between his abdominal muscles.

Wait. When did he get abs?

"Did I miss anything important?" he asked.

Tearing her gaze from his midriff, Ellen passed him the paper bag. "Not really. Just the regular Monday meeting stuff."

The schedule for the week, an overview of recent incidents, Void activity reports—the latter of which had been on a decline since the Diamond awoke in October. Initially, they suspected pure magic might be flowing in from the Domain and combating the wickedness leaking out of the Void. Based on what Kyani had been told of the Suit hierarchy, however, the Diamond's seal, like the Club's, had merely functioned as a floodgate, meaning the Domain and any magic it contained would be locked behind the still-intact Heart seal.

Thus, their theory had been debunked, and they were left scratching their heads for another explanation.

As Iori peeled the cellophane off his sandwich and bit into the tuna-stuffed bread, Ellen knocked her shoes together, debating whether to address his outburst. After the one-two punch of a disturbed night followed by bad news, she didn't want to go sticking her nose in where it may not belong.

She didn't have to, though.

"Sorry for making a scene," he said. "I know it was rude to storm out, and I'll apologize to the masters later. I just couldn't stay in that room." He made a gripping motion at his gut. "This anger I have is poison, and I don't have the stomach for it anymore. If I had swallowed it down like Howard told me to, like I always used to, it would've made me physically ill."

Ellen had witnessed that firsthand. When his memories of Wiseman resurfaced, they left him barely able to function in his waking hours, and sleep had to be induced by Dr. Cellier's hypnotic abilities or else he wouldn't rest.

"I'm sure they'll understand," she said, confident already that they did. "I'm glad you've found a healthier way to manage it."

The corner of his mouth quirked upward. "Can't say I'm used to having an audience."

Internally, Ellen squirmed. "I didn't mean to intrude. It's not like you've never performed for an audience, though. You played piano for a room full of strangers at the ball, and you danced with me there too."

"When I'm playing piano, the audience isn't focused solely on me. They're invested in the music. The instrument. I'm just a piece of that instrument, like you were a piece to a pair in our waltz. Here, it's just me," he said. "I'm the whole show, and . . . I don't know. Dancing is a very intimate thing for me. Feels like you caught me doing something risqué." He lifted his sandwich for another bite. "I did also *choose* to perform for an audience on both of those occasions."

The hint of laughter in his words only heightened Ellen's guilt. This was becoming a habit. A bad one. Staring at scars and marks, eavesdropping on his singing, watching him dance uninvited. Glances stolen out of curiosity, because she wanted to know more about him. Wanted to see the sides he was so reluctant to show. But he had reasons for that reluctance, and by sneaking peeks, she had robbed him of the chance to share those sides with her when he was ready.

She rubbed her arm. "I'm sorry . . ."

He balled up the empty cellophane wrap, elbows perched on his knees. "It's fine. Really." A mollifying warmth softened his features. "I don't mind that it was you."

There he went again, catching her off-guard with unexpected tenderness like that evening by the fountain after a strenuous honing session. *"She would have adored you,"* he'd told her of his mother. That tenderness had been present in his eyes then, too.

No matter the emotion, it would be magnified tenfold in their depths—the deep crimson of a wound, raw and open and unobstructed by his walls. A peephole into his soul.

When he looked at her with those eyes and uttered such simple yet potent words, were those the sparks Tatiana spoke of? The love Alexander saw? There was a form of affection there, certainly, but could Iori really have *that* kind of affection for her? A boy brimming with talent, a boy whose adventurous spirit couldn't be tamed, whose daring and confidence vastly outpaced her own . . .

No. A boy like that could never fall for a girl like her.

An alarm jolted Ellen from her thoughts. She whipped her phone out to silence it, the incident alert glowing indigo on her screen. She swiped right to read the details.

CODE: *INDIGO // ALPHA*
ADDRESS: *22 Maple Lane, Upper District*
DETAILS: *Inkblot attack. Multiple persons trapped.*

"Duty calls?" asked Iori.

"Yeah. Bad timing, as usual." She sprung to her feet, slotting her phone into her purse. "Oh! Speaking of timing, your appointment with Dr. Bristol is in an hour. You might want to get cleaned up for that."

Iori scowled, ears flattening. "*Ugh.*"

"Don't make that noise. She's nice. You'll be fine." Ellen had the pleasure of meeting Dr. Bristol when Alexander used to see her. Two sessions in, he'd sworn off therapy altogether and agreed only to speak to Dr. Cellier, the in-house counselor, when necessary. Hopefully Iori wouldn't be so quick to throw in the towel. "Anyway, I've gotta run."

"Be safe."

"I'll be in good hands. See you later!" She slung her purse over her shoulder and jogged for the exit. It was just a standard low-threat call. After her chaotic six months on the job, a few Inkblots couldn't scare her.

CHAPTER FIVE
NOVEMBER 22 | CARDPLAY HEADQUARTERS

BATHED IN MIDMORNING SUN and smelling of aged parchment and wood, the serenity of Hikaru's office was a stark contrast to the video on his computer monitor. There, shadows pooled in corners and stone walls glistened coldly. The surveillance camera footage captured the full width of the cavernous chamber beneath the Blackjack complex, carved out for the express purpose of awakening Suits.

On a low platform to the right stood the Rending Machine, an atrocity of coiled copper and steel framework; and to the left, chains trailed from a metal ring embedded in the floor to the ankles of a young man. He slumped against the wall, draped in the tattered remains of his father's tuxedo.

Alexander.

The Players would cart him in, kicking and cussing, and string him up in that ghastly contraption. Electricity would ravage his body, amplified volts battering the seal of his dormant Suit. And when it was done, the session complete, they would drag him out with much less fuss.

About a month in, that chamber became his new cell. Rather than cart him back and forth, they left him there to rot, piece by decaying piece.

Despite knowing how this movie would end and hardening himself in preparation for the inevitable decline, each video dealt a blow to Hikaru's armor. He braced for another as a shaft of light spilled across the screen, cleaved by a tall shadow. Blackjack's manager, Kane Kros, entered the cell, dangling a glass bottle bearing a hazard label by its neck. A yellowish liquid sloshed within.

The most recent addition to his disciplinary paraphernalia.

Alexander's heels scraped the floor as the man neared, humming a gleeful tune. *"Don't."* He spat the word like a warning, not a plea. *"Stay the fuck away from me."*

Kane snared him by the ankle.

"Let go of me!"

Acid lapped at the bottle's rim.

"DON'T—"

A tap of the space bar cut Alexander short and froze both men in place, a wicked joy contorting the ashen visage of the elder while the younger battled fear as much as his assailant.

Hikaru clasped his hands in front of his mouth, taking in the freeze frame. Usually he could detach emotionally to inspect a crime scene and the grisly details therein, but this was his *boy*—not by blood, but by heart—and it stirred a sickly concoction of pride and pain in him to watch Alexander resist.

Over and over and over.

A shower, a lavish room, a hot meal, a walk outside— every luxury they offered in exchange for compliance, he refused. Spat. Cussed them out. Put up a fight even though it would only lead to another beating. Another blade. More suffering.

Was it an effort to maintain his dignity? Inborn defiance? Or . . . could he have thought he deserved it? Hikaru wasn't sure he wanted the answer to that.

With any luck, the answers he did seek would be on this flash drive.

He tapped the escape key to minimize the video player. A folder lay open on his desktop, containing hundreds upon thousands of files. Photographs from the retrofitted asylum, written analyses, records, and countless other videos. Blackjack had documented *everything*. Every experiment . . .

Ink Infusion_Trial 22
Ink Infusion_Trial 56
Ink Infusion_Trial 68

. . . the studies of the dormant Club and its awakening . . .

Oto_Garden 02
Oto_Garden 13
Oto_Session 07
Oto_Session 15
Oto_Awakening

. . . and the rending process of the Diamond.

Jane_Session 03
Jane_Session 26
Jane_Session 47

Many had been corrupted, damaged by the electric-type Player, Felix *"Flick"* Taggert, in her attempt to erase the data before Cardplay stormed the complex. It was thanks to Naomi Toi's intervention that they were able to recover any of it at all. By short-circuiting Taggert using her own high-voltage powers, she had successfully halted the purge.

However, two major events were missing: the Diamond's awakening, and the creation of the Inkwraith horde. The events Charles Wiseman would have been present for. General surveillance of the property had also been tampered with over the duration of his visit, ensuring his alibis were upheld.

Hikaru tossed his glasses onto his desk and rubbed his eyes. There had to be a crack. A clue. Something among these documents that could dethrone the man or, at the barest minimum, bring him down from his fortress.

A knock interrupted Hikaru's fretful brain-wracking. He collected himself, his glasses. "Come in," he called, and his chest clenched when none other than Alexander Jane walked in. Chin held high, well put-together in a crisp white shirt and freshly-pressed slacks. He'd drawn his hair into a tuft of a ponytail, and gold studs and rings had been neatly arranged along his ears. No longer that frail shell of a boy.

Clearly, Hikaru appeared less put-together.

Alexander jabbed a thumb at the door. "I can come back later."

"No, no. Now is fine." Hikaru cleared his throat, tried to shake off the film of despair. "How are you?" He'd intended a single question, but more tumbled out unbidden. "Are you adjusting alright? Do you have everything you need at home?"

"I'm—yeah, I'm good. You don't have to worry about me."

Didn't he? "I wasn't expecting you back so soon. I thought you'd be resting."

"About that . . ." Alexander rubbed his collarbone. "I'd rather make myself useful here than waste time sitting around at home. I know I fucked up. *Messed* up," he amended politely. "My behavior was unprofessional and irresponsible, and I'll understand if you can't approve my request, but if you can give me another chance, I want to be a Joker again. Even if I have to start from the bottom."

Not a full day after discharge and already looking to pick up where he left off. "Is that wise?"

"I'm not asking you to put me on the field, just back on the roster so I can work in an official capacity. Elizabeth and I were talking on the drive home yesterday and she suggested I assist her with student training. Then in a couple of weeks once I've regained my strength, I can go out on patrol again."

Lizbet suggested that? Alexander had spent the past several days bedridden in the infirmary, barely able to move. What was she thinking, putting these ideas in his head? He should have been focusing on recovery, not work.

"Can you not look at me like that?" Alexander's voice sliced through Hikaru's thoughts.

"Like what?"

"Like I'm a *victim*."

But moments ago on-screen he was, and that wasn't some distant past. Although his injuries appeared long-healed due to his Suit's regenerative abilities, to Hikaru, they were fresh. "Alexander . . ."

"We won the battle, not the war." He pointed to the window. "Wiseman is out there biding his time. We have no idea what his endgame is, but he's got two pawns and a wildcard left." The Player pair still at large, and the magical entity known as the Sundered Star. "We need to be prepared for when he makes his next move, and you can't afford to have me sidelined when he does."

It wasn't arrogance that shaped Alexander's words; he'd been dubbed star Joker for a reason. His innate impulse to protect and his unmatched prowess in magical combat made him perfect for the role. As Keeper of the Diamond, one of four chosen by the divine to guard the mundane world, his potential would be even greater. And should Wiseman launch an attack, they would need their best battle ready. Elizabeth had the clarity of a more logical mind to see that.

Stowing his paternal concerns, Hikaru yielded. "I will approve your reinstatement request . . . on two conditions."

Alexander straightened attentively at that.

"Firstly, you must pass a psych evaluation."

A nod.

"Secondly, Ryone must be agreeable to it." The two appeared to have allayed the antagonism between them, but sharing a home and a workplace could rekindle that animosity. Hikaru had to be certain that Iori, being the former object of Alexander's fury, would be content with the arrangement.

Alexander opened his mouth, closed it. "That's fair. Should I . . .?"

"I will speak with him this evening. You should have your answer by day's end."

Another smaller nod.

This amicability felt strange from him. Within and outside of professional settings, Alexander had a tendency to domineer, and while the change at first struck Hikaru as sudden, he realized this was the result of months of introspection. The apologies Alexander made had not come lightly, his head made level only by the burdens weighed in his moral scales.

Now it made sense, in a poignant sort of way, why fate dictated he must bear all that he had. Not all roads to the ideal future were themselves idyllic.

"I am proud of you, you know," Hikaru said.

"Yeah, I know." Somewhat hesitantly, Alexander pivoted on his heel. "I'll let you get back to work. Are you sure everything's alright?"

Hikaru willed himself to smile. "Quite," he lied. The last thing he needed was for his kids to worry about him when they already had troubles of their own. "Hurry on, then. Dr. Cellier should be in."

With a final dip of his chin, Alexander made for the exit. Behind him trailed a strand of gold—the tightrope of life he walked, invisible to all but one. Prior to the paramedics wheeling him out of the Blackjack complex after the raid, Hikaru hadn't been able to see it.

Hadn't been *allowed* to see it.

The office door clicked shut. Hikaru swiveled to the large picture window and cast his gaze past the azure veil to the imperceptible realm beyond.

You didn't let me see because you knew I would intervene.

Somewhere out there, he imagined that a star winked in resigned confirmation. Everyone had to stay on their correct paths—this, Hikaru knew. But must they shoulder such tremendous suffering in order to restore the balance?

Deep down, he knew this as well, and there would be more hardship yet to overcome.

Fate was a cruel mistress, indeed.

CHAPTER SIX
NOVEMBER 22 | CARDPLAY HEADQUARTERS

CARDPLAY'S INFIRMARY REMINDED KYANI of the test chambers at the Blackjack complex, and of the facilities she'd frequented after her father's stroke. All sterile white and linoleum with chrome accents, with the exception of the pastel zinnias on her bedside table. The room's only saving grace.

Where the flowers had come from was anyone's guess. They arrived yesterday by courier, no message to accompany her name on the card. The possibility that Cardan McConnell had sent them had crossed her mind. He'd been kind to her as a handler, and lenient at a risk to his own wellbeing. He would bring her dinner when Kane forbade it, absorb himself in a book instead of monitoring her in the conservatory. Sometimes he would even sit outside her sleeping quarters, the pair of them on opposite sides of the door, and trade stories in the moonlit hours.

But would someone send such a beautiful bouquet to the person who took advantage of their benevolence to betray them?

A wisp of remorse licked up Kyani's spine. To remind herself why she did it, she brought her fingers to the ring emblazoned on her neck. To the feathered ends of the short bob that remained after Wiseman sawed off her ponytail. She twisted one of the longer strands in front, a shade darker than the smears of blight marring her skin.

The Sundered Star had threatened to cut off her wings next if she didn't divulge the contents of her clandestine meetings with the Keeper of the Spade. Mercifully, he didn't get the chance. He and Wiseman fled at the alert of incoming police boats, after which Cardan dragged Kyani indoors, chastising her for recklessly throwing herself into danger.

Cardan had always saved her from her random acts of rebellion, but this rebellion had been neither reckless nor random. It was a leap of faith.

Her only regret was not jumping sooner.

Movement in the hall drew Kyani's attention, and excitement fluttered in her chest when a young man appeared in the entrance to her room. "Alexander, hi."

"Hey," he replied in a more tepid tone. "Mind if I sit?"

At the shake her head, he pulled a squat chair up beside her bed. Even under the color-leaching fluorescents she noticed the healthier glow to his face, no longer a deathlike pallor. "You look better," she said.

"Thanks. I feel better."

A palpable tension unfolded between them. He hadn't popped by until now to see her, even when the only thing separating them was a long stretch of hallway. Him at one end, her at the other. Not that she expected different; she figured he would cut contact once he was home safe.

While she became a lifeline for him at the complex, she was also the person who put him there. The person who'd tricked and lured and poisoned him, both the cause of his trauma and his escape from it.

"I understand if you're angry with me," she said. "You have every right to be."

"I'm not angry. It's . . . complicated." He circled one thumb over the knuckle of the other. "This line of work requires us to compartmentalize events, sorting them into boxes so we can unpack them in our own time. And I'd be lying if I said the box I dumped the Blackjack shit into wasn't threatening to tip over by me being here, but I don't want *them* to be the reason I lose *you.*"

An updraft of relief lifted Kyani's wings. Was he really saying what she thought he was saying?

"We can't start over after what we went through, and it'll take time to get back to where we were, but I think we can get there. We are going to be seeing lots of each other in the future, so it'd be best if I'm not awkwardly trying to avoid you."

They shared a faltering laugh. Kyani's gaze then fell to the black blotches covering her body, and her wings sank to her sides. Dressed as she was in a sports bra and shorts, most were exposed for careful monitoring, and if she stared long enough, she could almost see them wicking across the ample curves of her stomach, arms, and thighs.

In the future, huh?

The time Alexander needed was time she didn't have. This disease, this blight—stemming from her corrupted Suit—was rotting her from the inside out. Dr. Fornell predicted that with rest and recuperation, the unsuppressed Club could fend it off. After all, Empowered had a natural resilience to the disease, and Kyani was no ordinary Empowered. But every day that she watched her own magical aura darken, so too did her hopes. The marks didn't even hurt anymore, just filled her with this terrible bone-deep *cold.*

At least she shouldn't have to worry about endangering those around her. Mundane folks turned rapidly, behavior shifting before the disease became visible to the naked eye. Empowered simply perished. She'd witnessed it in Kane's lab: the blackness would spread, and once every ounce of light had been consumed, the body would shrivel and die.

If the Club couldn't stop it, that same demise awaited her.

Her fingers curled into loose fists. "Can I ask for a favor?"

"Yeah, go ahead."

"If I don't get to speak to my father again, could you tell him I'm sorry?"

Alexander recoiled. "What's with the deathbed talk?"

"That's what this is, isn't it?" She patted the mattress. "I'm dying, Alexander. I knew the price to bring down Blackjack would be high, and I've made my peace with that." She could rest easier with the headmaster's assurance that her father would be cared for.

But Alexander boldly declared, "You'll be okay."

He was a realist with pessimistic inclinations. Naïve optimism wasn't his style. Why sow seeds of hope into a girl who knew she was nearing her end?

Before she could inquire, Cardplay's chief physician, Dr. Simone Fornell, entered the room with a clipboard under her arm. "Hate to interrupt. It's that time again."

Every day at six hour intervals, the doctor would come to evaluate the blight using an ocular ability that enabled her to track its spread layer by layer—like an MRI without the scanner, which suited Kyani. She'd developed an aversion to giant, raucous machines.

"It's fine. I have stuff to take care of." Alexander rose from his seat. "Is Cellier around?"

"Procrastinating in the nurse's lounge," Fornell told him.

He thanked her and returned the chair to its original spot, then said to Kyani, "We got an update on the investigation. I can swing by later to give you the rundown, if you're up for it."

Based on his tone, it wasn't a fruitful update. Nonetheless, she welcomed the opportunity to speak with him again. "I'd like that."

Alexander motioned to the flowers on the table. "I'll bring some water for those, too. Looks like they could use a drink."

Kyani regarded them from afar, longing but afraid to touch their wilting petals lest she spread her disease to them. "You know, we rarely carried zinnias where I worked. They're an underappreciated breed. Most people buy arrangements to express romance or condolences, but zinnias symbolize friendship. That deserves flowers too, I think."

"Does that mean you like them?"

She smiled. "Very much."

"Thought you would."

Kyani looked up in time to catch the fleeting traces of an uncharacteristic softness on Alexander's features before they settled into their typical impassivity.

"I'll swing by in a few hours," he said. "Hope the examination goes well."

"Bye," Kyani tried to say, her voice getting lost along the way. Of all the people to buy her flowers, she never would have guessed Alexander.

Dr. Fornell watched him go, twists of bleached hair swishing with the shake of her head. "That boy can be a real sweetheart when he wants to be." She sighed. "Been a long while since he wanted to be." Turning to Kyani, she conjured her big round X-ray spectacles. "Shall we get started?"

CHAPTER SEVEN
NOVEMBER 22 | CARDPLAY HEADQUARTERS

WINTER-BARE CHERRY TREES GLISTENED outside the windows of the second-floor lounge—the same strip of grove Iori could see from his dorm. A monotonous drone seeped up from the infirmary below, vying with another frequency he could compare only to a synthesizer preset.

The warped hum of the tarnished Club.

His own Suit's droning corruption reigned supreme over the pipe organ howl of its surviving purity. If he weren't here for an appointment, he would have liked to smother it with that piano across the room.

The black grand had been moved upstairs, rescued from a life spent mostly in storage. Iori hadn't revived his daily playing habits yet, and he'd had to force himself to the keys after the gaps in his memory filled, threatening to drag music into that abyss where the most harmless things became untouchable. But it brought comfort to know he could play on the occasion he got the urge, or when nothing else could clear his troubled mind.

Hopefully the former would soon outnumber the latter.

Iori's ears perked at the thump of footsteps on the foyer stairs. Two women entered the lounge a second later: his social worker, Mira Hodge, and a shorter woman with close-shorn hair and cool ebony skin. With her vibrant florals, chunky jewelry, and mild demeanor, she wasn't at all the shrewd image of a psychologist Iori had envisioned.

"Hello," said Mira in a singsong tune as Iori rose from one of the sofas, back in his street clothes with feline traits concealed beneath a beanie and cable knit cardigan. "Arynne, meet Iori Ryone. Iori, meet Dr. Arynne Bristol."

Iori dipped his head in greeting.

"Pleased to meet you." Bristol spoke in a posh accent akin to Hikaru's, only stronger. "How do you prefer to be called?"

"Uh, either name is fine." So long as neither was preceded by *master*. "Are you staying?" he asked Mira.

"Oh, no, I have business with the headmaster." She paused. "Unless you'd like me to?"

Embarrassment prickled along Iori's neck. "That won't be necessary." Although, it might've been nice to have company he'd done this dance with before. The fact he would have to omit certain details to maintain confidentiality took off some of the pressure, at least.

Mira's job as a magical polygraph examiner alone wasn't what gave her access to classified information. As Iori had learned, she was an alum of Cardplay. She'd studied magic here, honed her ability to read moral compasses within these very walls. The reason she hadn't been put off by his fangs, ears, or tail when they met was because she knew who and what he was from the start.

Monster.

Thief.

Keeper.

Dr. Bristol, on the other hand, hadn't a clue about Keepers or Suits or a cat-eared boy cursed by wickedness, only that *this* boy had experienced a great deal of suffering as a result of the Reemergence—and he'd been instructed by the headmaster to keep it that way. Outsiders couldn't be let in on these secrets yet. Not even the trusted ones.

To Bristol, he would be no more than a run-of-the-mill shadow-bender with a heaping pile of baggage.

"I'll leave you to it, then." Offering him one last look of encouragement, Mira left, pulling the door shut behind her.

Iori returned to the sofa, plunking down on a folded leg as Bristol made herself comfortable on the matching piece of furniture opposite him.

She retrieved a notepad and pen from her purse. "Are you nervous?"

"Should I be?"

"You've been scratching your nails since I walked in."

His thumbnail scraped to a halt. Little of yesterday's polish remained, much of it reduced to a sprinkling of black flakes on his skin and jeans. He pulled his hands inside his sleeves, a fresh wave of embarrassment tickling his ears. He'd been too busy analyzing Bristol to realize what he was doing.

"It's normal to be anxious. Most new clients are," assured Bristol. "I promise, I don't bite."

Iori's tail twitched against his hip, wrapped like a belt under his cardigan's weighty folds. "I don't think *biting* is the problem."

"No, it's more the talking-about-your-troubles part, isn't it?" she said, and his tail flicked again. "You don't have to worry about that yet. Today, we're just going to have a conversation. I want to be sure we're compatible."

Iori relaxed slightly at that. "Am I allowed to ask questions?"

"Be my guest."

There was one that had been nagging at him since Mira first mentioned her. "I was told you specialize in Empowered cases. Obviously they don't teach that anywhere, and you're not Empowered. How can you be an expert in a field that doesn't exist?"

"Technically, my specialty is trauma in youth. However, many of my clients after the Reemergence were Empowered teens struggling to control and come to terms with their new abilities. Very few psychologists were willing to tackle the issue, but we had a position that desperately needed filling, so I filled it. And through young Empowered such as yourself, I've learned and continue to learn much about the influence of emotions on magic."

All Iori could think was: *you've never worked with someone like me.* "What's your success rate?"

She chuckled deep in her chest. "I have a rating of four-point-eight on *Yap*. In all seriousness, I can't give every client what they need. It also depends how receptive they are to treatment." She inclined her head toward him. "Why have you sought counseling?"

He counted off the reasons, sarcasm sharpening his tongue. "Let's see: dead parent, kidnapping, brutal torture resulting in memory loss, magic instability . . . Didn't you read my file?" She should have received Mira Hodge's assessment, minus the redacted parts.

"I did. More, I was inquiring as to what you hope to take away from this. What are your goals?"

"To function like a well-adjusted human being?"

She scrutinized him, pen seesawing between her fingers. "Why don't you tell me about your history? Start with where you grew up."

Was she asking out of curiosity, or baiting him into talking about his deep-seated familial angst? He shrugged. "Not much to tell. I did most of my growing up in Hildegrand. Went to school. Didn't have a lot of friends, didn't really care." Even in childhood, he valued his personal time. "First few years here were great, and then . . . well."

Bristol hummed in understanding. "Where were you before?"

"Hokawa, Jeida. I was born there." In a quaint rural village by a lake. There he spent the first six years of his life swimming and catching frogs and listening to his grandmother tell stories on the porch while the aroma of steamed pork buns wafted from the kitchen. Those were some of his best memories, and now they felt like half-remembered dreams. A life he hadn't lived in a body that wasn't his.

He wanted it to be, though.

"What brought you to Hildegrand?"

"My mother. She wanted to travel, open her own dance studio. When the opportunity came up in Hildegrand, she jumped on it, and we were on a plane by the end of the week."

"That's fast," remarked Bristol.

"Living with my aunt and grandmother made it easy; all we had to do was pack and go. Pretty much started from scratch when we got here." They lived out of suitcases in a tiny apartment prior to moving into the red-shingled house that would become their home. He faintly recalled their first night there—blank walls and barren halls, shadows painting ominous shapes on the hardwood floor. How safe he felt in the cocoon of his mother's arms.

A different memory of her arms around him stalked at the borders of his reminiscence, one where ominous shadows turned solid, sharp, and lethal. Bristol's next question chased it away, but the discussion maintained its decline into unpleasant territory.

"Are you close with them? Your family?"

"I . . . was." Iori rubbed his neck, ears shifting downward under his beanie. "We kept in touch after the move, video calls every other day. Nothing since the Reemergence." Since a couple of months earlier, to be precise. A sourness churned inside him. "Can we talk about something else?"

"Of course." Dr. Bristol jotted in her notepad—a subject for later?—then asked about his hobbies, his lifestyle, his interest in music and dancing. Even as she praised his creative outlets, her scribbled notes terrified him, for they warned of hard work ahead.

Try as he might to keep his fragile pieces together, most were too small and worn and shook loose at the slightest wince—triggers like a spoon tap, tap, tapping at the hollowed-out shell of an egg. A nightmare, a name, an unnerving image invading his brain. The point of this, though, was to find a glue strong enough to hold those pieces in place. To fill his cracks with the gold of healing so that those close to him didn't have to keep collecting him off the floor.

To do that, he had to confront his past.

Opening up would be a grueling process, with this psychologist or any other, but if he could push through it, overcome his doubts and let Dr. Bristol in, he may just come out stronger on the other side.

Ellen, Mira, and Hikaru had vouched for her. If he could trust them, he could come to trust her too.

CHAPTER EIGHT
NOVEMBER 22 | HILDEGRAND, UPPER DISTRICT

So MUCH FOR A STANDARD CALL.

Ellen's scythe struck asphalt as the Inkblot she'd been chasing around the grocery store parking lot continued to evade her attacks. The critters were known to be slippery, but this was downright comical.

It chittered at her from a distance, the sweep of its liquid tail painting smears of black across the lot.

Was it taunting her?

"Get back here!" Fastening her grip on the ivory-white snath of her scythe, she lunged at it again. The Inkblot ducked under a car, scurried back and forth and back and forth from front to rear, then bolted onto the roof of a neighboring vehicle. When she finally caught it, snagging it midair, she was too worn out to celebrate.

To that point, she wasn't sure if she should.

The creature splashed to the ground, writhing as its reptilian body evaporated into particles of light. Those that rose shone the same vivid scarlet as her crystal-edged blade. Others winked out on the pavement, electric blue like the palm-sized galaxies that filled the eye sockets of Blackjack's Inkwraith horde.

A deafening boom rattled Ellen's eardrums, and another Inkblot burst at the concussive force of Sabaa Faizan's

Thunderclap technique. Her gray-blue frock shirt billowed over her breeches, metallic embroidery like lightning woven into a stormy sky.

Thunderhead was her power's callsign.

Her clap had resounded throughout Hildegrand during the Reemergence, accompanied by the cannonade of heavy artillery. Ellen remembered hearing those distant rumbles from outside the cordon, the tremors in the shelter floor. It was the sound of pandemonium, and the drumbeat of victory when at last the influx had been contained.

"Was that the last of them?" called Oskar Trey. He'd fought in the Reemergence too, his aquatic powers bringing the rain to Sabaa's storm. He lumbered over in cork sandals and a turquoise tunic adorned with ornamental knots of rope. On his heels were Tatiana and Soren, decked out in their full kits as well. A fluttery purple dress and scissor blades, and a golden cloak and light-bending scepter.

Tidal Wave, *Midnight Monarch*, and *Sunbearer*.

A dozen puddles speckled the ground around them, parked cars spattered in black goo. With the scene secure, the Jokers dismissed their weapons, and Oskar waved to the civilians in the storefront window. They'd locked themselves in when the Inkblots arrived.

As they trickled out in wary streams, Ellen focused on the perceived temperature of the air, feeling for that telltale chill of contamination. When the last person passed without any change, she blew a breath and gave her team a thumbs-up. All clear.

Erring on the side of caution, Sabaa asked, "Was anyone bitten or scratched?"

Several heads shook. Parents checked over their children.

"Most of us were inside when they came," reported the store owner, a spindly middle-aged man. "The ones who weren't—those creatures herded them in."

"Herded? They didn't attack?"

"No. Didn't try hard to get in either. Pounced at the glass, made a racket. Scared the living daylights out of us. I don't know what would've happened if you hadn't shown up." The man took Sabaa's hand gratefully in his.

"Just doing our duty." There was a hesitant hitch in her voice that told Ellen the situation sat about as well with her as the rest of the team. "We're going to have to tape off the area. You can reopen after the cleanup crew's been by."

That responsibility fell to the National Guard. They would collect the residual ink in a small tanker truck and cart it off to a hazardous waste facility, or to a lab for study.

Knowing the connections the Wiseman Corporation had to them . . . Could that have been how Blackjack managed to obtain so much ink? By bringing the cleanup crew in now, would they be continuing to supply the enemy with the secret ingredient to whatever disaster they were cooking up?

The store owner left to tend to his patrons, and Sabaa went to put in the call.

"Never in all my years on this job have I seen Inkblots toy with their prey," muttered Oskar. Typically, they were frenetic in nature, lacking preservation instincts and attacking with only one goal in their hive of a mind: infect, consume, spread their blight. But these had conducted themselves in a manner that implied a certain level of intelligence.

Soren fingered his wrist uneasily, where beneath his gilded sleeves lay a beaded bracelet. "Did anyone else notice their coloring?"

"The blue light?" Tatiana asked.

"I saw it too," said Ellen. Though no one said it, their thoughts seemed to align. If these Inkblots carried the same glow as the Inkwraith army, chances were they'd been touched by the Sundered Star. What that meant exactly wasn't clear. Were they simply more powerful, more calculating, or did he have control over them? Could he be using them to spy on Cardplay from afar?

Whatever the implications, they couldn't be good.

Oskar swept a hand over the stubble on his scalp, suspicious brown eyes scanning the parking lot. "We'll stay here and wait for the cleanup crew," he said of himself and Sabaa. "You three report to headquarters. Ritsuo's gonna wanna hear about this."

The unsettling news Ellen returned with had instilled an urgency in Alexander that sent him to the gym. Having talked to Cellier and Kyani, the most useful thing he could do while awaiting the verdict on his reinstatement was start getting back in shape.

Sweat ran in rivulets along his arms, which trembled under the weight of a barbell. The overhead lights fluctuated to the beat of his pulse, too strong and quick for the time he'd put in. He'd only been here for thirty minutes and spent even fewer on the bench.

Three more, he thought. Three more reps to complete the set, and then he could take a breather.

He brought the barbell down, shoulders and biceps quaking, and when he lifted it again, the burn in his muscles intensified to a searing pain. He didn't make it halfway before his elbows buckled and the barbell clanged onto the safety catch, the sound ringing out in the empty gym.

Alexander slid out from under the bar and slouched on the bench, the floor wavering beneath his shoes. He rested his face in his palms, waiting for the vertigo to pass.

Strength, body mass, stamina . . . It would take months for him to regain what he'd lost.

"It helps if you keep your sugar intake up."

Alexander lifted his head to find Iori lurking by the entrance, a towel draped around his neck and cords trailing from his ears. He must've come from the showers after his evening training session with Elizabeth.

Exhausted and exasperated, Alexander's arms flopped over his knees. "I'm not new to this. I don't need workout tips."

Iori blinked at him, then let out a waning chuckle. "I'm not giving you basic workout advice. I'm talking about your Suit." Removing his earbuds, he hitched a shoulder on the doorframe. "You know how magic feeds off the user's energy levels?"

"When it's active, yeah." Studies showed that magic drew its strength from blood glucose, hence the importance of Cardplay keeping their Jokers well-fed. The prepaid full-service cafeteria headquarters boasted wasn't so much a luxury as a necessity.

"Well, our Suits are active even when they're not engaged. Right now yours is probably more active than it normally would be because your body is still in recovery mode. Muscle hypertrophy is enough to trigger the healing factor unless you have more serious wounds, in which case it'll divert energy to those." Iori twisted the earbud cord around his fingers. "Just some lessons I've learned along the way. I'd also prioritize cardio over strength building exercises."

"Um. Thanks," Alexander said, and felt he should say more. Felt Iori wanted to say more, too, but both remained unspeaking in their respective positions, unsure how to traverse the bumpy terrain between them. Aside from a brief heart-to-heart, they'd hardly spoken—not for lack of trying on Iori's part. At dinner and throughout the day, he'd made efforts to be genial. Meanwhile, if Alexander managed more than a couple words, they came out serrated and biting.

It wasn't that he didn't want to treat Iori affably, merely that he didn't know how. Their earlier interactions had consisted of arguing, crude taunting, or physically fighting—on the streets, in the Cavity, around headquarters, at the ball. Fights nearly all of which Alexander had instigated. And where he hadn't instigated, he had provoked. Out of rage for the things he had lost, and out of fear of losing those he still clung to. Unfounded, in both instances.

How was he supposed to speak to a person he had wronged so deeply? How could Iori approach him after everything he'd done? This felt too easy, like he'd been let off the hook.

Or maybe Iori's payback was yet to come, in the form of a rejected reinstatement request if he decided he wasn't amenable to it. Odds were, he wouldn't be. It would be presumptuous to assume otherwise.

That discussion must have happened by now, right? Hikaru had promised an answer by end of day, and Ellen was currently in the office filing her shift report. It wouldn't be long until they were headed home.

Seeing as Iori was here now, he could just ask.

The second Alexander went to speak, Iori did as well, and the pair of them snapped their jaws shut.

"You go," Iori invited.

"Has Hikaru spoken to you yet?"

"Ah, you want to know what I said." Iori crossed his ankles, rolling an earbud in his fingertips. Alexander couldn't decipher the upward curve of his mouth. Amusement, maybe, or smug satisfaction. "I told him to approve your request."

That was so opposite to what Alexander expected that he blurted out a baffled, "Why?"

"Should I not have?"

"No, I just . . . I thought you hated me."

"There is one person in this world who is deserving of my hatred, Alexander, and you are not him. What's that saying, the enemy of my enemy is my friend?"

"Okay, but I tried to ruin your life. Why *not* ruin mine?" Fighting fire with fire had always been his go-to. Eye for an eye, tooth for a tooth. He wasn't sure how to react when the opposing party was trying to douse him with water.

Iori's gaze slid to the floor. "I believe you've paid your dues." His tail swished by his calves. "Grief makes us do stupid things. I should know; I spent the past few years gambling with my life. But our mistakes don't define us, and I'd be a massive hypocrite if I didn't think you deserved a second chance. What matters to me is what you do with it. So"—his fangs flashed in a grin—"don't blow it."

With that, Iori reinserted his earbuds and peeled away from the doorframe. Alexander looked down at his fists, clenching and unclenching them. Weak, but no longer shaking.

Carbs and cardio, huh?
Worth a shot.

CHAPTER NINE
NOVEMBER 22 | CARDPLAY HEADQUARTERS

THE MANSION'S WOODEN SKELETON CREAKED and shrank as the cold of night set in. The students had gone, the dayshift as well, and with the nightshift asleep in their dormitories, the time too had come for the masters to retire to their suite. And as Hikaru lowered himself onto the side of his bed, he couldn't help relating to the old, weary building.

Apparently, he wasn't alone.

"I don't know where those kids get their energy." Elizabeth shed her clothes on her way in, flinging blouse and bra onto a squat chair in the corner. The mattress dipped with her weight behind him. "At this rate, they're going to turn me gray before I'm fifty."

Hikaru gave a thoughtful hum as he untied his robe. "I think gray would suit you." He pressed the button on the inner thigh of his prosthetic leg, painted gold to match its filigree design. Air hissed from the vacuum seal. When Elizabeth didn't respond, he turned and met her heavy-lidded olive eyes.

"'*Stress would look good on you*' isn't the compliment you think it is."

"More of a reassurance, really."

"Nice recovery." She whipped the elastic out of her hair, letting it tumble over the burn dressing on her neck—an injury from the raid, inflicted by the Diamond's flames. "To their credit, they keep things interesting. Not sure what I'm going to do with myself after they graduate."

Her way of saying she would miss them. In the past, she'd always had more students to train. A pool of magic-touched hopefuls that seemed ever-growing—until three years ago, when it began to shrink inexplicably. Now it appeared the last dregs were about to dry up.

Enrollment rates had plummeted to zero, and the majority of Empowered who weren't already on government contracts or employed by Cardplay had chosen either to suppress their magic or been incarcerated. The current state of affairs being what they were, there may not be an organization for future prospects to join.

Between the Crown's variable support, pressure from other world powers, and new aspersions being cast on Cardplay as a result of the investigation into the Wiseman Corporation, their existence hung in the balance. Mayor Hargrove was doing his best to placate the situation, but he could only do so much.

And to add to that were these reports of abnormal Void activity. A steep decline followed by Inkblots bearing the Sundered Star's light . . .

"This world was doomed from the moment he reentered it," Kane Kros had said on the security footage from his lab, where he'd been cornered by Alexander, Ellen, and Iori during the raid. Chief Gardner chalked it up to the ravings of a madman.

Hikaru knew better.

A snap brought him back to reality. Elizabeth was leaning across the bed, hand outstretched to his ear. "Where did you go?" she asked.

"Not far." Seventeen years they'd been together—she his rock, and he her soft place to land. She always noticed when he went adrift, and knew him well enough to deduce why.

"You're thinking about the case again, aren't you?"

"I haven't stopped." Ellen, Alexander, Iori, and Kyani— they were depending on him to fix this. It was his *duty* to fix it. "Their future is in my hands, Lizbet, and every second I'm not making progress, I can feel it slipping away. Falling for Valerie's charade was a colossal failing on my part. I need to make it right."

Elizabeth shifted closer. "What you need is rest," she insisted, rubbing his arms. "We'll figure something out. We always do."

"They've been through so much . . ."

"Whatever troubles they've had to overcome to get to this point, they are right where they need to be. And they're here because of *you*. You've done more for those kids than they'll ever know." She pressed a kiss to his shoulder. "Now get some sleep, or you'll be of no use to anybody." She sank beneath the covers and switched off the lamp on her side of the bed.

With a sigh, Hikaru set his prosthesis aside with its silicone liner and shrugged out of his robe. Yes, he had done many things to preserve the safety of those under his care. Things unremarkable, and things unspeakable.

He turned off his own lamp.

But it's not enough.

MEMORY THREAD //
RADIANT
MAY 22, 2020 | 7 YEARS AGO

If ever a place truly qualified as the middle of nowhere, Hikaru was standing in it. Endless white stretched in all directions, no rooms or windows or doors to speak of. Just a vast emptiness crisscrossed by looping filaments of gold, which shone like dew-spotted spider's silk in the morning sun.

A place so far removed from reality, yet the first question that sprung to his mind was not where or why or how, but *who*.

Who brought him here?

Sirens wailed somewhere in the depths of his subconscious, and an echo of pain traveled up his right leg. Looking down, he discovered a woven casing of light in place of his limb, spun together from the same threads that surrounded him.

How peculiar.

Something tugged at his chest. Pivoting to the pull, he found another string spanning the gap between him and a shining starburst of an object he hadn't the words to describe. Taller than it was wide and much larger than he, it was composed of a myriad of interlacing crystalline plates that shifted through one another unobstructed.

Captivated by its ceaseless motion, Hikaru approached, and without thought or intention, almost on instinct, he reached out to touch it. Felt the atmosphere shiver around it.

His fingertips made contact, and the glasslike panes froze, their vibrations resonating now through his bones.

The object collapsed inwards, folding and shrinking until it had been reduced to a fraction of its original size. A radiant star, cupped in the palm of his hand. And as he held it, that vibration became a voice. Mild yet authoritative, reverberating in his subconscious.

By my light, guide them.

The object flared. Brightness consumed Hikaru's vision, blotting out the dream world—what must have been a dream world—and set his very atoms abuzz. It filled him to the brim, made him weightless and pleasantly numb.

And just as swiftly, plunged him into darkness.

Weightlessness became leaded veins, numbness, a damp and feverish chill. After a minute, the dark lightened to fluctuating reds and greens, and a beep punctuated the murmur of ambient conversation.

A vague sense of knowing skirted his awareness, the whats, wheres, whys beset by a dense fog of delirium. Hikaru forced his eyes open and tried to decipher his surroundings without his glasses: creamy walls, an open doorway, the guardrail of the bed he lay in. A hospital bed?

Slouched beside it was Elizabeth Howard, her own glasses illuminated by her phone screen. Her uniform shirt was a hazy black smear over the arm of the chair, the badge at her hip a blurry silver blob. As Hikaru stirred, her attention shifted up from her phone.

"Hey, easy." She scooped up his hand.

His palms still tingled from the dream. "Where are we?"

"Dumont General Hospital." Dumont, a town outside of Hildegrand. He frowned, and she tried to jog his memory. "You're probably groggy from the anesthesia. Your squad was attacked. Do you remember? Gardner sent us looking for you when you didn't report in." She squeezed his fingers. "Hikaru, what happened in that house?"

House? Which . . .

It all came rushing back then—the chaos, the call, the golden thread connecting him to a little boy looming over a dismembered corpse—and Hikaru jerked forward. "Where is he?"

"Who?"

"The boy. Where's the boy?"

"What are you talking about? What boy?"

"Th-the *boy*, Lizbet. There was a boy at the house." Black hair, red eyes, drenched in—what? Oil, tar? The sick had been bleeding and vomiting that same viscous fluid, the same matter those monsters terrorizing the streets were made of. And the shadows at his feet, on the walls, they'd *moved*. Could he have been affected the way others had been?

Elizabeth pressed him down toward the pillows. "Hold on, you can't be moving around."

Her words didn't register. Hikaru's mind was buzzing, full of strings and light and sprawling white. That strand had lured him into the den. Somehow, he and that boy were linked. "I have to find him." Ignoring the tug of tubes and sensor wires, he swung his legs off the bed. "I need to—"

He lost his balance. Elizabeth intercepted his fall, and his breath halted with his momentum when his gaze landed on the floor. Both feet were planted there, he was sure of it. He could feel it—the cool linoleum under both soles, the waxy texture of its polished surface. But where his right foot should have been, had always been, there was an absence. The limb now stopped above the knee, and the remaining stump had been wrapped in elastic bandages.

Gone.

Hikaru fell back to the bed, unable to take his eyes off it.

Sitting next to him, stabilizing him, Elizabeth explained. "The damage was too severe. They had to amputate." She pored over his face. He must've looked like a ghost. "Hikaru, there was no boy at the house."

"He ran . . ." After he crossed the threshold into the den, guided by that strand of gold, the shadows lunged and the boy took off—past him, past his squad. He remembered staring at the ceiling, a deathly quiet encroaching on him as he lay there, blood leaching into his clothes. His blood, and more. "Where are the others?"

"James is in the ICU. They brought him out of surgery an hour ago." Elizabeth clasped his wrist. "You were the only ones who made it out. I'm sorry."

Hikaru nodded slowly, struggling to process it all. He'd lost people in the past. Fellow officers, even, in the line of duty. This was different. Preventable. If he'd resisted the urge to enter the den, heeded the child's pleas, they may have lived.

You can't bring back the dead, Gardner once counseled.

And no, he couldn't, but there was one thing he could do.

By my light, guide them.

He had to find the boy.

CHAPTER TEN
NOVEMBER 22 | WISEMAN ESTATE

CARDAN MCCONNELL LAY ON THE FIRM chesterfield sofa in the salon—the designated meeting room, and one of few areas in the Wiseman Estate he and Sybil could occupy unsupervised. As always, they were early, because the boss could never be late. Whenever he arrived, he would be on time, regardless of what the grandfather clock in the corner said.

While Sybil made targets of the bookshelf ornaments, firing spitballs at them through a straw, Cardan recounted the events that led him here. It all started on May 21st, 2020.

The day his life changed forever.

As a man from humble beginnings who stocked shelves for a living, Cardan had envisioned himself performing menial tasks for minimum recompense until the day he died. Fate, it seemed, had other plans.

He was at work when it happened. There'd been chatter on the radio about a virus, evolving later into gossip about a second strain correlating with bizarre incidents. People igniting fires without starters, moving objects by sheer power of will. Causing blackouts, floods. Someone had been caught "levitating" on camera.

Bollocks, he thought, until a shelf collapsed at work and suddenly he was halfway across the stockroom with a woman in his arms. That shelf would have crushed her. *Should* have crushed her. Cardan hadn't been near enough to save her, and yet there they were on the floor together, the busted shelf and its dropped load several meters away.

The manager sent them to the office, both shaken like soda cans. *"Keep calm,"* he'd told them. *"There must be a logical explanation."*

Keep calm because I don't want you to run, was what he meant.

A hazmat team showed up shortly thereafter. Cardan's intuition told him to bolt, and his body listened. Fear triggered another jump through the fabric of space, this time dropping him on the apron out front, and he'd legged it from there.

The National Guard netted him like a stray later that evening and carted him off to quarantine. Thing is, when you're among the first afflicted by a strange magical plague, you become the guinea pig. And nobody gave a shite about guinea pigs.

There were no caregivers at the facility, just scientists. Consent—what was that? Needle jabs in arms, legs, and spine. Extractions, injections. X-rays and scans. Piss in this cup, spit in that one. Most of it was a blur since they'd kept him doped-up on sedatives to prevent him from engaging his powers. Then one day when they were understaffed and overrun, someone forgot to change his IV bag. The drugs wore off and he escaped his cell.

Only for the guards to catch him at the exit.

About three months in, some bigwig in an ivory suit came bearing gifts in the form of magic management technology. Patients were outfitted with collars and bracelets, the rooms with copper wire mesh. And so began the tests.

That bigwig, Cardan later learned, was Charles Wiseman, and the point of the tests was to unmask Keepers by exposing their *tells*. He would have uncovered the

Diamond then if Thelonious Hargrove hadn't ordered Alexander Jane's release a month prior.

If only those mayoral powers had reach enough to bail out more than the child of his departed assistant.

Freedom did knock at Cardan's door eventually, though. Distinct lack of Suit aside, his teleportation abilities and track record of breakout attempts caught Wiseman's attention. He paid him a visit off the record, said he was recruiting young Empowered for his cause. *"They've hurt you. You're angry. This would be an opportunity to make use of that anger."*

"What's the cause?" Cardan had asked, not much caring about the *what* if it would get him out.

Magic, Wiseman explained, had been a part of their world long ago, and he believed it was time for humanity to reclaim that power. Said he wanted to elevate the Empowered to a higher status, reshape society, and promised Cardan a seat at the table—not if, but when he achieved his goal. The rest could either conform to this new order, or be crushed by it.

Tired of being the underdog, the decision was a no-brainer.

And so, Blackjack was born. Cardan was transported with twenty others from the facility to the retrofitted asylum on Camrand Island. Management was dubious, coworkers a mixed bag, and the moral compass pointed wherever it needed to. But for once in his life, Cardan belonged—and he belonged to something that *mattered.*

Shame it didn't take long for it to start falling apart.

With the rise of Cardplay and the Wiseman Corporation forced to equip local authorities in order to keep up the guise, Blackjack couldn't maintain their numbers. Several were arrested, injured, or killed. A few deserted the cause. Pretty soon, only Cardan and Flick remained from the original group, and eligible Player recruits were about as rare as hen's teeth.

Now they were hunkered down in the cliffs with a few scraps of a plan, and their numbers had been reduced to four: Cardan himself, a self-serving sniper with no scruples, an aspirant king content to keep his court in ignorance, and an alleged deity with a suitably god-sized complex calling the shots—which may not have been a critique if shots were actually being called.

Nearly a week after the raid, and all Circ had done since unveiling Ellen Amelia Jane as the Heart's Keeper was put on Inkblot puppet shows in the city. Surveillance, he called it, as if Wiseman didn't already have eyes in Hildegrand. If Cardan had to guess, the little sneak was playing games while he bided his time—for *what* was what Cardan wanted to know.

Why did he feel like he was on the bottom again?

Another spitball dinged off an ornament, and Cardan shot upright. "Would you give it a rest?"

Sybil made a mocking face at him, lips curled and pushed out. She went to load another spitball into her straw, then swiped it out of view when the head of the house and his celestial advisor arrived. A tall sophisticated man of extravagant taste, and a shrimpy bare-chested imp whose gait appeared incompatible with the space he inhabited.

Those feet of his, bare and black as if dipped in charcoal, weren't made to walk this mortal plane. Most often, he would float on a miniature nebula of a cloud and phase between locations as needed. For him to be on the ground, he must've been preserving power.

Running low after another puppet show, perhaps?

Cardan swung his legs off the sofa. "Please tell me you have work for us."

The frustration pervading his words stopped Wiseman at the threshold. His pale, predatory eyes raked over Cardan, debating whether to rip into him or let it go. A fine line separated the man's good side from his bad, and it didn't take much of a misstep to cross it.

At last he said, "Soon," and proceeded through the glass panel doors, combing strands of platinum blond over his mangled ear with a glove that likely concealed an equally mangled hand. The damage sustained to his right side in the Spade's awakening may well have been the one sore spot he had.

Good-side standing maintained, Cardan risked another pointed question. "How soon?" After sticking it out this long, he and Sybil deserved answers. "What are we waiting for?"

"The Waning," said Circ.

"The what now?" Sybil flung herself onto the sofa beside Cardan, just about smacking her noggin into his.

Having tolerated the floor long enough, Circ hopped into the air, the gradient of his loose-fitting pants blending into the undulating blue-black cloud beneath him. "There's a natural barrier separating your world from mine. Like your moon, it waxes and wanes with the passage of time. The Waning refers to the annual period where the barrier thins, allowing magic to flow freely between the realms. Before the seals were put in place, that is."

The Suit seals, erected eons ago by the former Keepers to cut the mundane world off from magic. They'd been placed on Elysian Tower—the dimensional bridge connecting the realms—and one by one, Blackjack had been breaking them by forcing the Suits to wake in their human hosts. First the Spade, then the Club, and most recently, the Diamond. Only the Heart remained.

In theory, that one would unleash a flood of pure magic into the mundane world, infusing the global population with the very power they were determined to stamp out. The Empowered would achieve equality by becoming the majority, and no one else would have to suffer the inhumane treatment Cardan had.

One thing didn't stack up, though. The Wiseman family had been preparing for this for generations. "If this happens annually, why have we waited until now? Why not last year? Last century?"

"Because this year is special." Circ drew an infinity loop from his vaporous cloud, light braiding with shadow. "Stardust runs in cycles. Life is born from the Aether and returns to it upon death. Of course, your kind has been recycling the same dust ever since your link to the Aether was severed, but I digress. While this cycle occurred mostly undetected in your world, in the Domain, it made for a momentous affair.

"You see, every three thousand years, Stars are remade. We shed that we are composed of, and are reformed from the celestial streams. It is also plausible that a deceased Star could be reborn during this cycle."

"To put it plainly," said Wiseman, as sick of Circ's verbal roundabouts as anyone, "the seals were never meant to last. What the original Keepers created was a timelock that would commence a graduated release leading up to the rebirth. This began ten years ago when the Suits acquired new hosts, and was set to end with their simultaneous awakening during the Waning. Corruption and ranking made it possible for us to trigger premature awakenings in the Spade, Club, and Diamond. The Heart's purity and status, conversely, make its seal virtually invincible. Only its Keeper can wake it prior to the release of the timelock."

"Can't we just wait for the rebirth to happen?"

The question had barely left Cardan's mouth when Circ growled, "*No.*" Smoke slithered between his bony knuckles, the whirling loop smothered. "If the rebirth proceeds, it would imperil our plans. We must prevent it by infiltrating the Domain *before* the Waning reaches its peak."

Two Stars were better than one, Cardan would have thought. Seeing as he'd already come close to crossing one dreaded line today, he opted not to probe any further. So long as he could do his job, he didn't need the details. Less for him to worry about. "Right, okay." He hunched forward, freckled elbows on denim-clad thighs. "When is this *Waning*, then?"

Wiseman's shoes clumped past the sofa to the window spanning the salon's southerly wall. From this altitude, poised on the edge of the cliffs, the city of Hildegrand could just be made out in the distance. "The barrier will dissipate over the course of the Starlight Festival. The rebirth is set to occur on the seventh day."

The Starlight Festival?

January 1st marked the beginning of a week-long New Year's celebration that traced back as far as history had been recorded. Although its exact origins had been lost in the Cataclysm together with the magical era, the title and the timing . . . It couldn't be a coincidence.

"Our window of opportunity may be small," Wiseman continued, "but I am confident that when it opens, we will be ready. You should also be aware that Valerie Renard will be rejoining us."

Sybil groaned. "You're bringing that hag back into the fold?" They could put aside their differences for work. Behind closed doors, the pair bitched and moaned about each other constantly—Sybil about Valerie's officious conduct, Valerie about Sybil's rudeness and blatant disrespect for authority.

"That *hag* had her uses." Charles Wiseman was the inventor and procurer of stardust, but Valerie Renard was the entrepreneurial engineer who improved and distributed his creations. She had connections he lacked, notably in the supply chain, and they'd had several projects in development at the time of her arrest—primarily in the weapons department. "If you two wish to busy yourselves, I recommend using these next weeks to hone your skills. Your magic, and your aim."

That last point was directed at Cardan, whose marksmanship left much to be desired compared to Sybil the deadeye.

Wiseman angled a stern look at them over his shoulder. "Cardplay has not forgotten us, and when the gauntlet drops, you'd best be prepared to remind them why."

CHAPTER ELEVEN
NOVEMBER 23 | JANE RESIDENCE

STEAM CLOUDED THE FROSTED GLASS CONFINES of the shower as hot torrents streamed over Alexander's back—devoid of sensation in some areas, while in others the water evoked pinpricks of cold or seared like liquid flame.

Or acid, he thought bitterly, studying his marbled hands against the wall tiles. Nails warped, prints erased. His feet were the same. The only greater pain he'd experienced was the Rending Machine—ironically, the one device that hadn't left a mark on him.

His gaze traversed the scars on his limbs and torso, his body a patchwork of painful reminders. The canvas upon which Kane had produced his gruesome paintings.

Blades had been the man's tool of choice. Serrated, straight edge, saw and raker, and each had left its own unique mark. Most of those wounds had healed in fine lines, some in jagged slashes. The few that healed rapidly in the Diamond's awakening had bubbled into keloids.

And where there weren't scars, there were scales—polished flakes of alabaster trailing cobblestone-like paths across his cheeks and shoulders, and down neck and arms and thighs. Nigh-impenetrable organic armor, fused to his skin as if it had always been a part of him. He wished it felt that way.

Very little of his skin felt like his anymore.

At least his creature traits hadn't come with the raised black marks of corruption that accompanied Kyani's scales and raven wings, or Iori's ears and tail.

Alexander twisted the faucet off and carefully dabbed himself dry with a towel before stepping out of the shower and wiping the mirror clear. When he'd first taken in his unclothed image after the raid, it disturbed him to see how Blackjack had changed it. Even now, several days later, the sight made his stomach clench. But he would not satisfy the ghost of Kane Kros by allowing these changes to become a burden.

He would wear every one as a medal.

Once he'd treated the still-maturing scars, he got dressed and collected his medallion from his desk. He ran a thumb over the word JOKER engraved in its rippling banner, over the card suits centered in the decorative windrose above it.

The ping of the object striking the ballroom floor resounded in his memory.

That was the last time he'd called on *Emberguard,* in an alcohol-fueled rage that engulfed his senses in bright and burning red. Its dual pistols and royal military-style garb were still stowed inside the medallion. For close to half a decade, he'd served Hildegrand in that uniform. Wielded those pistols against the wickedness invading their world.

Emberguard used to be a symbol of strength and hope, notably among the young Empowered population, and it had been scorched by his own willful ignorance. But with the Diamond came a chance for redemption, and going into Cardplay Headquarters today, cleared for duty and fully reinstated, he intended to make his image anew.

He pinned the medallion to his belt and went downstairs, wrinkling his nose at the harsh scent of solvents drifting from the living room. Nail polish, so pungent he could practically taste it. He followed a more pleasant aroma into the kitchen—tonight's dinner, already in the slow cooker.

"Are you about ready to go?" he asked Ellen.

"Almost." She slid a container of leftover vegetables into the fridge. "First, I have something for you!"

"What kind of something?"

She snatched an item off the dining table before shuffling over to him, stockings sliding on hardwood and tile. "Here." She presented him with a thin black box, the type you'd buy a necklace in. "Open it."

He took the box and Ellen teetered on her toes in anticipation as he lifted the lid. On a bed of satin inside was a silken ribbon, identical to hers except for the metallic gold beads adorning the ends.

"I wanted to get you a reinstatement gift. I wasn't sure what, but I noticed you'd been wearing your hair up, and it gave me an idea." She ran her fingers through the uneven streamers of her own ribbon, the one she'd worn every day since the crash—if not in her hair, then on her wrist or around her neck. He clued in then to what she'd done.

This ribbon she'd gifted him didn't just look like hers. It *was* hers. A length she'd cut off to give to him.

"I don't know what to say . . ."

"You don't have to." Delicately, she removed the ribbon from its box. "It's a good luck charm. I thought you could use one." She lifted it toward him, and he turned to let her gather his hair into a ponytail. "This might sound silly, but wearing mine's always made me feel closer to them."

To their parents, she meant. Hers was a spontaneous gift from them, an item she'd become obsessed with in a souvenir shop when they vacationed in Ammolitia. Back in the days they were allowed to travel.

Ellen tugged his ribbon to secure it. "You don't need to let go of them, you know. I think when you lose someone you love, a part of them is bound to stay with you. Maybe don't hold on quite so tight from now on, though, okay?"

The beads clattered when he nodded, and Ellen went to kick Iori into gear. Alexander still couldn't talk to her about their parents' deaths and the complex emotions wrapped up in it for him. The fact that he couldn't save them, that he wasn't there when their father passed, and couldn't be there for her afterwards.

Someday he would, when it wasn't the cause of such recent strife.

Someday, when this would all sound like some wild story.

Only a few patches of snow remained at headquarters after the thaw, scattered amidst the grove and hedges and in corners the sun couldn't reach. Deprived of it not too long ago himself, Alexander relished every ray he could catch between the parking lot and the mansion's overshadowed porch.

Walking through these oaken doors yesterday hadn't felt especially momentous. Today, however, as he clasped the handle, medallion at his hip and a full title to his name, it held a certain significance.

A new day. A new Alexander Jane.

He took a breath, pushed the door inward, and—

"SURPRISE!"

Confetti exploded on either side of him and he stopped dead in the entrance. A WELCOME HOME banner hung from the indoor balcony, metallic letters shimmering against a black backdrop. Streamers and balloons had been strung along the double staircase, and beneath the crystal globe chandelier, the dayshift had gathered.

Ellen beamed, taking in all the decorations as Iori slipped in more quietly after her. Alexander was still processing the scene in front of him. "What's going on?"

"Read the sign, bozo." Naomi approached with Aryel and Ikkei, her phone pointed at him.

"Are you recording?"

"Don't tell me you're camera shy all of a sudden."

"I'm not." Twice he tried to swipe the phone from her, twice she evaded. "I just don't want to be filmed when I'm not prepared for it." Finally, he wrested the device from her grasp and went to delete the recording.

"Hey, don't! That's for Kyani," she said, and Alexander's finger paused over the trash bin icon. "I promised I'd record it for her since she couldn't join us."

Denying Kyani that would bruise more than his dignity. For her sake, he returned Naomi's phone.

The rest of the Jokers moved in to greet him, the scent of lavender hitting him like a perfume store delivery truck when Aryel pulled him in for a hug. He tried his best not to get choked up, and it had nothing to do with the gesture. The smell was literally choking him.

Last came Ikkei's crushing embrace, complete with a kiss pressed firmly to the cheek. Alexander's efforts to wriggle free were futile. "Ugh, Ikkei. We did this already. Stop."

The instant they'd heard he was conscious, the gang had swarmed him in the infirmary. Fresh from a grueling period of solitary confinement in which his only physical interactions had been—put mildly—*unpleasant*, he'd found their shower of affection overwhelming.

Still found it overwhelming.

"We've got a lot of time to make up for. I missed you." Ikkei withdrew, restoring a much-needed portion of Alexander's personal space. Wouldn't kill him to return a fraction of the affection, he supposed.

Letting out a huff, he patted the burly arm draped over his shoulder. "Yeah. Missed you, too."

With the surprise segment of the party complete, Naomi ushered everyone into the cafeteria. Several tables had been pushed end-to-end to form a single long one, upon which lay a lemon and blueberry icebox cake big enough to feed the whole building. Conversation bubbled as they dug in, stories of missions past evoking cringes and laughter and muffled *oofs* around bites of melt-in-your-mouth cake.

Alexander eased into the casual simmer of socialization, akin to testing the water before getting into the bath. At first too hot, but once acclimated, he would be hard pushed to get out—which was why he lit a fire under it when the possibility of attending Ulridge Academy arose.

He'd come to see Cardplay as a second home, and the people here as family. Ikkei and Naomi were damn near siblings to him, with Aryel being like the charismatic brother-in-law. Even Hikaru and Elizabeth, though he'd vehemently rejected them early on, were a part of that family. Being his legal guardians didn't make them replacements for the parents he'd lost, and it took him far too long to realize they were never trying to be.

But growing accustomed made the idea of leaving unbearable. His city needed him. His friends needed him. Most of all, he thought, his sister needed him. So, unconsciously, he'd set the water to a boil. Made staying more unbearable than leaving. And he would've boiled alive if his family hadn't saved him.

So now, deliberately, he chose to cherish what he had. Life didn't need to happen in leaps and bounds. For now, he would take it one step at a time.

Metal clattered on china as Naomi set her utensils on her plate. "We noticed you're not on the roster," she said to Alexander. "Is Ritsuo keeping you on a leash, or did you just feel naked without your medallion?"

She wasn't entirely off the mark with the last part. "Focusing my efforts in-house, that's all. Doing demonstrations and stuff."

Aryel plunked his chin in his hand. "Aw, you're gonna be a teacher! The students can call you *Mister Jane*."

Alexander recoiled. "They'd better fucking not." The only people who called him that were reporters and interviewers, and he hated it. *Mister Jane* was his father. On him, the epithet was a too-tight tie, a pair of shoes that would never fit. "It's a short-term thing anyway. Figured I'd make myself useful till I can get back to the field."

"I think you'll be a great instructor," Soren spoke up from the other side of the table. When Alexander looked at him, he retreated bashfully into his shell. "We—I mean, the students—they look up to you. They'd be lucky to learn from you."

Between him and Ellen, parked on the tabletop itself, Tatiana cracked a sly grin. "Do we have an Alexander Jane fan in our midst?"

Soren waved frantically to dispel the notion, Ellen giggling next to him. "N-no! I'm just saying there's a lot to learn from the senior Jokers, and he's one of the best."

It was a fair point. Oskar and Sabaa taught Alexander more about magical combat than Elizabeth had. She made an exceptional battlemaster, but magic held nuance she as a mundane person couldn't easily comprehend. "There's nothing stopping you from sitting in on the demonstrations if you want," Alexander said.

Soren's eyes went round. "Really?"

"As long as you keep your phone volume low. We can't have incident alerts disrupting the lessons."

The boy gave him an enthusiastic and unexpectedly gratifying nod. Alexander had always had mixed feelings about the role model status being foisted on him, but if he could use it to be more than a recruitment ad or some random teen's heart throb, perhaps he could come to appreciate it.

He fetched up his lukewarm apple cider and went to slug back the last of it—just as Aryel bumped him in the midst of an overly-emphatic storytelling session. He caught most of the spill on his face. "*Dude.*"

"Oops, my bad."

"I am begging you to develop some spatial awareness." Alexander grabbed a napkin to dry his chin, licking the sticky residue off his lips, and when Ikkei did a double take, he realized with a jolt of mortification that he *saw*.

"What was *that*?"

Alexander feigned ignorance. "What was what?"

Excitedly, Ikkei reached for him. "Open your mouth."

"The hell is wrong with you? Get away from me—"

Attentions honed in on their close-quarters wrestling match. A stupid tussle over a stupid secret that was bound to come out eventually, and Ikkei wouldn't rest until he'd uncovered it. Rather than let the spectators draw their own embarrassing conclusions, Alexander stuck out his tongue, giving the briefest glimpse of the shallow split in the end before pulling it back in. "There, happy?" He shoved Ikkei away, the man gawking at him like a kid in a toy store.

"Since when are you into body mods?"

"Forget that," Aryel interjected, "when did you get it?"

"Probably when he was blowing us off," said Naomi.

Alexander readjusted his shirt. "I'm not, I didn't, and if it were my choice, I wouldn't have it." Opposite him, Ellen radiated concern. Before he could quash her worries of the worst, Iori guessed the cause.

"The Diamond gave you that, didn't it?"

Even though the others had resumed eating, Alexander was keenly aware of their listening ears. "It did," he replied gruffly. "And it royally fucked up my sense of taste, so I can't say I'm happy about it."

"How so?"

He motioned to the contents of the table. "Everything's stronger. Not flavors, exactly. It's more like . . . scents in the air." The cake's fruity fragrance and the tart aroma of apple cider currently overpowered all other scents in the room, except one. "I also keep getting this weird metallic taste. It was stronger at the complex, but it comes and goes here and at home."

"Well," said Ellen, "Kyani can see auras, and Iori can hear magic. Maybe the Diamond gave you an enhanced sense, too."

"You're implying I can taste magic? Or smell it, or whatever?" The jury was still out on which sense had been affected. His brain logged it somewhere between the two.

"It's possible!" Ellen sounded much more excited about the prospect than he was. "If you're only getting that metallic taste in specific locations, you could be detecting Void magic."

Tatiana let out an obnoxious bark of laughter. "Oh my god, you can taste Iori."

"Terrific, so he can leave a figurative *and* literal sour taste in my mouth."

A smirk crossed Iori's lips. "Kinky."

Alexander grabbed a stack of disposable foam cups and hurled them across the table. Lightning quick, Iori hiked up a leg, teetering off the back of the bench seat to deflect the harmless projectile with an acoustic blast from the sole of his boot.

At the same moment Elizabeth entered the room.

Both of them froze. Foot still stuck in the air, Iori pointed at Alexander. "He started it."

Alexander leveled a glare at him. "You are such a child."

"I am *two* years younger than you."

"Then act like it!"

The battlemaster put her hands up. "I don't have the energy for this. Ryone, if I catch you using magic outside the permitted areas again, you're getting penalized." She stomped off to the serving counter as Iori returned his foot to the floor where it belonged.

Ready for a change of scene, Alexander scooped up a plated slice of cake and a fork and stepped away from the table.

"Where are you running off to?" asked Naomi.

"To have an intelligent conversation," he said faux-haughtily, and she jabbed him playfully in the side on his way by. He crossed the foyer to the infirmary. Here, pungent chemical cleaners saturated the air, and that metallic tang returned when Alexander entered the secure ward—indeed, sharpening the closer he got to Kyani's room.

If the poison eroding her Suit tasted so foul from afar, how must it feel inside her?

Pretty terrible, based on the tight curl of her body beneath the bedcovers. She pushed herself up when she saw him, loose feathers falling from her wings. More littered the sheets.

"Sorry, I didn't mean to wake you."

"No worries," she said, the creamy quality of her voice thickened by sleep. "I've just been feeling a bit dozy. How's the party going?"

Alexander walked over, passing up the chair in favor of the side of the mattress. "I'm not much of a party person. Or a surprise person. I'm enjoying hanging out with everybody, though." He raised his plate in offering. "Cake?"

"For breakfast?"

"It's got fruit and organic cream. That qualifies as nutritious." He held it out to her. "Go on. After all the crap life's thrown at you, don't you deserve to indulge a little?"

She brightened at that. "Alright, you've convinced me." She accepted the cake and cut off a portion, humming in delight the instant it hit her taste buds.

"Good, right? Naomi ordered it from the local bakery."

"It's *amazing*." Kyani carved out another bite. "Your friends are really thoughtful, going to all this effort. It's obvious how much they care about you."

"I hear they've been keeping you company, too. Hope they haven't been pestering you."

"Not at all. It's been nice, actually, coming here and having them be so welcoming."

Alexander's row wrinkled. "How did you expect them to treat you?"

"Like an outcast, I guess. Ignoring my involvement with Blackjack, I've always been sort of an outsider. Talking to plants will do that." She nudged some loose chips of almond onto her fork. "Other kids called me weird, adults used *quirky* to be polite. And yet, odd as I was, I rarely left an impression."

"I find that hard to believe."

"I was small and quiet. I could skip school and no one would notice, speak and no one would hear me. For the first eleven years of my existence, I was practically invisible . . . until the rumors started, and then I wished I could disappear." Kyani smiled sadly. "I'm sorry. That's not a fun story."

"You don't have to apologize." The Kyani Oto he met in the spring was a character she'd fabricated to get close to him. There were glimpses of her in that character, and she revealed her true—albeit, downtrodden—self at the Blackjack complex, but so much of her was still a mystery. "If you're willing to share, I'd like to hear it."

Her eyes flicked up to his. "Are you sure?"

"Nobody's story is perfect. Mine sure as hell isn't." Alexander laid a hand on her arm, marbled similarly to his skin, only hers was black on brown whereas his was pink on white. "I want to know you, Kyani. The real you."

She studied him. Then, as she chipped away at her cake, she told him of the time she became painfully visible, when gossip made her an outcast of a different sort—maligned for shortfalls not of her own, but her family's.

A childhood fraught with turmoil. An emotionally abusive mother who transformed into a physically abusive wife to a husband who'd been struggling to keep them afloat. The further finances dwindled, the worse it got, and husband and daughter both bore the blame.

"He was weak, I was a burden. He wasn't trying hard enough, and I was another mouth to feed. And I was always interrupting something." Work, a conversation, a train of thought—so often that, for a while, she didn't speak at all. Except to her father, to whom she wrote letters even at home.

The rumors started after a neighbor filed a noise complaint and her father showed up to work late with a questionable bruise. In the span of a week, Kyani had gone from being an afterthought to the talk of the neighborhood, and a couple weeks later, she'd come home to find her father on the porch, suitcases packed. One for him, one for her. Chrysanthemum yellow and daisy-spotted blue.

"He loved her. He *tried* to love her," Kyani said. "He thought if she could change for the worse, she could change for the better. But she didn't, and he was scared she would hurt me, so he left her. That was the hardest, bravest thing he's ever done, and he did it for me."

"What happened after that?"

"The Reemergence. We were in a motel for one night and evacuated the next. After the lockdown lifted, my mother filed for a divorce, left for Opalia, and my father and I moved into this tiny studio apartment. Then my powers manifested, got us evicted, and back into the financial sinkhole we went.

When I was twenty, he had a stroke. When I was twenty-two, Blackjack found me. And . . . now I'm here."

"Now you're here," Alexander echoed.

Kyani set her fork on her emptied plate. "I dropped the 'best friend' bomb on you pretty soon after we met. I meant what I said, though. You were the first person in years besides my father to treat me like I genuinely mattered, and not because of my magic. I can't express how . . . how much—" She attempted to stifle a cough and broke into a hacking fit.

Alexander transferred her plate to the bedside table. "Hey, are you alright?"

Shakily, she lowered her hand, and Alexander's stomach dropped when he saw her palm and lips were speckled black.

With *ink*.

They exchanged a look, and the face of the girl in front of him now was not the face of a girl who was ready to die.

Alexander rushed to the alarm on the wall, unlatched the case, and pounded the big red button inside. The door slid shut, sealing the room airtight to stop contaminants from leaking out—and to contain its occupant in the event that her blight turned her violent.

Outside, alarms blared. Emergency lights in the hall tinted Dr. Fornell's and Cellier's coats pink as they hurried into the secure ward, trailing a flock of nurses. Alexander met them at the door, separated by a pane of bulletproof glass.

"Get Hikaru," he said. "Bring Ellen, too."

CHAPTER TWELVE
NOVEMBER 23 | CARDPLAY HEADQUARTERS

ONCE AGAIN, ELLEN FOUND HERSELF at an infirmary room window, hurting for the person on the other side of the glass. Unlike Iori and her brother, however, Kyani wasn't out of the woods yet.

Dark stains streaked her chin. She hadn't coughed up any more ink, but her body jerked involuntarily and her breaths came in shuddering gasps. She could barely lie still enough for Dr. Fornell to conduct her scan.

Iori and Hikaru waited patiently with Ellen for the results while Alexander paced behind them, stirring the apprehension in the hall—stopping only when Fornell exited the room, leaving Kyani in Cellier's care.

She dismissed her horn-rimmed lenses in a glittering plume of particles much prettier than the diagnosis she brought. "The blight has spread throughout her system. It won't be long until it smothers her Suit completely."

Hikaru thumbed the ring on his pinky. "How long, by your estimation?"

"A few hours. A day, if she's lucky." Fornell glanced at Kyani through the window, the girl hugging her knees, weak wings sagging lower as Cellier spoke with her.

Alexander crossed his arms. "She was stable yesterday. What changed?"

Fornell pursed her lips, shrugged. "Something may have exacerbated it, accelerated the spread. Or her Suit could be caving under the pressure. No way to know for sure."

"Alright, so we purify her."

"It's not that simple," said Ellen. "We were relying on her magic to ward off the blight because I thought she might be too far gone. If I try to purify her, we could lose her and the Club." The more severe the corruption, the more likely that purification would lead to extermination. Even those who survived often did at a cost—the erasure of all memory between the point they contracted the disease and the present.

How much did Kyani stand to lose? Everything since the Club awakened in May, since her powers manifested seven years ago? No one could say how long the Suits had lain dormant in their Keepers. Their only hint was Wiseman identifying Iori prior to the Reemergence. What if they were chosen at birth, or conception?

Her whole identity could be wiped out in an instant.

But Alexander made a valid argument: "The longer we wait, the further gone she's going to be. If we don't do this now, we'll lose them both for sure."

Ellen rumpled the pleats of her skirt. He was right. She knew he was right, so why was she paralyzed by indecision?

A hand rested on her shoulder—Hikaru's, firm and encouraging—and alleviated the tension in her body. There was only one decision to make.

She swallowed the lump in her throat. "I'll do it."

Dr. Fornell whisked past them, headed for the reinforced door at the end of the hall. "I'll prep the chamber."

After a hasty discussion, Hikaru led Alexander into Kyani's room to inform her of a last resort experimental treatment. In the interest of adhering to protocol, they wouldn't reveal the details yet. Should enough of her survive the procedure, then would they tell her the truth: that Ellen's psychosomatic powers enabled her to cleanse Void matter.

With the others gone, Iori's silence became impossible to ignore. Not a peep out of him since they arrived, and he hadn't moved from the window. His ears were folded, pupils contracted in the fluorescent glow of the infirmary lights.

Ellen leaned into his field of view. "Iori?"

His jaw flexed. "What if I'm next?"

It dawned on her then that his concern wasn't purely for Kyani. The Club wasn't the only tarnished Suit in the deck.

Both of theirs had been corrupted by unknown means, afflicted already upon awakening. But their experiences with that corruption were incomparable. Iori had always maintained a degree of separation from it. He exhibited none of the standard symptoms of blight, and for the most part, his external marks were unchanging. Hard, blackened scars and a Void-filled eye that bled ink in moments of great duress.

The Club had been infecting Kyani from the start.

"You can't think like that," Ellen told him. "Just because the Club couldn't withstand it, that doesn't mean the Spade can't. It's protected you this long, hasn't it?"

His attention remained glued to the window. Ellen tugged his wrist to drag it away, and she was taken aback by the sheer fright in his eyes. Around and around it swirled, draining gradually as he searched hers. Fortunately, he didn't search too long, otherwise he might've seen that she was scared, too.

Scared because the chill of his corruption was much colder than Kyani's. Scared because if this attempt failed, purification would never be an option for him. Even if she succeeded, even if she saved Kyani, it wouldn't guarantee she had the power to save him. They just had to hope the Spade could ward it off.

But all things had a breaking point.

One problem at a time, Ellen reminded herself.

Once the room was ready, operating theatre reconfigured into purification chamber, she followed Hikaru and Dr.

Fornell inside—Iori right on her heels despite being repeatedly advised to wait in the hall.

"If this goes wrong, you won't want to be there," Ellen warned him.

Even knowing that *wrong* meant a person reduced to ashes on the floor, he replied simply, "I'm staying."

It was unclear whether he felt obligated to be there to support an ally and fellow Keeper, or if he came hoping for a glimpse at salvation.

Last to arrive was the girl of the eleventh hour, carried in by Alexander. Her arms were looped round his neck, the few patches of unmarred skin on her body rapidly shrinking.

He lowered her onto the operating table. Surgical lights shone from above, deepening the fretful lines on her brow as the doctor instructed her to lie flat. Alexander offered her some words of consolation and a squeeze of the hand, then retreated to the edge of the room with Fornell, Iori, and Hikaru.

Light pooled around Ellen and Kyani, alone in the center.

Kyani stared up at her in question, in despair, the inky blotches surrounding her irises making their lavender color vivid. Full black indicated a devoured soul, the body hollowed out to make room for the Void. There was still white in hers.

Standing at the head of the table, Ellen brought her fingers to Kyani's temples. "Close your eyes. Try to relax."

With a fraction of hesitation, her lids fluttered shut.

Ellen closed hers as well, concentrating on the pulse beneath her fingertips. Magic rose from her reservoir and spilled down her arms into the sickly girl on the table, pervading the fabric of her subconscious. Seeping into the darkest corners of her mind.

Blight fed primarily on misery and anger, sinking its fangs first into the most vulnerable memories—familial plights, self-loathing, shame, trauma. Appetizers. The bittersweet made for a delectable main course, and then it would treat itself to happiness for dessert.

Purification was the process of cleansing the memories the disease had latched onto, and the recipe for success called for joy. For light. The lesser, the dimmer, the lower the odds.

Kyani's was a bright but distant flicker, a beacon at the bottom of a muddied well. Determined to reach it, Ellen plunged into the archive of her life.

The Void flowed icily against her own magic, ushering in images of a slanted house, raised fists, brutal machinery, and raven feathers dripping black onto a linoleum floor—ghostly flashes that roused emotions in Ellen as real and visceral as if they were her own.

The earliest deep purification Ellen performed had left her in a borderline catatonic state, struggling to process the overload of information. To this day, nobody understood why, because she hadn't told anyone about this part. If the sick knew she could flip through their history like a photo album, they may be reluctant to accept help.

So she kept it to herself. Tucked the albums of the lives she hadn't lived into the attic of her brain, and ensured their secrets were secure. The same would go for Kyani's. All her growing pains and moral stains, the guilt that wore on her conscience. Every piece Ellen touched, she would clean and polish and put back where she found it.

She pushed through the turbulence of Wiseman's manipulation, the torture, the desperation that led Kyani to Blackjack, and the remorse tangling up her interactions with Alexander. Ellen faltered at the glimpses of her brother in the complex—a dangerous slip in the presence of the Void.

She hardened herself against them and kept going.

Scarlet blooms cleared a path to that enduring beacon at Kyani's core. But when Ellen's magic infused the fog surrounding it, something changed. The memories swirling about her now were on the verge of forgotten. Hazy recollections of strange people and strange places, and a fizz of anguish that felt somehow detached from Kyani's, yet it enshrouded her soul all the same.

Because these were parts of a life that didn't belong to her.

The imprint of the Club's former Keeper.

And then it was gone, overtaken by Kyani's brilliant glow—the warm emerald of sun-stroked leaves. The second Ellen made contact, all that pain and misery from earlier was chased away by an outpouring of love and joy and untempered wonder that filled Ellen's head again with pictures of her brother, and of Cardan, but mainly of a beaming, balding man.

Kyani's father.

He was her constant. Her light.

Please, Ellen begged, *let it be enough.*

Her soul grew brighter and brighter, spurred by Ellen's magic. Brimming, overflowing. And when Ellen opened her eyes, scarlet particles a reverse snowfall around them, she found Kyani's staring straight into hers—wide and white.

Awake.

Alive.

Aware.

No loss of memory or self either, judging by how she sat up to inspect herself. She rotated her arms, scanning every inch of skin within view. Even the hardened Void marks that once encircled her wings and scales had vanished.

Both girls burst into tearful laughter, and as Kyani pulled Ellen into her embrace, no goosebumps broke out on her skin. She couldn't detect the slightest tingle of a chill besides Iori's, increasing as he and the others neared.

Withdrawing, Kyani leant into Alexander's side hug, a shaky bundle of emotions in his caring hold. "I told you you'd be okay," he said.

"I don't understand how this is possible. We were told blight was incurable without the—" Kyani paused. Swiftly, she took Ellen's hands, beholding them as if a priceless artifact. "Healing touch. I didn't know what it meant before, but it's you, isn't it?" She looked into Ellen's perplexed face, that untempered wonder unfolding on hers. "You're the Heart."

Three words to dispel the reverent bliss of the atmosphere.

Iori's shock was a reflection of Ellen's own; Alexander's expression like a sheet hung to dry. And Hikaru—Hikaru hung like a grim spectre at the perimeter of the pooling light, not a hint of shock to be found behind his lenses.

Why did he look like that?

As the dust of that bombshell settled, Dr. Fornell moved in to examine Kyani, whose wonder gave way to confusion as she read the room.

"That can't be right," Alexander said.

"It must be." At the doctor's request, Kyani spread her wings. Though still frayed, her feathers didn't sound so brittle anymore. "The Heart's tell is said to be a healing touch. What else could that refer to?"

Tells were the subtle signs of a dormant Suit Wiseman had used to identify the Keepers. Iori's was his musical talent, Kyani's her green thumb, Alexander's a unique fire resistance that made him immune to all its forms—not merely the flames he conjured. The Heart was the only Suit that hadn't been identified, the only one Wiseman was still hunting for.

Before they could delve into further speculation, the headmaster stepped in and addressed Ellen, Iori, and Alexander. "Would you three kindly give me a moment alone with Miss Oto?"

Without protest, they exited the purification chamber and went to wait in Kyani's room. Parked on the side of the bed, staring past her dangling shoes, Ellen half-listened to the conversation between Iori and her brother, who'd resumed his earlier pacing. They were talking about her like she wasn't even in the room.

For all the presence she could muster, she might as well not be.

"Healing hands could be anything."

"It really can't," Iori drawled jadedly.

"A literal healing ability. For wounds or broken bones. She *can't* be a Keeper. What are the odds of that?"

"We can't ignore the evidence." Leaning against a counter, Iori gestured to Ellen. "What she can do is unheard of. It also explains why she can detect Void matter. I can hear it, you can taste it, Oto can see it. She can feel it. Don't tell me that didn't strike you as even remotely coincidental when we were talking about it this morning."

"You and Kyani can sense pure magic as well, though."

Iori tilted his head, tail tip twitching. "Can't help noticing you excluded yourself from that equation. If you can't sense it either, that kind of makes it a null point."

"There has to be another explanation." Alexander's shoes passed in front of Ellen again, then his steady pace faltered, tripped up by a revelation. "The rest of us didn't gain our senses until *after* our Suits awakened."

A lackluster revelation. He was grasping at any straw, no matter how short, that could debunk the theory that his baby sister was the Heart's Keeper. However, the more she thought about it, the more she believed she could be. Stringent rules, strange phrasing, and scattered pieces of reasoning that previously seemed unnotable had begun to assemble into a whole and hard to swallow truth in her head.

"You, my dear, have been gifted with something truly special."

That was what Hikaru told her when her powers manifested, after she'd cleansed an Inkblot bite on his arm.

From that moment on, he had made it his mission to keep those powers hidden, going so far as to fudge her documentation—labeling her pyric instead of psychosomatic, the same way he'd disguised Iori's corrupt acoustic magic as *umbric*. Shadow manipulation. It was only when Ellen learned to mask her abilities by funneling them through a weapon, her scythe, that he'd allowed her to graduate.

All things considered, she had to wonder . . .

"What if he knew?"

Both boys' heads swiveled to her.

Her brother asked, "Who?"

"Hikaru," she said quietly. "It would make sense, wouldn't it? All the secrecy, all the times I've been pulled off duty."

Alexander looked almost as flabbergasted by her supposition as he had been by Kyani's. "Your powers are unique. Lots of people would want to exploit them. Doesn't that make perfectly logical sense by itself? You don't really think he'd lie to us."

Ellen shriveled at the notion. "Not *lie*. It's not like he's ever denied knowing." No one had ever thought to ask, and why would they? They'd always assumed the extent of his knowledge was contained on his bookshelves, in the handwritten journals he used to teach magic history.

"If he *was* aware you were the Heart's Keeper..." Caution edged Alexander's tone. "Would he have known I was the Diamond's?"

Neither of them wanted to go down that rabbit hole. The implications on the surface were discomforting enough—that he might've known from the start that both of his adopted children harbored legendary magics. That he may have known before adopting them.

Iori stopped them from staying too close to the hole, lest one of them slip in. "I don't think so," he said, elbow in hand and chin resting on his knuckles. "I had to convince him I fought the Diamond at Elysian Tower. Why keep up the act after that?"

Coming from Iori, the most distrusting person in the building, that gave Ellen a sliver of faith to cling to. Still, she couldn't decide which outcome she'd prefer—that Hikaru knew, or that he didn't. That she was the Heart, or that she wasn't. It would lend more importance to his actions, but what purpose would it serve to keep this from her? And if he had been withholding it all this time, what else could he be hiding?

She smothered her anxious thoughts. She couldn't let this speck of doubt recolor her entire perception of him. Whatever secrets he held, she had to believe he'd withheld them for good reason.

Groaning in frustration, Alexander interlocked his fingers behind his head. "We won't know anything until we talk to him."

Ellen detected movement beyond the window blinds and hopped to her feet as Dr. Fornell helped a wobbly Kyani back to her room, the headmaster tailing them in.

"Well?" prompted Alexander.

"We're going to keep her under observation for twenty-four hours to be on the safe side," said Fornell, "but from the looks of it, the purification was a success. No residual signs of blight, or any indication of cognitive impairment. A few days' rest, and she should be right as rain."

"And once Miss Oto has been discharged," Hikaru added, much less grave than before, "I am pleased to say she will be moving into the dormitory hall."

Excitement blossomed in Ellen's chest. "You're staying?"

Kyani dipped her head appreciatively. "Your headmaster made me a very generous offer of residency, not contingent on my admittance to the rehabilitation program."

"There's no way *he* gets in and you don't." Alexander flung a look at Iori, who stuck his tongue out in response.

That got a mild chuckle out of Hikaru. "Her placement in the program is all but guaranteed. I'll put in a call to Mira this afternoon and we should be able to make it official next week. First and foremost, there is paperwork in need of my signature." He pivoted on his prosthetic heel. "Ellen, would you join me upstairs when I've finished?"

That only sounded mildly foreboding.

Ellen murmured in subdued compliance, feeling as if she were about to be reprimanded. Dr. Fornell then passed Kyani over to Alexander's sturdy hands and led Hikaru to her office, leaving the four of them in the disquieted room.

"Well, here we are," said Iori. "Four of a kind."

CHAPTER THIRTEEN
NOVEMBER 23 | CARDPLAY HEADQUARTERS

AFTER BEING SHOOED OUT OF KYANI'S ROOM, Ellen climbed the steps to the headmaster's office. Having had time to play through various scenarios in her head, she'd come to the conclusion that she had nothing to be afraid of.

This was the man who took her and her brother in when no one else would, who stood in their defense when the world turned against them. Though he couldn't fill the hole of her parents' absence, he'd made it less of a chasm. Raised her as his own, taught her the hard lessons of life.

Always, he'd had her best interests at heart. But she was old enough now to decide where her own best interests lay.

Ellen knocked twice and poked her head into the office. The headmaster was at his desk, pen scratching away at never-ending paperwork. He waved her in, promising to be with her momentarily, and the door clicked shut with the weight of her body against it.

She waited patiently, semi-patiently, the handle clutched at her back. A moment was all Hikaru requested, and Ellen had nowhere else to be, but she had a question burning on her tongue, and if she held it too long, she feared she may lose her nerve and swallow it down.

Screw patience. He'd kept her waiting long enough. She took a breath and asked, "How long have you known?"

Hikaru lifted his gaze. The light reflecting off the parchment from below painted him like an old portrait. He set his pen in its holder and pushed his papers aside. "Come here," he beckoned, reclining as she approached. "I had intended to tell you when the time was right. It would seem that time has been chosen for me."

So he had known. "Why not tell me before? Why wait?"

Conflict tugged at the upward curve of his lips. "How does one tell such a small child that she bears the weight of the world on her shoulders?"

For that, she had no answer.

"I was afraid of the ramifications," he said. "How it would affect you, what might happen if the wrong ears overheard." Ellen couldn't claim she wouldn't have let it slip after she'd blurted out the truth of her Void-cleansing powers to Iori within minutes of meeting him. "When your powers manifested, I'd only recently learned what you were. I had no idea what you would be capable of, or what that would mean for you. All I knew was that I had to keep you safe."

Ellen wrung her hands. "What about Alexander? Did you know about him?"

His shoulders slumped. "Oh, child, no. If I had, I would never have put him in harm's way." He pushed up from his chair and rounded the mahogany desk. Then, with a note of amusement: "Whether I would have been able to keep him out of it is another matter."

Alexander was the one who'd insisted on the premature graduation. Hikaru's reluctance had been outweighed by a need for more Jokers.

He invited her into a one-armed embrace. "I am sorry I couldn't tell you sooner. I forget sometimes that you're no longer a little girl with her head in the clouds. You're growing up, and you're coming down to Earth." His voice rumbled in his chest, a murmur in her hair. "Can you forgive me?"

She nodded, mostly satisfied with his explanation even though it still stung that he'd kept it from her in the first place. "How did you find out, though?" Of all the Suits, they knew least about the Heart. Most poems spoke only of its Keeper and her moonlight trysts with the Spade's.

Ellen tried not to draw comparisons between that and her more personal predicament.

Hikaru smoothed his waistcoat. "I had access to materials others did not. They were destroyed for your protection; however, it appears Charles Wiseman managed to obtain his own information elsewhere. That in mind," he said, "I advise you keep this within our circle. I've already ensured that Miss Oto understands the seriousness of the situation. Please instruct your brother and Ryone to do the same."

Another nod. *What's one more secret?* Recognizing the importance of keeping her other friends in the dark didn't make it any less disappointing. "Where do we go from here?"

"Stay the course. This changes nothing. As of yet, we have no reason to believe Wiseman is aware of the Heart's location, but he will be watching us closely, and any diversion from our current trajectory could alert him to the fact we have it." When Ellen said no more, he asked, "Was there anything else?"

She shook her head.

"Run along then. I'll be here if you need me."

Despite ending on a high note with the purification of the Club, the emotional rollercoaster of a morning had left everyone emotionally drained, and the party had been disbanded. They still had energy to babble, though, and babble they did well into the evening. But amidst the many voices that had churned around Iori, Ellen's silence had spoken the loudest.

Her Keeper status had lent clarity to a number of former unknowns. Why she could do what she could, feel what she felt. Why the headmaster had kept a side of her locked in the highest room of the tallest tower, hidden from the world.

Clarity, however, wasn't always sunny.

A cool draft greeted Iori when he walked into Ellen's bedroom, carrying two steaming mugs of cocoa. Winter air slithered through the ajar balcony door. Ellen was outside in a bowl chair, wrapped in a knit blanket, watching effervescent stars twinkle in the black pitcher of night. The very image of melancholy.

Iori had years to come to grips with what he was. Even Kyani and Alexander had received ample notice. But the truth had been dropped on Ellen late in the game, leaving minimal time to strategize.

He toed the sliding door open further, its rasp drawing Ellen's attention as he stepped onto the balcony. The evening was mild by November standards. Not mild enough to be forgetting to close doors.

Ellen rubbed her nose, pinkened by the cold. "Hi."

"Hey." Iori presented both mugs. "I made hot chocolate." He passed her the one in the shape of a polar bear and kept the festive red-and-white for himself. The brush of her icy fingers against his should not have been worth cataloguing, but that didn't stop him from filing it alongside the other totally-not-significant touches. Playful shoves, the accidental knock of knees and occasional head-on-shoulder lean, or the rare delight of a handhold.

He wished he could pluck up the courage to reach out and take hers now. To warm them. To hold her and comfort her as she'd done for him. A hug wouldn't likely expose his feelings, but the minute possibility that it could kept him from making any physical gestures of consolation.

Hopefully the hot beverage would suffice. Her small gifts of treats and trinkets always cheered him up.

"Are you okay?" she asked. "You looked pretty shaken up earlier."

Funny, I was going to ask you the same thing, thought Iori, resting against the balcony's wooden railing. "I'll live." He'd seen blight worse than Kyani's. Although, none of those had stemmed from a corrupted Suit. "How are you?"

Ellen tracked the marshmallows swirling in her drink, the buoyant lumps of sugar and gelatin dissolving into frothy trails. She didn't reply.

"It's bothering you, isn't it?"

She stroked the polar bear mug's ceramic ears. "I feel like someone put me in a snow globe and shook it, and now I can't tell which way is up."

"That's a seasonally appropriate simile." Iori's attempt to lift her spirits only resulted in her sinking lower into her woolen blanket. "Which part are you struggling with?"

"All of it," she said. "Hikaru told me this changes nothing, but it changes *everything*. How I interact with people, how I view the world. At dinner, I kept thinking how useless the alarm system is. Would it go off in time to stop a teleporter from kidnapping me? Can motion sensors even detect magical entities?" She was referring to Cardan McConnell and the Sundered Star. "Then I started wondering how they'd force the Heart out of me, and what might happen if they did . . ."

One hypothesis was that waking the Heart would lead to an influx of pure magic from the Domain—as opposed to the Spade, which had previously dammed the Void and unleashed a flood of darkness when it broke. But none of them could fathom why the Sundered Star, a being of darkness himself, would want that. The more likely scenario was that breaking the fourth and final seal would trigger another Cataclysm. A magical disaster of such magnitude to end the world as they knew it.

"Are you aware what was sacrificed to imprison him? What it took to seal the realms?" echoed Kane's dying words.

It couldn't be a fluke that the two events were connected. As for how an awakening might be forced, at least there was comfort in knowing the Rending Machine was out of order and Blackjack didn't have the resources to build or fuel another.

"On top of everything else," Ellen said, voice taut with frustration, "I don't get why it chose *me*. Alexander's a natural fighter, Kyani's always had this intimate connection to nature, and your bones might as well be filled with music instead of marrow. What's so special about me?"

It pained Iori to see her so lost and low on morale. Combat may not have come easy to her, and perhaps nature and rhythm were mere acquaintances in her life, but here was a girl who'd gone to great lengths to protect her loved ones. Who gave hope and care to all in need, even at a detriment to herself.

With or without magic, she had the power to save lives.

And she had saved his—more than once.

Scents of cinnamon and rich cocoa coiled under Iori's nose, and he smiled, because the answer was obvious. "Your heart," he told her. "I'd argue it's the most important part. We may trust our guts, but we follow our hearts. We know by them, thank from the bottom of them. Cross them to pledge our deepest, most solemn oaths. They're where we keep our courage, and our affections..." He touched his chest, felt his own beating behind his ribs. "You lead with yours. Every bond forged is an artery, and you're the thing that keeps the blood pumping through them. I don't know about you, but that sounds pretty special to me."

When he lifted his gaze from his mug, he found Ellen's brimmed with an emotion he couldn't identify. Bafflement, probably, at the load of absolute besotted drivel that just spilled unchecked from his mouth. "What I'm saying is: you don't need some fancy talent to be worthy. You already are, just by being you."

She clutched her drink closer, rosy cheeks rounding.

"If it helps," Iori added, "you're not alone. Besides an ear for music, what do I have to offer? I never wanted to be anything more than ordinary. My pursuit of music wasn't motivated by fame or money. If I could make people *feel*, my job was done." He ran a thumb along the rim of his mug. "But for better or worse, this is the duty we were entrusted with. All we can do is rise to the occasion."

"I suppose you're right," Ellen agreed.

"When have I ever been wrong?"

"Do you really want me to answer that?"

He laughed through a shiver, the cold beginning to seep into his socks and his sleeves. Living someplace dry with actual heating these past few months had made him more sensitive to the elements. Seeing as he had no need to harden himself to it, he yielded to the desire for warmth. "I'm heading in. You coming?"

Ellen gathered her blanket, more cheerful than he'd found her, and followed him indoors.

CHAPTER FOURTEEN
NOVEMBER 26 | JANE RESIDENCE

IT WOULD HAVE BEEN MESMERIZING, how the light flickered between his lashes, if Ellen didn't know it to be a warning.

Iori squirmed in bed beside her, the stiff hunch of his shoulder outlined by the city glow pervading the balcony curtains. His ears twitched to sounds unheard, face contorted in shadow. And with every heaving breath, every surge of emotion, that violet flare of magic shone brighter.

Usually, Ellen could take his hand as she did now, his fingers curling instinctively to her touch, and ease him through the worst of it. Quelling terrors, however, was a battle she couldn't always win.

The twitching traveled into his limbs, eyelids crinkling as erratic breaths pushed a voice to his lips. The combination of mumbled speech and the fact he often reverted to Jeidish made it difficult to decipher what he was saying, but she had learned one phrase that frequented his sleeping tongue.

Help me.

All around, ink flowed—from the barkless trunks of decaying trees, the shriveled funnels of calla lilies. More bubbled from fissures in the stone floor, pooling in the middle where Iori stood.

No matter how he willed his feet, they would not move.

The gems clutched in the bars of the gates encircling him were dark, the two previously lit having lost their luster and the Heart's still deep in slumber. Behind him, the glow of his throne's own amethyst dimmed.

A sluggish beat throbbed in his skull, crawling thickly through his veins. His gaze snapped down to his arms, and his blood would've run cold if it weren't already freezing. Where there should have been faint blue-green trails, black paths wove instead, creeping up to his shoulders and leaving ugly bruises in their wake.

No, no, no . . .

He blinked, and tears of liquid onyx trickled down both cheeks. Tried to inhale, and found his lungs full. Opened his mouth to scream, and ink smothered his voice, spilling over into palms open to catch it.

No, please—

It beaded on his skin, seeped from his pores. Leaked from ears, nose, and cascaded from the gaping void in his chest. He couldn't move, couldn't breathe, couldn't speak. Couldn't hear past the laboring thump of his dying pulse.

Help me.

Black tendrils snaked into his corneas, threatening to consume his vision.

Help me!

The world darkened, but through the thickening shadows, a glimmer of red. A spark in the depths of the ruby heart.

HELP—

A shout erupted from Iori's throat. He sat bolt upright, grabbing at his tank top and the mark underneath—no longer a gaping, gushing wound, but the firm slash of vitrified ink it had always been. He patted his cheeks, dry save for the clammy film of sweat on his skin. Examined his arms, veins untainted.

The foggy realm of the dreamscape had been replaced by four pastel walls; the gates with a balcony window, a closet, and a bedroom door; and the decaying forest with furniture.

He was home, safe, and Ellen confirmed it.

"It's okay," she said. "It was just a dream."

Iori lay back on the sweat-dampened sheets, Ellen watching him closely. *Home. Safe. Just a dream,* he told himself. A new mantra. But as the frantic beat in his ribcage slowed, the ice-laden panic from the nightmare began to thaw, and despite his efforts to hold it in, it was the pitiful sound of his own voice that unlatched the floodgates.

Everything came pouring out in hot streams, and each whimper he failed to suppress only made him cry harder. Made him sweatier and shakier and more sorry for himself than he already felt. These tears did nothing to eradicate the curdling distress in his stomach.

How could anyone call this therapeutic?

"I hate this," he croaked between hiccupped sobs. Hated this feeling, hated that his mind was a beast he couldn't tame. Hated that his disturbed sleep disturbed Ellen's, and that his screams must disturb her brother's as well. How humiliating.

Ellen's thumb swept back and forth in soothing arcs on his upper arm. "Was it the same one again?"

He managed a nod, nails tensed against his brow. Every night since Kyani's close brush with the Void and in every wink he'd tried to catch between, he'd been tormented by visions of blight. He almost preferred the haunts of Wiseman's still-living ghost. That monster was too far away to do any real harm. The Void, conversely, remained ever present—a parasite entrenched in his soul, waiting for his Suit to drop its guard.

"You could try sleeping aids," Ellen suggested.

"No. I don't want to mask these." Iori combed back his fringe, resting his other hand on his chest. "I can't shake the feeling that they mean something . . ."

"Like what?"

He shrugged. The nightmares he'd been having lately were different than usual, and not only because of their dreamscape setting. In every recurrence, they showed him the same scenario: the place flooded with ink, all gates dark, his gem dimming in the background. Although, he couldn't recall the Heart's gate glimmering before.

The first time, he'd been convinced he went there. That what he'd seen was actually happening. A quick trip to the dreamscape upon waking had proven it was fine, if it could be called that in its decrepit state.

Still, it felt as though the Spade were trying to communicate with him.

He curled his fingers over the hardened ridge of Void matter beneath his shirt.

What are you trying to tell me?

CHAPTER FIFTEEN
NOVEMBER 26 | HILDEGRAND, MID DISTRICT

"WE DO ACTUALLY HAVE TO TALK FOR THIS TO WORK."

Dr. Bristol sat across from Iori, notepad in lap, her tweed chair a match to the sofa he slouched in. Her mid district office was a cross between cozy and clinical. Too bare to feel like a home, homey enough that he could almost forget he was undergoing a mental dissection.

Originally, these appointments were to be held at Cardplay Headquarters, but Iori had made a last-minute request to move them off-site, not wanting the lounge—a location he visited to de-stress—to become contaminated by the feelings these sessions would surely rouse.

Then again, he wouldn't have to worry about rousing anything if he didn't let Bristol in. Though he should've been open and honest and responding to questions with more than noncommittal grunts, hums, and shrugs, he couldn't seem to unlock his jaw to do so.

He propped an elbow on the sofa's arm, resting his head on his wrist. "I know. I'm just . . . tired." A half-truth. He may have been more cooperative if he'd slept better. "If it's not anxiety keeping me up, it's the back-to-back horror movie marathon."

"You've been having nightmares?"

Iori murmured in affirmation, and a pen rasped on paper. Dr. Bristol was scribbling in her notepad, long acrylic nails claw-gripping a ballpoint pen. Should've known better than to mention dreams. Psychologists ate that shit up.

She leaned forward, attentive. "Tell me about them."

If she wanted to analyze the demons in his head and get to the root of the issue, he'd already been there and done that, and she wouldn't have the means to decipher their latest show. But if she could give him some guidance on how to shut them out, it might be worth sharing.

She jotted more notes as he described the dreamscape, excluding its status as an existent even if non-physical realm. Told her about the gates while omitting their real world connections, and about the ink and the blight. Mumbled about a friend who'd had a scare when Bristol inquired as to what provoked these terrors.

Plenty of people were scared of getting blighted or losing loved ones to the disease. Such was the risk of living in Hildegrand. Dr. Bristol said as much, stating that his fears were not unfounded but the chances of contracting it were low, especially for an Empowered person such as himself.

If he told her he already carried it, droning like a swarm of hornets in the deepest cavity of his body, he'd be locked up in quarantine. He couldn't tell her that his friend's case was unique, or that the demon he feared was real. And no one could assure him he would be okay, because no one knew if he would be.

The Void was static in him now. What about tomorrow?

They spent the remainder of the hour talking about fears and triggers and how best to manage them. When their time was up, she gave him a faux leather journal and recommended he write his dreams down to better process them, then sent him on his way.

Tucking his scarf into his jacket and smoothing his beanie over concealed ears, Iori exited the clinic—his belt of a tail puffing when a maroon minivan honked at him from the curb. The *whoosh* of pneumatic magic told him who the driver was before the window rolled down, revealing Tatiana Kosta.

She flashed him a peace sign. "Yo. Need a ride?"

Iori eyed her dubiously. "Who gave you a license?"

"I am perfectly capable of driving a motor vehicle, thank you very much." She rapped her knuckles on the steering wheel. "This baby is the result of two years of concerted effort. No more carpooling with Soren's parental units or inhaling B.O. on the bus. It's gonna be sweet." When Iori made no move towards the van, she snapped, "Are you getting in or what?"

Might as well.

That new used car smell of freshly washed upholstery enveloped Iori as he climbed into the passenger seat. The padding was a tad worn, and there was a dent in the dash. Somehow, that seemed fitting for her.

"Safety first, please." Tatiana wagged a finger at the seatbelt. "I am not getting fined because your twink ass decided to live dangerously."

"If you get fined, I doubt my *twink ass* would be to blame." Iori fastened his seatbelt and they pulled away from the clinic, hot air blowing from the vents.

They drove for several blocks in silence, a beaded mirror accessory jangling at every turn and traffic light. Then Tatiana's hands flexed around the steering wheel, and he could tell she was gearing up to break some ice.

"So," she began, "first impressions of therapy?"

"Well, I've officially been diagnosed as a disaster, so that's fun." Strictly speaking, he hadn't *officially* been diagnosed yet, but Dr. Bristol suspected post-traumatic stress disorder and generalized anxiety based on the file Mira Hodge had provided. How about that? His issues were so blatant they could be garnered from a piece of paper and two sixty-minute meetings. Of course, that file probably mentioned the repeat breakdowns he'd had after discovering the man responsible for his torment was, in fact, not a corpse.

"It'll get easier," Tatiana said, to which he gave an incredulous look. "What, you think you're the only one who needs professional assistance sorting out your problems? Join the club."

"Oh yeah, what are you in for?"

"It's not *prison*. Jeez." She flipped on the indicator and switched lanes. "We survived a magical catastrophe, dude. People don't come out of that without a few screws loose. Or a few wound up too tight, in my case. Therapy's not a nice experience, but it can help—if you let it. You can't expect proper treatment without telling them where it hurts."

Iori slumped in his seat.

"Don't be a sour puss," chided Tatiana. "I have just the thing to cheer you up." She brought the van to a stop at the side of a road in the older part of the mid district, where the buildings were age-worn, antiquely adorned, and slanting on their foundations.

"This isn't headquarters," Iori observed flatly.

Tatiana pulled the keys from the ignition. "I thought we could take a detour. It's been a while since you and I had a one-on-one."

Yeah, there's a reason for that.

After some increasingly annoying verbal persuasion, Iori got out of the car and followed her to a corner café with an engraved wooden sign. *The Humble Bean.* Its chalkboard standee on the sidewalk welcomed customers in from the cold and listed their specials for the day—a selection of warm beverages and soups.

A bell announced their entry. The place, filled with the caramelized aroma of brewing coffee, boasted a wide variety of baked goods. Fresh bagels, sandwiches, doughnuts, and muffins. Plenty to choose from for the modest crowd occupying its tables, most of whom were huddled behind laptops or scrolling on their phones.

Tatiana bounced up to the counter and dinged the bell in rhythmic repetition. Iori hissed at her to cut it out, but she waved him off. "Chill. This is my moms' café."

A stout woman emerged from the back a moment later, carrying a fresh tray of pastries. She was a few shades closer to olive than Tatiana, with frizzy black hair compressed under a net and smears of flour on her apron. "Tati! We weren't expecting you until dinner. Everything go smoothly with the car?"

"Yep, decided to spend my lunch break catching up with a friend." She hooked her arm with Iori's and dragged him closer to the counter. "Ma, this is the guy I was telling you and Mo about."

Great, she's been talking about me.

"Iori, right?" The pastry rack rattled into the display case, and the woman straightened up. "I'm Rosa. I'd shake your hand, but . . ." She waved hers in the air, dusted with more flour.

Disconnecting from Tatiana, Iori stooped in greeting.

"What can I get you two?"

"I'll have one of those solstice hot chocolates with the peppermint flakes. Ooh, and a cinnamon roll," said Tatiana, her mother punching the order into the register. She turned to Iori. "Whaddaya fancy? You like chai, right?"

"I'm good, thanks."

"Give him a chai latte. If he doesn't drink it, I will."

Iori narrowed his uncovered eye at her and Rosa's smile lines deepened, no stranger to her daughter's antics. She had half-siblings, too. Were they all as loud and rambunctious as her? Iori couldn't fathom living in a house full of Tatianas.

They shuffled over to another counter to wait for their order. "I never mentioned liking chai," Iori said. They'd talked about a lot of stuff. Personal stuff. Skipped over the introductory elementary school-style sharing of favorites and jumped straight into the deep end of the topics pool.

"You were living off those chai drinks a couple months ago, weren't you? It's gotta be in your top five."

At his lowest, his appetite had been nonexistent, and Ellen, worried he'd waste away, had convinced him to try meal replacement shakes. For days, they were all he could keep down. "Why do you know that?"

"I work random shifts here. Remembering a regular's order makes them feel appreciated, and I do café runs for folks at HQ, so I try to take note of what everyone likes. Soren's forever loyal to the blueberry pastries, Ellen's a strawberry-anything girl. I could even tell you the masters' orders."

So committing those details to memory was how she showed she cared, like Ellen's acts of service or the headmaster's offerings of tea.

Rosa placed their drinks on the counter with a brown paper bag. "Stay out of trouble," she said, then went to tend to the next customer.

Iori and Tatiana took their refreshments to the vacant patio. The metal table and chairs had been warmed by the sun, a blinding ball of white in the clear blue sky. Before they could even get comfortable, Tatiana burned herself on her drink.

"There is literally a warning on the cup telling you it's hot."

"I know, but I'm thirsty." She fanned her scalded mouth, which subsequently twisted into a smirk. "Speaking of *thirsty*."

Iori pointed a finger at her. "First of all: I am not *thirsty*. Second: you really waste no time, do you?"

"Hasn't it been long enough? I miss our talks, and we've gotta get you back on the love horse."

The love horse. "Eh . . ." It hadn't felt appropriate to discuss in months, what with the carpet-bombing of bad news, and in the break, his reservations had grown.

"Your crush didn't wear off, did it?"

"No." *Crush* was too diminutive a word for it, like cramming a too-large object into a tiny box—his heart being the box, and his feelings the contents close to bursting it. "With everything that's going on, I just wonder if I should even be pursuing a relationship."

Tatiana made an affronted noise. "Why the hell not?"

"Look at me, Kosta. My baggage has baggage, and someday—maybe not today, maybe not tomorrow—she's going to get tired of lugging it around." How many more sleepless nights could Ellen tolerate? How long until the panic attacks became too much for her?

"It's not baggage. It's a life and you've *lived*." Tatiana leaned on the table in a rare instance of calm sincerity. "Has Ellen ever said or done anything to indicate she's even the teensiest bit fed up?"

Her question rewound Iori's mind to the same period as his diet of chai shakes, when he'd cloistered himself away in his dormitory—leaving only when necessary, or when Elizabeth hauled him out for a training session. Ellen had often been there when her presence wasn't required elsewhere, but it was the day after his initial breakdown that left an impression.

She'd brought a cloth and a bowl of water to his bedside and had him sit while she washed the ink stains from his face. There, with his chin steadied in her hand, barely able to hold himself vertical, he'd asked, *"Why do you put up with me?"*

"I'm not putting up with you," she'd told him. *"I'm here because I want to be."*

The tears that flowed then had tasted different from the rest—not of bitter ink or salt-soused anger, but sweet release.

She'd already seen him at his worst, all his damaged parts laid bare. He could weep openly in front of her and be vulnerable without it being tantamount to pulling teeth.

Tatiana continued. "Don't forget how hard she fought to keep you around. She wouldn't spend ninety percent of every day with you or let you sleep in her bed if she didn't care loads about you." Tatiana lifted her cup to her lips and blew on it. "Plus, she thinks you're cute."

Iori's ears shifted under his beanie, warmth traveling up to them from his cheeks. "She said that?"

"Well, no. Not with words," she clarified, and his expression flat-lined. Bubble burst. "She's always giving you heart eyes, though. It's obvious she likes you."

"How can you be so sure?"

Tatiana proudly put a thumb to her chest. "As her best friend, it's my job to know these things. And it's not just me. Soren's noticed, too." She shook her cinnamon roll out of its bag. "Why don't you ask her out, see what she says?"

"I . . . can't."

"I don't see why not."

"What if she says no?" challenged Iori.

"What if she says yes?" countered Tatiana.

If the general vibes Iori got were accurate, she could very well, but he didn't want to make assumptions. It wasn't the idea of unrequited love that scared him so much as the chance that it would make things awkward between them. He didn't want to jeopardize the friendship they'd built, the closeness they shared. Losing that would be worse than any rejection.

Tatiana peeled off a piece of frosting-coated pastry. "You should've told her how you felt on your birthday instead of texting me."

"Oh I'm sure that would've gone over great. 'Hey, Ellen, sorry your brother's missing. P.S., I'm in love with you.'" Iori rolled his eyes and sipped his latte, creamy with a kick of ginger and spice.

"Did you just say *in love*?"

Iori nearly choked on his drink. "Wait, that's not—"

"Don't you dare take that back!" Tatiana grinned ear-to-ear. "You said it was a crush. You never mentioned the L-word!"

"Because I didn't want you to do *this*."

"What, be happy for you?"

"Make a big deal out of it." Iori loosened his scarf to let out some of the heat. "If you get excited, I might get my hopes up, and then if it goes wrong . . . Even if it goes right, there's no guarantee it'll last." His chest clenched around the scars of a once-broken heart. All of his frustrations rose to his throat in a feeble moan, and he bowed his head to the table's surface. "I've ruined so much. I don't want to ruin this, too."

Tatiana scrunched his beanie. "You love her, right? Doesn't that make it worth the risk?"

He craned his neck to glare at her. "I don't know, does it?"

Her friendly scrunching ended in a hard pat of rebuttal. "Quit grumbling. With the love guru on your side, you've practically got this in the bag. I'm responsible for the super adorable couple that is Dax and Miriam. I also set Aryel up with Naomi through a very elaborate secret-admirer note game, and rumor has it he's getting ready to propose."

"That's it?"

"I might be new, but my track record is flawless."

"Uh-huh. If you're so good, why aren't you and Brozak an item?" She'd .been pining after the "shield-maiden" for ages and had yet to make an actual move.

"That's a work in progress. The woman just came out of a long-term relationship; gotta wait until we're clear of the rebound zone." Tatiana stripped off another piece of cinnamon roll. "Not to mention, I'm too busy sorting out your love life. The role of a matchmaker demands sacrifice."

Iori supposed he could consider himself lucky that his matchmaker was one of his love interest's closest friends. "Fine, genius, what did you have in mind?"

"Have you ever been to the Starlight Festival?"

"Once. When I was little." His mother had taken him to commemorate their move to Hildegrand and immerse themselves in Amethistian culture. There were variations of the event around the globe, influenced by a multitude of cultures. Typically it was composed of games and food and colorful parades, and capped off with a display of light. Lanterns, pyrotechnics, ceremonial bonfires. Here, it was fireworks.

Tatiana clapped. "Okay, so, Cardplay organizes a group trip every year. Ellen, Soren, and I always go together. If you join us, we could arrange some *alone time*." She wiggled her brows. "The event just exudes romantic energy. It's all about new beginnings and taking chances. It's perfect for a confession! But first . . ." She perched her chin between her forefinger and thumb, evaluating him. "We're gonna have to spice up your wardrobe."

"What's wrong with my clothes?"

"You have, like, eighteen identical sleeveless black turtlenecks."

"That's not true," said Iori. "Some of them have zippers."

"Look, you're going on what will effectively be your first date with Ellen. Dressing to impress matters. Trust me, I know what I'm doing."

CHAPTER SIXTEEN
NOVEMBER 26 | KABR RESIDENCE

EVEN IN THE "RICH DISTRICT," the divide between upper-middle and upper-class was clear. A short jaunt from Ellen's house, the Kabr family's small mansion of a home almost put Cardplay Headquarters to shame. Heated pool, basement theatre, a two-tiered deck, and a tailored garden that left plenty of backyard to spare. Nearly the entire place was outfitted with smart devices, including voice assistants in every room except for Soren's. His quiet rebellion.

Most of his rebellions were, really.

The Kabrs were steeped in politics. His father was a statistician, his mother a communications director, and both sides of the family had been politically involved for decades. They'd expected Soren to follow a similar path until becoming Empowered put a wrench in it. An out for which he was grateful.

Their house made for a fun hangout spot, at least. But fun wasn't the only thing on Ellen's mind today. While Tatiana was picking up her car and Iori was in therapy, she had gone to confide in her more levelheaded friend about a different heart-related issue that had been plaguing her.

"How's your day off going?" asked Ellen, snatching a large and unfeasibly adorable ram plushie off Soren's bed as she plunked down on the carpeted floor of his room. A row of stuffed animals lined the headboard. Every year, Tatiana and Ellen each bought him another for his birthday, meaning the collection was soon to grow with January around the corner.

Soren grabbed a pair of gaming controllers. "Crampy and hormonal, but junk food and cartoons make it tolerable." He turned on the television and sat next to Ellen in his oversized sweats. "How's work?"

"Uneventful. We've only had two alerts today, and one was a prank call."

Soren gave a conflicted *hrmm* and pressed a button on his controller, sparking the console to life. A decline in Void activity would've been a promising sign if the unknowns surrounding it didn't make it more of a concern. "Is that why you've been kinda down and distracted lately?"

Ellen never had been good at masking her emotions. "It's not that. There is something I wanted to talk to you about, though." There were several things she wanted to talk to him *and* Tatiana about, but those were confidential. "Would you mind keeping it between us?"

Worry crossed Soren's rounded features. "Okay," he said, wariness elongating the word.

"It's not bad. I've been thinking about what you guys said at the ball—about sparks and stuff." Ellen squidged the ram plushie's stubby hooves. "I didn't give it much thought at the time, but Alexander made a weird comment the other day and I've been overanalyzing ever since."

"What'd he say?"

"He thought Iori and I were *together* together."

Soren tilted his head. "I mean . . ."

"You know we're not!"

"No, I know. You two just have this chemistry that not-so-low-key reeks of romance from an outside perspective. Why aren't you talking to Tatiana about this, though? Isn't this her area of expertise?"

Ellen shifted uncomfortably. "She doesn't always listen." Her good intentions regularly got trampled by her tendency to get carried away. "If I brought this up with her, she'd only try to convince me that I have feelings for him."

"Don't you?"

"No!" was her knee-jerk response. When Soren flinched, she amended her reply to an exasperated, "I don't know." Iori was sweet and funny. She could be unapologetically herself around him, and in his company, silence was comfortable as any conversation. She felt similarly about Tatiana and Soren, but not the same, and she couldn't quite put her finger on why. "How do you tell the difference between a friend crush and a romantic crush?"

"The fact that you're asking?"

Ellen pouted at him.

"I don't have much more experience than you do. I had one crush in high school that led to two weeks of sweaty handholding before we realized we were better as friends." That was still one crush more than she'd had. "If you can't flat-out deny it, don't you think that's a sign something's there?"

"Even if it is, that doesn't mean he likes *me*." She couldn't imagine someone having those kinds of feelings for her. Couldn't picture anyone—least of all the quick-witted, wild, artistic boy she rescued off the street—viewing her that way. Especially when she knew he had trouble getting close to people.

Soren passed her the second controller and loaded up a 2D platformer game they were both awful at and had never finished. "You could just talk to him about it. Have an open and honest discussion."

There was a terrifying thought. Iori would probably think her silly for entertaining the assumptions of onlookers. Or she could fumble her words so badly that he would mistake them for a confession. Worse yet, what if she left him under the impression that she didn't like him at all?

"Sorry." She'd come seeking advice and shot down every piece she'd received so far. "I thought this would be easier."

"You don't have to figure it out right now," Soren said. "It's okay to be confused, but you're not doing yourself any favors by refusing to believe there could be feelings on either side. Maybe you should take a real hard look in the mirror and ask yourself: what do *you* want?"

♥ · ♥ · ♥ · ♥ · ♥

The question became a third wheel to their hangout, a pesky insect buzzing in Ellen's ear all the way back to HQ. Unable to bat it away, she'd awkwardly avoided Iori for the rest of the day, and now as she stood in front of the bathroom mirror in her pajamas, perhaps taking Soren's suggestion too literally, she finally asked herself:

What do *I want?*

Her reflection stared uselessly at her. Maybe if she envisioned it, tried to picture what a romantic relationship with Iori could look like, it would give her some clarity. What kind of partner would he be, what kind of life could they make together? Where would it take them five, ten, or twenty years from now?

Roadblock, roadblock, roadblock. Mental barricades at every turn.

She had witnessed love from the outside, watched people fall in and out of it. Saw it between her parents and the masters and her friends and their partners. But how could she picture herself in love when she hadn't had so much as a crush?

Briefly, she wondered if she could be aromantic like her brother. *No, that's not right.* She didn't need to be actively in pursuit of romance to know she was capable of romantic attraction. Desired it, even. She just didn't know how it felt.

Something set her connection with Iori apart. They shared a closeness unlike that of her other friendships, and it wasn't the closeness of siblings. And even with that, her actions towards him weren't without refrain. *I love yous* came effortlessly to her. When she loved people, she supplied those affirmations generously—at most every farewell, and frequently in between. Yet she'd never said those words to Iori, fearing he would take them the wrong way.

What is the wrong way?

She almost wished for that spark of sexual attraction, another box to tick, but the concept of viewing someone through that lens struck her as foreign. Under certain circumstances, maybe . . . For now, all she had to go on was sensual and aesthetic attraction, of which neither could be tied solely to romance. She'd always cuddled with friends. Had admired Naomi's athletic figure and bold fashions, and thought Kyani was drop-dead gorgeous. And Iori—

Well, it would be a lie to say she hadn't noticed the feline allure of his eyes, or how his curls framed his face. It would also be a lie to say she hadn't replayed the memory of him dancing, enamored by his form and flexibility. The grace with which he moved.

That same grace imbued his hands when he played piano.

She'd sat next to him on the bench the morning after the ball, watching his fingers draw beautiful notes from the keys with delicate yet purposeful strokes. Veins shifting to the pull of tendons, trailing up over thin wrists and slender forearms to where his sleeves had been rolled to the elbow.

A roadmap to the heart.

If she traced them from the valleys between his knuckles, would they lead her there? Let her see inside so she could know where she truly resided?

Heat rushed to her face.

Okay, okay. It was clear in the details, now she just had to admit it to herself. *Without* blushing. If she could do that, it would prove there was nothing there, right?

Ellen leaned on the counter, staring herself down in the mirror, and willed the redness to clear.

Admit it.

The color deepened. She puffed her cheeks, indignant.

He's attractive.

He is.

He's a nicely-formed human being and there's nothing wrong with acknowledging that.

So why did her head feel like a kettle about to boil? She patted her face, trying to stamp out the embers prickling under her skin.

"Ellen, are you almost—"

She whirled to the bathroom door at the intrusion, armed with the nearest item she could grab: a tube of toothpaste, thrust at Alexander like a deadly knife. He eyed her choice of weapon, bemused.

"What're you doing?"

"Nothing!" She lowered the toothpaste, turning redder by the second. "Why didn't you knock?"

"The door was open."

"Oh."

Alexander blinked at her, and she blinked at him.

"Should I be con—"

"No!" she replied, too quick.

To her relief, he couldn't be bothered to probe into his kid sister's weird behavior. "Well, could you hurry it up? Other people would like to use the bathroom when you're done . . . whatever it is that you're doing." He maintained his suspicious squint a moment longer, then carried on down the hall. Ellen waited for him to disappear into his bedroom before slouching over the sink, counting her lucky stars that it was her brother who walked in on that mortifying display and not the boy at the center of her internal debate.

Feelings are hard, she whined inwardly. If only her parents were here. Theirs wasn't a story fit for the silver screen, but surely they would've had some tips for her.

Or maybe they'd tell her to stop wasting energy on potential romantic prospects when more important things were at stake.

She looked into the mirror again, her complexion cooling. Regardless of whether Iori liked her, he probably had too much on his plate to commit to a relationship. Therapy, Wiseman, the Spade and its corruption . . . It would be selfish of her to add more to the pile when she couldn't even unscramble her feelings. His heart had been broken once already, smashed by a boy who'd made empty promises. What if she hurt him because she made a wrong choice?

Better to spare them both the hassle. She would only end up disappointing him anyway.

ACT II

WHAT THE HEART WANTS

CHAPTER SEVENTEEN
DECEMBER 2 | HILDEGRAND, MID DISTRICT

A HARSH DECEMBER RAIN HAD DESCENDED on Hildegrand. Icy droplets pattered on Hikaru's tan topcoat, its collar upturned to ward off the cold, but the damp still seeped into his bones, setting off an ache in his right leg.

A reminder of why he'd come.

Past the streams pouring off the wide brim of his hat stood a brick building, its façade molded into an arch. The aged brass sign mounted there bore the words POLICE DEPARTMENT, and decaled on the thin strip of a window above its recessed entryway was 7TH DISTRICT.

His old haunt.

He climbed to the entrance, two feet to a step. The temperate air indoors, saturated with stale coffee and hints of mildew, evoked a sense of nostalgia in him. History papered these walls. Late nights and long hours, grave losses and great triumphs. When Hikaru first set foot in this building, he'd been barely more than Alexander's age. A rookie aiming to make a difference.

Here, he'd found purpose.

Today, he hoped to find answers.

The desk sergeant, Martina Ortiz—the stocky and devoted mother bear of this unit—called merrily to him as he approached. "There's a face I haven't seen in a while! Where've you been?"

"Busy," he lamented, removing his rain-soaked hat. He'd purposely kept his distance from the station in light of the Wiseman Corporation's involvement with the Reemergence and Blackjack. Best to avoid drawing more attention than necessary to himself or his allies. "Is Clive in?"

"Not even gonna ask your old desk lady how she's doing?"

In his haste, he'd neglected the usual pleasantries. "Forgive me, I'm in a bit of a hurry. Shall we catch up at a later date? Over a meal, perhaps?"

"I'll hold you to it." Ortiz picked up a pen, jabbed it over her shoulder. "Clive's in his usual spot."

With a nod of thanks, Hikaru proceeded past the front desk to a room whose window blinds were permanently stuck half-shut. An Amethistian flag hung in the corner of the cramped office, tinged yellow from a combination of time and tobacco smoke—a lingering mark of the former police chief.

Chief Clive Gardner left his own marks in the form of cup rings on his desk, the stains of too many forgotten coffees. There was a mug by his elbow now, neglected while he perused his computer screen. He looked up when Hikaru stepped in, and the hand that had been scratching his balding scalp flopped to his desk. "Why do I get the feeling this isn't a social visit?"

Because it wasn't. "I need a favor."

"No. No more favors, Ritsuo. I told you, I'm out."

"One more is all I'm asking."

"You checked out the files I gave you?"

"Twice," said Hikaru with a sharpness not intended for his comrade. Few things rattled his composure, but this case had him at his wit's end. "If there was any damning evidence on those servers, it has been erased."

Gardner slouched in his chair.

"Please," Hikaru pressed. "You know I would not be here unless I needed to be." He stressed that sentence, a pluck at the golden thread between them that Gardner couldn't see but would now realize was there. This strand led Hikaru to the precinct today for a reason, and he had a hunch as to why.

"I'm not sure what you want me to do," said Gardner. "We've exhausted our options."

"Not all of them." Hikaru paused for a last-minute internal debate. Once made, this favor could not be retracted, and the fallout could be devastating. For him, for Gardner. For both of their families. However, as long as Wiseman and the Warden of the Void held the strategic advantage, danger loomed large over all of them.

The price of justice may be steep, but the cost of doing nothing would be steeper.

"Put me in a room with Valerie Renard."

Every stern line on Gardner's face smoothed. "Please tell me you're not going to do what I think you're going to do."

Now that her transfer had been approved, it would only be a matter of time until the patrol wagon came to collect her. "This could be our last chance to get information out of her, Clive. Our last chance to indict Charles Wiseman. We are talking about a man who abducted and tortured multiple people, including my boy. And if he did kidnap Master Ryone with the intent of awakening his magic, if he willfully triggered the Reemergence, then it's not merely their blood on his hands. It is the blood of over *a thousand* innocent lives, and there will be more if we do not stop him." Hikaru brought his hat to his chest, clutching its pinched crown.

"Grant me fifteen minutes, and I will never ask a favor of you again."

Gardner blew out a breath. "Your funeral. Don't expect me to bring you flowers."

They made their way to the holding cells in the basement, Hikaru's cane a hollow tap on the concrete steps. Water stains painted wavy lines on the ceiling and floor, more opaque where flood waters had pooled one exceptionally rainy year.

Each cell had four solid walls and a green metal door with a small slot of a window to see through, permitting their occupants a modicum of privacy. Chief Gardner led Hikaru to the third cell down and unlatched the door, a rusty squeak ringing out from its hinges.

"Renard. You have a visitor."

Within the narrow box of a cell, on a rickety cot that made Hikaru uncomfortable just to look at, sat a woman in drab prison garb. No jewels, no gold, her once kempt and conditioned hair falling in frizzy waves about her. It brought him a kind of satisfaction to see her stripped of her glamor, afforded only the barest necessities.

"Well, well." The cell encapsulated her husky tone. "What did I do to earn a visit from the esteemed headmaster of Cardplay?"

Gardner glanced sideways at Hikaru. "Fifteen minutes," he said. "I'll make sure no one knows you were here." He lumbered off, and Hikaru waited for the click of the lock at the top of the stairwell before entering the cell, halting midway when Valerie swung her legs leisurely off the cot.

She returned his unblinking gaze, a guileful twist to her unlacquered lips. "Are you angry at me? Come to give me a talking-to?"

Hikaru didn't respond, didn't react.

"How does it feel knowing you essentially received compensation for the abduction?" She rocked to and fro on the side of the cot. "I bet you've already surrendered my donation to the authorities—an honorable citizen such as yourself has principles to uphold—but that doesn't change how you've been living off the corporation's money. Using our wares, supporting our mission . . . You should be grateful we didn't have you implicated as well."

If they'd tried, he would have taken it to court, which was precisely the reason they hadn't. It would have caused them far more trouble than it was worth.

Valerie tilted her head. "Nothing to say? I thought the speechmaker would have a few choice words lined up after what we did to your golden boy. How is he doing these days? Alexander?"

She was trying to provoke him, drive the nail deeper. What she failed to recognize was that Hikaru was already full of nails, and it would take more than she had for him to fracture. "Did I ever tell you why I resigned from the department?"

"You didn't have to. You tell the same sappy story every goddamn year." On the anniversary of the Reemergence, during the opening segments of the graduation ceremony, he would reiterate to the public how he'd retired from police work to pursue Cardplay.

"That's the official story." Only a handful of people were privy to the truth, and for a moment, she would be too. "In actual fact, I continued my work off the books as an interrogator. I'd developed a certain aptitude for persuasion, you see, but I wasn't fond of what that job was turning me into."

Valerie grunted. "Do you really think your cheap intimidation tactics are going to work on me?"

"I would hesitate to call them cheap." Hikaru lifted his right hand to show the ring on his pinky finger, the silver band bisected by a thin copper strip. "Do you recognize this?"

"It's a ring?"

"One of your earlier designs," he said, and her expression flashed from confusion to trepidation. "Your technology operates similarly to an Empowered individual's natural resilience to offensive magics, utilizing stardust to create a barrier. Reverse that barrier, and you get a suppression field. Applying this to ordinary accessories is effective . . . though, impermanent." As he slipped the ring off over his knuckle, a warmth of power unrestricted flowed through him.

Valerie shifted uneasily on her cot. "I already confessed," she said on the edge of a breath. "I have nothing else to say to you. Guard! *Guard!*"

No one would come. Only Gardner would be watching from the surveillance room.

The golden string binding Hikaru to Valerie pulled taut, and he closed the gap between them with one final tap of his cane. The woman shrank in his shadow, a drop of fear rippling the dark oceans of her eyes. Confronted by a foe she didn't know, the lioness had become a petrified lamb.

He pressed his palm to her forehead. "If you value your intellect, Miss Renard, you will tell me everything you know about Charles Wiseman."

MEMORY THREAD //
JAMES
MAY 24, 2020

Dumont General Hospital was locked in a state of bedlam. Medical staff buzzed about in an exhausted frenzy, patients overflowing into corridors. And the *noise*. Everywhere Hikaru went, the wailing followed—alarms and people, wounded and scared and distraught and angry.

The dissonant chorus continued as Elizabeth wheeled him into the intensive care unit. Machines hummed louder here, many of the occupants either comatose or sleeping off anesthesia. Families sat vigil by their loved ones, praying for them to wake.

The patient Hikaru had come to see already had.

"There he is," came Officer Grayson James' gruff voice. "I was starting to think you were avoiding me."

Perhaps that was because he had been.

Elizabeth stooped to Hikaru's ear. "I'm gonna grab a coffee, let you two talk." She rubbed his shoulders, then left him to roll the rest of the way into James' shared room. He maneuvered his wheelchair into his comrade's semi-private space, separated from the other beds by a thin curtain.

They hadn't been the best of friends; *agree to disagree* summed up the majority of their interactions. As fellow squad members, however, Hikaru felt an obligation to check in, and seeing the condition the man had been left in stirred his guilty conscience all over again. Both arms were bound in casts, head bandaged, and a catheter led from his chest to a container of cloudy yellow fluid hooked to the side of his bed. A medical report wasn't necessary to know the damages were extensive.

"Hey, don't give me that look." James forced a crooked smile. "We're the lucky ones, right?"

"You shouldn't be here. If I hadn't—"

"*Don't*. Don't you dare. You didn't do this."

"I could have prevented it."

"You can't predict the future, Ritsuo. None of us had any idea what that thing was." James screwed up his mouth, the beep of his heart monitor climbing. "I swear, if I see that monster again, I am going to give it a taste of its own medicine."

It. Monster. Thing.

"You're talking about the child we saw at the house?"

"Child? No, no, no. You saw it yourself. Children don't have killer shadows, Ritsuo. You see what's happening out there, don't you?" He pointed imprecisely, referring to the upturned world beyond these howling walls. "This isn't a virus, it's an *invasion*. Those demons are breeding other demons, taking our people and wearing our skin. That kid was one of them. And the government—the government's trying to hide it. They came by your room too, right? The public deserves to know what's really going on. We need to tell them."

But Hikaru couldn't see, not through the same lens. Communications had been restricted and authorities placed under a gag order, yes—in the interest of avoiding panic and civil unrest. If this news spread too quickly, the whole of Amberlye would be thrown into chaos. It wasn't as if they were trying to sweep the incident under the rug. They couldn't.

Sooner or later, the world would know.

Dubious administrative strategies aside, he couldn't bring himself to believe that small child was no different from the creatures hunting humans in the streets. The boy had begged him to stay away. *Begged.* If he'd intended to harm them, why run? Why not stay and finish them off?

What's more, Hikaru couldn't ignore the thread that tethered them together.

By my light, guide them.

He didn't understand it, couldn't explain what force compelled him to seek out and protect this child. Something strange was going on, undeniably, but Hikaru could not condone the violent retribution his comrade sought. He had to get him to forget this wild idea. Somehow, he—

Alerts blared, James' vitals going haywire.

Hikaru tore his hand from the man's forehead, unable to remember reaching out in the first place, let alone rising from his wheelchair. He fell back into the seat as James' eyes rolled, convulsions rattling his bed frame.

Gold filaments scattered between them. Another thread, broken before Hikaru could properly register it.

Nurses rushed in and he wheeled out of their way. When they inquired as to what happened, he could only stutter uncertainties, watching in a daze as they crowded around their patient. His fellow officer.

There was a tingling sensation in his palm.

Did I . . . ?

Stories had been circulating about people who could bend the laws of physics to their will. Hikaru had witnessed them himself that night in the city—seen the earth move for a young man, seen windows shatter at the clap of a woman's hands. And that same glass had melted at the touch of another, who wielded it against the monsters like molten rain.

Health officials were calling it a second strain. Could he have contracted it?

James stilled in his bed, unconscious.

The tingling faded.

What have I done?

~ • ~ • ~ • ~ • ~

Memory was a fickle thing. The human mind could only store so much data, and would automatically discard the old and insignificant in favor of the new and noteworthy. But with the right touch, they could be rearranged or removed manually. Fabricated events could even be implanted in their place, blocks of code shifted and rewritten.

However, tampering with another's memory came at a cost to one's own.

By the time Hikaru returned to Cardplay Headquarters, the drive from the precinct had been reduced to a series of too-bright snapshots in his recollection. The sequence grew during the climb to his office, moments stitching closer together as the side effects gradually wore off.

Temporary lapses were normal. This sensitivity to light and sound and the disorientating sway of movement, on the other hand, was rare. Every bulb burned like a flare. The clang of his footsteps on the spiral staircase to the suite rang sharp, and so too did the clink of a teaspoon on china.

Elizabeth was in the kitchen making tea. Even her nonabrasive tone pounded on his eardrums, muffled as though he'd been submerged in an aquarium. It became clearer mid-sentence when a peculiar sense of buoyancy overcame him, a release of pressure from his head, and it occurred to him then that he hadn't absorbed a single word she'd said.

"Did you get that errand taken care of?" she asked, the electric kettle whistling next to her.

What errand? He wouldn't have revealed where he was going or why; she wouldn't have let him leave if he did.

It took a moment for the reply to trickle down from his brain to his tongue. "It's done," he told her in as minimal detail as possible.

A blink like a camera shutter. Suddenly there was a cup of tea on the counter next to him, and Elizabeth was partway through a story about student antics. Another lapse. Hoping to play it off until he recovered, he reached for the cup . . . and was betrayed by a violent tremor in his right hand. Not only that, his pinky finger was bare. He'd forgotten to put his ring back on, and Elizabeth zeroed in on the faint tan line where it should've been like a hawk.

"Hikaru, where were you today?"

He opened his mouth, unsure whether to fess up or attempt a lie. Before he could decide, a wave of dizziness knocked him off-kilter. He bumped against the fridge, cane clattering to the tiles. Elizabeth caught him and eased him to the floor.

There was a tickle on his upper lip. Dabbing it, his fingers came away glistening and red.

That was new.

Frustration hissing through her teeth, Elizabeth swiped a wad of tissues from the box on the kitchen island and held them to his nose. "Goddamn it, Hikaru. What did you do?"

The explanation came out slurred breathless, his head sloshing like a fishbowl. "I had to do something, Lizbet. They're depending on me to fix this. She was the only lead I had access to."

Elizabeth started to ask who, and then clued in. There was only one *she* it could be. "You *didn't*," she snarled, a warning delivered too late.

Shame and desperation clenched Hikaru's throat. "I didn't know what else to do."

Elizabeth pinched the bridge of her nose. The creases in her brow shifted, softened. They'd been in this position several years ago when she convinced him to resign from the HPD. His role as an interrogator had turned him neglectful and impatient, but duty-bound as he was, he hadn't the resolve to pull the plug. Elizabeth had done it for him.

"Did you at least get anything useful out of her?"

That was the worst part. "Nothing. Not a bloody damn thing." He'd scrambled her memory the way he'd been compelled to scramble James' and she let him, preferring to lose herself than be labeled a traitor. If only he could read minds instead of merely tinker. "I saw the thread, Lizbet. *I saw it.*" His arm flapped weakly.

Fate had never led him astray. Could he have read the strings wrong?

No, he would've been given a sign, surely.

This had to be right.

This has to be right.

CHAPTER EIGHTEEN
DECEMBER 3 | CARDPLAY HEADQUARTERS

KYANI HAD SPENT THE BETTER PART OF HER LIFE scraping by and making the best of the worst. So to stand before the assembly in the foyer after so many false starts and false hopes—free of blight, free of Blackjack—and be able to say in confidence that she was on the right path . . .

What a blessing.

With the headmaster indisposed due to a seasonal cold, the responsibility of the formal introduction fell to his spouse, Elizabeth Howard. To Kyani's relief, the news of her enrollment in the rehabilitation program and her pursuit of a permanent position at Cardplay got a warm reception.

It was nice to have people on her side for a change, rooting for her. Looking out for her. Iori had given her a rundown of what to expect prior to her polygraph test last week, in which she'd met the acclaimed Mira Hodge. Later, Alexander had taken her on a tour of the facility and rallied his friends to help decorate her dorm. And his sister, currently situated between him and Iori, had been a bottomless well of goodwill from the beginning.

"In short," said Elizabeth, bringing the introduction to a close, "be respectful, be professional, and if anyone has any objections, I don't want to hear them."

Iori's tail twisted into a mischievous curl. "Riveting."

The battlemaster scowled at him. Her intro had been rather brusque. "As much as we all would've preferred Hikaru's eloquent speech, he's not here. You have me. Deal with it." With an upward sweep of her arms, she released them from the grips of formality, and the crowd dispersed.

Naomi and Aryel headed out for the afternoon patrol. Ikkei was already out on a call with Oskar Trey and Soren Kabr, tracking an Empowered suspect in a burglary.

The few Jokers and Jokers-to-be whom Kyani hadn't properly met yet welcomed her in turn, the youngest of the students clustering around her last—a girl with braids called Xiaolin, and the identical Hein twins Haden and Sem. One of the boys had a gap tooth. Kyani couldn't remember which.

"Are your wings real?" asked one.

"Can we touch them?" asked the other.

Xiaolin's black eyes shone. "Can you fly?"

That Kyani had wondered herself as her feathers regrew, fuller and healthier and unburdened by corruption. Maybe, just maybe, she could. "I haven't tried yet," she admitted, wings drawing inward self-consciously. If she were honest, the attention was a bit overwhelming.

Tatiana sniggered to Iori. "Move over, puss. You're old news."

He cringed at the nickname. "I'd rather be old news than a walking exhibit."

The students' questions kept coming, an unrelenting torrent of curiosity until Alexander shooed them away. "Don't you have a class to get ready for?"

"They do," said Elizabeth, patting one of the twins on the head as they sulked off to the locker room. "And you're going to join us. But first, I want a word with you four." She addressed the Keepers, leaving Tatiana looking like a deflated sixth wheel.

"I have therapy in twenty minutes," said Iori in mild protest.

"And this is going to take *two*. Please do not test my patience today, Ryone. I have very little of it."

The battlemaster was known for her snappish attitude, but the way the group collectively flinched suggested this was excessive. Quietly, Tatiana offered Iori a ride to his appointment and promised Ellen they would catch up later, then went to wait in her car.

Once alone, Elizabeth got to the point. "We've decided to accelerate student training over the winter holidays to make up for missed classes. As a result, I won't be able to devote myself to Oto's rehabilitation or Ryone's individual sessions. However, seeing as Alexander is still recuperating and Ellen is aware of her Keeper status, this presents an opportunity for a team-building exercise."

The idea of working alongside them as a real team gave Kyani the most delightful rush.

"Starting Monday, you'll be training together for an hour every day after shift. Alexander's competent enough to handle combat, and I'm putting Ellen in charge of honing." The siblings nodded in unison, Alexander sharply and his sister with a bounce of enthusiasm. "Oto, I'd like you to contribute any knowledge you may have to this as well. And Ryone"—he recoiled—"you have the most experience as a Keeper. I expect you'll coach the others on what you've learned."

Before Iori could respond, Alexander interjected, mouth twisting like he'd tasted something bitter. "I'm not taking lessons from him. He's three ranks below me."

"Not on the Suit hierarchy, I'm not," Iori intoned, earning a reproachful look from Ellen. "Luckily for you, I had no intention of giving lessons anyway. It's not in my skill set."

The battlemaster's hand went to her brow. "The one time you blockheads actually agree . . . " She inhaled deeply, one stray spark from a blowup. "Look, the four of you are a unit, and I need you to be a cohesive one. I know it's hard to grasp the stakes, but it's not just a city or a country at risk here. There is a reason pre-Cataclysm history was forgotten, and that's probably because very few people were left to remember it. Whatever differences you have, you need to put them aside so that doesn't happen again. Do you understand me?"

That sobering reminder lent a new weight to the atmosphere, cooling Alexander's temper and taking the bite out of Iori's snark. Ellen rubbed her arm stiffly, and Kyani's wings sank. Without active battle, it was easy to forget they were in the midst of a silent war, both sides plotting their next move.

Sometimes, Kyani wished she'd played a more willing pawn for Blackjack. If she had been in Cardan's shoes or Sybil's, she would've had considerably more valuable information to bring to the table.

Iori hunched his shoulders. "What could I coach them on that they don't already know?"

"You'd be surprised." Elizabeth regarded him with a weariness that implied she knew precisely what he had to offer, even if he didn't. Dumb luck didn't get him this far. His was a wisdom garnered from years on the streets, learning by trial and error rather than example. "At any rate, I don't just want you to spar. I want you to communicate. *Bond.*" She interlaced her calloused fingers. "Prove to me that you can be a team."

After a beat of silence, the challenge set, Iori jabbed a thumb over his shoulder. "Does that mean I can go?"

The battlemaster huffed. "Yes. Scram."

Ellen and Iori exchanged a wave, and it wasn't lost on Kyani how the girl watched him go—forlorn, almost. She seemed troubled lately. Worried about him, perhaps. But as Iori was heading out the door, her close friend Soren returned from his call, and she perked up and jogged over to meet him.

They all had plenty to be troubled about, Kyani supposed.

"Are you gonna be alright on your own for a few hours?" Alexander asked, touching her lightly on the shoulder. "Classes usually run until seven."

The sentiment was sweet, but didn't he realize? "I have been doing life by myself for a while now."

"Right." He shifted uncomfortably, then pointed in the direction Elizabeth had gone. "I'd better get going then."

A request almost forgotten sprung to Kyani's mind. "Oh, Alex, there is one thing I could use your help with when you're not busy." A thing which required an escort, as per the terms of the rehab program. "While our situation is stable, I was hoping to visit my father?"

He pondered that, fingering the strap of his messenger bag. "That can probably be arranged, yeah. How about we aim for next Sunday?"

Excitement and nervousness fizzled within Kyani. "Next Sunday would be perfect."

After all this time, she would finally see her father again.

CHAPTER NINETEEN
DECEMBER 3 | HILDEGRAND, MID DISTRICT

IORI'S ORIGINAL POST-THERAPY PLAN had been to join Ellen in the courtyard for lunch, as had become their habit. Naturally, with Tatiana being his chauffeur, those plans got upended, and he texted to let her know he wouldn't make it.

Iori: Kosta's dragging me along for holiday shopping. Raincheck on the lunch date?

Date. *Date.* Damn it, he actually said *date.*

Don't panic, he told himself. He'd made similar joking comments in the past. Hopefully she wouldn't read into it beyond the platonic context he'd intended.

But when the chime sound effect came, notifying him of her reply, he wondered not for the first time: *Does she know?*

Ellen: That's okay! You two have fun! I'll see you later

It wasn't the verbiage that roused his suspicion—any oddities there could be blamed on hiccups with the translation software morphing her Amethistian text into Jeidish. More so it was the disappearing, reappearing dots resulting in a contrastingly short message devoid of emojis.

Am I being paranoid?

A scroll through their message history told him he wasn't. Her texting tone had shifted about the same time her behavior changed in person. She'd been ultra prone to fluster, flaking on meet-ups, and spacing out more than usual. And if Iori wasn't mistaken, she'd been dodging him at work too. Last week, she literally hid under the stairs when she saw him coming and made up an excuse when he confronted her, claiming she'd lost the black ring that was still clearly on her middle finger.

He would've ascribed it to the Heart conundrum if she hadn't been acting normally around everyone else.

He cast a sidelong glance at Tatiana, who was low-key jamming out to a pop song on the radio while she drove. "You didn't say anything to Ellen, did you?"

"About?"

"What do you think?"

"Why would I? That'd ruin the confession plan."

Iori swiped to the most recent message again. "If you didn't, why has she been acting so weird lately?"

Tatiana snorted. "Dude, you are not subtle. You probably gave it away. Half of Cardplay's gotta know you've got the hots for her by now."

His tail twitched irritably. "Don't say it like that." If Ellen *had* sussed out his feelings for her, the behavioral change could be her dropping hints that she didn't have any for him. Then again, it could be evidence that she did. After all, the more his feelings grew, the more of a bumbling idiot he became.

The minivan bucked over a speed bump.

"Hey, don't get in your head about it," Tatiana said. It was annoying how easily she could read him. "Ellen's weird when she's stressed, and she's got a lot to stress about."

More than you know, thought Iori.

"But today we're focusing on your romantic future, so tell your anxiety brain to zip it." She pulled into the parking lot of the midtown mall—a packed, two-story shopping center that would only get busier as the solstice closed in.

In preparation to brave the public, Iori poked his ears under his beanie, folding them in such a way that they wouldn't ache from the compression and his earring wouldn't dig in anywhere. Then he coiled his tail around his waist. Not the most comfortable arrangement, but more tolerable than the stink-eye he'd receive otherwise.

Tatiana took in his transformation from mutant cat person to regular human boy. "Why don't you just let it all hang out?"

"*Phrasing.*"

"I'm serious. People aren't going to think you have actual cat parts. They'd probably assume you're in cosplay."

"Yeah, no." Iori unrolled his shirt over his tail and re-zipped his jacket. "Besides, they're the only unique identifying traits the local authorities have on me. Without them, I'm just another skinny, black-haired, East Coraldan kid."

"With an eyepatch."

"With an eyepatch." Not much he could do about that. Removing it wouldn't do him any favors.

They exited the vehicle, exhaust fumes sharp in the air, and Iori braced for the sensory overload as he tailed Tatiana through the revolving doors.

The whole mall had been decorated in tinsel, lights, and cotton wool snow, and oversized baubles hung in a spiral formation beneath the skylight. Fortunately, the towering evergreen in the center was fake, or else he would've had to take a wide berth to avoid the pine scent—an inconvenient trigger during this time of year. The swarms of people in too-close proximity were disconcerting as it was, and Iori instinctively found himself plotting escape routes. Sizing up security, taking note of potential threats.

A switch he wished he could turn off.

He followed Tatiana to the wayfinding kiosk. "Where to?"

"Depends," she said. "What's your style?"

"You're looking at it." There'd been no point in developing a style on the streets. Functional and cheap or whatever he could nab off a clothesline were his go-tos. Shades that didn't stand out too boldly. Nothing restrictive, nothing scant. Crop tops were about as adventurous as he was willing to be with his current wardrobe, and he wouldn't be caught wearing those outside the arena yet.

Tatiana assessed him long and hard. "Alright. I can work with this." She pointed forth. "Onward!"

They boarded the escalator to the second floor, whimsical holiday tunes playing as it carried them past the ornamental baubles. Even more gargantuan up close, they sparkled in the sunshine from above, red dusted white and green dusted gold. After the solstice, they'd be swapped out for silver and cobalt stars.

"So," said Tatiana, "you mentioned a while ago that you were in a relationship once. How long did that last?"

"Couple years. I was fourteen when it ended."

"Aw, young love! Anyone I know?"

She'd asked in jest, but she did. Know *of* him, at least. "Noah," he told her. "Pinciotti."

She gasped. "The kid who ratted you out to the cops? He went to the same school as my half-sister!" Upon reaching the second floor, Tatiana stopped Iori by the guardrail. "Hold on, hold on. I want details. Was it serious?"

"For me, it was." Not serious in a planning-a-future-together or a he-could-be-the-one sort of way. More in the sense that, for those two years, his entire world had revolved around a boy who'd taken pity on him—much like Ellen had.

Tatiana propped her elbow on the railing. "Do you miss him?"

He cast his gaze to the solstice display below. "I miss when we were happy. We had fun, and he cheered me up when I was at rock bottom." Until he put Iori there himself. "I don't regret our time together, but . . . no. I don't miss him. Our relationship wasn't healthy. I kept things from him, depended on him too much, and he was an impulsive troublemaker. A bit like someone else I know."

"*Hey.*"

Iori indulged in a laugh stolen at Tatiana's expense, then sighed. "Noah and I weren't compatible long term, but I think we needed each other. I just wish he could've been there for me through my shit the way I tried to be there through his. Instead, when it mattered most, he left. He hurt me, and I carried that hurt for a long time." If he were honest, he was still carrying it now. "I don't blame him for leaving. He was scared. We both were. Problem is, you can't run from the monster when the monster is you."

"*Woof.*" Tatiana puffed her checks. "Did you ever see him again?"

Iori shook his head. "He moved out of the city. Probably for the best." The Pinciotti house went up for sale a month after the Langston High incident, and their once-merry band of ruffians split. The only one he encountered again was Camille Langdon, who'd been recruited by Blackjack to hunt him down because she had a vendetta against him.

"Yeah, you're right." In a mortifyingly public display of solidarity, Tatiana thrust her middle fingers over the guardrail and yelled, "FUCK YOU, NOAH!"

Iori snagged her by the collar of her jacket. "Come on, you're gonna get us kicked out."

They went on to browse the mall's wares, Tatiana encouraging him to maintain an open fashion mind. So far, all he'd learned was what he *didn't* like. Pointed studs and skulls were overtly hardcore for his taste, neon colors gave him a headache, and whatever was going on with the "trending" displays was an affront to society.

The accessory rack in the pop culture shop absorbed their attention far longer than it should have, several minutes wasted trying on creatively shaped sunglasses and headbands neither of them planned to buy. Iori did, however, purchase a squishy strawberry charm from the rack as a solstice gift for Ellen.

Tatiana *awwed* loudly during the transaction.

The next shop they visited offered printed dresses, shirts, pants, and blazers in a range of colors and monotone shades. A sort of understated chic, formal and fun without being too audacious or kitschy.

Tatiana bee-lined to a butterfly-printed dress near the front. "Oh, this is nice." She then flipped over the price tag, cringed, and sang "No it's not," as she returned it to the rack.

As she ventured deeper into the store, Iori rifled through a few shelves by himself. He picked out a pair of houndstooth pants and merlot-colored chinos. Nothing exceptional, just a diversion from his standard stonewashed denim.

He wandered over to a rack of button-ups, fingers gliding over the fabric—cool and satiny to the touch. A few designs caught his eye: white ferns on gunmetal, rusty orange with pale autumn leaves. The one he couldn't pass without a closer look bore dark pink florals on black with a hint of ashen green for leaves. Classy, yet casual.

"And here I was starting to think you had no appreciation for color." Tatiana appeared at the end of the row with an armful of clothes. "Ready to try stuff on?"

Thankfully, they had the changing area to themselves. Iori stepped into his unlocked stall and hung Tatiana's prearranged outfits in the order she'd insisted on. The door clattered when she rested on it, heels visible through the gap at the bottom, and when Iori lifted his head, he found his reflection staring back at him on the inside.

If there were one relationship more complicated than his with Noah, it was his relationship with mirrors. Or any reflective surface, for that matter. Even photos he dodged, because as much as he wanted to capture moments in this new life he'd begun to build, he couldn't bear to have his image immortalized.

But he couldn't hide from himself forever.

Hesitantly, he undressed. Removed his beanie, his jacket, and unwrapped his tail from his waist. Leaving the eyepatch on, he stripped down to his undergarments. And he dared himself to look.

Actually *look*.

At the black slash that spanned from left clavicle to right pectoral. At the incision line on his abdomen, and the ghastly twist of tissue on his right shin where a dog's gnashing bite had just about skinned him. He unveiled the char-like marks around his ears, hidden by his hair, and twisted to look at the ones reaching up his spine from his tail.

It wasn't just the scars, though. Or the eye. Or the fangs, ears, or tail. Arriving at Cardplay, he'd been an anemic bag of bones relying on magic to keep him upright. He'd felt it, of course, the steady decline with every year that passed and every inch he'd grown. And he'd ignored it, because what could he have done?

Asked for help, he supposed. Hard to do when he couldn't distinguish enemy from ally.

On the plus side, his skeleton no longer appeared to be trying to break out of its flesh prison, and he had muscle definition where there'd previously only been sinews. The hollows of his cheeks had filled in, regained color, and he felt better. Stronger, happier, more energetic, and most of his nagging pains had gone.

He couldn't quite see past that frail boy in the glass yet, feeding off a power that in turn fed off him.

One day, he would.

I can work with this, he thought, echoing Tatiana's declaration. With that, he grabbed the first of her outfit combinations off the rack.

"We should brainstorm confession ideas," she spoke through the door. "There's the good ol' verbal kind, which you have the vocabulary for ... but seeing how you struggled to tell *me* about your crush, I'd say that's a no-go." Iori took offense at that. "What if you slipped a handwritten note into her pocket? That could be sweet."

"If by sweet you mean *illegible*." Iori pulled on a pair of dark red jeans with a row of silver eyelets down each leg. "I can't write in Amethistian, and she can't read Jeidish. I'd have to explain it to her."

"I could write it!"

And have the personal touch taken out of it? "No, thanks."

"How about memes?"

"Too corny."

"Ooh, you could serenade her!"

Iori laughed dryly. "Not a chance."

"Why not? She told me your voice is pretty." He could picture the teasing smirk on Tatiana's face, and was glad for the door between them so she couldn't see the flush on his. Thinking back to that morning after the ball, had Ellen been trying to flirt?

Probably not. She didn't seem the flirting type.

Fully dressed, Iori took a second to appraise his outfit in the mirror and didn't need any longer to know it was wrong. "I don't want to be showy about it," he said, peeling off the long-sleeved shirt. "Neither of us are showy people."

"Gotcha, gotcha." Tatiana's foot tapped in thought. Iori had gone through another outfit and a half when she asked, "Who confessed, you or Noah?"

"Uh. There wasn't a confession, per se."

"What does *that* mean?"

The gang had scattered after a convenience store robbery. High on adrenaline and forced into close proximity by their hiding spot, it just sort of . . . happened. "He kissed me"—Iori pulled on another shirt—"and I kissed him back." And suddenly, all the fluttery feelings he'd been having made sense.

Tatiana clapped outside the stall. "That could work."

"What could?"

"A kiss! Think about it: the music, the atmosphere, the whole festival sparkling. It's perfect."

Perfect might've been a stretch, but it was the only suggestion so far that hadn't put him off. He and Ellen had already established a physical closeness, and where words might fail him, a kiss wouldn't leave much room for miscommunication.

"Just keep your tongue in your mouth," Tatiana advised. "Ellen finds that gross."

"Who goes for tongue on a first kiss?"

Her defensiveness said it all. "Lots of people! Don't act like it's weird because you didn't do it."

After fighting his way out of the tight vinyl pants and jacket of the third pre-arranged outfit, Iori decided to mix and match. He selected the floral shirt he'd picked out, cuffed the sleeves and buttoned it, then grabbed the loose high-waisted black pants from Tatiana's second combo.

When she spoke again, his ear twisted to a note of unease. "Hey, you're not asexual, are you?"

"Not in the slightest." He slipped his feet through the silky pantlegs, tucked the shirt into the waistband. "I don't mind if she can't look at me that way, though, if that's what you're worried about." The affection she regarded him with already made him melt. If ever she looked at him with lustful intent, he might fully evaporate.

Tatiana rubbed her ankle with the heel of her boot. "Just wanted to make sure you're not hoping for more than she's willing to give. Like, sex and stuff. That's not to say she's sex-*repulsed*, just that she's expressed a disinterest in having a lot of sex, and—"

"*Kosta.*"

"What?"

"I don't think you should be telling me this." He'd already heard more than he wanted to.

"Nah, Ellen wouldn't mind. It's for a good cause."

"You're not listening." Iori leaned in close to the door and directed his words, hushed, through the seam. "*I'm* not comfortable talking about it. Whatever Ellen's told you, she told you in confidence and probably wouldn't want you sharing with me. It's personal, it's private, and it's for us to discuss if we ever have that conversation." His voice softened. "I would never pressure her into doing anything she doesn't want to. Even if she decides that's off the table, it wouldn't change how I feel about her. You don't have to worry, Tatiana. I promise."

His matchmaker became unusually quiet.

"Are you sulking?"

The moody "No," from the other side of the door told him otherwise. Tatiana scuffed her shoe on the floor. "Me and my big mouth, huh?"

"You care about her. I get it."

"It's not that I don't trust you to treat her right. Ellen's just not so great at taking care of herself."

"Must be a Jane thing."

She scoffed. "You've got that right."

Two sides of a coin, and simultaneously two peas in a pod. Alexander had set his own downfall in motion by neglecting his troubles in favor of protecting his sister, and she tended to do the same, taking on the burdens of others whilst her own fell by the wayside.

A little less sullen, Tatiana asked, "Are you gonna let me see any of those outfits or what?"

She'd gone to the effort of driving him here and taking on the role of his personal stylist. She deserved to see at least *one*. Iori unlatched the barrel bolt, and when he pulled the door open, Tatiana's jaw hit the floor.

"Holy shit, you look amazing."

Caught off-guard by her reaction, he flushed again, shrinking back into the cubicle. "I mean, it fits okay, I guess."

"*It fits okay, I guess.*" Tatiana grabbed him and turned him stiffly toward the mirror. "Get a load of yourself, dude. You're gorgeous." His ears went flat, and she smooshed her cheek against his shoulder. "Aw. You're cute when you're bashful."

Iori smiled despite himself. "Piss off." He shoved her away, but she was back immediately, grabbing at his buttons.

"Wait, wait! I know what'd spice this up even more. These always look better if you undo the first couple of— buttons . . ." Tatiana stared at the Void mark she'd uncovered. Iori snatched the shirt closed, and she grinned sheepishly as he retreated into the stall. "That's the one, right?"

He grunted in mild disinclination. "I think I'll stick to my regular clothes. There's a lot riding on the festival as it is. I'd rather not add constantly-fretting-over-how-I-look to the list." Familiar fabrics supplied a layer of comfort he would need if he were going to confess with a kiss.

"Ugh, seriously?"

"She wouldn't even see it. I'll be wearing a jacket."

Tatiana moaned in disappointment but didn't fight him.

Normal human boy disguise donned once more, they shifted the clothes to an empty rack nearby—all except for the floral shirt and black pants, which Iori held out of Tatiana's reach when she went to take them from him.

"I thought you weren't getting anything new?"

"I said I wasn't going to wear anything new to the *festival*," he clarified with mock affectedness. "This is for future special occasions."

In the future he was determined to see.

CHAPTER TWENTY
DECEMBER 3 | CARDPLAY HEADQUARTERS

AN ASSORTMENT OF EQUIPMENT LAY on the workbench in front of Alexander, another pile by his feet. Busted practice swords and chest protectors, scuffed shin guards and plastic shields. Friday evenings were for taking inventory—cleaning and repairing gear and listing items that needed to be replaced.

When pitted against magic, mundane materials like foam, plastic, and wood were bound to break, and the students burned through them like nobody's business. Some more literally than others.

The Hein twins shared a pyric ability. *Sparks*, they'd nicknamed it, alongside their official call signs of *Red Jester* and *White Jester*. As the nickname implied, they could generate burning particulates using friction, and the pair's destructive tendencies had escalated after receiving their specially-crafted weapons from Pavati Varma.

Yoyos, complete with rotating blades sandwiched by their outer halves. A terrible idea, in Alexander's opinion.

"You left quite an impression," said Elizabeth on her way back into the arena. "Work on that temper and you could make a fine battlemaster yourself someday."

"You think?" Alexander replied, incredulous. Which had left the impression: his demonstration or his temper? He'd lost it more than once, at one point bringing Layla to tears because his instructions weren't sinking in. They were straightforward, he thought. Even so, he shouldn't have taken his frustration out on her.

He picked up a wooden haft covered in thorns. They'd sprouted at Layla's botanic touch, forcing Benji to drop the weapon and causing him to dissipate involuntarily. His somatic powers enabled him to disperse the molecules of his body; it only lasted a few seconds, but that was plenty to dodge a blow or phase through a wall. Perfect for a stealthy infiltration, which was Xiaolin's specialty. Her ability to spin clouds from the moisture in the air made her a slippery target even her battle buddy Aziz couldn't catch with his magically-enhanced speed.

There was so much talent in this room, and they deserved to hone their skills in a nurturing environment. Alexander had to do better if he was going to make these next few weeks memorable rather than miserable.

"Would you ever consider it?" asked Elizabeth as she drew up to the work bench. "Taking up the torch when I retire?"

Alexander discarded the haft in the recyclable pile. "I'm having a hard time picturing you in retirement." This was the only Elizabeth Howard he'd known, a woman of steely resolve whose tongue was as sharp as her blade. Soldier, drill instructor, officer, battlemaster.

"I'm serious. Teaching isn't so different from leading, and you've proven your capabilities there. You are good with the students when you're not yelling at them."

"As if you never yell."

"It's about knowing *when* to yell." She inclined her head toward him. "Being a battlemaster requires a degree of stringency. Your intolerance for bullshit can be useful. Get a grip on that, and you could be better at this job than me."

He looked her in the eye. "You don't believe that."

She scrunched up her face. "I don't. But I'd welcome a bit of friendly competition if you want to stick this out with me until graduation. It'd give you a proper break from field work. A chance to *breathe*."

Ideally, he'd aimed to return by the new year, but more and more he was being told to slow his roll, and he couldn't help feeling swayed by Elizabeth when she bore the mark of his burnout. Uncovered now, her dressings removed, the nape of her neck still glared an angry red—kissed by the Diamond's fire.

By *his* fire.

He had come within an inch of taking her life and couldn't even remember it. Ikkei had filled him in on the details, told him of the immense power he'd radiated at the complex. Unfathomable compared to his current output. He could barely maintain a small flame, which he didn't realize until it went out in the middle of his demonstration. They'd had to switch techniques. Shorter bursts, lesser magical discharge.

Taking it easy wasn't as easy as he'd hoped.

"Why don't you head out? I can finish up here," Elizabeth suggested as he lifted a practice sword from the workbench. One of the few intact pieces.

"You sure?"

"Inventory's been a solitary task for me for years. Unwinds me so Hikaru doesn't have to listen to me bitch and moan about you lot." She ruffled his fringe, and he ducked away. She always had to go for the hair. "Plus, I want you well-rested for the coming week. That's where you'll really be putting that Diamond of yours to work."

Right. Keeper training.

Alexander yielded, passing her the sword.

"Oh, by the way," she said, "if you're wondering what to get me for the solstice, you owe me a new coat."

Her emotional wounds couldn't be too deep, otherwise she wouldn't use the damage he'd done to get a replacement trench coat out of him. If she could joke about it, maybe he was the fool for lugging around these sandbags of guilt.

"Noted," he said, no guarantees. "G'night."

"'Night."

He retrieved his messenger bag from the locker room and texted Ellen to tell her he was heading home. She'd clocked out early after the evening patrol and walked back with Iori.

As he shrugged on his shearling jacket in the foyer, Ikkei jogged out of the cafeteria. "Hey, Alex. Got a sec?"

"What's up?"

"Just wanted to talk."

Did that phrase ever precede a positive conversation? "I don't like where this is going."

"Relax." Ikkei threw on his own puffer jacket and ushered Alexander onto the porch. They descended the steps to the driveway, gravel crunching underfoot. Ikkei dug out a pack of cigarettes and a metal lighter engraved with an abstract howling wolf design, then lit one rolled stick of tobacco between his lips.

Stuffing pack and lighter back into his pocket, he took a seat on the bottom step and patted the unoccupied space beside him. Alexander accepted the invitation, the cold of the concrete seeping into his jeans.

When Ikkei pulled his hand out again, a set of keys dangled from his finger. He flung them to Alexander, exhaling a mixture of smoke and misty breath. "Notice anything different?"

A guessing game? Alexander shuffled through the keys, intermingled with a collection of gas discount tabs. Car, apartment, locker, the polka-dot spare for Naomi and Aryel's house. He didn't recognize the cobalt key. "What's this for?"

Ikkei took another puff from his cigarette, the tip glowing red against the night-dark backdrop of the yard. "You, my friend, are looking at one of Hildegrand's newest homeowners."

"You bought a house?"

"Yup. Nice spot in the mid district. Two stories, two bedrooms, a garage big enough for billiards. Even has a patio that'll be perfect for barbecues in the summer. Not bad, eh?"

The key ring rested more heavily in Alexander's palm. "When did that happen?"

"Place went on sale in October, closed on it middle of last month. Owners were looking for a quick sale. The lease on my apartment doesn't end until the twentieth, though, so I'm taking the time to clean it up and move my stuff over."

"How'd you manage to afford that? I thought you were broke." Last Alexander heard, car repairs had made a substantial dent in Ikkei's savings account.

The tendons in his neck pulled taut in a grimace. "I didn't. Naomi co-signed the mortgage. Gonna be indebted to her for a while."

Alexander was flabbergasted. The Toi siblings used to share an apartment, but after Ikkei failed to cough up his half of the rent several months in a row, Naomi cut him off. Kicked him out. Swore she'd never loan him another cent. That was what landed him in that cruddy hovel downtown. Didn't keep him from splurging on bad habits, just stopped them from becoming somebody else's problem.

"I have you to thank as well," he said.

"What did I do?"

Ikkei craned his neck to the sky. Smoke coiled lazily into the starless expanse. "You disappearing put a lot into perspective. Messed me up real good, too. I think that's why Naomi took pity on me ... You scared the shit out of me, you know that?" His smile belied the sadness in his eyes. "I could *feel* you pulling away, but every effort to keep you close seemed to push you further out, so all I could do was watch."

Shame soured in the pit of Alexander's stomach, recalling the weeks leading up to the charity ball. The fury and vitriol he doused every interaction in. "Wasn't my brightest moment."

"I'm not saying this to make you feel bad, Alex." Ikkei slid an arm around him and squeezed his shoulder. "I'm saying it because *I love you.* We all do. And you can talk to us when life gets tough. You don't have to be this brave, stoic leader all the time."

A small but earnest nod earned Alexander a kiss on the temple, and for once, he didn't shy away. He let himself slouch into his friend's side, let the tension drain from his body. There was something to be said for the comfort of actually *physically* leaning on someone.

"You stink of smoke," Alexander muttered. Stronger than ever with this enhanced sense of his, an acrid taste at the top of his throat.

Ikkei chuckled. "Yeah, I'm working on it." He stamped his cigarette out in the gravel with the steel toe of his workman's boots. "Back on topic: I'm throwing a little housewarming shindig on the nineteenth. You're welcome to invite Oto, if you want. There'll be snacks, games. Booze. You in?"

Alexander clutched the keys. "I'll be there."

CHAPTER TWENTY-ONE
DECEMBER 3 | CARDPLAY HEADQUARTERS

HIKARU'S HEAD FELT CLOSE TO SPLITTING. The throbbing pressure came and went in waves, periodically obscuring his vision with zigzag mosaics. Unrelenting in its assault, the migraine had bound him to the recliner in the den for most of the day.

Curtains had been drawn to block out the piercing sun. The lack of light bleeding through now told him that dusk had come. A whole day gone, hopefully not wasted. Having had time to reflect, he'd concluded that the *nothing* he obtained from Valerie may well hold importance unbeknownst to him.

His actions must have had some impact, must have altered the trajectory of their future. If the strings willed it, there had to be a reason. He merely wished, for the sake of the brain he'd bruised in fate's service, that he knew what.

It was fortunate that his abilities hadn't been required elsewhere. There'd been no civilian blightings in almost a week.

Though Elizabeth had insisted he cease magic use altogether after resigning from the HPD, he hadn't the luxury. Duty trumped pain, but at least sporadic memory erasures imposed minimal strain. Taking things out was simpler than putting them in or jumbling them about.

He tilted his head back, encouraging the pressure to drain, and lifted it again at the clang of footsteps on the suite's spiral staircase. Elizabeth rose from the stairwell, recognizable though bleary without his glasses. Even in a crowded room, no lenses to aid him, he could pick out her tall, sturdy frame from a distance.

She paused in the middle of the den, displeasure scrawled on every square inch of that frame. "I really don't enjoy having to lie for you."

Hikaru resituated himself. "I know. And I hate that I've put this on you, but I—" Another stabbing throb behind his eyes, and he bowed his head into his hand, justifications dammed by gritted teeth. Only the same old excuses.

It's terrible, but I must.

It's troublesome, but I must.

It's tiring, but I must.

I must.

I must.

For how much longer?

Sighing, Elizabeth sat on the arm of his chair. It may have been a coincidence that the pain eased when she rubbed his back, or perhaps she had a magical touch too. "How's the head?"

"Improving." At a snail's pace.

"The kids were worried about you this morning."

Ellen more than Alexander, Hikaru imagined. Not for a lack of care on Alexander's part, but an overabundance of it on his sister's. The girl used to worry herself silly whenever her brother fell under the weather. "What did you tell them?"

"That you're sick and contagious."

Contagious? "You could have let them see me, Lizbet. To put their minds at ease."

"Hikaru, if they saw you, their minds would be anything but *at ease*. You look like death warmed up."

That confirmed he looked as poorly on the outside as he felt on the inside. "Rest assured, I'll be at work tomorrow."

"Oh, no you won't. You're not going near that desk until you're fully recovered."

"There is work to be done."

"And I will handle it," Elizabeth pointedly cut in. "Take the next couple of days off. The world's not going to implode over the weekend."

You don't know that, he almost said, and held his tongue. Without a finish line in sight, the endgame up in the air, he'd gotten absorbed in trying to predict and thwart his opponent's next move. If he pushed too hard, he was going to sabotage his own game.

His slouch deepened. "You must think I'm mad."

Elizabeth hummed, threading her fingers through the loose coppery reams of his hair. "Can't help that," she said. "We're all mad here."

CHAPTER TWENTY-TWO
DECEMBER 6 | SANGMOR, ATTIKA

A FEW SHINY DOLLARS IN AVARICIOUS POCKETS had accelerated Valerie Renard's transfer to the Federal Correctional Institution in Sangmor—a prairie township northeast of Hildegrand. Bribes couldn't buy her freedom; she was in too deep for that. What they could buy was a private cellblock in which to conduct business.

Although, Cardan doubted they could conduct business with her in this condition.

The woman paced her cell like a captive animal, twitchy and off-kilter. A disheveled mimicry of the person she used to be. She pressed herself to the bars, crazed focus glued to Wiseman. "I told them you would come. They didn't believe me, but I told them. You still need me, after all."

Her ego appeared intact, but Cardan knew inflated egos to be an undesirable trait in Wiseman's eyes, and right now, those eyes were full of steely ire. "What happened to you?" he asked, the question devoid of concern.

Valerie's brows pushed upward, a wavering innocence on her cracked lips. "I'm not sure what you mean."

Wiseman wrapped his black-gloved fingers around the bar next to her face and leaned close. "Do not lie to me. You've been touched by magic. I can sense it on you." He could what? "Someone has done this to you. Who was it?"

"I don't . . . I c-can't remember."

"*Think.*"

She retreated into her cell, biting her once-manicured nails. Some had been chewed to stumps.

If magic was the cause of her condition, someone must have gotten to her at the precinct. But to Cardan's knowledge, none of the officers stationed there were Empowered, and what kind of power could unravel a person this way? All of Valerie's hard-earned marbles had been spilled on the floor.

She stopped her nail-biting. "There was a man," she said, one marble recovered.

"Who?" Wiseman pressed. "Give me a name."

"I don't know. I don't know, I don't know, I don't—"

Wiseman slammed the cell door, startling both her and Cardan. "A *name*, Valerie."

"Can you remember what he looked like? How tall he was, what he was wearing?" Cardan prompted more gently. Scaring her wasn't going to get them far.

Valerie scratched vigorously at her scalp, further matting her hair. Whatever buried treasure she was digging for, it wasn't there anymore.

Back at the bars, groveling, the last of her dignity leaked from her tear ducts. "It's there. I swear it's there. It's this place, Charles. It has me all mixed up. Just take me away from here. Please." She went to grab his hand and he retracted it briskly, shaking it as if to dispel some vile filth.

He lifted his chin, inhaling deeply, his composure a capricious thing. Hard to hold on to. Then he smoothed his vest and unclasped his right cufflink. "McConnell," he said evenly. "Watch the door. Ensure that no one enters."

"What are you going to do?"

He rolled up his sleeve. "Tie up a loose end."

In this business, that phrase carried only one grim definition, and one that struck Cardan as gratuitous in this scenario. "Why don't we take her back to the estate? She's no good to us dead."

"Nor as a liability." Finger by finger, Wiseman began to remove his arm-length glove. "Do not make me repeat myself."

For the first time since he walked in, Valerie locked eyes with Cardan. Her tears had dried up in her horror. Initially faced with a life sentence in federal prison, now hurled onto death row because her mind, her most valuable asset, had been damaged.

This was the woman who helped Wiseman build the original Rending Machine, who assisted in distribution of the corporation's magic management tech. She took the fall for his transgressions, for fuck's sake. Was he really going to toss her to the curb like a defunct appliance?

Am I any better for letting it happen?

Smothering that thought and ignoring Valerie's mouthed pleas, which became audible when he turned away, Cardan did as he was told and assumed his position by the door.

Off came the glove with a whisper of vinyl. The lights dimmed and shadows rose to dance on the wall, sending a chill down his spine. And in that hole where he buried his woes, he laid his morals to rest.

For the good of the cause.

A necessary evil.

"No, please! I can be useful." Desperation lent a harshness to Valerie's tone, and Cardan fought the urge to cover his ears as she pleaded her hopeless case. "You can't do this to me, Charles. You wouldn't be where you are without me! You *need* me! I'm—"

A wet crunch and splatter silenced her.

Bile rose, burning, to Cardan's throat. He clamped a hand over his mouth. Faint gurgles and gasps radiated from the cell behind him, the dying breath of a playing piece he'd previously thought indispensable. Another nauseating squelch, and a thud signaled a body hitting the floor.

Loose end tied.

There was a sigh, a rasp of fabric—the shadows contained—and the too-even tap of Wiseman's approaching footfalls. "We're leaving," he said, unnervingly calm. How could he be so unruffled when Cardan couldn't stop shaking?

"*Swiftly*, McConnell. Before someone sees something they shouldn't."

Knowing that would mean more wanton bloodshed, Cardan shuddered free of his shock. If he could stomach Kane turning convicts into ink soup, he could stomach this.

Refusing to look back, he placed a hand as steadily as he could on Wiseman's shoulder and pictured the place he intended to go: the parking lot outside the brick and barbed wire fence. And just as they came, they went.

Out of sight.

Out of mind.

CHAPTER TWENTY-THREE
DECEMBER 6 | CARDPLAY HEADQUARTERS

"Nervous?" Iori pulled on a pair of fingerless gloves as he joined Kyani in the arena's sandy pit. She wore her own athletic garb: a halter top and shorts, forgoing any form of foot covering. Full gear wasn't necessary; today, they'd just be flexing their magical muscles. And this would be the first time Kyani had flexed hers since the purification.

"A little," she admitted. Though she masked it well, he could detect faint shivers in the black vanes of her wings. "I know how pure magic feels, and I want to feel it again, but I worry that using it could bring back the blight."

"If it does," said Iori, "we have an extinguisher."

Kyani puffed through her nose, amused. Jokes aside, he hoped it wouldn't come to that. Suit cleansings were unexplored territory. They couldn't be absolutely certain the Club was clean until they put it to the test.

The clap of shoes on the upper level preceded the rest of the training group. Elizabeth had donned her battlemaster gear, Alexander a maroon tank top and joggers.

Ellen's crop tee and capri combo sprung a leak in Iori's attention span—a leak he promptly plugged. Yes, she looked cute in her little black and lilac getup with her hair drawn into a messy bun. Acknowledged, move on. If Tatiana were here, she'd be winking and nudging him like there was no tomorrow.

"Before I leave you to your own devices," Elizabeth said once they'd gathered in the pit, "I'm going to supervise this session to ensure you know what you're doing and can work together without biting each other's heads off. I am looking at *you two*."

Iori and Alexander recoiled in discomfort. Their last and only duel had ended in a violent provocation of the feral Spade. A lot had happened since then, though—lessons learned, amends made—and Alexander had made it clear he had no intention of instigating such violence again.

"We can live together, we can work together," Alexander said, albeit with a grumbling undercurrent of reluctance.

With that, Elizabeth laid down the guidelines and explained that this would serve as orientation to the unofficial training course she'd dubbed *Keeper 101*. These freestyle sessions would allow them to test their cooperative ability, determine strengths and weaknesses, and in the case of the more recently-awakened: get comfortable with their Suits.

"Any questions?" When no one replied, Elizabeth commenced their preliminary session with a clap. "Alright. First and foremost, we need to test the Club."

Kyani stepped forward, a rigidity in her posture. "What do you want me to do exactly?"

The battlemaster put a couple meters between her and Kyani. Better to err on the side of caution, even if she was wearing magic-repellent threads. "Just call it like you normally would."

Kyani exhaled slowly, the others watching in anticipation. Praying for the best, preparing for the worst. "Awaken, *Withered Club*."

The summon rang clear on her tongue, and what should've come next was her transformation into the masked Keeper Iori met at Elysian Tower. However, no stunning visual display followed, and after a brief increase in volume at her initial command, her magic's hum plunged to an idle frequency.

A second attempt yielded the same disconcerting result.

"I don't know what I'm doing wrong."

"It may not be you," Elizabeth said. "It's possible the purification wasn't as successful as we thought."

"But it worked!" exclaimed Ellen, and Iori's chest panged at the sag of her shoulders. "I was sure it worked . . ."

He wouldn't believe it hadn't. "The Club is still there. I can hear it." Its frequency had changed, the drone of corruption erased. If it had been eradicated, it wouldn't have any hum at all. "Did you call the right name?"

"I think she would know," Alexander put in bluntly.

"Don't start." Those bonds Elizabeth had wanted them to foster wouldn't be easily forged. "Oto, please answer Ryone's question."

"It's the only name I've known it by." Her voice dropped to a murmur. "I don't think I could forget after how it made me call it."

"*Made* you? You didn't summon it willingly?" asked Alexander, who'd reportedly called on his Suit for aid during a duel with Charles Wiseman—a ploy likely intended to achieve just that. Not that he would've given Alexander much choice.

"When I couldn't take the Rending Machine anymore, the Club brought me to its dreamscape and tied me to the throne." A shudder rustled through Kyani's feathers. "I had no idea how to summon it until the words were coming out of my mouth."

Coerced, magically influenced. Either way, one element went unchanged. "You still had to call yours by name . . ."

Iori had been under the impression that at least he and Kyani shared an awakening experience.

She frowned at him. "You didn't?"

Easier to show than tell. They had their marks, and he had his. In arguably his least dramatic reveal yet, Iori tugged down the collar of his sleeveless hoodie, and Kyani blanched at the sight of his scar. "It didn't need me to," he said. All it took was a man and a machine. Cracked him, his seal, and the Void open, and let the darkness come gushing out. No dreamscape, no summon. To the corrupted Spade, he had been a vessel ripe for the taking.

Elizabeth tapped her chin. "It's conceivable that purifying the Club flipped a reset switch and caused it to retreat into a state of dormancy. If that's the case, it could require a reawakening." She looked at Iori over the top of her oval lenses. "You taught yourself to summon the Spade. Would you be willing to share your methods with Oto?"

Methods seemed a generous thing to call them. Months of one-sided conversations that made him feel like he was going insane, until one day the monster inside him decided to give him its name. Granted, with its purity restored, the Club might be more responsive.

He agreed to try, and the battlemaster waved him over to Kyani. There was an expectancy on her face he wasn't confident he could live up to, a faith he felt undeserved, but on the off chance it could help, he'd give her his best shot.

"It's not too complicated," he said. "The Suits aren't sentient, but they're not totally insentient either. If you speak to it right, it'll listen."

"Out loud?" she asked.

"Doesn't have to be."

"Like meditation, then?"

He shrugged. "Sure."

"That's how I accessed my dreamscape." Kyani's gaze fell to her scaly toes. "I made a dome like yours using plants to help me concentrate. I don't think I can make it here, though." Her connection to the foliage outdoors would be blocked by the mesh-lined concrete barrel of the arena, and there were no plants inside she could use.

But she'd taken a page out of his book. "*That* I can assist you with." He looked to Elizabeth for permission, and she motioned for Ellen and Alexander to move back. Once they were clear, Iori brought a hand to his chest and drew a rivulet of ink from his well, unending until he clipped it. So far, the only limit he'd encountered was the amount he could control.

A twist of the wrist sent the liquid down and around, catching up granules of sand from the arena floor. Kyani pulled her wings close to her body as it circled them.

"Is that safe?" Alexander asked, ever the skeptic.

"Safe as it's ever been." Iori cast a teasing glance at him through the widening ribbons of ink. "Be a dear and don't shoot me this time?"

He caught an irate twitch in Alexander's expression and a less funny hint of disapproval in Ellen's before the dome whirled shut, isolating him and Kyani from the outside world. Their own private bubble, shaped by his internal rhythm. The last time they shared this dome, they were fighting on opposite sides, and he'd spirited her away to his dreamscape.

Evidently, cats and birds could be friends.

The interior had its own ambient light, a faint purple from the magic infusing his ink. That combined with the steady whoosh of its constant rotation should make for a more propitious environment.

"Try now," he said. "Pretend I'm not here."

She closed her eyes, hands folded neatly in front of her. For a minute, nothing notable transpired. She simply stood there, breathing in and out and in and out, and Iori wondered if his presence was too much of a distraction.

Then the synthesizer tone of her magic fluctuated, dipped and wavered. If the Club wasn't talking to her yet, it was listening.

Sensing the increase in magical output, the Void strained against Iori's control. Hungering for it. He increased the Spade's volume to keep it at bay.

Kyani's hum rose to a warble. A glow permeated her eyelids, the soft hue of fresh grass after a thaw.

She had it.

Now, thought Iori, *call it.*

Her lips began to move to the incantation. "Awaken," she whispered, and with her next breath she called her Suit by a different name: *"Verdant Club."*

Magic bloomed green and bright, her body a beacon in this dome of night. Her wings fanned wide, and the Club took the threads of her athletic attire and spun them into a familiar shape. A skirt of downy barbs plumed at her hips. Vine-like tendrils traced a three-leaf clover on her bust. And over the upper half of her face, a mask unfolded, intricate designs engraved in its long wooden beak.

It happened in a moment, and ended in a flash.

A gust like a spring gale slammed into Iori, blasting open his dome. Kyani leapt back, nearly taking flight, as her tutor hit the sand. He propped himself on an elbow, tingling from head to toe, and couldn't tell if it was the adrenaline or an aftereffect of the magical explosion.

They stared at each other. Then at Ellen and Alexander, and at the battlemaster who'd gone paler than Iori had ever seen her. And Iori burst out laughing, because his good deed for the day had inadvertently turned into a dance with danger. His dome had been obliterated, his corrupted magic chased into hiding. Power like that could do a real number on him.

He picked himself up, winded from the exhilaration. "Well, that worked." He dusted off his pants. Kyani hadn't moved. "Well, go on. Show us what you can do."

CHAPTER TWENTY-FOUR
DECEMBER 6 | WISEMAN ESTATE

How much value did a pawn hold to a king who had slain his own queen?

About as much as that shattered whiskey decanter on the floor, Cardan reckoned.

Sybil lounged on the sofa he stood next to, eating chunks of fresh-cut mango off a knife while Circ hovered on his ominous cloud, waiting for Hurricane Wiseman to blow over. It reminded Cardan of his father's drunken rampages, except Da's fits never escalated beyond stomping and yelling.

When Mr. Wiseman got angry, he broke things—inanimate objects and people alike. He'd had reason to expel Valerie Renard, but if the woman's undying loyalty hadn't been sufficient to maintain her seat at the table, what would it take for Cardan to lose his? At what point did lackeys become expendable?

"Cardan, he is using us."

Lately, his conscience had taken on the persona of Kyani Oto, this little bird sowing seeds of doubt in his mind and singing louder every day.

"What are we doing?"

"This isn't right."

"Think about it."

"Who's next?"

"Are you finished?" asked Circ when Wiseman's tirade petered out. "While Valerie's death is unfortunate, her condition, as you describe it, has confirmed my suspicions."

"What suspicions?" Wiseman growled.

More withheld information. Brilliant.

The Warden dispelled his cloud and sauntered past the sofa. "Haven't you wondered how Cardplay is always one step ahead?" He reached over the back, pinching a slice of mango from Sybil. "Why the odds seem to be in their favor?" His stroll around the salon brought him to Wiseman, whose crooked jaw showed no enthusiasm for the buildup. "It's because they have a *Guiding Light*. A failsafe, I believe you would call it." He bit into the fruit's juicy yellow flesh as Sybil indignantly carved another slice.

"Meaning?" prompted Cardan.

"Meaning my sister chipped off a piece of herself and cast it into the mundane world, not unlike the fragment I left to the Wisemans—only hers grants its host the ability to manipulate the strings of fate."

"Are you saying someone out there has the power to change the future?" One would think seven years and a metric ton of magical nonsense later, none of this would surprise Cardan anymore. Especially when the entity it came from was bloody malice incarnate.

Circ chewed on that. "More the power to alter paths based on the probability that they will lead to an ideal outcome."

Sybil grunted. "Sounds OP to me."

"Are you certain of this?" inquired Wiseman, massaging his gloved hand. Cardan still wasn't quite sure what lay beneath that black vinyl covering, but their trip to the Sangmor Institution had revealed it to be a damn sight more than scars.

Kyani once said he had an aura, bleaker than a starless night. Was the Spade responsible for that too, or was that a part of his deal with the devil?

"You know as well as I that breaking the Spade's seal should not have heralded the return of pure magic. Waking it before its time must have triggered my sister's contingency plan and stirred the quiescent magic in the mundane world. Even in death, her light shines."

"And you didn't think to tell me?" The bite in Wiseman's tone drew a sidelong glare from Circ. "This is my family's legacy. We didn't devote the past millennia to this mission just to pass the reins to an impulsive juvenile. If you had listened to me from the start, we wouldn't be in this position. We would still have the complex. An army. We would have two Keepers under our control, and Valerie—"

At an almost imperceptible gesture from Circ, Wiseman choked on his rant. His right leg buckled and he caught himself on the coffee table, giving Cardan and even Sybil a start. Nearly nicked her lip with her knife when she jolted against the cushions.

Inky veins crept over Wiseman's pallid skin as Circ stooped to his level, teasing Void-strung strings with a subtle flex of his fingers. "Do not presume to speak to me as though I am your servant or spawn," he hissed through razor teeth. "I am your Lord Warden. What you need to know and when you need to know it is up to *me*."

"If you don't—"

A clench of the fist strangled that rejoinder. Whatever marks Wiseman had, whatever demonic transfiguration he was hiding, the Sundered Star had taken control of it.

"Need I remind you that your life is dependent on mine? The only reason the Void has not consumed you is because *I* command it. You breathe because *I* allow it." Circ leaned in close to him, eyes gleaming something sinister. "Know your place, Wiseman, or you will be king of nothing."

He relaxed his grip, released his hold, and as Wiseman sucked in a ragged lungful of air, Cardan felt as if the oxygen had been siphoned out of his. Up till now, Circ had maintained a level temper, faced every hurdle with a nonchalance tantamount to indifference. But one overstepped boundary had put Wiseman's head on the chopping block. There'd been more order under Kane, for fuck's sake.

"What are we dealing with here, a living god?"

There was Kyani's echo again.

"Why was he locked up in there?"

As Wiseman gathered himself, trying his best to appear unaffected, Circ continued where he left off. "The Guiding Light is an obstacle, but not an insurmountable one. If we can obtain it, the plan can move ahead accordingly. What we are looking for is a well-connected individual. Someone in a high-ranking, influential position. A philanthropic type who's not afraid to make difficult choices."

A name sprung to mind, and Cardan's conflicted conscience coiled around it. This person could pull strings no one else could, and would've had access to Valerie Renard. When you held the keys to the city, there was nary a door you couldn't open. But that person had also been a champion for the Empowered, had made leaps and bounds in the pursuit of equality. On the one hand, divulging their identity could secure Cardan's seat here. On the other . . .

"Could be that old lug, Hargrove." Sybil beat him to the punch before he could decide if wanted to swing. "He's the one who pulled flame boy out of quarantine. Dropped him and his sis in Ritsuo's lap right before giving the go-ahead on the magic school. All Empowered documentation goes through him, too. Bet he knew both kids were Keepers and fudged the Heart's papers to keep her hidden."

Trust the stab-happy first-year Cardplay expellee to throw one of their kind's biggest supporters under the bus.

What would become of Mayor Hargrove if he really was in possession of the fragment?

Judging by the broad and disconcerting smile pulling at Circ's lips, nothing good. "Tell me more about this Hargrove."

Wiseman answered, still working out the kinks Circ had put in the right side of his body. "Thelonious Hargrove is the Mayor of Hildegrand." Effectively, the man in the fancy chair he sorely desired. "Engstrom's assessment is accurate. He's a known proponent of a united mundane and magical society. If there is a Guiding Light, he would be a prime candidate."

Sybil's knife glided along the inside of the mango's red-green skin. "Want me to pop 'im?"

The utter lack of concern she approached taking a life with disturbed Cardan.

"Your willingness is duly noted but your services will not be required." Circ might've patted her on the head if he didn't avoid human contact like the plague. "Extracting the fragment is a delicate process. If he dies, we risk losing it to a replacement host. I will take care of him myself."

CHAPTER TWENTY-FIVE
DECEMBER 12 | HILDEGRAND, MID DISTRICT

OVER THE CAR STEREO, Kyani listened as enthused radio hosts reflected on the blessings 2027 had bestowed on them. New babes in the family, good health, low gas prices, and an unprecedented drop in Void activity.

Knock on wood.

But rarely could the topic of monsters come up without segueing into talk of the monster hunters, and today the discussion slanted towards their uncertain future. Before they could get into the bias-laden debate over whether Cardplay should remain in operation if the decline continued, Alexander turned the radio off.

Being the constant focus of public opinion must get tiring.

"When we get there, do you want me to come in with you?" he asked Kyani.

"Would that be weird?"

"Only if it's weird for you."

In the passenger seat, Kyani tried to roll the tension out of her shoulders. "This whole situation is weird for me." They were headed for the care home her father resided in, a trip she'd been looking forward to until she was getting ready this morning.

It started with the mascara, a slight upset in her stomach, worsening when she applied the concealer to her scars, and turning to dread as she struggled to bind her wings. Cardan always assisted her in the past, wrapping them while she pinned the feathery appendages to her flanks. Disguising them under a half cloak was the rotten cherry on top.

On that note . . . "Are you comfortable showing your scales in public?" The bone-white flakes on Alexander's hands were hidden by a pair of gloves, but the ones on his face glinted in the midday sun, no measures taken to conceal them.

"If anyone asks," he said, "they're body mods."

He did already have the split tongue and an array of ear piercings to reinforce that claim, and the scowl he often wore would scare off more inquisitive people than his charming looks could draw in.

"It might be nice to have company, then," Kyani decided.

Soon, they arrived at the Woodridge Long Term Care Facility. The reception area had been decorated for the solstice. Holiday spices masked the hospital smell that usually laced the air. Wreaths hung on every door, and tinsel lined the front desk where a lush poinsettia sat with its striking variegated bracts.

The staff had changed since Kyani's last visit. She didn't recognize the young receptionists at the desk, who appeared unsettled by Alexander. It was hard to tell what put them on edge: the scales, the aforementioned scowl, or the fact a defamed Joker had entered the establishment.

"How can I help you?" asked the brunette in a pointy festive hat.

"I'm here to visit a resident," said Kyani. "Jabari Badawi?"

The other receptionist, whose dark eyelids had been painted to mimic candy canes, wheeled their stool to the computer while their desk partner gathered information. "What's your name and relation to the patient?"

"Kyani Oto. I'm his daughter."

"Can we see some ID?"

They'd increased security, too. Kyani didn't have to show identification before. She and Alexander dug out their government-issued cards, stamped to denote their Empowered status. The candy cane-eyed receptionist took both and resumed typing.

Alexander rested an elbow on the desk. "Badawi?"

"Oto is my mother's name. She insisted on it when I was born." Ironic considering how easily the woman let her go. Kyani had contemplated switching to her father's surname but chose not to. For one thing, name changes were expensive. For another, Oto belonged to more than her mother. It was her history, her heritage—a tie to a southeast Coraldan country she'd never been to and a family she'd never met. But that lineage belonged to her as much as her mother.

One foul limb didn't mean the tree had to be uprooted.

Identification verified and visit logged, Kyani and Alexander boarded the elevator to the third floor. The premium care level. A nurse met them at the top and guided them through the spacious halls.

The differences on the surface weren't vast. Private rooms, cushier furnishings, higher grade tech. The most notable disparities were in the type of food and care patients received. Assigned nurses and specialists, superior rehab services, organic protein-rich meals instead of canned or frozen produce. Things that could drastically influence a patient's recovery.

Things Kyani hadn't been able to afford on her own.

On her pittance of an income, she'd faced the eventuality of becoming her father's caretaker in their cramped studio apartment. She would've had to forfeit her job, live off welfare scraps. Without Wiseman's *generosity*, he wouldn't have gotten the care he needed.

But she didn't need Wiseman or his money anymore. Through Cardplay, she'd attained the funding to cover the medical bills, and with her prospective career as a Joker, in-home support in an actual house had become a real possibility.

Dare she hope for such things?

Rounding the corner, Kyani spotted a security guard outside a room midway down the hall. That had to be her father's. The guard must've been part of the security detail Cardplay had hired per the terms of their negotiation.

The realness of the situation rushed in like a squall, stopping her in her tracks and whistling scorn in her ear.

You don't deserve to see him. You haven't earned this.

When he finds out what you did, it'll ruin him. Hasn't he suffered enough?

How selfish can you be?

To make matters more disconcerting, she didn't know what condition he'd be in. Some days when she used to visit, he'd be lucid, but often his mind would be far away—sometimes, so far that he would forget who she was. That she was his daughter. That he *had* a daughter.

She'd been gone so long, maybe he'd forgotten she existed at all.

There was a light touch at the small of her back, Alexander urging her on. "You're alright," he said, and she wanted to believe him.

If she had the strength to defy the man who'd deceived and manipulated and tortured her, she could face the man who'd never raised his voice or hand to her.

The nurse entered the room ahead of them, and there by the window, Jabari Badawi observed the healing gardens below from his wheelchair. Thin black hair wisped about his sun-spotted scalp, and the knitted shawl he once swaddled a much smaller version of Kyani in was draped over his shoulders.

"Mr. Badawi." The nurse bent to speak to him. "You have company."

He followed her sweeping gesture to Kyani and Alexander, and recognition swirled in the rich sepia of his eyes. He beckoned Kyani closer with outstretched arms, and eager strides carried her straight to him. She dropped into a crouch and took his weathered mechanic's hands in hers.

"Hi, Baba."

"*Haslah, bibi,*" he replied in Peridi. *Hello, my child.* His fingers drifted to her short hair, a question on his lips. They opened, closed, pursed—the phrasing lost to him. He'd never been much of a talker, but the aphasia brought on by the stroke had rendered his few words fewer.

"A story for another time," she told him. "Right now, there's someone I want you to meet." She waved Alexander into the room, and Jabari squinted, tapping his lip as if trying to place him. "Do you remember him from the news? This is Alexander Jane. We're going to be coworkers from now on, Baba. I'm going to work for Cardplay."

Letting out a weepy *ohh*, he clasped Alexander's hand in greeting and gratitude. "She's a good girl, my Kyani. She'll make you proud."

"She already has," Alexander said. "She's a hard worker, and her powers show a lot of potential. She'll be a perfect fit."

There was the charm that captivated the public, the articulate candor and hard-won smile of a boy who'd seen too much for his years and persevered in spite of it. He could be hot and cold but seldom in between, and what a privilege, thought Kyani, to be close enough to feel that warmth without fear of getting burned.

The nurse left them to socialize and they spent the next couple of hours talking about the future, the past, and a censored version of how Kyani's path crossed with Alexander's. Jabari absorbed it all with attentive nods and crinkling crow's feet, and when the thrill of the reunion had leveled out, he took his turn to share.

Picking words like cherries, searching for just the right ones, he told her about the nursing staff and movie nights with the other residents. Stuff from two, three, four months ago. He even remembered the police coming by in the summer and explaining to them that she was in Barsair—a tale she'd fabricated over where she'd really gone: to Camrand Island for a *classified magic study*.

Technically impossible with the Empowered travel ban, but he didn't need to know that. Not yet.

Fumbling in his excitement, he informed her that he'd received her letters and spoke affectionately of the nice fellow with the lyrical accent who would deliver and read them aloud—a fact Kyani hadn't been aware of. Cardan was meant to leave the letters for the nurses to find.

In and out, that was the rule.

Before Jabari could inquire as to the young man's whereabouts, the nurse returned to collect him for physiotherapy, and Kyani was able to kiss him goodbye knowing she would see him again soon. She lingered behind as Alexander followed them out of the room, unable to ignore the persistent murmur of the flowers on the windowsill.

Alstroemerias, a long-lived lily-like perennial. These were at the end of their bloom.

She hadn't had a chance to exercise her untarnished green thumb on any plants yet. If she were honest, she was afraid to. The last time she did, they shriveled and died, overtaken by blight. But the *Withered Club* was no more.

She reached out to stroke their wilting petals, and at the brush of her fingertips, they shivered back to life. Clusters of patterned pink and yellow flourished at the top of firm, leafy stems, no sign of disease to speak of.

Delight thrummed in her chest. Now she could go.

When she turned to leave, she found Alexander watching her from the door, jacket hooked over his arm. Caught red—or rather, green—handed using magic unauthorized outside of the permitted grounds.

Rather than mention it, he continued down the hall. Kyani jogged to catch up to him, a worm of culpability wriggling in her conscience.

They took a detour through the healing gardens, along footpaths flanked by young maples. The warm sunshine trickling through their branches cast a latticework of shadows on the bare flowerbeds underneath, where decaying leaf litter would provide a nutrient mulch for the vegetation come spring.

If Kyani concentrated, she could sense their roots winding beneath the paving stones, faint in their hibernation. Evergreens held the most prominent presence in the winter, but all were clearer than ever with her senses no longer dulled by the Void. She'd almost forgotten how beautiful the language of flora could be.

She hooked her arm in Alexander's. "Thank you for coming with me today." She hung her head. "And for not reporting me back there."

"Who says I'm not going to?" Kyani looked up at him, and him down at her—straight-faced, unreadable. "I'm kidding," he clarified, adding insistently when she remained unconvinced, "For real, it was a joke."

"You're not funny." The smile she failed to repress implied otherwise.

"Seriously, though, I wouldn't get you in trouble for a minor misdemeanor." Regardless of his obligations as his escort? "The laws are there to keep magic from upsetting the balance of mundane life. I can't fault you for perking up some flowers."

"I couldn't resist. It's been ages since I could interact with plants without hurting them, and they seemed so sad. I wanted to give them a pick-me-up, even if it's only temporary."

"How long does it last?"

"For them, not long. They'll be gone tomorrow. My one rule is that I can't interrupt the natural order of things. Interfering with that cycle by forcing plants beyond their intended lifespan would upset a balance more vital than mundane life." There she went, off on a tangent again. "Listen to me getting philosophical on you."

He hunched a shoulder. "It's a sensible rule. We have a responsibility to set boundaries on magic use. The current laws are too strict, but it's better than having no laws at all. And so we're clear: you can get philosophical with me any time."

She appreciated how receptive he could be. It was strange, in a pleasant way, how well the two of them fit together. How well they all did. And it reminded her of a heavy hitter of an existential topic she'd been pondering more and more lately. "Then answer me this, Alexander Jane: do you believe in fate?"

"Like, everything happening for a reason and predetermined ends and all that?"

"Not in an inescapable sense. There's a saying: *the stars incline us, they do not bind us.* To me, it implies we each have a role, and we get to choose how we play it."

Alexander mulled over that. "What do you think?"

She tipped her face to the plane trails streaking the cloud-cluttered sky. "I think we were meant to meet," she said. "For the four of us to come together with this shared purpose, it feels too significant to be an accident."

"I don't know if I'd call it fate, but I'm glad we met." Alexander squeezed her arm against his side. Their shoes scuffed a shallow slope, the parking lot sliding into view. "Speaking of coming together for a shared purpose . . . I was wondering if you'd wanna come to Ikkei's housewarming party next weekend?"

"How many people are going?"

"Just me, him, and Naomi and Aryel."

That she could do. Kyani held onto him a little tighter. "I'd love to."

CHAPTER TWENTY-SIX
DECEMBER 19 | HILDEGRAND, MID DISTRICT

THE WEEK FLEW BY, as time tended to during the holiday season—further accelerated by a steady schedule of class demonstrations and after-shift Keeper 101 meet-ups. Alexander still couldn't believe that cheesy title stuck.

For the most part, it had been productive. Fun, even, sparring with his sister and showing Kyani the ropes. What she lacked in melee combat, she more than made up for in archery and evasion tactics, and when she began the honing process this Monday, they would see what she was really capable of.

Taking the reins of Iori's training also turned out not to be the ordeal Alexander had envisioned. They had their spats—over techniques and proper form and just because Iori liked to push his buttons—but most sessions went smoothly, and as Iori's control continually improved, Alexander regained his.

His magic stores were refilling. Flames reinvigorated, strength and energy levels on the rise. Though loathe to admit it, Iori's unsolicited workout tips had helped. Alexander wasn't about to give him a reason to brag by admitting it out loud, though.

Cocky bastard.

Rewarding as it had been, Alexander was looking forward to a break before jumping back into the thick of it tomorrow. Tonight, he planned to leave all his worries at the door.

Ikkei's door, specifically.

He struck the knocker and retreated a step. Next to him, Kyani cradled a bamboo plant—something simple yet ornamental and fuss-free, because when she'd asked what type of plants Ikkei liked, Alexander blanked. Far as he was aware, the only plants Ikkei cared for were the kind that could be smoked, eaten, or happened to be tattooed on a hookup's skin.

Aryel answered the door and invited them in from the cold. There was an underlying hint of fresh paint in the hall, smothered by the woody, vaguely minty scents of camphor, eucalyptus, and cloves.

Candles—Aryel's gift. Naomi's was essentially the house itself. She and Ikkei greeted them as they shed their outerwear, and Kyani meekly presented her gift to Ikkei, explaining that in Zirca, where bamboo held symbolic value, these six bound stalks represented prosperity, peace, and longevity.

"Aw, that's so thoughtful!"

"And smart," added Naomi. "It won't keel over and die if you forget to water it."

He hugged the plant protectively. "I would *never*."

Seeing as he'd never nurtured another living thing, Alexander wouldn't bet on it, which was why he'd chosen a gift that could put only Ikkei's wellbeing in jeopardy. He produced an anchor-shaped bottle of peach and ginger vodka from his bag. "Make it last."

Ikkei gave a deep, throaty laugh, the plant pot in one arm and the bottle in the other. "I will, I will. By the way, you're welcome to crash on the couch if you want. It's not the shitty one; it's a sectional. Courtesy of the parents."

Whereas Alexander would've readily taken him up on that in the past, the idea of spending a night away from home right now set him on edge. Kyani probably wouldn't want to stay on her own either. "I think we're just gonna head out after."

"All good." Ikkei jerked his head. "C'mon, I'll give you the tour."

After he'd shown them around, Alexander went to assist Naomi with drinks while the others dug into a Coraldan-style snack spread Ikkei had prepared in the living room. Edamame dip and peanut sauce, rice crackers, mochi, diced papaya, and an assortment of cheeses and skewered meats.

When Ikkei Toi was in charge of the food, eating well was guaranteed, and his sister's cocktails deserved equal praise.

She broke out her mixology kit alongside a selection of booze and mixers, then cracked open a bottle of gin and got to work. Watching her in action, a well-oiled machine, Alexander felt his help would only impede her flow.

Help wasn't really the reason he'd caught Naomi alone.

They hadn't spoken much since he got back, and their last interaction prior to that had been a shouting match on *Duels Day*. She had called him out and ratted him out, and he'd blamed her in part for his suspension. Acknowledging now that she was in the right, he owed her an apology. A proper discussion. Something.

The most he could muster to start was, "Hey, we're good, right?"

A flash of gold behind straight-cut bangs, an upward glance from her meticulous work. "Why wouldn't we be?"

Because of a million reasons neither of them knew how to talk about. Ikkei and Aryel were pros at this kiss-and-make-up crap. How come he and Naomi only settle disputes by arguing or ignoring the problem until it faded into obscurity?

Alexander made another attempt. "We left things kind of rough. It's my fault. I can own that, and—"

"Oh god, am I the next stop on your apology tour?"

"That's the direction I was going in, yeah."

Naomi's head sank between her shoulders. "Look, Alex, you don't owe me shit. Got it? Sure, you were an immature brat parading around with a raging ego—"

"Okay, ow."

"—but I'm not proud of how I handled the situation either."

Was this her attempt at being vulnerable or was she trying to get him to drop it? "You had your reasons."

"So did you. They didn't make sense to everybody, but they made sense to you, and you're forgiven. You better have forgiven me too, or we're gonna have a problem." All ingredients in the shaker, Naomi slapped the lid on and shook it, her bracelets jangling to the gyration. "What I *would* like to know is if you and Ryone are getting along."

Alexander leaned on the granite countertop. "Well enough, I guess. He makes it his job to be a pain in my ass, but he's just annoying." A huge step down from *monster*. "I'm more concerned about things with Ellen. It's still kinda weird between us."

Though they'd bridged the divide, they stood on opposite sides, Ellen waiting for him to come to her and him too chickenshit to meet her halfway.

In order to respect her boundaries, he'd had to wrestle his instincts into submission. Repress the sense of duty that had been ingrained in him as the eldest. *Look after your sister, take care of your sister.* He used to walk her to and from school every day, watch her until their parents got home. Now she was in more danger than ever, and he was supposed to just stop?

A pink mixture splashed into stout cocktail glasses. "You'll get through it," said Naomi. "Siblings fight.

Sometimes I wanna cave Ikkei's skull in, but at the end of the day, we stick like glue. If he and I can make it, so can you and Ellen." Alexander hoped that was true. "Now, give me your drink order. And don't say 'surprise me' or I'll give you a pint with everything in it and you'll be stuck here for the night."

Good talk.

Drinks made and trayed, they brought out the games. First up: *Q & Effin' A*, a card game that prompted players to share stories and fun—or not-so-fun—facts about themselves. Aryel called it *platonic speed dating*. Alexander would sooner liken it to hazing. Regardless, Kyani was eager to play even after Ikkei's warning that he had no shame, which was met with a resounding "WE KNOW."

Halfway through the deck, the booze set in. Alexander fiddled with Ikkei's lighter as Naomi slurred through a tale about the polyamorous triad she'd been a part of in high school. A queen sandwiched between a prince and a peasant girl, was how she described it. Her being the queen, of course.

By the time she finished, they'd forgotten what her prompt was, and Kyani drew the next card. "'*In counter-clockwise order, each player must share an embarrassing story.*'"

"Drawer goes first," declared Ikkei.

Kyani placed the card face-down in a separate stack. "Okay, well...when my powers manifested, I almost demolished our apartment building by accidentally accelerating the growth of a fig tree."

Aryel gulped a mouthful of vodka soda. "I saw that on Bleater! It was trending under *Magic Mishaps*."

A social media hashtag Alexander refused to explore on the rare occasion he logged in. Originally started to connect Empowered, it quickly devolved into a cesspit of pranksters, bullies, and anti-magic activists, and caused more trouble than it was worth.

"Honestly, Oto," said Naomi, crunching on honey-roasted almonds, "you have nothing to be embarrassed about compared to the shit these idiots got up to."

Alexander flipped the lighter's lid shut. "Don't lump me in with them."

"You participated in their dumbass experiments. Isn't that how you figured out you were fireproof?"

"It's how we *confirmed* it." A month post-graduation he responded to a call involving a pyric arsonist who'd set fire to a building. After escaping from the blaze impossibly unscathed, they decided to investigate further. "We did a harmless candle test. I didn't fucking condone Ikkei and Aryel trying to drown Oskar in a hot tub."

Ikkei flapped his lips. "We weren't *trying* to drown him."

Kyani gaped at them, entertained in an aghast sort of way. "What were you trying to do?"

"Test elemental immunity," Aryel explained. "Since Alex was immune to fire, we wanted to see if all elemental types were immune to the matter we can manipulate, or if it was limited to conjured matter." He sighed, twisting his necklace's blue teardrop crystal. "They locked me in the kitchen freezer."

"Thus proving that cryogenic types are not immune to subzero temperatures." Ikkei held up a judicious finger, then pointed it accusingly at Naomi. "Also, fuck you and your high horse. You participated as well."

"Not by choice. You *tased* me. Electricity's not even an element!"

Brother and sister descended into Jeidish bickering, Aryel trapped in the middle plugging his ears. If the rumors floating around headquarters were true and he was gearing up to propose—he'd declined to comment—Alexander wondered how long he could survive the Toi family dynamic.

Alexander tossed a weary look at Kyani. "My *friends*," he muttered in sarcastic presentation. He'd worried they might be too much for her. Too loud, too overbearing. To his relief, she seemed to have melded fine with the group, and even brought a level of calm to their chaos.

The bickering grew louder when Naomi flicked an almond at her brother. Knowing they'd never finish the game if he didn't stop them, Alexander intervened. "Alright, shut up. Ikkei, it's your turn."

"What're we doing?"

"Embarrassing stories. Go."

He threw back a multicolored shot and slouched forward, chin propped on his knuckles. Thinking hard, digging deep. An obscene groan of delight then rose from his chest. "Remember that time I found you tied buck naked to a bed?"

Mortification struck Alexander like a wet fish, and Kyani nearly choked on her drink. "What the fuck, Ikkei? You're supposed to tell *your* embarrassing stories, not mine!" He never would have volunteered that one. It had taken a monetary bribe to zip Ikkei's mouth in the first place.

And three beers, a cocktail, and a tequila shot to unzip it.

"I was embarrassed *for* you. It counts. Anyway, who goes for a bang sesh and leaves the door unlocked? Should be thankful it was me who stumbled in and not Ritsuo or your sister. That would've been awkward."

As if it wasn't already. Alexander hid his face in his hands. "Please, for the love of god, stop talking."

"It's not a big deal," Kyani spoke past poorly-suppressed laughter. "We all have embarrassing stories from when we were young. It's a part of growing up."

"It was last year."

"Oh."

They'd organized a dorm party at headquarters to celebrate the solstice. Long story short—he couldn't remember the longer part—he drank too much and snuck off to one of the unoccupied rooms with Javi, a Second Classer from the night shift. Later on, Ikkei found Alexander bound to the bedposts and Javi lounging fully-clothed in the bathtub.

The benefits part of his and Javi's friendship ended there. Actually, so did the friendship part, if it even qualified as that. Acquaintanceship, more like.

Suddenly, Alexander regretted volunteering to be the designated driver. Non-alcoholic coconut rum couldn't save him from this.

CHAPTER TWENTY-SEVEN
DECEMBER 20 | HILDEGRAND, MID DISTRICT

Kyani wasn't used to being invited to parties, and since meeting Alexander, she'd been invited to three. The first she'd attended with an ulterior motive, the second she'd spent at death's door, and the third she wouldn't soon forget either—but not because it plagued her.

This one would be a black-eyed Susan, pressed into her life's scrapbook. A source of motivation and encouragement, cherished for years to come.

As the night wore on, games slowed and conversation dwindled. Naomi and Aryel eventually retired to the guest bedroom, too exhausted and inebriated to socialize any longer, and Ikkei lumbered off soon after, leaving Kyani and Alexander to lounge on the sectional.

Tucked in at one end, her legs extended over his lap, Kyani watched him draw absentminded lines along her shins. Up and down over her obsidian scales, his head tipped back and eyes closed. She hadn't taken him to be a tactile person. Generally, he tended to shy away from anything more than a hug. However, the closer they grew, the more physical his affections became, and lately she'd caught herself longing for his touches when they were apart. There was comfort in them, a sort of unspoken validation.

And as his fingers crested her knee, they reminded her that these weren't the only touches she'd been craving. Another desire had been secretly budding inside her, and after their revealing game of cards, she wondered if this closeness had opened a door for it. But was it greedy to want such a thing from someone she'd already taken so much from?

Her actions, be they unwilling or not, had robbed him of his freedom, his safety, and nearly his life. She had forced him to a brink no person should ever have to stand on. Yet, he had given her all of that and more. Freedom, safety. Amity. A chance to rekindle a life she'd thought lost.

All she had done was save him from the dire straits she put him in. So where had she scrounged up the gall to want this so badly that she couldn't cast it out of her mind?

She chewed on her lower lip. Surely there wouldn't be any harm in putting the idea out there. He could always say *no*, and it wasn't like she'd be toying with his heart; there wouldn't be any strings attached. It would just be two friends enjoying each other's company.

She'd taken plenty of chances already. What was one more?

"Hey, Alex, can I ask you a personal question?"

His head tipped toward her. "Shoot."

"You mentioned earlier about your past . . . dalliances." *Hookups* sounded too salacious for her. "Did that last encounter put you off for good, or would you still be open to that sort of thing?"

"Why, are you interested?" It was a joke—she could tell by the drowsy chortle in his voice—and when she didn't respond to it, he lifted his head to look her dead in the eyes, fingers faltering in their languid path. "*Are* you interested?"

No sense beating around the bush if he'd already caught on. Might as well lay it all out. Kick the ball into his court, so to speak. "I'm going to be really candid with you," she said.

"I like you, Alexander. A lot. You make me feel good about myself, and I'm attracted to you in a way I don't experience often. I know romance doesn't appeal to you, and I'm not looking for that, but if you were up for a different sort of arrangement . . ." Noting the lack of change in his expression, she trailed off. "I'm being too forward again, aren't I?"

"No. No, you're fine. I'm just taking it in." His gaze dropped to her shins. "I'm not gonna lie, the thought has crossed my mind. Didn't think you'd be interested after, well, everything." His thumb traced contemplative circles around her ankle bone. "What does it mean to you? The act."

The *act*? Was Alexander Jane seriously too shy to use the word? "You mean *sex*?"

He gave her a long, dramatic blink. "Yes."

Stifling her amusement, she ruminated on that. "I view it as a way of expressing affection. It's fun, it can be relaxing. For me to show that side of myself to someone, I need to feel connected to them on a deep emotional level, and I feel that with you. Don't feel pressured to agree to it, though. I'd understand if you'd rather not."

An almost imperceptible laugh rocked Alexander's body. "This is gonna sound corny, and it might be the post-party fatigue talking, but . . . you told me you used to feel invisible, and I want you to know that you are important to me. I *do* see you. And if you want to show me, Kyani, I would be happy to see all of you."

The—indeed, exceptionally corny—sentiment filled her with the fuzzy warmth of a dandelion clock, soaking up the sun-like shine of Alexander's aura. "Would you mind if I kissed you, then? For real this time."

Keen to oblige, Alexander leaned in. Their lips met gingerly in a test of physical chemistry, followed by a second, and a third just to be sure—each a little hungrier than the last and torturously tender. So unlike the poisoned kiss she'd forced on him at the construction site.

This, she hoped, would make up for that.

Alexander must have decided more hands-on research was necessary. Wandering fingers traveled from ankle to calf to inner thigh, turning Kyani's skin to gooseflesh, and he eased her back against the arm of the couch. His friend's couch in his friend's house, right in the middle of the den.

Before they could get too absorbed, Kyani gently pushed him back and came up for air. "Wait, should we?"

He looked confused, somewhat feverish. "Should we not?"

"Here?"

"It is a housewarming party. We haven't sufficiently warmed the house yet." He swallowed dryly. "Unless you don't want to?"

Everyone else had gone to bed, and the curtains were drawn. No one would see. And she really, really didn't want to stop, so if Alexander thought it was fine to fool around with his friends a floor above, that was good enough for her. "I do. I definitely do." She grabbed him by the shirt collar and pulled him in again.

The sweet aroma of coconut engulfed her, and she tasted it on his tongue when she parted her lips to let him in. The small notch in the tip, split flawlessly by magic, felt larger in her mouth than it appeared in his.

Her left wing was squashed, but she couldn't be bothered to move, her focus fixed elsewhere. On the firelight in her peripheries, on the sensation coiling low in her abdomen. On Alexander's hand sneaking further up her thigh, pausing at the hem of her dark cyan dress—a request for permission she would've granted if they weren't interrupted.

"Ooh! What did I just walk in on?"

They parted in haste, Ikkei's interjection a storm breaking the humidity between them. He was standing shirtless in a pair of ratty old sweatpants, halfway to the kitchen when he must have spotted them.

Alexander hurled a cushion at him. "Fuck off."

"Hey, hey, no need for violence; I just wanted a glass of water. Not my fault you got caught." Ikkei chucked the cushion back and proceeded to the kitchen. The fridge opened, bottles clattering in the door. Water trickled as the light perspiration on Kyani's skin cooled. Then the fridge thumped shut, and Ikkei reappeared with a filled glass, waggling his fingers in a wave. "You kids have fun."

When the creak of the stairs faded, Kyani's eyes slid to Alexander, and she snorted behind her hands, struggling to contain herself.

He quirked a brow at her. "What're you laughing at?"

"You're so red." All the way from his nose to his pierced ears, like someone had taken a marker and colored him in. He struck her playfully with the cushion. On the plus side, he'd have a brand new embarrassing story to share for future games.

He checked his phone, the screen with its geometric-patterned wallpaper a vivid rectangle in the dimly-lit room. "We should probably get going. It's past midnight." He patted her leg. "Do you want to continue this at my place?"

Walking into the Jane house, Kyani could feel the magic in the air—that subtle mundane type of magic ushered in by the holidays. Tinsel and twinkle lights framed doorways and windows, and adorned the faux fir tree in the living room.

Like a snapshot from the solstice films that used to cause the green to spread beyond Kyani's thumbs, filling her with a different breed of poison called envy.

More than the abundant gifts and decorations, it was the picture-perfect families versus her broken one that made her envious. As she grew older, however, she'd come to cherish what she did have, even if she wished that little girl had more.

Security system reset, Alexander and Kyani tiptoed upstairs. Passing the second door in the hall, she detected two auras inside. Iori and Ellen, violet and scarlet—the shadows mixed with the former dimmed by the luminosity of the latter. The way they enveloped each other, they couldn't have been far apart.

Alexander led Kyani to the neighboring room. It was all very *him*, clean-cut and organized, a few personal touches dotted around. One such item was a photo on his desk. Kyani stooped for a closer look and gasped at the young boy in the lower left. "Is this you?"

Those frosty lashes rimming goldleaf eyes couldn't have belonged to anyone else. He and his sister stood in front, proud parents behind. Alexander had his mother's terse smile and nose, free of bumps or dips. Ellen got her pointed chin, but the apples of her cheeks were as round and red as her father's, plucked from the same basket. And both had his snow-white hair, like sheep's wool on his head and sparse cotton along his jaw. Their mother's was straight and mousy.

"Hm? Oh, yeah." Alexander was rummaging through his nightstand. "That's from *The Tines Vineyard* in Ammolitia. Our last vacation before shit hit the fan."

"You two are such a perfect blend of your parents." Kyani bore a likeness to her father, more and more with each passing year. Her mother despised the resemblance.

"We got a fairly even spread of the genes. Personalities, not so much. Ellen got Dad's sunny disposition, and I got

Mom's short fuse. Not surprising I ended up a pyric type. Always did have a knack for inflaming situations."

There was a crinkle of foil. Alexander slouched on the bed, rotating a thin square packet between his fingertips. Now wasn't the time for him to be getting dour.

As Kyani stepped into the gap between his knees, he craned to look at her. "Fire isn't only a force of destruction." She combed back his coarse white waves, let loose from their ribbon. "Many cultures view it as a source of life or a symbol of hope." Alexander pulled her against him, a coaxing tug of the waist. His lips found her collarbone, her throat, and the electrical burns that ringed it. "It can also represent desire . . . and passion . . ." A whimper escaped her at the scrape of teeth on sensitive skin.

Alexander's breath plumed hot against her neck. "How far do you wanna take this?"

She bit her lip, running a thumb over the studded lobe of his ear. She'd had a taste of freedom and now she couldn't get enough. "All the way," she said.

Their mouths met again, needy hands making savory work of removing clothes. One by one, Kyani unbuttoned Alexander's shirt, then smoothed her palms over the scars charting the broad expanse of his chest. The wounds she'd tended. Next, her fingers trickled past his navel, guided by a snowy trail of hair to his belt buckle.

In turn, he subjected her to the same torment, teasing the spaghetti straps off her shoulders. He followed the descent of fabric to the supple slope of her breast, open-mouthed kisses igniting an urgency within her.

She didn't want to wait any longer.

They parted briefly to shed the last of their clothes, flower-embroidered dress and russet pants and undergarments haphazardly discarded on the floor. Alexander shifted back on the bed as Kyani settled on top of him, straddling his thighs. His arms around her middle, her wings encircling them both—malleable curves sinking against sculpted muscle. Two battered souls, seeking solace in each other's fissures.

For all their misery, all their pain, they had earned this.

Tonight, Kyani would have her celebration.

CHAPTER TWENTY-EIGHT
DECEMBER 20 | JANE RESIDENCE

DAWN STRETCHED THROUGH Alexander's bedroom window, bringing out the blue-green iridescence of Kyani's feathers. She lay on her stomach, wings draped over the bed, as he stroked their vanes in fascination. The longest of them rivaled the length of his arm, the rest growing shorter and softer closer to the base.

She'd flinched when he first touched her there, where wing met flesh, and then leaned into it, shivering at the graze of his misshapen nails. Similar shivers coursed through him when her mouth explored the healed lacerations on his ribs, the X carved into his abdomen, the scales dotting his hip bones. Together, creating new associations for their marks. Replacing pain with pleasure.

Was that coping, or another form of avoidance?

"Did it hurt when you got your wings?" Alexander asked as his fingers slid near that sensitive spot again.

Her gaze traversed the underside of her feathered limb. "Apart from pressure, I didn't feel much of anything until later. I went into shock, apparently. What about you?" she mumbled drowsily. "Your scales."

He lay his hand on the arm he'd tucked under his pillow, the white flakes on his knuckles stark against his burns. "I don't remember much. I know I went numb, but that wasn't from shock. That was . . ."

"When Valerie took control," Kyani concluded when he couldn't finish. He hadn't taken the time to sort through that box yet. It was stored in a cupboard of hazardous contents with a *fragile* warning scrawled on the flap, and unpacking it with his sister, the masters, his friends, or even Cellier would require him to provide context.

That was the hurdle he couldn't get over: retelling the horror story he'd lived so that others could understand it.

But Kyani already had the context. She had been there to witness what he went through, had experienced some of it herself. Maybe she was the right person to open the box with.

"I think having her in my head messed me up more than I realized." More than he wanted to acknowledge. "Sometimes I wonder if I'm actually still there. At the complex."

He could almost smell it now. The stale air, the sweat and blood and filth impregnating his clothes. The closest he'd gotten to clean in captivity was a frigid bath of sea water delivered by a high-pressure hose, which Sybil delighted in. She got a kick out of watching his temperature fluctuate using her thermal vision—a power she'd thoroughly abused in her brief enrollment at Cardplay.

He kept waiting for that blast of cold to wake him up. For the bite of a blade. The sear of acid. For hands viciously knotting his hair, grabbing his face, wrenching him out of the dream. "I feel like any minute, the rug's going to be pulled out from under me. Like being with you and being home is just me inventing scenarios in my head. When shit goes bad, that's how I can tell it's real. That *I'm* in control. And I hate that part of the reason I'm struggling is because I have to refrain from hovering over Ellen." Alexander rolled onto his back, knuckles bumping against his brow. "How fucked up is that? I can't dictate what my sister does, so I'm driving myself up the wall."

"Have you told her?"

"No. She's got too much going on between Iori and all this Heart crap, which is another topic we haven't discussed." She hadn't brought it up with him, and he was too afraid of overstepping boundaries to bring it up with her. If she wanted to talk to him about it, she would, right? Alexander huffed. "We used to talk about everything. Then the accident happened and she got a sorry excuse for a brother back from quarantine."

Kyani propped herself up. "You were in quarantine?"

"For about two months. Fifty two days, to be exact. Fun fact: Blackjack weren't the only ones to put me through the ringer with their *tests*." The government's methods were more subtle and conducted under the guise of research, but they still cut him. Stuck him with needles. Pumped him full of god-knows-what and hooked him up to noisy contraptions. "I was *twelve*. How is a twelve-year-old supposed to cope with that?"

The car accident made him road-wary.

The Reemergence made him world-wary.

Quarantine, well . . . that was a can of worms he hadn't quite gotten to the bottom of. And Blackjack had renewed all of that trauma and more. He couldn't even handle a static shock off his car without being thrown mentally into the Rending Machine.

Alexander dragged his hands down his face. "Now who's talking whose ear off?"

"I don't mind. I'm glad you can confide in me, and I'm happy to provide a distraction when you need it." Kyani bent to kiss him, her honeydew fragrance clearing the grime from his gray matter. A drop of sweet nectar on his tongue.

Getting up and getting on with the day suddenly seemed far less appealing.

Two fingers to her chin, he put an inch between them. "You're more than a distraction to me." He looked up from her lips to her deep-set eyes. "If we're going to make this a regular thing, I wanna be clear that I'm only doing it with you. I have no intention of trying to tie you down; you're free to do whatever, but I'll be keeping it exclusive on my end."

"Ooh, *exclusive*."

"You like that?"

"It's got a nice ring to it. I like the idea of having you all to myself." She folded her arms atop his chest. "And just so you know, I wouldn't object to you tying me down occasionally."

Alexander chuckled. "Noted."

Despite her best efforts, Ellen had become hopelessly obsessed with whatever was or wasn't between her and the boy slumbering beside her. She tipped her head to look at him, so close his fringe brushed her shoulder. One of his spindly arms stretched over her, and a knobbly knee against hers.

Often, they would end up like this, twisted like a pretzel. Whoever woke first would do their best to slip out of the bind unnoticed, but neither were heavy sleepers, and when they did stir simultaneously, they would pretend it didn't happen. That it didn't mean anything.

Could it?

He loves me.

He loves me not.

He loves me a little.

He loves me a lot.

Normally the person playing the game would be seeking reciprocation for their own affections, but Ellen didn't know which affections she sought reciprocation for. Was she looking for an everlasting friendship, or something else?

"What do you *want?"* The question nagged at her again, her own feelings a riddle she couldn't solve. Her attempts to comb out the tangles only resulted in more knots, and the harder she tugged at them, the more she floundered around Iori. With his acute observational skills, he was bound to notice soon if he hadn't already.

When he was asleep, she didn't have to worry what he thought. If he believed she liked him or not.

"Don't you?" Soren had asked.

If she couldn't say *yes*, did that mean *no*?

If she couldn't say *no*, did that mean *yes*?

Frustration clawed at her insides. She was going in circles.

Carefully, she slid out from under Iori's arm and made a quick trip to the bathroom before heading downstairs. The smell and burble of brewing coffee reached her from the kitchen, accompanied by voices. Turning the corner, she saw her brother at the dining table with an unexpected guest— Kyani Oto, dressed in one of his racerback tanks and a pair of his shorts. Feathers ruffled.

"Oh, hi."

"Hey," replied Alexander, thumbing his phone screen.

Kyani offered a warm, "Morning."

"Did you stay the night?"

"It was a last minute decision."

"It was more convenient," Alexander put in.

Except it wasn't. Nearly all routes from Ikkei's house to home would've taken him past headquarters, where he'd originally planned to drop Kyani off. Ellen chose not to pry; she didn't need the details of her brother's escapades. "I was going to make fancy egg bread. Do you want any?"

That piqued Kyani's interest. "Fancy egg bread?"

"Highly recommend it." Alexander sipped his coffee. "Might as well use up the loaf. We can pack leftovers for lunch."

Excited to introduce Kyani to one of her favorite breakfasts, Ellen dug out the ingredients: the remainder of the brioche bread, a bottle of pure maple syrup, the freshest berries as you could get this time of year, and a box of organic eggs. She gathered the lot in her arms and deposited them on the counter. "What time did you get in?"

"Late," came the answer, but not from either of the people she'd asked. Without a sound to precede him, Iori had sauntered in, cardigan thrown over his tank top and pajama pants, and hair toeing the line between *sloppy* and *I-woke-up-like-this*. His ears pointed knowingly in Alexander's direction. "Sleep well?"

Alexander glared at him while Kyani sought refuge in her mug. "You realize I could still kill you if I wanted to. I know where you live."

"Eh, you tried that already. And you failed. Twice." Iori swiped a bottled milkshake from the fridge and took a seat, leaning his chair back on its rear legs. "Maybe next time you could be more considerate of your housemate's sensitive hearing?" He flicked the peel-off seal across the table.

Alexander flicked it back. "If your hearing is that sensitive, you should invest in earplugs."

The boys continued bickering in the background as Ellen cracked eggs into a bowl. Kyani stepped up to the counter a moment later, fleeing from the war zone to avoid getting caught in the crossfire. The steam rising from her mug carried the herbal tartness of licorice.

"Need any help?"

"No thanks, I've got this under control." Her parents wouldn't have stood for it—putting a guest to work. Plus, Ellen relished the process. This was her own kind of therapy. She added a few drops of vanilla, a splash of milk, and a teaspoon of sugar to the mix, then whisked it into a rich yellow froth.

Kyani watched the conflict unfold at the dining table. "Are they always like this?"

"This is an improvement." Their harmless verbal tiffs had become the ambience of the home. It was a game to Iori, and her brother kept getting played. Ellen had to wonder if some part of him enjoyed it. "At least Alexander's not bullying anymore."

"Actually, I think he's the one getting bullied."

The pair of them giggled. Ellen placed a pan on the stove, a turn of the knob and a rapid click-click-click resulting in a plume of flame from the burner. While she waited for it to warm, she slopped slices of brioche into the egg custard. "I'm glad we can all be together like this."

Kyani murmured in agreement. "I owe it to you. And Iori. If he hadn't thrown me a rope, I'm not sure how things would've panned out for me. Or for your brother."

That was one what-if Ellen wouldn't let herself entertain.

The boys' voices sharpened. Their bickering had escalated to a battle of insults, in which Iori's weapon of choice was his mother tongue.

"*Koharou*," he drawled mockingly.

Alexander shot back, "I can understand Jeidish, dipshit."

"I'm aware. Amethistian just doesn't have the same *edge*."

What Iori didn't realize was that he was up against a polyglot.

"You want an edge? I'll give you an edge, *ju mes paton*." Alexander switched to Malchais, the language of the country Ulridge Academy resided in. It was known for its unforgiving vocabulary, particularly when compared to their father's home country, Thulia, where insults flaunted about as much zest as a floppy-wristed slap fight.

Grimacing at the severity of Alexander's vocal bombardment against Iori's nonchalant jabs, Kyani leaned over to Ellen. "Should we stop them?"

"Nah, they're fine." She forked custard-coated brioche into the pan. "They're bonding."

A crash caused both girls to jump. Ellen spun to find Iori on the floor, his chair toppled over, and her brother's leg stuck out under the table. She put her fists on her hips. "Alexander!"

"Don't *Alexander* me, I barely nudged it."

To be fair, it would've been hard to resist when Iori's precarious positioning had already been tempting gravity.

"I deserved it. A little." Iori rubbed the back of his head, letting out a pained hiss as he picked himself off the floor. "Lucky you didn't knock me unconscious, though."

"So much for cat-like reflexes," Alexander muttered.

Kyani's wings perked. "Oh! Speaking of consciousness," she wrenched the conversation onto a different track, "there's a subject we haven't touched on in training yet. I was actually hoping Iori could coach us."

He righted his chair. "Coach you on what, exactly?"

"Dreamscapes." Ellen tended to the sizzling breakfast as Kyani explained. "Alex hasn't visited his since the Diamond awoke, and I haven't been to mine since the raid. Ellen will need to know how to access hers, too, if her seal breaks. And you make the transitions look so effortless. If you can show us how to do that, we could use them to stay in touch."

"Isn't that why we have cellphones?" asked Alexander.

Ever leery, Iori pointed out, "Cellphones can be traced and hacked. I think she's suggesting something more under the radar."

A bob of Kyani's head verified that. "We don't know what'll happen in the next few days or weeks, but we do know Blackjack won't go down without a fight. We should be prepared for anything they might throw at us. With that said: will you teach us?"

Iori shrank under their collective attention. "I guess I could give you the crash course, yeah."

CHAPTER TWENTY-NINE
DECEMBER 20 | CARDPLAY HEADQUARTERS

AFTER ANOTHER ABNORMALLY UNEVENTFUL DAY, Ellen, Iori, Alexander, and Kyani congregated around the coffee table in the headmaster's office for their next training session. The eve of the solstice meant Hikaru and Elizabeth had gone to Mayor Hargrove's annual holiday jamboree.

And when the masters were away, the Keepers would play.

Ellen sat next to her brother on the sofa, Iori seated opposite her on the ornate area rug with Kyani, both favoring the floor over the perfectly fine chairs flanking the table.

"Alright," said Iori, tail tip curling behind him, "before we dive in, literally, let's establish some ground rules."

"Wait, we're going in? Now?" Apprehension laced Kyani's tone.

"I figured that'd be best. The dreamscapes are sort of a non-physical plane where Suit and soul meet. Exploring them and spending time there is how I fostered the connection to mine. Learning to enter them on a whim isn't actually too different from mastering any other skill."

Alexander grumbled, chin in hand. "This better not take ten thousand hours."

"That'll depend on you." Not giving Alexander a chance to retort, Iori carried on, more animated and articulate than one would expect from his earlier diffidence. "I thought we could do a round trip, get acquainted with each other's dreamscapes. Seeing as not everyone has access to theirs"— Ellen became the personification of the smiling sweat drop emoji—"I'll lead the expedition. That way we can start in the same location."

"Can you take that many people?" Kyani asked.

"We're about to find out." He'd only ever taken one at a time. Ellen for a few trips, Kyani once. "Rule number one: apart from the ground and the gates, don't touch anything that's not yours. Rule number two: don't wander off the edge of the world, because I don't know what'll happen if you do. Lastly, it's probably best if we don't interact with the Heart gate, because if by some fluke we trigger its awakening—"

"We're fucked," Alexander surmised.

"Most likely."

"So how do we do this?"

"Physical contact." Iori extended his arms to either side. "If the four of us are linked, I should be able to pull all of you in at once." Kyani took one of his hands and one of Ellen's, and Ellen clasped her brother's leathery palm. Iori then flapped his still-empty fingers, urging Alexander to close the circle.

"I am not holding your hand."

"Why," crooned Iori, "afraid you might like it?"

With a great effort of a sigh, Alexander grasped Iori's awaiting hand. "There. Now what?"

"Close your eyes. I'll count us in."

No telling how long their physical bodies would be left sitting for, Kyani uncrossed her legs and moved into a more comfortable kneel on the rug. "Don't we need the dome?"

"That's more for security than anything. Outside disturbances can pull you out of the dreamscape. Loud noises, external interactions. Since it's just us here, we shouldn't have to worry about getting interrupted." He firmed his grip on his fellow Keepers. "Ready?"

Firming hers likewise, Ellen shut her eyes, and Alexander squeezed her fingers—for her comfort or his, she couldn't tell—as Iori began the countdown.

"Three . . . two . . . one."

There was a brief lapse in sensory input before that haunting melody welcomed Ellen to the Spade's dreamscape, plinking like a distant music box. The song Iori performed at the charity ball, the one that, by his account, Wiseman used to make him play until his fingers went numb. And when the fog cleared, she found herself where she always did: in the center of the concentric rings engraved in the floor, facing Iori's throne. Kyani and Alexander, backlit by their gemstones, had spawned outside their respective gates.

The Heart's stood unlit several meters behind Ellen, leaving her woefully displaced—somewhere on the boundary between ordinary and extraordinary, and unsure which she'd rather be.

Alexander covered his nose and mouth as if he'd caught a whiff of something rotten. He must've tasted the corruption on the air. Kyani would've been able to see it, too—an aura of darkness enveloping the floating landmass, tangible to Ellen as a dense, damp chill.

With a clap to break the uneasy quiet, Iori pushed up from his throne. "I'll admit it's not the most hospitable locale, so let's not hang around longer than necessary." He descended from the dais. "Oto has some experience traveling between dreamscapes. Why don't we start with the Club's? You lead, we'll follow."

Put on the spot, she stiffened. "How do I let you in?" Due to her limited time unsupervised at the complex, she'd always been the one to call Iori for their covert meetings.

"It works on the same principle as other techniques: will and intent. You'll hear us ring the doorbell. For me, it sounded like a gong. All you have to do is will the door open. Worst case, we get separated and you'll have to ring me to let you back in."

The group gathered at the Club gate.

Kyani lifted her hand to the clover-shaped emerald. "Just a matter of will and intent . . ." She bowed her head in concentration, and on the gem's second pulse, she disintegrated—startling Alexander back a pace as her particles funneled into the gleaming stone. Unlike Iori, he was way out of his element.

"Don't worry," said Ellen, "it's just a magic trick." It surprised her when she first saw it, too. "Do you wanna go next?"

Shaking off the discomfort, Alexander approached the gate. "It's all fake anyway, right?" That wasn't strictly true, but if it gave him peace of mind, Ellen wouldn't argue. He copied Kyani's motion, and a few pulses later, he burst into a cloud of glittering gold.

Then came Ellen's turn. Iori had to go last; without him in it, his dreamscape would dissipate and eject her. She'd experienced that once already and had no interest in repeating it. She touched the emerald as Kyani and her brother had, feeling the vibration of magical energy within.

One pulse, two, three, and off she went.

Transitioning from one dreamscape to another was smoother than entering the non-physical plane from the real world, but it still took Ellen a moment to regain her bearings. And once she had, the environment struck her with awe.

Trees reached to lofty canopies of yellow-limned green. Dust motes drifted on the rays piercing their leaves, which dappled the mossy stone floor in gold. Ivy crept through the knots and channels carved into it, and twined around a great sycamore throne whose roots spilled over its dais, snaking off into vegetation so dense Ellen couldn't see beyond it.

Emerging from the Spade's gate, Iori materialized beside her. The other two were ahead in the clearing, taking in the sights and the refreshing scent of damp earth.

Face tilted to the canopy, Kyani pivoted on her toes. "This forest was sick before. Now look, it's thriving!"

The Club's dreamscape would've been corrupted like the Spade's. The purification must have reversed the effects on it as well. But with that revelation, the temperature to Ellen's left dropped, Iori's own corruption stirring with a decline in mood. A tangible stroke of misery for what Kyani could have that he could not.

Hoping to take his mind off it, Ellen prodded him for more educational tidbits as they explored the forest. Here, he explained, they were completely cut off from the outside world. Technology couldn't be used, and neither could magic except for the purpose of travel. They'd been stripped down to their fundamentals. Their essence, their dust. Avatars within their Suits within themselves.

Ellen got dizzy thinking about it. Iori advised her not to.

After a brief jaunt through the dewy undergrowth, they moved on to the next location. More cheerful than when they arrived, Iori strode up to the Diamond's gate and rapped a knuckle on its vine-woven bars. "Let's see what's behind door number three."

"Can you not?" Shooing Iori aside, Alexander raised his hand to the chunk of yellow diamond with its pointed ends and sides, shaped like the Suit it symbolized . . . and paused a hairsbreadth from contact.

Iori stooped towards him and jeered, "What's the matter, got performance anxiety?" But the smirk slid from his lips when Alexander didn't deliver the expected riposte.

"Alex?" prompted Kyani.

His jaw shifted. He was frozen, and Ellen could hazard a guess as to why. The last time he set foot in the Diamond's dreamscape, he'd been sent there against his will and made a prisoner of his own mind. Kindly, she reminded him, "We don't have to go if you're not ready."

At that, his expression hardened. "No. We're here. I'm ready." He planted his palm on the gem's central facet. Light flared within, dazzlingly bright, a single strong pulse that took him with it when it dimmed. The rest of them waited a minute before following him through, and this time they reformed in a realm Ellen knew.

Fluffy clouds like daubs of paint dotted a pale afternoon sky, and rolling fields of wheat rippled in a hot summer gale. Nigh harvest season. She could almost hear the cicadas.

Like the Club's seemingly infinite forest, the Diamond's horizons stretched to unseen limits. No drop off point, no rim to the world. If one were to wander, would they wander for eternity, or end up back where they started? Maybe the scenery in the distance was an artful illusion, and they'd be blocked by an invisible barrier video game-style.

At the top of the dais, Alexander gingerly stroked the marble arm of his throne. Ellen stopped midway up the shallow steps. "Do you remember when we were here last?"

He frowned. "We?"

"You pulled me in at the complex." Unintentionally, she presumed. The way she'd found him, in a daze after Valerie's and the Diamond's spells had been broken, she wasn't surprised the memory eluded him. From what he'd told her, he couldn't even recall plunging his blade into Kane Kros' blight-riddled body. The entire raid had been erased, save for that precious moment they shared on the checkerboard floor, safe in each other's arms. Reunited at last.

If he were only ever able to remember one thing from that night, Ellen would be glad it was that.

Iori beckoned them to the clearing for a final lesson. "It's worth noting how easy it is to lose time here. Dreams move faster than reality, so you'll want to get a feel for the differential. The upside is that these expeditions shouldn't cut into our usual training period much."

"You said the domes are a security measure," Alexander spoke up. "If there's a chance we might be using the dreamscapes to communicate in hazardous situations, we should practice those formations."

"Probably wise, yeah." The curl of Iori's tail warned of a quip to come. "I'd recommend practicing yours in the arena. Wouldn't want to accidentally set the building on fire."

A growl rasped in Alexander's throat. Perhaps to evade his wrath or simply bring the trip to a close, Iori suggested they take the train back to the station and went to his gate. Sprigs of wheat swayed at the base. He reached out to the amethyst, its shine dulled by the blazing sun, and vanished the instant his fingers brushed it.

Corrupted or not, the connection between him and his Suit was clearly much stronger than Kyani's and Alexander's. For him, this stuff scantly required a thought.

The four reconvened in the Spade's autumnal wood.

"And that concludes our tour," announced Iori. "If anyone has any questions, the Q-and-A portion is now open."

Kyani raised her hand as if in class. "How did you learn about the dreamscapes in the first place? I haven't seen any mention of them in my magic studies, and there's no record of them in the extracurricular material either."

His ears folded slightly, an uneasy laugh in his chest. "I saw it in a dream," he admitted. "I'm not sure if I actually went there, but it felt real enough that I tried to go back after I woke up, and I kept trying until it worked."

No wonder the night terrors troubled him. If there was even a remote possibility he could travel there in his sleep, who was to say the Spade's dreamscape *wasn't* caving under the Void's corruption? The only way to be sure was to check upon waking.

Ellen had noticed it weighing on him more and more—the fear that his Suit might consume him as Kyani's had tried to consume her. How it hadn't already was a miracle itself, far over the line as he was. And Ellen was the one person in the whole wide world with the ability to bring him back.

But she couldn't.

Purifying Kyani and the Club had drained her reserves, and she couldn't pause in the middle of a procedure to recharge. At her current maximum output, the most she could do was eradicate the Spade, and the risk that Iori would be lost with it was too great.

The group's discussion faded into the background, Ellen's focus drifting to the Heart gate. If she were to unlock its full potential, would it grant her the power to cleanse him? Would there be no soul beyond saving, no more too-far-goners?

Her feet carried her across the clearing to the gate, mist eddying around her ankles. Apart from the ambient light bouncing off its polished surface, the ruby delicately held in those wrought iron bars was dark—the emptiness within it amplifying that within her chest. That hollow which ached with every failed purification.

She clutched the pleats of her dress.

How did it look, that place on the other side? Would it be as lush and beautiful as the Club's forest, as warm as the Diamond's fields? Or could the hidden realm inside her be desolate like the Spade's, cold and unmoored—a graveyard for the souls she couldn't save?

A touch might afford her a glimpse. It was a choice after all, wasn't it? For pure Suits like hers and her brother's? He'd been coerced, but he made the decision to take the throne and call its name.

Surely a peek couldn't do any harm.

Just as her fingers twitched toward the gem, someone caught her by the wrist. She twisted and met Iori's steady gaze—crimson on white and bleeding into night, both intent on her. "We can't," he said softly, having predicted what she was about to do. "Aren't you always telling me we can't be too careful?"

She looked past him to Alexander and Kyani, who regarded her from afar. Waiting, and concerned. Then her eyes wandered back to the gate, its molded heart of ruby faintly reflecting her image. A hazy, unknowable version of herself imprisoned in the facets.

If they were to meet, would all her doubts become certainties?

Iori gave her wrist a gentle tug. "We should go."

CHAPTER THIRTY
DECEMBER 24 | HILDEGRAND, MID DISTRICT

"All living things have an end, Rishi."

"Even me?" He sniffled.

"Mm-hmm, but not for a very long time."

He peered up at her then. "Even you?"

His mother swayed, him snug in her lap, contemplating the withered orchid on the windowsill that he'd been mourning. "Someday," she told him. "When I do, just remember I'll always be with you. In here." She rubbed his chest above his heart, wherein it thumped a rapid little beat.

The organ thumped slower but stronger now as the memory ebbed, leaving Iori staring at the purple-freckled orchid on Dr. Bristol's shelf while he massaged that same spot on his ribs. Today's session had taken them below the near-present troubles of the surface to dredge the depths where he'd sunk his past. Ironically, he'd brought it up. Family had been at the forefront of his mind since the solstice, and it came out naturally in the pleasantries.

Bristol had asked how he observed the day, which he'd spent with Ellen, her brother, and the masters in their suite. Daring to reminisce, he'd segued from that into how he used to spend it—with trips to the hot springs in Jeida, fried squid on the deck, and later, video calls linking his family across two different time zones.

The squid didn't taste as good in Hildegrand.

Bristol decided to delve deeper. "The day we met," she said, watching him meander about her office from her chair, "you mentioned you were no longer in touch with your extended family. Why is that?"

Because look at me, he wanted to say, and tear off his normal human disguise to show her how the Spade had disfigured him. He may have been coming to terms with the changes on a personal level, but what would his aunt and grandmother think? Never mind his bad reputation and the fact it was *his* magic that took from them a beloved sister and daughter.

Technically, they could carry on believing that she'd been killed by an Inkblot. But Iori didn't want to live a lie.

Would the truth scare them? Would they label him a monster, too? He could reach out, only to be disowned when they learned of the ugliness that shaped him.

All of that internal rambling to produce a simple short statement: "I thought they were better off without me."

Dr. Bristol didn't do short and simple. "*Thought.* Past tense. Have your feelings changed?"

"Not . . . changed, exactly." He completed his cycle around the office, coming back to the couch. Ready for it or not, the past he'd been running from was about to catch up with him. "I graduate in May," he said, and Bristol's *ahh* implied she understood.

Cardplay's graduation ceremony was a televised event. A global spectacle. His name would be broadcast for the world to hear, and he didn't want his family to discover he was alive through the media. Even if they didn't tune-in the day of, it wouldn't take long for them to find out. Their village community in Jeida had always been tight-knit. Everyone knew everyone, and news traveled fast.

"So you're feeling pressured to make contact."

A barely perceptible nod.

"What makes you think they would be better off without you?" When Iori couldn't rally a response to that, Bristol tried a more direct route. "Do you feel responsible for your mother's death?"

He opened his mouth, closed it, forced a swallow past a lump in his throat. Put plainly, no, he didn't hold himself accountable. Blame couldn't be pinned on any singular person or thing, and he couldn't have known a hug would kill her.

"What happened was out of my control. I realize that." But did *she?* "It doesn't change that if I hadn't gone home, she might be alive."

Bristol's deep brown eyes bored into him. "Would you say you've grieved for her?"

"I—yes?"

"Properly?"

"Define *properly*."

She crossed her legs, reclined in her chair. "You've displayed a tendency to withdraw and become defensive when you talk about her, if you don't evade the subject altogether. Your file details similar patterns of avoidance, and the insomnia you've described in combination with your other symptoms are also indicators of unresolved grief."

They could also be side effects of *constant impending doom*.

"It's not unexpected. You lost her at a tender age after escaping a deeply traumatic event, and you were thrown immediately into another one. Growing up alone, having to fend for yourself . . . You've been in survival mode for a significant portion of your youth. Grieving takes time, and time is a luxury you haven't had."

Being analyzed on such a level made Iori want to curl into a ball and vanish. "Can we skip to the part where you tell me how to get over it? I thought your job was to take notes and offer solutions."

"My job is to help you become a well-adjusted human being." Bristol's maroon-glossed lips curved faintly upward. "That was your goal, wasn't it?"

Using his own words against him. Clever.

She glanced at the wall clock. "We're done for today, but there is an exercise I'd like you to do this week." *Oh good.* "I want you to imagine what your mother might say to you if she were here and jot it down in that journal I gave you. I'd also encourage you to consider reaching out to your family. Picture how that might look. Reconnecting with them could be beneficial to your recovery."

"Or it could be detrimental to it." Iori wished he'd bitten his tongue on that one. Balking only proved her point.

"They may surprise you," Bristol said. "Remember, your aunt didn't only lose a sister that night, and your grandmother didn't only lose a daughter. They also lost a nephew. A grandson.

"Iori, they lost *you.*"

The journal remained untouched in Iori's duffel bag. Clasp closed, pages blank. However, while he couldn't bring himself to have a pretend conversation with a dead woman, it was high time the living heard from him. He had considered it long enough.

Arriving at headquarters the next day, he headed straight to the second floor lounge—to the piano, the instrument that had always given him a voice when he couldn't find his. He studied the keys, scratching at the polish on his thumbnail. Ellen's paint job, alternating red and silver for the solstice. She'd helped him prepare this morning, psyched him up.

Now, which song to play?

Music could convey a powerful message with the right notes. For this, the rhythm couldn't be too lively nor too blue. It had to be a piece that held significance to its intended audience, something they'd recognize. Something they would associate with him.

Recital tunes were too impersonal, whereas an original composition would be far too personal—an embrace when all he wanted to do was say, *"Hi, it's me. I'm okay."*

Another few pondering ticks, and it came to him.

He settled on the bench and set his phone to record—audio only. A view of the keyboard would've been nice, but he wasn't ready to be seen yet to any extent. For the time being, all he could offer was his sound.

He brought hands to keys and song to mind, and then began to play. A light and slow intro, gaining power and pace and volume towards the middle. There was grief wrapped up in these chords. Resilience, too. They illustrated a story of moving on, of moving forward.

This piece had been a favorite of his mother's. He used to watch her dance to it—could picture her now, barefoot on a woven rush mat, layers of sheer fabric swirling about her. Sunlight pouring in through open doors, a wind bell chiming in the breeze. Could almost feel her with him while he played, same as when he danced.

A lingering impression of the life they'd shared.

It hurt to draw the fingers of recollection over that impression. So much that, in the past, he'd preferred to cast those memories out. These days, he let himself feel them. Let them hurt, because they became a little less tender with each plaintive stroke.

Healing wasn't a painless process, and although he would carry the scars for the rest of his years, these wounds would heal.

And so would he.

~•~•~•~•~

As Hikaru climbed to the foyer balcony, the last person he expected to find loitering outside his office was Iori. "Evening," he greeted with an inquisitive rise in pitch. The boy seldom dropped by of his own accord, and he was behaving markedly suspect—ears back, uptight, avoiding eye contact more than usual.

There was a small black object pinched in his fingertips. "Hey, um . . . do you have a minute?"

A minute, a few. However many he might need. Something had clearly agitated him. Curious as to what, Hikaru invited him inside. "Certainly. We can speak in my office." But as he reached for the handle, Iori stopped him.

"That's—that's not necessary. I just had a favor to ask." His gaze fell to the flat, rectangular piece of plastic he held. A storage chip, from the looks of it. "With graduation coming up, I've been thinking about the ceremony and how it's pretty much unavoidable that my family's going to learn I'm actually *not* dead. Or missing."

"That is highly probable, yes." If Iori had been a year younger, their consent would've been required for him to graduate. At eighteen, the choice to notify them was his. However, unless he wanted to change his name, this game of hide and seek was nigh at an end. And when his family did inevitably learn that he was in Cardplay's care, Hikaru would have to own up to breaking his promise to keep them apprised.

A meager penalty to pay.

Iori tapped the chip with his thumb. "I recorded something for them. A song. Figured if the news were going to break, it should come from me. Or from me via you." He passed it to Hikaru, his message in a bottle. "It didn't feel right uploading it to Chatterbox even though that would've been easier, and I know that doesn't make sense, but ... I was wondering if you could send it? Since you offered to contact them before."

Hikaru eyed the device as if he'd been given a long lost antique. He'd heard the music this morning, emanating from the lounge. It must've taken Iori most of the day to drum up the courage to bring this to him. "Are you sure you're ready?"

"I don't think I'm capable of being ready. That's why I'm asking you." Iori swept a hand over his ear and tasseled earring, fingers lingering briefly on its two purple beads before sliding to his neck. "This is me ripping the band aid off."

"I see. Do you have a letter to go along with this?"

"I was hoping the song would do the talking. Just make sure they don't go booking flights right away or anything."

Hikaru nodded. "I understand." A step was a step, no matter how he decided to take it. "I'll inform you if they respond."

Iori thumped his knuckles lightly against his palm, at a visible loss for what to do or say next. After a moment, he mumbled his thanks and excused himself. Hikaru tracked him down the steps to the ground floor, then a glimmer in his peripheral tugged his attention downward.

Strings. They wove a golden sleeve around the storage device, tracing the contact pins and the grooves in the plastic. *Not yet, not yet,* they seemed to whisper, advising him to hold onto it for the time being.

Their insistence weighed on Hikaru's conscience. At a glance, he couldn't see a simple email having any significant impact. But then, you never could tell how far a thread might travel until you pulled, and before you realized it, the seams could be coming undone.

Resignedly, he closed his hand over the chip.

Not yet.

CHAPTER THIRTY-ONE
JANUARY 1 | CARDPLAY HEADQUARTERS

"HUDDLE FOR WARMTH, HUDDLE FOR WARMTH." Soren tottered over to Ellen like a penguin in his pompom toggle coat. They and almost two dozen others had amassed outside Cardplay Headquarters. With any luck, the impending crowds, games, and hot food and drink would ward off winter's touch, because the Starlight Festival was upon them, and Ellen had no intention of staying indoors.

Tatiana bounced on her toes to keep her blood circulating. "I am going to consume so much sugar," she said, not so much a prediction as a vow. She and Iori were borderline twinning in their red jackets—her in her red trucker with the brown sherpa collar, and Iori in the leather bomber Ellen had gifted him.

His unexpected gift to her, a strawberry charm she'd attached to her phone, dangled out of her pocket. *"It's not much,"* he'd said when she unwrapped it. Where he got it, how big it was, how much it cost—none of that mattered. The gesture alone had jerked tears.

Then again, she rarely made it through the solstice without shedding a few.

While they waited for their ride to the festival, Soren polled the group. "They've got a ton of new attractions this year. Which ones are you guys most excited for?"

"I know which one Iori's excited for." Tatiana nudged him, and he returned a withering look. It gladdened Ellen to see how buddy-buddy they'd been lately, hanging out one-on-one and riffing off each other's jokes at lunch. At last, Iori was spreading his social wings.

He hiked his shirt's zipper to the top of its turtleneck, tail fluffed against the cold. He'd taken advantage of the costumes the event was known for to leave his feline traits exposed. "Navigating hordes of noisy people just to spend most of the time in line isn't what I'd call *exciting*."

"You don't have to go if you don't want to," said Ellen, knowing how allergic to crowds he could be. He and Soren had that in common, but Soren wouldn't be kept from the fun.

Iori flashed her a smile. "It'll be worth it."

A whistle cut through the chatter in the yard. Hikaru was poised on the mansion's porch with Alexander, the whistler in question. With an appreciative pat on the arm, the headmaster sent him back to his friends at the bottom of the steps.

"I don't mean to rain on the parade," said Hikaru. "Given the current state of affairs, however, I must remind you all to remain vigilant this evening, and to keep an eye on your peers. While you are unlikely to encounter trouble at such a highly populated event, we mustn't allow ourselves to become complacent."

A honk from the end of the driveway announced Elizabeth's arrival in the rental bus that would take them to the market square.

Hikaru motioned toward it. "There's your lift. I've said my piece. Be safe and enjoy yourselves; you've earned it."

Whether it was the new attractions, the low Void activity, or a result of the magical disaster that shook the globe being another year past, the Starlight Festival had drawn record numbers. The closest available parking spot put them six blocks away, and attendees flowed well outside the boundaries of the market square.

Hikaru had framed the crowds as a benefit. An array of watchful eyes to dissuade nefarious business and phone cameras aplenty to capture it, should any be so daring. But to Alexander, the masses posed risks of their own. The noise, the lights, the congestion in the walkways—would anyone notice if something happened? Would they be able to react quickly enough in an emergency?

He also couldn't help thinking, *What a perfect place to stage a massacre.*

"Are you planning on playing bodyguard all night?" Naomi called from the balloon darts booth. Aryel and Kyani were up, throwing needle-tipped projectiles at a wall of balloons while Ikkei—a one-man cheer squad—rooted for whoever happened to be winning at the time.

Currently, that was Kyani. Unsurprising when she could hit a bullseye from across the arena.

"Somebody has to," Alexander replied.

"Yeah, the people who are being paid to." She pointed out three guards in the immediate vicinity, dressed in plain uniforms and armed with magic-suppressant stun guns.

"I'm not relying on a bunch of dime-an-hour security guards who aren't even equipped to take on an Inkblot." They might be able to take on a couple of Players, but Void entities? Without protective gear, they'd be ripped to shreds.

"Then rely on the entire bus load of magic users we brought with us—three of whom are Keepers."

Four including his dormant Suit-bearing sister, and he didn't want to get started on that. For one thing, he'd been forbidden from talking about that with his friends. For another, if he let his worries get the better of him, he'd wind up helicoptering her for the duration of the event.

Another popped balloon, and Kyani claimed her prize. Aryel never was a good judge of distance and couldn't throw straight for the life of him, hence his specialty in area-of-effect techniques. Determined to win at least one round— he'd lost three so far—he challenged Ikkei to a match and called his prospective fiancé-to-be over for a good luck smooch.

He still refused to comment on the proposal rumor. To Alexander's knowledge, Naomi hadn't caught wind of it yet.

Kyani left the competitors to their game and joined him at the corner of the booth, arms around a stuffed purple octopus. "She has a point. We're not helpless," she said. "I know you're scared, but—"

"I'm not scared. I'm being vigilant, like Hikaru told us to."

"Even if Wiseman decided to launch an attack tonight, isn't that what we've been training for? We're ready, Alex. As ready as we can be. You can afford to have some fun."

He clenched his teeth, the ache in his jaw a sign he'd been grinding them far too much lately. The more time that passed without incident, without change, without any sort of noteworthy development in the situation, the higher his stress levels climbed.

Something was creeping up his arm.

The octopus, puppeteered by Kyani, had wriggled onto his shoulder. "If you won't do it for yourself, will you do it for Mr. Octopus?" She prodded his cheek with a fuzzy tentacle tip.

"How do I always make friends with the weirdest people?"

"Birds of a feather flock together?"

His mouth twisted into a shape between a grimace and a smile, not least because of the cringe-worthy bird pun. "Did you just call me weird?"

She shrugged, hugging the stuffed animal. "You are a bit. But I like weird, and you're in good company."

The mournful moans of a defeated Aryel begged to differ.

"Hey, Alex," Ikkei hollered as his sister criticized her boyfriend's throwing methods. "I know what'll loosen you up." Grinning broadly, he pounded a fist into his palm. "You wanna go ape and break some shit?"

Nice to see the power trip from his victory had gone straight to his thick skull. "Do you *want* to get us banned from the festival?"

"Oh no, I'm talking about totally legal, organizer-sanctioned destruction. They've got wreck rooms this year."

Wreck rooms—a space dedicated to going wild and demolishing every inanimate object in sight. Now that was an activity Alexander could get behind.

CHAPTER THIRTY-TWO
JANUARY 1 | MARKET SQUARE

AN ESCAPE ROOM AND SEVERAL AMUSEMENT booths later, Iori, Ellen, Tatiana, and Soren queued up at the concession stands. A colorful assortment of savory treats and sweetmeats filled the racks. Freshly-spun candy floss and glistening caramel apples, fried seafood and poutine drowned in gravy, and star-shaped cakes oozing a variety of mouth-watering fillings.

"I'm buying," Ellen declared, retrieving her wallet. "What do you fancy?"

"I could eat the whole stand." Tatiana was virtually gorging on the food with her eyes. When Soren couldn't decide and Iori politely declined even though the hunger pangs were setting in, she proposed ordering a platter to share. "And while we wait . . ." Iori jolted when she linked arms with him. "You, come with me. I need to pee."

He dug his heels into the cobblestones. In an abundance of caution, the masters had enacted a buddy system for the lower-ranking magic users in the group, so she had to choose *someone*. "Why me?"

Her nails bit into his arm. "Ellen is busy and Soren's not intimidating enough."

The growling emphasis she put on each word told him what this was really about, and at another tug, he surrendered.

"Back in a minute!" Not so skilled in the art of subtlety herself, Tatiana hauled him off through a band of costumed entertainers. As soon as they were out of sight, she confronted him. "Why haven't you made your move yet?"

"Cut me some slack. I'm waiting for the right moment."

"You're gonna miss your moment if you wait too long. The clock is ticking." She tapped her wrist, devoid of any watch. "I literally could not have given you more opportunities."

Through trickery and deceit, she'd orchestrated numerous *moments* for him and Ellen to be alone. Abandoned them on the ferris wheel, gotten them lost in the funhouse together, insisted on going two vs. two in the escape rooms—a terrible decision on her part. She and Soren solved their room first and had to wait twenty minutes for him and Ellen to get out of theirs. They'd been alone, sure, but he refused to go for a kiss under the surveillance of the game masters.

Her relentless efforts were sucking out all the fun Iori was trying to have, and Soren and Ellen hadn't a clue what was going on. Dragged wherever Tatiana saw fit, both of them looked as frazzled as Iori felt. Too much more of this, and he'd cave.

"Where did that suave guy from the charity ball go?"

"Nowhere." Iori untwisted his sleeve. "You can't force this, Kosta. It needs to be organic."

"Organic, my ass. If you don't do this tonight, you two are gonna be dancing around each other for the foreseeable future—or until you lose her to somebody else. You still love her, don't you?"

"Of course I do." So much that it hurt. And if his hesitation cost them the chance to see what they could have been, the wondering and the regret would gnaw at him forevermore. But it *had* to feel right. "I just need you to lay off a bit. Let me figure this part out on my own."

Tatiana groaned. "You are not making this easy for me."

"If it makes you feel better, it's not like I'm paying you." he said, earning himself a punch in the arm. For what it was worth, he did appreciate her taking on the pro bono matchmaking gig. He jerked an elbow the way they came. "Shall we head back?" If they were gone too long, Ellen and Soren—worrywarts, the pair of them—would wonder what had become of them.

"Probably," Tatiana agreed. "I actually do need to pee, though. That part was true."

Predictably, when they did finally regroup at the concession stands, Ellen and Soren had begun to worry.

"You guys were gone awhile," remarked Ellen, sagging with relief as Soren pocketed his phone. He must've been drafting a check-in text.

"Sorry. We got lost." Tatiana jounced to a stop. "What'd you get? Aside from candy." Soren had purchased several bags of candy floss and gummies. He clutched them like a dragon guarding its hoard.

"They seemed busy, so I kept it simple and ordered nachos." Ellen was about to explain what kind when Tatiana started teasing her for always being so grossly considerate, and she laughed through her defense.

Listening to that bubbly sound, watching her eyes crinkle with joy, Iori felt silly for stressing over the time, the place, and the setting. He didn't have to wait for the stars to align to make a moment with her. Some of their fondest memories were formed when it was just the two of them, hearts bared, talking about nothing and everything and all the nonsense in between.

What made it special was her, was them, the connection they shared—a solid foundation upon which they could build a beautiful life together, if only he'd get out of his own way.

If he could reach out to his family, he could do this.

He jumped in at the next gap in dialogue, praying his tightening coil of nerves didn't show. "Hey, Ellen. The fireworks should be starting soon. Do you want to find a spot to watch from?"

"No worries there, we always go to the same place."

He offered her his hand. "Show me?"

Tatiana swooped in for what would hopefully be her last act as wingwoman. "Good idea! It's super busy this year, wouldn't want to lose our spot. We can take care of the food." She threw an arm around Soren, the boy flabbergasted once more. "You two go lay claim to the territory."

"Um. Okay." Ellen's suede glove slid into Iori's palm, and they set off into the market square. Their stroll took them along the emptier paths that skirted it, where foot traffic ran thin enough for them to walk side by side.

Iori couldn't tell if the firmness of her hold was intended to soothe what she presumed to be anxiety in him, or if his nervous energy had set her on edge. Hoping to diffuse any tension, he broke the silence that had fallen over them. "Having fun?"

"Yeah," she said brightly. "Alexander and I usually spend most of the festival together, so this is different for me, but I'm sure he's having a good time. And it's never dull with Tatiana and Soren." She readjusted her grip to a friendlier squeeze. "I'm glad you decided to come."

Iori squeezed back. "Me too."

Idiot, he chided himself blithely for the infusion of joy this gave him. They'd held hands before; only this time, it wasn't a bandage for emotional wounds or a means to ground him. This was a show of affection, plain and simple, and for once, he had initiated it.

Ellen led him to a souvenir shop, an end cap to one of the larger multi-story buildings encircling the square. They went straight through, climbed the rear staircase to the as of yet unoccupied rooftop, and she jogged up to the parapet.

The festival was a field of shining color below. Metallic accents, gaudy signs, entertainers in big feathery hats and platform shoes encrusted in glitter. Attendees had donned horned headbands and animal ears much less convincing than Iori's. Still, no one questioned the periodic flick of a tail when many wore mechanical wing harnesses.

From up here, he could distinguish the layers of noise. The plinky attraction tunes and more distant fanciful melody of a local band, the rush of the kiddie rollercoaster along its tracks, and the squeals of children therein. Magic hummed near and far, Ellen's chime nearest of all aside from his ever-present dual tones.

"Is this the spot?"

"Yep!" She hoisted herself onto the parapet and pointed seaward. "They launch the fireworks from a barge over there. It's a perfect view." The breeze teased at her hair, loosening a few strands from her scarf. "We used to come every year. Watched the parade, rode the teacups, got our faces painted . . . then we'd all go for Moose Hooves before the fireworks."

"What in the world are *Moose Hooves?*"

"You've never had them? They're these big fried dough pastries." She mimed an oval. "Dad and Alexander always got banana chocolate or apple pie, and Mom liked the cinnamon and sugar with lemon. Strawberry strudel was my favorite." That tracked. "You'll have to try one."

"Which flavor would you recommend?"

"Hm. I bet you'd like coco vanilla."

An educated guess. "I'll hold you to that."

Every so often, in instances like these, talking about parades and pastries, Iori marveled at the shape his life had taken on. Edges smoothed and hollows filled in, dark corners illuminated by an influx of love and support he previously believed unattainable.

Love, he'd thought, was for other people. Better people. Stability and control were idealistic fantasies, not meant for gray folks like him. Now he was mending ties, planning beyond tomorrow. Celebrating the dawn of a new year when, in the past, the passage of time had been reduced to another row of striked-out tallies on a wall.

What shape would it be if Ellen hadn't been there to mold it?

"Iori," she said then, pulling him from his reverie. "Are you doing okay? You seem kind of off tonight."

He leaned a hip against the concrete. "You noticed, huh?"

A slight nod. "You know you can tell me if something's bothering you, right?" she asked in that whisper-sweet voice that made him want to divulge it all. And, sure enough, the ball of anxiety his restless mind had spun began to unravel.

"Uh, well . . ." He rubbed his neck. "It was less of a *tell* and more of a *show* thing."

If ever there were a moment, this was it.

In a bout of surety, Iori leaned in and brought a knuckle to her chin, tilting it up. Her cheeks, made rosy by the cold, darkened a few shades further, and his warmed too as he searched her eyes. Wide as they were, they captured all the hues of the festival lights—blue and white and pale yellow, sparkling on the surface of two jewel-like discs of scarlet.

Those brief seconds stretched to an eternity, an unspoken question on the wisps of barely held breath between them. And, Iori thought, an answer. Before the nerves could return to claim him, he let his eyelids drift shut and pressed a kiss to her chilled lips.

The festival melted away, noises fading to a faint reverberation in the back of his senses while Ellen's chime became amplified. For that impossibly small yet hugely significant moment, the whole world shrank to this vacant rooftop on the outer limits of the market square.

Alas, spells were bound to break.

When Iori withdrew and reopened his eyes, he found Ellen's still wide and unblinking. Her expression hadn't changed, save for the slight parting of her lips—as if she wanted to speak, but couldn't.

Was she even breathing?

The warmth drained from Iori's cheeks, leaving cold, colorless panic in its place. He'd wanted to take her breath away, but not like this.

He jerked back. "I-I'm sorry. I don't know why I did that."

Except he did. He did it because his pulse soared at the sight of her. Because she was his best friend, his favorite person. He did it because she was his home and his solace, and as sappy and bloody desperate as it sounded, he couldn't imagine a life without her in it. And he wanted them to share that life, through thick and thin.

For months, he'd been picturing this moment. Now it had come and gone and it was all so wrong. He should've waited, should've asked. Shouldn't have gone ahead with the plan based on the assumptions of a biased friend trying to fulfill her own selfish goals.

Speak of the devil.

The steel door to the rooftop swung open, Tatiana loudly proclaiming her and Soren's arrival with the food. Iori retreated another pace from Ellen, who still hadn't moved a muscle.

Run, urged a voice from the recesses of his mind. The one he swore he'd never listen to again. Maybe he wouldn't have if the buddy system had forced him to stay, but he wouldn't be abandoning Ellen. She'd be safe with her friends, and her brother and the others would be along shortly.

So, he listened. Turned tail and fled like he always did.

"Hey, where are you going?" called Tatiana as he whisked past her. "The fireworks are about to start!"

"I need air," he said. *Wow, great excuse.* They were outside. There was air everywhere.

And yet, he was suffocating.

The door hushed closed on its pistons, Ellen left frozen on the parapet. She brushed her fingertips across her lips, haunted by the ghost of a kiss.

It couldn't have lasted more than a second or two, but those were the longest seconds of her life, and somehow they'd passed too quickly for her to react. Before she could commit to one action or another, before she could will her mouth to move, Iori was gone.

"What was that about?" Tatiana asked, snapping Ellen out of her stupor. She and Soren walked over, carrying a steaming plate of nachos.

"I'm not sure." Truthfully, she wasn't. From the moment Iori leaned in to the moment he pulled away, static had consumed her brain. Swept her up in that snow globe again, somewhere between floating and falling. Even the butterflies in her stomach had ceased their fluttering.

Deep down, she must've known.

She'd been told. Time and time and time again.

He loves you.

He loves you.

He loves you.

Why didn't I say anything?

By choosing to ignore Iori's potential feelings and deliberately refusing to detangle her own, Ellen had done the very thing she'd been trying to avoid.

She hurt him.

"Should we go after him?" suggested Soren.

She shook her head hazily. "If he's not back for the fireworks, I'll go find him." They both needed a few minutes—him to cool off, her to gather her thoughts. Later, when they were home and in private, she would explain everything to him. Her uncertainty, her internal conflict. All of it.

She could fix this.

CHAPTER THIRTY-THREE
JANUARY 1 | MARKET SQUARE

A PEBBLE CLATTERED OVER THE COBBLESTONES, kicked by Iori's boot. He trudged through the network of alleys encompassing the market square, the maze of rusted pipes and weathered brick he used to frequent.

Idiot, idiot, idiot, he chided himself again, and this time he meant every biting syllable. Where did he get off thinking it would be a good idea to kiss her out of the blue? Could've gone for a peck on the cheek, at least. That would've made it less of a catastrophe.

Had to go for the mouth. Dumbass. He slumped against a wall. Rejection, he supposed, was an apt punishment.

Come to think of it, did Ellen's reaction count as rejection? In his panic, he hadn't given her the opportunity to respond, just bolted like a coward under the assumption that he'd irreparably screwed up.

How had that made her feel?

He raked his fringe off his brow. The fireworks wouldn't be starting for a little while yet. At the very least, he could give her a proper apology and promise to talk about it later so she could enjoy the remainder of the night.

A botched kiss wasn't the end of the world.

Rallying what courage he could, Iori peeled his sorry self off the wall and—

Halted at the ring of a bell.

He could've sworn it was right next to him, to his left, but all that lay in that direction was a narrow stretch of alleyway that led to an intersection. He listened for a minute, ears pricked, but didn't hear it again.

Until he went to leave.

Ring-a-ling, farther away.

His boots were already chafing the dry cobbles towards it before he'd decided whether to investigate, curiosity luring him down the lonesome alley.

Ring-a-ling, ring-a-ling.

Upon reaching the intersection, lit by a solitary lamp on the wall, the oddly alluring jingle stopped. Iori pivoted on his heels, ears rotating in search of the sound and its source. The range, the clarity . . . it couldn't have been a regular bell. The way it vibrated in his eardrums, it was almost like—

Ring-a-ling.

Magic.

"Here kitty, kitty."

Iori whipped around to find a boy had materialized atop a stack of wooden crates. And not just any boy. This boy appeared plucked from the night sky, constellations sparkling on mottled gray skin and hair infused with moonlight. His irises gleamed too, electric blue against unfathomable black.

The Void rumbled within him, a thousand unremitting bells alongside it—the same frequency Elysian Tower had produced after the Diamond's seal broke. Corruption and purity singing in discordant harmony.

A union of light and shadow.

"Pleased to make your acquaintance. The name's Circ." The boy's cheeks dimpled with a smirk. "Ring a bell?"

Circ. The Sundered Star, exiled Warden of the Void. This was the entity Kyani had warned them about, the creature Blackjack had released from its prison. And if he was here, everyone was in danger.

Iori had to alert the others, but he couldn't move.

Why couldn't he move?

"Clever trick, don't you think? Using your own senses to lure you here." The boy hopped down from the crates, unbothered by the cold stones under his bare soles. Even topless as he was, the frigid temperatures didn't seem to affect him. "Then again . . ." He ambled closer. "Those ears always were susceptible to my influence."

Iori's pulse quickened. *Damn it, move!*

Pipe organs blared—the Spade's battle cry, breaking the unseen chains that had bound its Keeper. Drawing ink from his personal well, Iori thrust both arms forth. A lethal corkscrew of black liquid went spiraling down the alleyway and—

Froze at the lift of Circ's hand.

Iori stiffened. *He stopped it?*

"Oh, ho, ho, so it's true! You actually learned to control it. Color me impressed." Circ tapped the corkscrew's sharpened tip, glasslike in the lamplight. He leaned past it to look at Iori. "Too bad it doesn't belong to you."

With another deft motion, Circ forced the ink back, back, into the inkwell. Iori gaped soundlessly, unable to fight it as the liquid turned to lead in his veins. His limbs grew weak and heavy, an invisible vise compressing his ribcage. Constricting his vocal cords.

"But you," said Circ, "belong to *me*."

A swift leftward swipe threw Iori against the wall. He crumpled to the ground, a pounding in his skull, and it took every ounce of strength he had to pull himself upright against the bricks. His skeleton had become an anchor, rooting him to the spot. Muscles seized, throat and jaw locked. Couldn't speak, could barely breathe—frightfully reminiscent of when the feral Spade tried to take the wheel, only now it had gone deathly quiet inside him.

Circ crouched in front of him, elbows perched on knees. "What's the matter, Star got your tongue?"

Refusing to let the Warden see how thick his terror ran, Iori did the only thing he could and glared. Nobody knew where he'd gone. Unless he could overpower the control this entity had over him, he was on his own. An animal, cornered.

Why did I have to run?

Thin silver chains slithered over the Warden's lean shoulders at the tilt of his head. "Vy used to give me that look. Ever heard of her? Vy Sentarus, former Keeper of the Spade? You remind me of her. Though, that's to be expected, *kindred spirits* and all. She had one of these, too." He tore off Iori's eyepatch, irises brightening at the sight of his marked eye. He pried the lids open further—much too close for comfort. "Fascinating. Vy lost hers prior to her ascension. The Spade must not have known what to do with two intact oculi, so it consumed one of yours instead."

There was a throb deep in its socket.

Someone had to come looking for him soon. They'd implemented the buddy system for a reason.

"But do you want to know what my favorite trait is that you share?" Circ trailed a white nail from jaw to jugular and collarbone. "Your . . . *openness*." He splayed his hand over Iori's chest, a layer of ribbed cotton separating it from the scar beneath. "They say that eyes are windows to the soul. If that's the case, then this is a door." Circ's gaze flicked up to meet his. "And I happen to have the key."

Panic spiked through Iori.

"Cheer up," said Circ. "You and I are going to have some fun." He snared the collar of Iori's jacket, hauled him up and over as if he weighed nothing, and dragged him sharply down—not towards the ground, but an opaque black puddle. A portal, shimmering with the light of the pentagram that spawned it.

They plunged into it, and next Iori knew, he was floating in a sea of liquid jet and nebulous sapphire. A vast, roaring emptiness.

The Warden's disembodied voice permeated the din. "You like music, don't you? Let me sing you a song."

From the undulating dark came a sound like a bow drawn low over the strings of a cello.

"Have you ever dreamt a twisted little dream,
Where demons roam and black eyes gleam?
Where blackened gates that tower tall,
Look down on fields where heroes fall?"

Something snagged Iori's ankle—an inky tentacle, reaching up from the abyss below. Adrenaline surged through him as more lashed out, grasping at his clothes and wrists.

The whole place was *alive.*

"And on those fields long stained with red,
We make our home in the devil's stead.
Our little band of merry frights,
We live for darkness and the night."

They spread his limbs and wrenched the zipper of his shirt open, baring his chest. Baring the mark.

A door. Circ called it a door.

"Welcome to the circus, welcome to the show!
Cast away what you think and everything you know.
I'll show you terror, I'll show delight.
What you'll see will sure excite."

Iori opened his mouth to cry out, but his shouts were lost to the void. Tendrils slammed into him, flooding the inkwell.

"Welcome to the circus, my pretty little thing!
My shattered little puppet, dangling from a string."

A numbing cold filled Iori's body, dulling his senses as Circ's lyrical intonation slowed, growing muffled.

"On this plane where souls have screamed,
I shall weave you

        a twisted

                little

                        dream."

ACT III

RAISING HELL

CHAPTER THIRTY-FOUR
JANUARY 2 | JANE RESIDENCE

AN EMPTY CHASM LAY WHERE Iori normally slept. He'd reappeared during the fireworks show and hung near Ellen like a dark cloud on a cold front. They didn't speak on the bus back to headquarters or on the drive home, and he'd opted to stay on the couch rather than join her in bed.

She couldn't blame him after the way she'd reacted.

She replayed the kiss over and over, running mental laps through alternate scenarios. If he'd asked permission, if she'd pushed him away, if she'd kissed him back, if she'd told him to stay. Reality was, none of those things happened, and now there was an enormous elephant in the room she didn't know how to address.

What do you want?

Ellen grabbed a pillow, his pillow, and wailed feebly into the stuffing. If nothing else, the kiss should have given her clarity, but all it did was make her more confused. How could she still not solve that maddening riddle Soren put in her head?

She inhaled slow and deep, face still buried in Iori's pillow, and caught the faint floral notes of shampoo mixed with traces of old leather. Always leather. It didn't matter how often he bathed, that scent was permanently stamped on his skin.

Her fingers tensed in the feather-stuffed lump.

What am I doing?

She flung the pillow aside with a *whumph*. The guy vacated the bed for one night after a poorly planned—though not necessarily poorly executed—kiss, and here she was drinking in his scent like he'd perished when he was a flight of stairs away.

Always, she had encouraged him to communicate his feelings to her. The least she could do was attempt to verbalize hers, however muddled they may be. This was no longer a *her* problem. It was theirs, and they could work through it together.

Ellen got to her feet and started downstairs, rehearsing what she would say and how she would say it—only to be confronted by an empty couch when she veered into the living room. It didn't even appear slept on.

Hearing activity in the kitchen, she poked her head in there. Still no cat-eared boy, just her brother unloading the dishwasher. "Hey, have you seen Iori?"

"Nope."

He must've gone before either of them got up. Ellen sagged against the doorframe. Was he avoiding her out of embarrassment, or had her inaction really hurt him so badly that he couldn't bear to face her? Surely he hadn't *expected* her to kiss him back, unless she'd misled him somehow.

But he'd apologized. Panicked.

"I-I'm sorry. I don't know why I did that."

Had he done it on a whim?

"It was less of a tell *and more of a* show *thing."*

Something didn't add up.

"Did you guys have a fight?" Alexander asked, transferring a stack of plates into the cupboard. "You both seemed quiet on the drive home last night."

He would know. Those boys couldn't be in the same vehicle without fighting over radio stations or Iori backseat driving for the purposes of his own entertainment. Quiet wasn't something they knew how to be in a confined space together.

Should she tell him? Alexander had no idea what she'd been wrestling with internally, and romance wasn't his area of expertise. He had experience in other types of relationships, though, and would be able to view the situation objectively without his own personal biases influencing his perception.

Maybe that made him the perfect person to talk to.

"We—" was all Ellen managed to get out before the doorbell rang. And rang. And rang, and rang, and rang.

Who could it be at this hour?

Ellen answered and was surprised, yet not so based on the doorbell abuse, to discover Tatiana and Soren on her doorstep. "It's seven a.m. What are you two doing here?"

"FRIENDTERVENTION!" Tatiana barged in and dragged Ellen upstairs without explanation, Soren tossing a hasty greeting to Alexander on their way through. He closed the bedroom door as Tatiana threw a discombobulated Ellen into her desk chair.

"Spill it!" she ordered, hands on hips.

"S-spill what?"

She let out a guttural groan. "You and Iori! Something went down on that rooftop, and I want to know what. You don't go from strolling off hand-in-hand to refusing to look at each other over *nothing*. I thought maybe he chickened out, but then you were acting spacey too, so spill the damn beans!"

Realization stabilized Ellen's reeling mind. "Wait, chickened out? Did you know what he was going to do?" She stood suddenly, causing Tatiana to bump backwards into Soren.

"Uh—"

"They've been having secret meetings," Soren piped up from behind her.

She clapped a hand over his mouth. "*Shh!*"

"That's why you two have been hanging out so much." It was starting to make sense—their sudden closeness, their post-therapy meet-ups. "Tatiana, what did you say to him?"

"Stuff and . . . things."

Soren pried her hand off long enough to say, "She told him you liked him," and color rushed to Ellen's cheeks—the rare sweltering red of outrage.

She hadn't misled Iori at all. *Tatiana* did.

"Why would you say that?!"

"Because I thought you did!" Tatiana released Soren from her makeshift muzzle. "Of course, if you two had let me in on *your* secret meeting weeks ago, maybe I would have exercised more caution." Did she even know the definition of that word? "And hey, hold up, does this mean he actually did it?"

"Yes, Tatiana, he *kissed* me." Ellen pointed to her lips. "On the *mouth*."

"Well, how did it go?"

She dropped back into her chair with a defeated huff. "Badly. He was acting nervous and twitchy, so I asked him about it. Then he gave me some cheeky one-liner, and the next thing I realized, his mouth was on mine."

"What did you do?" asked Soren, meekly.

"Nothing."

Tatiana blinked. "Nothing? What's nothing?"

"I froze, okay? I clammed up and he ran, because that's what he does when he gets scared. He runs." She recalled his expression, pallid and petrified. Cue the waterworks. "I didn't mean to hurt him, I just wasn't expecting him to do *that*. I didn't know he felt that way about me."

"Not like we didn't tell you a bazillion times," Tatiana muttered, and Soren shot her a reproachful look. Neither he nor Ellen could argue her point, though. If she had taken them seriously back then, they might have been able to avoid this.

She wiped a teary cheek with her sweater sleeve. "Even if he did, I couldn't imagine us working out. We're too different, and I thought he was into boys . . ."

Tatiana folded her arms. "Having an ex-boyfriend doesn't mean he's exclusively into boys, Ellen. I know you didn't assume that when your brother is bi. You're just searching for reasons for him not to like you. And *why*, might I ask?"

"Why would he?"

Soren exchanged a bemused glance with Tatiana. "What do you mean?"

Did she really have to spell it out for them? "I'm boring," she said. *Plain Jane.* "If Iori and I got together, sooner or later, he'd get tired of me and call it off. I don't have any interesting hobbies, and I'm not even skilled at the ones I do have. I'm exceptionally unexceptional."

"That's not true. You have lots of good qualities!"

"Give me one example."

"For starters, you're an amazing friend."

Ellen leveled the approximation of a glare at him. "That's basically a participation trophy."

A gasp from Tatiana. "I'm going to ignore the fact that you just slandered our friendship because you're upset, but what Soren is trying to say is: you're one of the kindest, most caring human beings on this planet, and you don't need to be more than that. Your bubbliness is contagious. You're fun and easy company, and you're always there when we need you—which, ironically, is also your biggest flaw." Tatiana crouched next to her chair. "You've spent your whole life living for other people. Maybe it's time you started living for yourself."

Ellen rubbed her arm. Looking back, she couldn't deny it. Throughout her life, her choices had been made based on how they would impact others. To please or appease and to be of as little trouble as possible, because everyone had their own problems and she didn't want to become another.

"And for your information," Tatiana added, "*boring* is not a word Iori has used to describe you." She rose and pulled out her cellphone, the case plastered in stickers of cartoon characters. "This is a gross violation of the friendship code, but you obviously need hard evidence." She thrust the phone at Ellen. "Here. Read."

The first text she glimpsed read:

> **Iori**: Could I talk to you about something, uh . . . personal?

She wiped her nose. "Wait, what is this?"

"Keep reading," instructed Tatiana, and so she did. Through Iori's hesitation and Tatiana's shameless prodding, noting the timestamp as his birthday. And there it was, clear as day. A confession.

> **Iori**: So, I may have feelings for Ellen

Followed by Tatiana's enthusiastic reception.

> **Tatiana**: I KNEW IT

> **Tatiana**: oh my god tell me everything

> **Tatiana**: when did you know?? was it the charity ball? It was the charity ball, right???

> **Iori**: Try a month earlier

Tatiana: OH MY GOD you were a smitten kitten from the start

Iori: I was not *smitten.*

Iori: And don't call me that.

Tatiana: yeah, yeah, whatever. Tell me what you like about her!!

Iori: That's . . . a long list.

As Ellen read on, knuckles pressed to her lips, her tears threatened to overflow again.

Iori: She's determined. Persistent, too. If she sets her mind to something, you'd better believe she's going to do it.

Iori: She loves unabashedly and without hesitation, and it's the sort of love you can just *feel.* And when I'm with her . . . I'm safe.

Iori: I know it's far-fetched, this idea of her and me. I'm a gamble. My life is a mess, and I'm sure as hell not the type of partner her parents would've approved of. But if there's even the tiniest chance that we could be together, I don't want to stamp it out, because I want her *so badly*, and it's been so long since I let myself want anything.

Iori: . . .

Iori: Are you there or am I rambling to myself now?

Tatiana: yeah no don't mind me, just sobbing into my cereal

Iori: It's almost midnight, why are you eating cereal?

Tatiana: I'M AN ADULT I CAN DO WHAT I WANT

Tatiana: Please, keep going. I am thriving on this.

For over an hour, they talked—about Ellen, about feelings, about past relationships and hopes and insecurities. They continued chatting sporadically over the next three weeks, too, the conversation taking a somber turn after the clash with Blackjack at Elysian Tower.

A few days later, their communications ceased. Right about when Kyani had ripped the veil off Charles Wiseman.

Ellen thumbed to the earlier texts again, the ones exuding unfiltered affection. It would've been surreal to see *anyone* speak so fervently about her, let alone the boy who kept his heart under lock and key.

"We started talking again in November. Decided to meet in person instead." Tatiana reclaimed her phone. "Ellen, the guy is *in love* with you. I might have gone overboard orchestrating the kiss—"

"I'll say," interjected Soren.

"—and I'm sorry for that," Tatiana said emphatically. "But I wouldn't have encouraged him if I wasn't convinced you had feelings for him. Was I really that far off the mark?"

Ellen still couldn't give a solid answer to that, but reading those texts had unclogged something in her brain, and her thoughts were flowing clearer now. If she could just sit down with Iori and speak to him about all of this, maybe they could—

The bedroom door creaked open, and Alexander leaned in. Ellen was about to rebuke him for neglecting to knock, then she noticed the grave smoothness of his features, and her insides constricted. "What's wrong?"

He hesitated, searching for the right words.

But there were none for what he had to say.

"Mayor Hargrove is dead."

CHAPTER THIRTY-FIVE
JANUARY 2 | CITY HALL

THE VIEW OF CITY HALL BOUND IN yellow tape brought an unwelcome realness to the situation. POLICE LINE DO NOT CROSS spanned every doorway, officers ducked in and out as they canvassed the premises. The last time Ellen saw this many cruisers on site was at graduation.

Only she and Alexander had been summoned. They dropped Tatiana and Soren off at headquarters on their way, and flashed their medallions to the rookie officer manning the door when they arrived. He gave them a leery once-over but granted them passage without hassle.

Police presence aside, the place appeared jarringly normal. People often milled about the main hall and stairwell. Of course, it should have been empty today with staff let off for the holiday, and their friendlier faces had been replaced by badge-wearing strangers.

The flow of bodies thickened upstairs as they neared the mayor's office. Between here and there, however, lay an intermediary room that Ellen hadn't visited in many years: her father's office.

Long scrubbed of him and redecorated to the tastes of his successor, it didn't look like his anymore, but it still felt like it.

A containment barrier, like a miniaturized section of the boundary fence, had been erected in front of the double doors leading into the mayor's office, and many of the investigators here were dressed in full protective gear—black hazmat-style suits that shone copper in the light. The brand worn by ink cleanup crews.

In plain dress, Hikaru and Chief Gardner stood out from the crowd. They put their conversation on hold when Ellen and Alexander entered, and Hikaru parted from his comrade to speak with them.

"Thank you for coming," he said, almost breathless. Seeing him shaken never failed to unsettle Ellen. Hargrove was an old friend of his. A good friend, and a devoted civil servant. This loss came as a devastating blow not just to Hikaru and Cardplay, but to the citizens of Hildegrand.

"What do we know?" Alexander asked.

"His assistant found him this morning after his son called to say he didn't return home. Apart from that, nothing yet. That's the reason I've asked you here. Your sister, specifically." Hikaru laid a hand on her arm. "Ellen, my dear, I am terribly sorry to subject you to this, but we need you to verify the cause of death. Can you do that?"

Her brow dimpled. "I thought you told Alexander it was blight?"

"We suspect so, yes." His thumb stroked her shoulder. He glanced up at her brother. "Come. Let me show you."

Once the headmaster had suited up and Chief Gardner had cleared his officers out of the room, they proceeded into the mayor's office. Blight presented itself distinctly in mundane folk. In stained skin, veins, and eyes, erratic behavior, and bleeding and vomiting of ink. Ellen had to see it herself to understand how they were unable to confirm it on sight.

The body slouched on the floor by an open window, brown skin blackened to a midnight sheen. Everything above the neck was gone, smeared over the windowsill in sharp icicle jags that resembled a blown glass sculpture. More spikes rose like stalagmites from its chest.

Ellen couldn't recognize it as Thelonious Hargrove. It scarcely resembled a person.

Alexander covered his mouth. "What did this?"

"I have a theory," Hikaru murmured, voice further muffled by his suit's face shield. "I'm hoping to deduce whether or not that theory is correct. Though, I can't say which outcome would be preferable." He looked to Ellen and motioned to the body. "When you're ready."

Slowly, she approached the warped mound of a man. A breeze rippled the curtain, scattering light over the surface. Wherever the shadows fell, it glittered blue. And when she crouched to touch his hand—the one that first pinned this medallion to her breast, that held hers after her parents died—she found it solid. Too cold, too smooth. Not like Hargrove at all. It was reminiscent of the material the Cavity was formed from, a product of the Void colloquially referred to as *onyx*. This radiated the same scalpel-sharp chill of malevolence, too.

"It's definitely blight," she reported. "I've never seen it like this, though." The closest comparison would be the Inkwraiths they fought at the Blackjack complex. Their horns and limbs, on otherwise fluid forms, had been similarly vitrified. But how had Hargrove wound up like them?

There were no paw prints in the room, no visible bite marks or scratches on the body. He could've come in contact with Void emissions . . . except, whether by airborne toxins or Inkblot attack, infections didn't feel like this. As a disease, blight emitted a chill like deep autumn fog, as if dampened by the very tears of misery it fed on.

But Ellen couldn't imagine Hargrove would've made for a viable conduit. Far as she knew, the Void couldn't lay claim to pure souls, and she refused to believe that his, deep down, had been wicked. Besides, conduit transformations originated from the inside, and based on the direction of those spikes where his head used to be, whatever inflicted this was external.

"I think someone did this to him," she said, rising from her crouch. And by the looks on Hikaru's and her brother's faces, it seemed they all shared an idea as to who.

Why was another matter.

What could Mayor Hargrove have done to incur the wrath of the Sundered Star, and what was he doing here last night? He should have been out of office on holiday like the rest of his staff—drinking beer and playing poker, counting down the seconds to the new year with his family.

He didn't deserve to die. Not like this, not ever.

Where Ellen's sorrow pooled, Alexander's fury roiled.

"They've made their move," he said. "Now we make ours."

CHAPTER THIRTY-SIX
JANUARY 2 | FOLKLAN CLIFFS

HOW INVIGORATING IT WAS TO BE *ALIVE*.

To feel winter's breath shiver through living flesh, every inhalation pulling it deeper, laced with the sweet aroma of pine—a scent that also roused a sort of exhilaration in this commandeered brain. Joules of terror pumping adrenaline through his bloodstream.

Existence as a celestial entity was numbing. Emotions virtually forbidden, spurred not by electrochemical signals but imprinted on the dust by which they were made. Concepts meant to be assimilated, not expressed. Scents were molecules, taste evoked no memory, sound was a simple vibration in the air, and touch no more than a collision of atoms.

In this body, Circ could feel it all unhindered. No dampers, no shackles. What a shame that for humans, these lives of blissful sensation were fleeting. But soon, he would give them something more. Something greater than they'd felt before.

Unity.

As he strode up the driveway to the Wiseman Estate, transported by a subterranean vein of Void matter, a red dot swooped across the gravel to land upon his chest. *Sybil.* Her aim was trained on him from one of those ivy-framed windows in the building's stone and stucco façade, and any second now . . .

A whoosh behind him—the fabric of reality rearranging to make room for a new object, followed by the click of a cocked gun.

"Move and I will blast you to kingdom come."

"You say that as if it's my life to lose," sneered Circ in a voice that wasn't his but an accent that was. He turned as realization washed over Cardan McConnell's freckled face. "Your reaction time has improved."

His pistol's barrel dropped a smidge. "Warden?"

"The one and only."

Holstering his weapon, Cardan stooped apologetically. "F-forgive me, Your Eminence. I didn't recognize you."

Eminence. He liked the sound of that. "If you had, that would defeat the purpose."

"Might wanna work on that accent if you're planning on going undercover." Sybil exited the estate, sniper rifle propped against her shoulder. Fully assembled, the firearm had almost as many inches as she did.

It occurred to Circ that he hadn't heard the Spade's Keeper speak. Didn't give him a chance, really. An acoustic type's voice could be lethal if properly utilized. Regardless, everything he needed for the perfect imitation was contained in muscle and memory. Nothing he couldn't master in an afternoon.

"What is this, anyway? An illusion?"

"Illusions are tricks of the mundane and the Domain. This"—Circ gestured to himself, his mortal shell—"is what you would call the *real deal*."

The Players' reactions were two opposing forces.

"That is fucking sweet." Sybil beamed.

Her associate gawped. "It's fucked up, is what it is. Underhanded maneuvers? Fine. But body-snatching?"

Cardan, Cardan, afflicted with that awful condition called humanity. Circ cast him a wry and weary look. "A conscience is a terribly inconvenient thing to have." He beckoned them indoors. "Join me, both of you. I have news."

Inside, other sensory details poked at the organ housed in his skull, trauma set deep in its crevices. The creak of the floorboards, the sight of the building's aged innards. The portraits in gilded frames that depicted Wiseman family heads dead and gone, all spotless in their attire with a delightful darkness hidden within.

These paintings only dated back a few centuries, but more were stored in the archives beneath the estate amidst carefully preserved relics and historical records—because while the rest of the world had been content to let the magical era fade into oblivion, the Wisemans had devoted themselves to immortalizing it.

"I'm back," Circ sang as he threw open the doors to the current head's study. If one could be considered head of a family they were the sole surviving member of.

Charles Wiseman mused at a mural on the wall, a stylized depiction of Elysian Tower as it once stood: the obelisk stark against a night threaded with silver, that black sea bleeding into pearlescent earth and carving out a hollow beneath it. One bright star shone at the tower's peak, another resting in the bottom of that cavity—dimmer than its counterpart.

North and south, radiant and sundered.

Dragging his focus from the mural, Wiseman did a double-take at Circ. His expression cycled through a range of emotions—a flash of shock, a spot of confusion—before an unnerving placidity settled over his angular features.

"What have you done?" His tone spoke volumes, none of them anger. Cardan and Sybil gave him room to circle and view the stolen body. This would be the first he'd seen of it in the flesh since he had the boy in captivity.

Circ struck a pose, jutting a hip and extending one languid arm. "You like? I nabbed it at the Starlight Festival."

"How?"

"I told you, didn't I? Anywhere the Void has touched, I can go." There were limits, of course, but the depth of the Spade's corruption had met the necessary requirements. Just like that cavity beneath the tower, this Suit had a hole in it too. A space for him to fill.

Wiseman reached for him then, as if to test the authenticity of his form, and Circ recoiled involuntarily— something sharper than his own personal distaste for physical contact bolting through him.

Humans, so at the whim of their somatic responses.

"No touching." He tried to shake off the feeling as Wiseman withdrew his curious hand, scrutinizing him like an appraiser who'd detected a fault. An imperfection. One that didn't belong to Circ.

"What of Hargrove?" asked Wiseman.

That was the reason he'd gone, after all, to nip that problem in the bud. A few well-placed calls was all it took to bait Mr. Mayor into the trap—and oh, the horror that shook his jowls when Circ sprang it on him. Gave him quite the start to learn he had company, and then he'd squinted and scratched his chin. What business did this Cardplay boy have in his office?

Pity for Hargrove that it was not the boy's business, but Circ's. He could still hear the mayor's squeals, his gurgles, his dying breath. Yes, even the Sundered Star could compose sweet melodies. His tastes just required a more organic breed of instrument.

Too bad his efforts were for naught. "Dead," Circ reported, moving past Wiseman to the mural. "He wasn't the vessel we were looking for."

Cardan's gob dropped open. "So you *killed* him?"

"What's the problem? With the mayor gone, Cardplay has one leg fewer to stand on. And by process of elimination"—Plus a few insider tips from the Keeper's memory—"we can infer who the Guiding Light's true beholder is."

He paused, leaving them on tenterhooks.

First to succumb to the anticipation was Wiseman. "Who is it then?" he demanded. *O ye of little patience.*

"The mayor oversaw Empowered documentation, but who wrote it? He approved the idea for Cardplay, but who conceived it?" Circ ran a finger along one of the mural's painted silver threads, reveling in how his subordinate's faces fell when he added indolently, "Who took two young Keepers into his care and had access to nearly every magic user the Reemergence spawned?"

Wiseman spat the name: "*Ritsuo.*" Mayor Hargrove's magnanimity and high standing had made a perfect shield for the unassuming magic professor, but now he had nowhere to hide.

Other pieces were beginning to click for Sybil. "That's what your undercover getup's for."

Her wits weren't as sharp as her shooting. "Not quite. While this will make obtaining the fragment easier, there is another reason I've taken the Spade's Keeper." Circ looked over the three of them, utterly clueless, and flashed a grin several fangs short of his own. "Don't you see? This is how we break the Heart."

CHAPTER THIRTY-SEVEN
JANUARY 2 | JANE RESIDENCE

ELLEN SPUN THE RING ON HER MIDDLE FINGER round and round, each twist of the black band winding her up tighter. In her left hand she held her phone, the screen's glow harsh in the dim living room; and on the coffee table lay Iori's, recovered from the sinkhole of the couch cushions.

That explained why he hadn't responded to her messages. Surely, though, if he'd gone to languish by his lonesome, he would've at least had the courtesy to let everyone know he was okay. He could have picked up a payphone, swung by headquarters . . .

Her phone buzzed then, and she gave a start—hopes soaring, and promptly plummeting when she saw it was just Tatiana checking in. Ellen had been instructed to watch for Iori at home with her brother, who was upstairs monitoring police scanners, while her friends had gone to keep an eye out with the evening patrol.

Tatiana: Any sign of him?

Ellen: No, not yet.

Tatiana: I swear, if that boy isn't dead, I'm gonna kill him myself.

Ellen started to type a reply, but didn't have the willpower to finish it. She held her phone to her chest and slumped against the arm of the couch. If only she could turn back the clock and stop Iori from fleeing the rooftop, maybe she would be curled up beside him instead of filling his absence with dismal speculation.

The scene from Hargrove's office bobbed to the surface of her thoughts again, his corpse left there like a gruesome effigy.

Like a threat.

What if Iori hadn't touched base because something happened to him? Blackjack used to keep tabs on him for Wiseman. What if they'd gotten to him, captured him? What if he needed her while she lay here waiting?

Her fingers wandered to her lips.

She knew Iori like a part of herself. With her, he'd shared some of his darkest, most delicate pieces. He wouldn't let her worry like this after the storms they'd weathered together. He just wouldn't. Not if he loved her the way that kiss told her he did.

Something *had* to be wrong.

Navigating to Hikaru's icon in her contacts list, she began to type a new message. There hadn't been cause for immediate concern since she'd explained, albeit in patchy terms, what went down at the festival, and when it came to flight or fight, they both knew Iori was prone to choose the former. But it was getting late, and every second could be—

A beep from the security system stalled her texting. She cast her gaze into the front hall as the door swung inward, and relief rushed through her when that tall, tailed shape she'd been missing walked in.

"Iori!" She hopped up, then teetered to a halt in the doorway when a biting chill rolled in to meet her. In his lack of acknowledgement as he slid off his boots, her voice became a small and docile thing. "I've been trying to contact you. Where have you been?"

"Out," he said.

"You've been gone all day."

He hung up his jacket, his scarf. "I needed space."

Space. He skipped out on training because he needed space, and he didn't even think to call? He could've done the bare minimum and notified the masters. "I was worried. We have people out there searching for you. Didn't you hear the news?

"What news?"

She almost couldn't bring herself to say it. "About Mayor Hargrove. He's dead."

Iori paused at the bottom of the stairs, hand on the railing. "Oh." His tone softened somewhat, then he slung a "Sorry," over his shoulder and continued up the steps.

"That's it?" She hadn't expected him to take her in his arms and grieve with her, but he knew how much Hargrove meant to everyone. To her and her brother. The man had been like an uncle to them. "I tell you someone important to me died, and that's all you have to say?"

"What do you want me to say?"

Why was he being so short with her? "He was *murdered*. This should concern you too!"

He turned to her, and the look in his uncovered eye reminded her of the boy she met at Elysian Tower. Flippant, aloof—a far cry from the person she'd come to know. "It's a grim world, doll. Better get used to it." *Doll?* "And if you must know, I won't be present tomorrow either. I have plans."

Plans for *what*? "We have a meeting tomorrow, and you have therapy."

"Oh, I'm done with that."

"Done? W-what do you mean you're done?" He and Dr. Bristol had been making progress. He'd told her as much himself. He'd been feeling better, braver, more in control, but the ghosts that haunted his slumber were far from exorcized. "What about the night terrors?"

His mouth pulled into an unsettling curve. "You could say I've . . . learned to live with them."

CHAPTER THIRTY-EIGHT
NEITHER HERE NOR THERE

I DREAM I'M DROWNING

fluid filling my lungs

a viscous flood

pitch as night

sullied blood

Iori jolted as if from a dream, only to find himself in a waking nightmare.

The festival grounds sprawled around him, laden in smog. Glitzy costumes lay deflated on the cobblestones, as if the people who'd worn them had evaporated into thin air, and there wasn't a light to make their sequins shine. Every last bulb had blown, gone out, and unfilled Ferris wheel cars teetered on squeaky hinges, rocked by the wind.

Unsure how he wound up on the ground, Iori rose slowly to his feet and scanned the market square. The unmanned concession stands, the motionless rides, the darkened buildings encasing it all. "Ellen?" His voice echoed across the deserted space, bouncing off cobbles and concrete. "Kosta? Kabr?"

Nobody answered.

Where had everyone gone? This place had been teeming with people. They couldn't have just vanished.

Iori pulled out his phone, the fuzzy pompom charm Ellen had gifted him dangling off its corner, and tapped the screen. Tapped it again. Clicked the buttons along its side. Nothing could bring it back to life, not even a forced restart. The battery must have died, or perhaps it had been damaged somehow.

Anxiety prickled in his extremities. He felt like a kid who'd meandered off and gotten lost, and couldn't recall how he got here. What happened after the bungled kiss? He'd fled from the rooftop, escaped to the alleyways, and then, and then . . . What brought him back to the square? And where had this smog come from? It swirled in grungy smoke-like streamers, braided through the framework of abandoned rides by howling winds and—

No. This howl wasn't a product of the wind. The smog itself was droning this all-too familiar tune, which tickled the fine hairs in his ears and drowned out even the hum of his own magic. These were clouds of vaporous Void, churning the atmosphere into a toxic soup.

There must have been an outbreak. An influx.

He had to get to headquarters. If the others had left in a hurry, that was where they'd be.

CHAPTER THIRTY-NINE
JANUARY 3 | CARDPLAY HEADQUARTERS

As promised, Iori was gone at the crack of dawn. Where to, he hadn't disclosed, and why, Ellen hadn't a clue. But his absence didn't go unnoticed.

"Where's Ryone?" Hikaru asked from the command centre stage as everyone gathered for the Monday meeting. He and Elizabeth were backlit by a map of Hildegrand on the projector screen. Several areas had been circled on it.

Ellen's initial impulse was to make an excuse. *He's sick, he's late, he had an errand to run.* But she wouldn't cover his tracks if she didn't know where they led. So, regretfully, she informed the masters that he would not be attending, and with some reluctance, they proceeded without him.

News of Mayor Hargrove's death had officially broken, and the people were clamoring for answers the authorities couldn't provide. To add to that, Void activity had increased overnight with no discernible trigger or pattern. Inkblots spawned at random, no host bodies accounted for. Ellen had already performed two purifications this morning, and twice, incident alarms interrupted the meeting. Yusuf, Miriam, and Heather had rushed out to tend to an Inkblot attack. Not long after, Sabaa took Iris and Tatiana to quash another.

It seemed their stint of moderate peace was over.

When the meeting wrapped, the masters pulled the three Keepers present aside. Under normal circumstances, Kyani wouldn't have been allowed in the command centre whilst in the rehab program, but Hikaru had overridden the rule, deeming this too important to miss.

"It's gotta be Blackjack," Alexander stated before his shoes even hit the stage. With the spike in Void activity on the heels of Hargrove's death, it was safe to assume the usual suspects were responsible. "We need to make our move before they get ahead of us."

Hikaru made a leveling motion. "I know you want to take action against Charles Wiseman, but this does not elevate us to a more advantageous position than we were previously in." Alexander went to interject, and the headmaster stopped him. "We cannot connect these incidents to him or his operatives, nor can we prove the existence of the Sundered Star. There is a law we must adhere to."

"You can't expect us to just sit here—"

"We're not," Elizabeth staunchly cut in. "I'm putting you on an upper district patrol with Naomi and Ikkei. Your sister will be joining Trey and Kabr in mid, and Oto"—Kyani straightened, attentive—"you're with me. Using your specially-tuned magic senses, we're going to try and pinpoint the source of these outbreaks. I was hoping Ryone would be here to help cover more ground. Does anyone know where he is?"

The three of them shook their heads.

"A day I can forgive, but two . . ." Hikaru exhaled through his nose. Time and again, he'd stuck his neck out for Iori. Shown leniency when Elizabeth urged discipline. If Iori needed space to reconcile his feelings, all he had to do was ask, but he hadn't bothered to grant them that courtesy.

Elizabeth clucked her tongue. "What could he possibly have to do that's more important?"

"You said you had a disagreement," Alexander recalled, addressing Ellen and putting her in the hot seat for the second day in a row. "What was that about?"

"It wasn't a disagreement, as such." She entwined and twisted her fingers, the truth gumming up her mouth like overcooked taffy. "He . . . he kissed me, and I didn't kiss him back."

Kyani uttered a small and sympathetic *oh*.

Repressed umbrage pinched Alexander's brows. "So, what, he's avoiding you because you rejected him?"

"I didn't reject him!" Ellen retorted, her outburst sending a ripple of surprise through the group. "I—I froze, and he bolted. I thought we'd just have an awkward patch to get through, but when he finally came home . . . he seemed different."

"How so?" asked Hikaru.

The vision of Iori in the stairwell crossed her mind, smiling sardonically as their reprieve split apart at the seams. "I told him about Hargrove, and he said it's *a grim world* and I should *get used to it*." It hurt enough to hear him speak of his own troubles that way, but hers? *Theirs?*

"The fuck's gotten into him?" muttered Alexander. Even he would realize that was out of character for Iori, and no doubt, he was resisting the urge to get involved.

At this point, Ellen was tempted to let him. The juxtaposition of this Iori and the boy who'd welcomed her into his bed—technically, hers—after her brother went missing made her feel like she was looking at two different people. Had the stress become too much and caused him to regress into his pre-Cardplay loner shell?

"Well he'd better have a damn good explanation." Elizabeth unknotted her arms and descended from the stage. "Next time you see him, send him to me. I won't tolerate students going AWOL. If he can't get his shit together, he can forget about graduating."

CHAPTER FORTY
JANUARY 3 | CARDPLAY HEADQUARTERS

THE SMELL OF BINDING GLUE AND PAPER wafted from the pages of Hikaru's journal, one of many packed full of photos and clippings with notes jotted in the margins. Questions, theories. Rough translations of scriptures that none other than he could interpret.

Guidance came in many forms. Not only did the strings lead him where he needed to go, they could also feed him knowledge when necessary—to help him decipher the ancient tongues of lost poets, or translate captions of old paintings. Occasionally, they even ferried messages via dreams.

He hadn't dreamt in some time, though, and since leads had been few and far between, he'd turned to his records in search of enlightenment. And therein, he discovered a pattern.

Most increases in Void activity could be tied to specific events. Blackjack's meddling, undetected blightings. The breaking of a seal further weakening the barrier between the magical and mortal planes. If he hadn't noticed the recurrence in prior years, he would've had to assume the present outbreak were a delayed influx resultant of the Diamond's awakening.

Rather, in winter, the Void appeared to become restless. Blighted succumbed more quickly to their disease, and the number of wicked made conduits rose. As far as Hikaru could tell, these annual upticks didn't coincide with anything of note, but after weeks of inactivity, there had to be a reason the Sundered Star had chosen now to make a move.

What am I missing?

A knock at the door interrupted his frenetic page-flipping. "Come in," he called, and was relieved when Iori ducked into the office, sagging presumably under the weight of a guilty conscience. "Ah, Ryone. I was hoping to . . . have a word." Hikaru frowned as a string, taut and fraying, shivered into existence above the boy's head. The last string to behave that way was Ellen's when she volunteered as bait to lure out her brother's captors.

A sign of trouble.

Hikaru clapped his journal shut and slotted it into its rightful place on the shelf. "You've had a lot of people worried about you, myself included."

"I know." Iori rested against the double doors, hands behind him. "Sorry for being absent the past couple of days. It won't happen again."

Hikaru predicted the boy would take accountability of his own volition, but if he'd come to make reparations, to what trouble did this string allude? He returned to his desk, motioning for Iori to take the chair in front of it. "Why don't we have a talk?"

He had to get to the bottom of this.

"Actually," said Iori, "I had a question for you." He parted from the doors, carrying on past the chair and desk to the large picture window overlooking the courtyard. "What inspires an officer of the law to get into the business of magic?"

Hikaru narrowed his gaze. "You know this story." It was included in Cardplay's mission statement and was a staple of his Reemergence Day speech. The city had needed order and protection, the Empowered a purpose, and no longer able to offer either with a badge, he had found another way to serve his fellow citizens. The strings may have tugged him in certain directions here and there, but every decision made was ultimately his.

"Just seems serendipitous, don't you think? That the man who founded the modern world's first magic academy had already taken not one, but two Keepers under his wing." Iori inclined his head to the darkening sky. "I suppose that's what you'd call . . . a twist of *fate*."

More was off about him than a wayward string. The modulation of his voice, the pride in his posture, the sureness of his gait. And when that string shivered again, Hikaru realized there were two—one coiled around the other, smothering it.

Two souls, one body.

It can't be.

"Master Ryone." Hikaru tested the honorific like a reflex hammer, and the lack of reaction was all the confirmation he needed. "Would you excuse me a moment? I need to make a phone call." He lifted the receiver to his ear and pushed the button to speed dial Elizabeth.

Halfway through the second ring, the call cut off as a black-nailed finger slid onto the switchhook.

"How rude. We were in the middle of a conversation." Iori's voice ticked up an octave, slipping into an accent that flowed with a rhythm of a time long lost. And when Hikaru looked up at him again, a stranger stared back through a pupil rimmed in blue.

The Sundered Star had infiltrated Cardplay Headquarters.

Hikaru did his best to silence the alarm bells tolling in his head. As of now, the building was virtually empty, their forces scattered across the city. He had to play this safe. "Why have you come here?" he asked.

"Oh, I think you have an inkling." The imposter delicately removed the telephone receiver from his grasp and placed it on the desk. "I have to say, you had me fooled. Your pal Hargrove certainly fit the bill, but I should have known better than to chase a red herring."

Fit the bill, a red herring . . .

The eyes Hikaru had fixed on Circ, hardened more by fear than defiance, sank gravely behind his spectacles. Thelonious Hargrove had become collateral damage in the hunt for the Guiding Light.

For *him*.

"I was your target . . ."

"Bravo, the detective solved his case!" Circ's applause slowed, his mouth sagging at the corners. "Too little too late, I'm afraid." He planted a boot on the lip of Hikaru's chair and grabbed him by the face, the alarms pealing louder as shadows leaked from under his palm. "I can see why her fragment chose you. She always did have a soft spot for the scholarly types. But my sister's reign is over, and it's time for you to relinquish that fragment to me."

Circ shoved him back, and Hikaru's hands flew to his assailant's arms as a biting, blinding cold enveloped his face. His skin stretched and ossified, crackling like a lake freezing over. A scream rose to his throat, and was swiftly smothered by the noxious cloud surging into his airways, racing for his core.

For the fragment.

In that moment, existence revolved around one paralyzing feeling: pain. So pervasive that he barely noticed the rattle of the door handle.

Locked—by Circ when he entered.

Voices called from the other side. Alexander and Naomi, returning from their patrol. That door was never locked; they would know something was wrong.

Circ flung a panicked glance their way, features contorting when the handle jiggled more violently. "If I can't have that fragment, no one can." He squeezed harder, driving that darkness deeper and deeper until Hikaru's vision began to tunnel. At another jarring rattle, he hurled the headmaster onto the floor. One of his lenses splintered, the carpet's burn on his cheekbone nothing compared to the malicious vapors churning in his lungs.

Shaking his hand, Circ cast off cobwebs of shadow as Hikaru gasped and shuddered at his feet. "Lucky you, I'm not done with this disguise yet, so you get to live another day. Though, this will be the last you're awake to see."

The shouts outside became muted, the hammer of fists a dull thump somewhere in the vanishing background.

Circ withdrew. "Ta," he said, and with a snap of his fingers, absconded in a whirl of Void and starlight.

Moments later, people crowded around Hikaru. Naomi and Ikkei, the latter of whom must have unlocked the deadbolt using his magnetic powers. Alexander was a smudge of white and gray kneeling at his side, shaking his shoulder.

A new string shimmered out the corner of Hikaru's vision, not tethering him to anyone or anything in particular. It trailed up from his body toward the ceiling, wobbling unsteadily.

His life, hanging by a thread.

CHAPTER FORTY-ONE
JANUARY 3 | CARDPLAY HEADQUARTERS

ELLEN BROUGHT TREMBLING FINGERS to the glossy onyx ridges on Hikaru's face, the glitter of starlight within dulled by the infirmary's fluorescent lights. The horrible marks spanned his mouth, left his lips cracked and statuesque, and crept up his cheek. More reached down his throat, past the endotracheal tube the doctors had inserted to combat the blackness in his lungs.

A blight even Ellen couldn't wipe clean.

Third time's the charm, right?

Under the watch of her brother and Iori, who'd finally decided to show, Ellen scraped the bottom of her magic barrel and tried again. Like her previous attempts, the marks only receded a centimeter or so before her power fizzled out—this time depleting the last of her reserves.

"I don't understand. I cleansed him before . . ." Years ago, after he'd been bitten by an Inkblot at an improperly-secured crime scene. "Why can't I do it now?" Too exhausted to contain her emotions any longer, Ellen yielded to the helplessness that had been building inside her, and Alexander held her while she cried.

"Don't beat yourself up," he said. "You've done everything you can."

She should've been able to do *more*, but for some reason, she couldn't access the temporal lobe where his memories were stored in order to perform a deep purification. And she shouldn't have had to. The blight was isolated, external. It didn't even cover a large portion of his body.

Again she was the only person in the room with the power to solve the problem, and again, the Void energy swirling around her was a chilling reminder that she couldn't.

Not Hikaru's blight, or the Spade's corruption.

Iori slouched in a squat chair across the room, radiating cold as if sculpted from ice. He'd been behaving more like his old self in a sorry way, withdrawn into his shell to hide from the crushing reality they found themselves in.

They faced one of two possibilities. Either they were dealing with a new and extremely virulent strain of blight, or the Sundered Star had broken into headquarters—into the headmaster's office, no less—without raising an alarm, and Ellen wasn't sure which scared her more.

There came a hollering from the hall, drawing their collective attention to the secure room's sealed glass door.

"Wait," said Fornell, closer now. "You can't go in there!"

Elizabeth stormed into view a second later with Kyani close behind, wresting her sleeve from the doctor's grasp. Both of them froze when they spotted the headmaster through the window.

Then Elizabeth lunged for the door.

Letting go of his sister, Alexander rushed to block her, barring her path with his body. She squared her shoulders to him, nostrils flaring.

"Alexander, *move*."

"I can't do that."

"Alex—"

"We don't know yet if this is transmissible." A fretful Elizabeth pressed the heel of her palm to her brow as he went on. "If he contracted it at City Hall, fully-suited, your gear may not protect you. And you and I are well aware that blight spreads faster between the unempowered. If you set foot in here—"

"He's not," Elizabeth blurted out.

Her interruption gave Alexander pause. "Not what?"

"Unempowered."

Alexander cast a look at Ellen, and she stared back glassy-eyed, equally as puzzled. "What are you saying?" he asked Elizabeth.

Conflict chiseled deep lines into her expression, her stony façade mere taps from crumbling. She gave an exasperated wave to her spouse, whose chest inflated with another mechanized breath. "He has magic. Wears a ring to suppress it. Has done for years."

Ellen's gaze fell to his ring on the bedside table, next to his cracked and folded spectacles. The tungsten band's inlaid copper strip shone more boldly now than it ever had, but somehow, the unveiling of yet another secret did not faze her.

"I thought you knew," murmured Kyani.

"Did you?" Alexander shot back in bafflement.

"He has an aura. He must've heard it, too." She looked to Iori, who contributed no more than a shrug. They must've assumed Ellen and her brother were aware, but Hikaru hadn't mentioned anything of the sort. Not in his classes, not in the privacy of their own home.

A sigh poured from Alexander's mouth. "Great. So we're officially the last to know. Again." He slammed the doorframe, causing Ellen to flinch. Hurt and confusion transformed his tongue into a lashing whip. "What—what is it, does he not trust us enough to tell us? Is that the issue?"

"He wanted to," said Elizabeth, more delicate than Ellen had ever heard her. "It's complicated. He doesn't use his powers often. He can't. And she knows, too." She thrust an almost accusatory finger at Dr. Fornell. "So does Cellier. So does Mira Hodge. So does Chief Gardner. It's not the kind of power you can flaunt around; he had to keep his circle tight."

"Why? What can he do?"

"That is for him to tell you *when* he wakes up."

"Is there anything else we should know?"

She hesitated, then set her jaw. "No."

"Are you sure?" Sparks flew between Alexander and Elizabeth like clashing blades, Kyani and Ellen nervous spectators to the duel while Iori watched unperturbed. "Because we don't need more bombs dropped on us when we're already—"

"Stop yelling!" Ellen interjected. She couldn't take it anymore. "Fighting won't get us anywhere, and you're missing the point: if Hikaru is Empowered, the blight had to have been forced on him."

Kyani's eyes widened. "Which means Circ was here."

For a moment, Elizabeth's fretfulness ebbed. "We've been compromised. We need to secure the premises."

"We already did," said Alexander.

"So check it again! You and Ryone take the yard, Oto and Ellen can search the building." She smoothed her hair, fighting a losing battle with her own composure. "Now would you *please* let me see him?"

"Not until we've confirmed it's safe." Dr. Fornell reached out as if to calm an agitated animal, retracting the gesture when Elizabeth recoiled. "We can't risk losing both masters. Someone's got to run this place. Why don't you call Gardner, let him know what's going on?"

Elizabeth pinched the bridge of her nose but surrendered to Fornell, and the doctor led her away.

Alexander thumped Iori's shoulder with the back of his hand. "Get up. Make yourself useful." He hit the button for the door and marched into the hall, tracked by a faintly offended look from Iori. Alexander was bound to give him a piece of his mind once they got outside.

"I'll meet you out there," said Kyani to Ellen before jogging after him.

As Iori rose to follow, Ellen stepped toward him. "Iori—" She stopped short. This wasn't the place for a proper discussion; she only wanted to put a bandage on the gash between them. But when his aberrantly empty gaze landed on her, she couldn't manage more than a few plaintive parting words. "B-be careful, okay?"

"You too," he said.

Even his voice sounded hollow.

CHAPTER FORTY-TWO
NEITHER HERE NOR THERE

IORI HAD ALWAYS THOUGHT OF HILDEGRAND'S alleys as a maze, but this was getting ridiculous. He'd been stuck in this labyrinth for what felt like hours, what could've been minutes, unable to escape via rooftop due to his magic stores being inexplicably drained. And every path he took brought him back to the same damn location over and over and over.

Market square.

Market square.

Market square.

Market—

Wait. That wasn't there before.

An enormous tent had been erected in the square. Aged off-white canvas striped with rusty blue, tattered flags flying high. The sign above its entrance spelled CIRCUS, each letter lined with spherical bulbs fogged in soot—blown like the rest of the festival lights—and a silver star topped its tallest peak. Impossible to miss, but an entire circus couldn't pop up from the ether.

The fluttering entry flaps beckoned to him.

Convinced he'd been sucked into some twisted illusion—did Blackjack have any illusionists in their ranks?—Iori emerged from the yawning mouth of the alleyway. A trap was only a trap if you didn't suspect it.

Besides, if this was an illusion, exploration might lead him to an exit.

A different kind of gloom shrouded the tent's interior. Strips of moth-eaten canvas looped across the ceiling, creating a latticework of shadow over an audience of platinum-suited mannequins in the grandstands. The circus ring lay before them, a sprinkling of azure and alabaster paint on the volcanic sands within.

Circuses were built to entertain. To inspire awe and astonish the masses with gravity-defying acrobatics, magic tricks, and stunts that taunted death itself. This place had been gutted of all that wonder.

This place was intended to breed horror.

Spotlights clanged on. A kooky tune wound up in the background, a worn record's grooves singing through the brass horn of a gramophone, and the audience clattered brokenly in applause as their marionette ringmaster took the stage. It stooped in a crooked bow, the brighter accents of its midnight attire sparkling under the lights. A wobbly smile and starburst eyes had been painted on its otherwise featureless face.

Not keen to witness just how much weirdness this illusion or dream or whatever it was could cook up, he slunk off into the neighboring tent. A dressing room. Costumes had been hung haphazardly on clothing racks, the vanity table smeared in more paint, and in the corner sat a cage on a wagon chassis.

There was movement inside, the rise and fall of an animal's sleek black flank. The creature stirred as Iori neared, its pointed ears pricking to the rasp of his steps on the straw-strewn cobblestones. A cat—larger than any Iori had seen. And as he got closer, he realized its coat wasn't merely sleek. It was *liquid*.

The oversized feline rounded on him, ink oozing from the cracked chunk of amethyst crammed into its right eye socket. The growl in its chest exploded into a furious roar and it lunged at the bars, rocking the wagon on its wheels.

Iori stumbled backward and fell through the flaps into the main tent, toppling over the throng of mannequins that had gathered outside. The ringmaster loomed over him, and his pulse leapt.

Kicking one of the mannequins in the head, he broke away from their groping ball-jointed fingers and bolted across the ring into the adjacent tent, pulling the drapes shut behind him. No door, no lock. Would that be enough to stop them?

He spun, hoping to see an exit, and was confronted by—

Himself.

Innumerable panes of glass captured his image—too many for this tent to house, he would've thought. At least he looked normal in them. Or as normal as a boy with cat ears and a puffed tail could look.

He wandered the hall, peering into the gaps between the mirrors. Taking in every scratch and scuff mark, poring for a flaw. He'd heard of the falsehoods Empowered illusionists could weave over reality. Some were even capable of manipulating a person's perception of time, squashing hours into seconds and stretching minutes into days. However, no illusion was perfect. Find the hole, and you could rip it wide open.

Locating it was the tricky part.

His reflection followed his every step, hanging in his peripherals. A comforting if not slightly disconcerting constant in this fabricated space.

Until it changed.

As he passed another mirror, a new figure matched his pace but not his posture. A silhouette whose ears stood taller than his, and whose hair didn't curl. Great tufts of fur adorned their shoulders, tapering into a cape, and though their face was veiled in shadow, they gave Iori the strangest sense of familiarity.

The stranger shifted in sync with his movements. Flicked an ear when he flicked his, inclined their head likewise. He placed his fingers on the glass, and they brought theirs to meet his, their gloved forefinger and thumb tipped with needle-thin claws.

"Who are you?" Iori's question reverberated like an echo through a telephone receiver, except the echo didn't belong to him. Grit where his was gravel, and pitched slightly higher. "Who are you?" he queried the silhouette again.

A pipe organ rent the stillness of the atmosphere, causing the mirrors to quake and rattle. And Iori remembered then, remembered the painting from his magic studies—of the cat-eared figure bent ceremoniously over a pool of swirling ink. An artifact from the era of magic, the sole link between him and the Spade.

The stranger in the glass was his Suit's former Keeper.

Their right eye cracked open, revealing gleaming amethyst where there should have been tissue. Iori quailed at the sight and covered his ears as their jaw unhinged to loose a monstrous yowl.

The Spade wept, oh wept . . .

Their tormented voice rose with the organ's cry.

. . . and lo . . .

Glass fractured. Ink seeped out.

. . . the darkness slept.

The mirrors burst, and Iori was swept away in the flood.

CHAPTER FORTY-THREE
JANUARY 5 | WISEMAN ESTATE

GUIDING LIGHT OR NOT, Thelonious Hargrove's fate was sealed the moment his name left Sybil's blabbering mouth. His death was part of a covert coup that Cardan hadn't been let in on because his associates knew he would have objected to it.

You can still leave, whistled the bird in his ear, reminiscent of his last conversation with Kyani. As he'd hauled her into the complex, police boats closing in on Camrand Island, she'd dug her heels in and begged him to desert the cause he poured seven years of blood, sweat, and tears into.

"Don't do this, Cardan, please! You can leave with me. We can go together. I'll tell them how you helped me and they'll take us both!"

He'd whirled on her then, her with the break in her voice and the burns on her neck and strands of cut hair clinging to her skin. *"We won't be together, Kyani. Don't you get that? They're taking you because you sold us out. All that's waiting for me out there is a life sentence, and I refuse to become another statistic."*

He hadn't considered what he would become if he stayed.

Wiseman's luxury sedan bounced against his back as Sybil hefted another duffel bag into the boot. Must've been half an armory's worth of munitions in there. Everything from tasers and stun grenades to lethal explosives and automatic rifles—a portion of which were prototypes from the project Wiseman and Valerie had been developing before he abolished her and it both.

Cardan had an idea who those stardust-filled shells were intended for, and it wasn't the Void-spawned monsters Circ had set loose in the city.

"Quit slacking and put this on." Sybil slung a smaller duffel at him and he caught it, fumbling the floppy bag in his arms.

"What is it?"

"Use your eyes, fucknut."

He rolled them, then put them to use as instructed and unzipped the bag. Stuffed inside was a uniform. Black trousers, steel-toed boots, and a beret the same vibrant red as the coat's lining and lopsided lapels. Every piece had been trimmed in silver to match the epaulettes.

A corporal's epaulettes.

"What am I supposed to do with this?"

"They're *clothes*. For *wearing*." Sybil had already donned the pants of her uniform and was slipping her tattooed arms through the coat's sleeves.

"So we're impersonating national guards now?"

"We can't waltz into Hildegrand looking like ourselves." She buttoned her coat, its own epaulettes and trimming a dull bronze in the gray morning. "If anyone asks, and they will, you're Corporal James Bennett. ID's in the inner pocket."

Couldn't even pick a Fluorantine name. "And who're you meant to be?"

She gave a mock salute. "Private First Class Allison West, at your service."

Shame her lower rank disguise wouldn't come with any respect for the chain of command. Cardan was still on the bottom, just as he'd always been. Forever the underdog, begging for scraps at the dinner table.

Sybil adjusted her beret. Its red flash, bearing Amberlye's coat of arms, complemented the frizzy dye-streaked coils of hair that poked out from underneath. "What's eating you anyway? We're about to harvest the fruits of our labors, and you're moping around like a flaccid balloon."

Better judgment advised he keep it to himself. Hot takes didn't garner much traction in this crowd. At best, you'd get the equivalent of a passive-aggressive *bless your heart.*

At worst, your viscera splattered up a wall.

"You're brooding over the loss of your idol, aren't you?"

Couldn't avoid it now that she'd honed in on his sticking point. "I'm not *brooding*." He placed the duffel bag on the roof of the car. "I just don't see how we're supposed to achieve equality for the Empowered when we keep killing our allies." Blighting convicted murderers and abusers was one thing. Slaying innocents and the few people actively aiding their cause was another.

Empowered or mundane, haters or supporters—it didn't matter whose side they were on. If they were in the way, Blackjack didn't discriminate.

Sybil sniggered, knuckles abutted to her hip. "You still think this is about equality? Man, you're more brainwashed than I thought."

"If not equality, then what is it about?"

"For Mr. Wiseman? Survival of the fittest. For Circ? Fuck if I know. I'm pretty sure he's using our boss to further his own agenda. And me? I'm here for the chaos, baby."

Cardan gave an exasperated wave toward the city. "Don't you care what happens to those people down there?"

"Down there, up here . . . meh." Sybil shrugged. "Caring about others never got me anywhere. The only person who matters to me is me, and if I get to watch this sad little world and its sad little people burn from the best seats in the house?" She put her index finger and thumb together to form an O and kissed it.

Cardan's arm flopped to his side in defeat.

"This utopia you're chasing is a poor man's fantasy, Cardan. If I were you, I'd adopt a more realistic mindset." She slammed the boot of the car shut. "Might wanna tuck that heart back under your sleeve while you're at it. You're starting to sound like Kyani."

CHAPTER FORTY-FOUR
JANUARY 5 | CARDPLAY HEADQUARTERS

ALTHOUGH CIRC HAD FAILED TO OBTAIN the fragment, as of yet lacking the power to extract it, his efforts were not entirely in vain. Immobilizing the host kept strings from being pulled, and unless the body regained consciousness or died, the fragment would remain trapped inside.

All he had to do was ensure it stayed that way.

Pretending to be moral support, he monitored the headmaster and the Jane girl from the discomfort of an infirmary room chair, watching in case he needed to prevent a purification. Ironically, his sister's fragment was doing a fine job of that itself by obstructing access to the man's memory archives.

Circ could sense it, the shield encasing him. A defensive mechanism triggered by the attack. But in trying to protect its host, the fragment had sealed his fate, for without a dive into his subconscious, the unawakened Heart could not cleanse him. That didn't stop its Keeper from trying, though.

Over and over, her carafe of magic would fill to the brim, and over and over, she would pour it into him. All of yesterday, all of today, parting from his side only to tend to her own bodily needs and the blighted—of which Circ had ensured there were many. The Void vents he'd opened the night of the festival had worked a treat.

Quietly recharging now, Ellen hunched by the headmaster's side, cradling his hand as though it might crumble.

Are you praying to the heavens for a miracle? pondered Circ. *I'm afraid your skies are empty, little doe.*

It was fortunate that her grief had distracted her from him. Fortunate, too, that the failed romantic pursuit by the Keeper he wore had provided reason to keep her at arm's length, no affectionate commiseration required. How nauseating it would have been to portray a doting lover, whispering sweet nothings into spoiled ears and wearing smiles that dripped of saccharine rot.

A flurry of visions blustered through his mind: red hair, rose lips, ruinous eyes, round hips—

He dug his nails into the padded arm of his chair, blotting out the sordid imagery. That devout fool's fragmented recollections were still entrenched in the Spade, her soulmate haunting him like a sorrowing ghost.

Soon, what dust remained of them both would be blackened by the oils of corruption. The process had already begun in this one. Drop by drop, more of this Suit and this body became Circ's. Became the Void's.

By the dawn of the seventh, it all would be.

The girl's phone chimed.

And so the bell tolls.

She retrieved the device and pored over the screen. "It's Soren. They're about to make the announcement." She stood, bending to kiss her dear adoptive father on the brow, then led the way upstairs.

The mayor's seat was empty, a throne for the taking—its previous occupant a bloated, blighted corpse in some mortuary's drawer—and the council had been mulling over candidates to fill the position in the interim. Now the day had come for them to name their selection.

For the sheer concentration it took to conceal his excitement, Circ thought himself deserving of an award.

O sister mine, your Guiding Light isn't the only person on this earth with the power to pull strings.

She always had been overconfident, his sister. Couldn't make a mistake; no, no, flawless as the heavens that birthed her. Perhaps she'd thought herself even more so. After all, those heavens had birthed him too, and seldom had a day gone by without her reminding him just how imperfect he was.

Well, perfection wasn't everything.

A small crowd had accumulated in the lounge: the Keepers of the Club and Diamond, Cardplay's battlemaster, and a handful of Jokers whose identities Circ hadn't bothered to memorize. The loud one, the muscular one, the one more timorous than a mouse. So on, and so forth. Most were busy cleaning up the messes he'd made.

While Ellen slotted herself between her typically chatty companion and her brother, Circ hung back by the piano to avoid detection. The gradual dose of poison would darken his aura, chill the air, and give off a scent of tarnished metal. The Keepers would have to weigh those levels against those previously exuded by the Spade's corruption, but still—better to err on the side of caution.

On the wall-mounted television screen, a stout councilor delivered a speech from City Hall commemorating the late and allegedly great Thelonious Hargrove. Yammering on about his aptitude and sincerity and blah, blah, blah, blah, *blah.* Circ couldn't care less about the schmaltzy drivel.

He'd come for the reveal.

"With this in mind," said the councilor, *"we intend to elect an individual befitting of the mold Thelonious left. Someone who has already demonstrated an admirable level of commitment and care for this city, and who embodies our true Amberlynian values. Therefore, I am honored to*

announce that, by unanimous vote . . . the council has chosen to appoint Charles Wiseman as Mayor of Hildegrand."

And the silence that followed—what music to these borrowed ears! Even the pigtailed chatterbox had nothing to say, and none could avert their eyes from the screen when their new leader graced the portico.

Once the city's savior, poised to become its king.

He assumed his position at the podium, a fog of breath enveloping the microphone as he addressed the people. His future subjects. *"Citizens of Hildegrand, it is both a privilege and a tragedy that I stand before you in the midst of this hallowed season."* His gloved fingers curled around the edges of the lectern. *"This week should be a period of renewal and celebration. Yet here you wallow in grief, robbed of your deserved peace."*

The public's throats had been made raw by their cries for action, and now that Wiseman had rolled into town offering honeyed syllables to soothe them, they would be lapping up every drop at a premium.

"Initiative must be taken if we are to control this outbreak. Thelonious Hargrove did what he felt was right, and I commend him for his benignity, but his compassion for those he deemed oppressed led him to place the wellbeing of this city in the wrong hands."

The brawny Joker with the blue quiff jerked ahead like he was about to fight the television. "What is he doing?"

Watch and listen, Circ advised inwardly.

"In the beginning, mundane folk had to rely on those who possessed magic to protect them from it. But with Hargrove's untimely demise, our city besieged by darkness, and Cardplay's own headmaster sick with blight, it has become apparent that they can no longer guarantee our safety. Therefore, my first act as mayor will be rectification, beginning with the enactment of martial law. As the city

enters an indefinite lockdown, I implore residents to shelter in place until this crisis has passed."

Wiseman turned to the camera, eyes boring into the lens.

"And I am hereby ordering Cardplay to cease operations immediately. All Empowered personnel are to convene at their headquarters. Any found outside past curfew will be dealt with appropriately."

The battlemaster clicked a button to shut the television off. "*Appropriately*, my ass." She chucked the remote onto a cabinet. It skittered over the side, nearly taking a full vase of flowers with it. Her temper almost rivaled the Diamond's.

"What just happened?" uttered a tall, bewildered man as the audience slipped out of their collective stupor. An earth-mover, judging by the dirt and dust that covered his brown skin from his last call.

A woman with a cutting jawline and hands large enough to be weapons themselves replied. "We've been made the enemy."

Ellen cast her concern toward Circ, and he did his best to imitate the traumatized boy smothered within, drooping the ears and letting his uncovered eye linger on the blackened screen as the room devolved into panic. The timorous kid worrying at his beaded bracelet, the Diamond's Keeper ranting about the council's unanimously ignorant vote.

Chaos.

"He was under investigation barely over a month ago. What the fuck were they thinking?"

"Wiseman must have gotten to them," the Club's doleful Keeper presumed correctly. Circ wished he'd rendered her flightless when he had the chance.

The battlemaster raised her voice above the rest, calling for order. Ironic considering hers was the first gasket to blow. "We are going to deal with this calmly and efficiently."

Finally, the pigtailed chatterbox opened her lid. "Wiseman just threw us under the bus. He's the mayor! How are we supposed to go up against that?"

"I am *thinking*."

How convenient that their Spade already had a plan. "Wiseman's rounding up all the Jokers . . ." Circ began, burdening his voice to the brink of a tremor. "What if he figured out we have the Heart?"

Here the Jane girl was lamenting for her beau when it was her own safety she should be concerned about. The realization swept the rosy hue from her cheeks, and from the cheeks of several others as well.

Pigtails gawked. "I'm sorry—*what?*"

Oops. Not everyone was privy to that detail.

"Since when?" demanded the burly fellow.

"A while. It's Ellen," Alexander told them. "I'll explain later. We only learned about it recently ourselves, and I don't see how Wiseman could have. We stayed the course like Hikaru told us to. We've been careful."

Not careful enough, thought Circ. Granted, Wiseman hadn't identified her. Circ had. To him, the Suit-bearers shone brighter than the rest, infused with his sister's resplendent light, and the Heart shone brightest of all.

"Are you willing to bet on that?" he pressed. "He must at least suspect we have it. We need to get her out of here." Away from her friends, from her family, away from the Guiding Light. "This place isn't safe for her anymore."

Alexander stabbed a disfigured finger at the floor. "This is her *home*. The military is going to be patrolling the streets. If you go gallivanting around the city after curfew and they catch you—"

"No, Iori's right." Ellen balled her little fists in determination, and her brother did a dismayed double-take. "I don't want to go, but if I stay, we might as well surrender the

Heart to Wiseman." She looked to her battlemaster. "We can't let Hikaru's work go to waste."

The austere woman rubbed her chin, the others tensely awaiting her decision. "Okay," she said at last, and the siblings echoed her—brother aghast, sister seeking confirmation. "Ryone managed to evade us, Blackjack, *and* the authorities for seven years. You'll only need to stay in hiding for as long as it takes us to find a solution." Bold of her to assume they would. "And should Wiseman come down on us, he'll come down hard and fast, which means we need to be faster."

Humans. Such gullible creatures.

Privately, Circ beamed. The pieces were falling perfectly into place, and he barely had to lift a finger.

CHAPTER FORTY-FIVE
JANUARY 5 | CARDPLAY HEADQUARTERS

IF ALEXANDER HATED ANYTHING MORE than the inaction of others, it was being forced into inaction himself.

"Be patient and let me sort this out," Elizabeth had told them before shutting herself in the headmaster's office. Being put under a government stranglehold while your city was under attack was hardly conducive to patience.

The temptation gripped him, not for the first time, to march on City Hall and rip Charles Wiseman out of the mayor's seat with his bare hands. *It would be easy,* seethed the vengeful devil on his shoulder. *Behead him like the monster he is, and it'll be over.*

Killing wasn't that easy, though. Kane had been deserving, had already been hurtling towards a self-inflicted end, and even then, the fact Alexander had run his blade through a beating heart disturbed him. Should he come face to face with Wiseman again, would he be able to do it? Or would he freeze?

If only his shoulder angel weren't spiraling into despair.

At a loss for viable ideas and hoping proximity to a natural problem-solver might inspire him, Alexander had paid a visit to the secure ward. From the hall, he watched Hikaru's vitals chart stable lines on the monitors.

It used to annoy him how effortlessly on-the-ball and organized the man was. Always had a solution prepared, and if you weren't ready to accept it, he'd hold onto it until you were—or until you were in no condition to refuse. More often than not, determined to solve his own problems, Alexander wound up the latter.

Now he'd finally come seeking advice, and Hikaru wasn't conscious to provide it. Bedbound but improving, blight reduced by thirty percent thanks to Ellen. Brain buzzing with activity, yet totally unresponsive. According to those wave forms, he should've been awake.

I'm ready, thought Alexander. *Where are you?*

Wings entered his field of vision.

"How is he?" asked Kyani, drawing up to the window.

He wished he had better news. "No change." Maybe she had a promising update for him. "Has Elizabeth made any progress?"

She shook her head. Figures. They were on a losing streak, and it seemed none of them had the power to turn the tables. Blackjack had executed the perfect coup, put Cardplay under house arrest, and forced his kid sister into hiding. What other tricks did they have up their sleeves?

Alexander withdrew from the window, dragging his hands down his face. "This is so fucked up. Maybe we should . . . I don't know, break curfew. Go out there and fight. I mean, what's stopping us?"

"The army," Kyani reminded him.

"They can't honestly think they have what it takes to fight the Void, can they? Whatever Wiseman's promised them, it's a lie. They're going to learn that the hard way when he no longer has use for them." Humanity was an ocean for the Void to pollute, and it wouldn't rest until it had spoiled every gallon. "They must realize we're the reason they're still kicking. If it weren't for the Empowered, they would've been wiped out in the Reemergence."

"Uh, Alex—"

"You'd think risking our lives on a daily basis to save their ungrateful asses would've earned us some respec—"

"*Alex.*" Kyani grabbed him by the arm and rotated him to the window. About to tell him to stop bellyaching over the inequities of the situation and focus not on what was right in front of him, he thought. And in a way, he supposed she was, because right in front of him, Hikaru had begun to stir.

His head rolled on his pillow, fingers twitching as the stats on the monitors climbed.

"Go get Fornell," Alexander said, and Kyani dashed for the doctor's office as he rushed into the room of wailing alarms. Heart rate elevated, blood pressure soaring. Hikaru's uncoordinated hands drifted to the ventilator tube he was gagging on.

Alexander intercepted them. "Whoa, hey, hey, hey. You're okay, you're okay." Hazel eyes darted to him, panicked and glassy. "You're in the infirmary. You've been out for a few days." Hikaru strained against his hold, but he didn't let go. "I get it, it's uncomfortable. Just hang tight."

A rush of footsteps announced Kyani's return with both doctors. She stopped at the foot of the bed, Fornell whipping out her magical spectacles while Cellier went to silence the machines.

"Hello," he intoned. "You're more alert than expected."

Alert enough that he should have understood why he couldn't extubate himself. "Can this tube come out?" Alexander asked as Hikaru continued to fight him.

Fornell popped her lenses on. "Not unless those airways are clear. Last I checked, they looked like the inside of a chimney." To the headmaster, she said, "We're going to run a few tests. Be patient with us."

With an attempted huff, more of a cough, Hikaru twisted his hands free. Before Alexander could retake them, he made a hasty pedaling motion with his index fingers and repeated it until Alexander clued in.

"What's that?" Kyani inquired.

"Sign language." Hikaru had been trying to communicate, and Alexander had essentially muzzled him. He apologized and sat back to observe while the doctors went about their business. "Go slow. It's been a while." He hadn't signed since high school.

<Where is your sister?>

Ellen's whereabouts being the first question Hikaru shaped upon waking from a coma didn't bode well. "She's not here. Why?"

<Where?> he asked again, a troubled crease between his brows.

That Alexander didn't precisely know. The most he could offer was, "She's safe. She's with Iori. We had to—"

Hikaru moved frantically, a tremor in his extremities, and as Alexander interpreted each sign and fingerspelled letter, his stomach plummeted.

<The Sundered Star has taken Ryone. Ellen is in danger. He *knows*.>

"I should've listened to my gut. I knew sending her off with him was a bad idea."

"They can't have gone far. We can still catch them," said Kyani, praying the same as she tailed Alexander through the infirmary halls. With their enhanced senses, tracking them down shouldn't be too difficult—provided Circ hadn't already teleported himself and Ellen to some remote location beyond their reach.

If only Kyani had brought attention to the altered hue of Iori's aura earlier. It would darken occasionally with his mood, but not only had it darkened, its violet color had dipped towards indigo. She'd excused it as a trick of the light. Ellen must've detected the change too and shrugged it off, or kept it to herself for fear of the worst case scenario: that the Spade's defenses were failing.

None of them could have imagined this was the cause.

Exiting the infirmary, they made a beeline for the headmaster's office to inform Elizabeth. Before they could even reach the stairs, Ikkei burst through the front doors, headlights streaming up the dusky driveway behind him.

Alexander spun around with a flap of his arms. "What now?"

"The whole damn motorcade just rolled in." There was a wry twist at the corner of Ikkei's mouth. "Guess who decided to drop by?"

The mansion guards were forcibly disarmed and relieved from their posts, and Empowered personnel assembled by rank in the foyer. Soldiers wearing ski-masked undersuits and hefting automatic rifles poured into the building in droves to keep them in check.

Someday, Kyani knew she would have had to confront Charles Wiseman again, but she had hoped it would be in a court of law—and not with him playing judge, jury, and executioner.

His aura preceded him up the steps, a bleak cloud licking its way across the porch. Reflexively, she averted her gaze, then lifted it at the glimmer of two familiar auras flanking the living shadow: blistering sunset and forget-me-not blue.

Sybil Engstrom and Cardan McConnell, adorned in the colors of the National Guard, marched in at Wiseman's side.

His freshly-minted right and left hands, serving in place of Kane's emphatic touch and Valerie's dexterous reach.

The battlemaster strode forth to meet their uninvited guests, carrying her own powerful aura—a mixture of righteous fury and borrowed magic in her new uniform. Thigh-highs, a navy blue trench coat, and a tricorne fit for an admiral. Each piece, hemmed in gold, had been crafted by none other than Cardplay's Pavati Varma. The sword at her hip, too.

A last-minute decision. More of an experiment, really. The seamstress had never dressed an unempowered person, and without the wearer's magic to support it, it was anyone's guess how long it would last. For this reason, it had been spun over a protective undersuit as not to leave her totally defenseless should it come unraveled.

Wiseman brought his palm to rest on the hilt of his own sheathed rapier, a threat veiled thinner than those reptilian lips of his. "Sergeant Major Elizabeth Howard. From decorated military officer to master of a pack of mutts. My, how the mighty fall."

"Better to lead wolfdogs than a flock of sheep." Elizabeth nodded to his soldiers, the embroidered patches on their arms. "That emblem used to mean something. Now it's just a brand burned into pampered hides." She gazed down the length of her nose at him. "I'm content with where I stand."

He hummed thoughtfully, narrowed eyes raking the assembled. The instant they landed on Alexander, his turned molten. "It's wonderful to see your star Joker back on the roster. You'll have to forgive me for not sending my blessings upon your safe return, Alexander. As you can see, I've been busy."

"If I were you, I'd start counting those blessings," he seethed.

Elizabeth uttered his name in warning, but Wiseman insisted on stoking the flames. "You must have me mistaken for someone else. Can't say I'm surprised after all you've been through."

Unable to simply stand there and let Wiseman float, Alexander lurched forward, his aura brightening to a bonfire glow—only to have it snuffed out by a taser that struck him in the chest.

As he went down, the soldiers' weapons snapped up, and Elizabeth threw an arm outward when several Jokers moved toward him. "Stay where you are!"

"Yes, obey your master. We don't need any more trouble." Wiseman watched Alexander's body spasm with aftershocks. Somehow, the boy still had the strength in him to glare. All Kyani could do was hold her throat, paralyzed by the memory of metal and electricity. A phantom sensation that was about to become painfully real again.

"Collar them. The whelps, too."

At Wiseman's command, the soldiers converged on them with suppression devices. Most submitted without a fuss. Only Naomi and Alexander put up a fight, which earned her a rifle butt to the stomach and Alexander a pinning knee between his shoulders.

It was Cardan who delivered Kyani's collar to her. An act of kindness, or retribution for the knife she'd driven into his back? She would have assumed the latter if he hadn't murmured "I'm sorry" as he fastened it around her neck.

"Are you?" she asked, because he knew how much she hated it—this corked bottle feeling. Knew how she despised Wiseman for all he had done to them, and all he had made them do. His manipulation, his lies, his false promises. If Cardan genuinely cared, how could he go ahead with this?

For a split second, their eyes locked.

"Bear with me," he said before returning to Wiseman's side, leaving Kyani feeling like a bird who'd flown into a window. What did he mean by that?

With the Jokers effectively neutralized, one step remained: to dismantle their leadership. "Private West." Wiseman called Sybil by a moniker that wasn't hers. "Please relieve the battlemaster of her weapons. She won't require them any longer."

"My pleasure." Sybil stripped the stun gun from her holster and the scabbard from her hip, taking a moment to admire the magic-forged blade within. Elizabeth's icy focus didn't drift from Wiseman for a second.

"Hildegrand needs us," she said. "You can't do this."

"Actually, I can." Wiseman produced a piece of paper from the inner pocket of his jacket. The official cease and desist order.

Elizabeth snatched it from him. "On what grounds?"

"Dereliction of duty."

"That's bullshit and you know it."

"It's all there in writing, Miss Howard. Don't forget to read the fine print." He tapped the top of the paper. "And please accept my condolences for the headmaster. Such a terrible mishap." Pivoting to the entrance, he addressed a bearded soldier. "Sergeant Moss, you have the helm. See to it that the rest of the pack is brought to heel."

CHAPTER FORTY-SIX
NEITHER HERE NOR THERE

"Iori?"

A voice caressed his ears, whisper soft.

"Iori."

Louder that time, rousing him from a drowsy darkness. The bed beneath him wasn't the cushy mattress that typically welcomed him to the world of the waking. It pressed at the bony blades of his shoulders, cold and hard against his scalp.

"Wake up."

The blanket of night didn't lift when he opened his eyes, but he could tell its starless depths stretched beyond the backs of his eyelids. He was on the ground again.

As he sat up, the floor shimmered like water trapped beneath glass, and that wasn't where the peculiarities ended. His street clothes had been replaced by formal attire. Polished shoes and pressed slacks, a waistcoat over a dress shirt—the entire ensemble composed of grays and blacks. Even his exposed forearms had been sapped of color.

Rising, he hiked up his sleeves, tugged open his collar, and peered under the cuff of his pants. Monochrome from head to toe, as if he'd been plucked from an old film.

"Iori."

There was that voice again.

He turned, markedly buoyant, expecting to find Ellen there. Her name slid to the tip of his tongue, but he held it when he saw the ghostly girl ahead. Masses of white hair drifted weightlessly about her, petite frame wrapped in a black dress that resembled an upturned calla lily. The petals fanned around her legs, floating too as if underwater.

Not Ellen. At least, not *his* Ellen.

This girl appeared crafted from porcelain. Skin polished to a glossy shine, no rouge upon her cheeks, and her eyes were blank—the same unblemished white as the rest of her.

"Hello." She spoke in a singsong tune that lacked the charming cadence he yearned for. The modest curve of her lips drooped, hair rippling with the tilt of her head. "What's the matter? Not happy to see me?"

"No," he said almost defensively; though, truth be told, there was a girl he'd rather see. "I just . . . thought you were somebody else."

She laughed, high and dizzy. "Silly. Who else would I be?" She padded over, hands clasped behind her. "You made me, didn't you? Conjured me up to escape that awful nightmare you were having."

Nightmare? His subconscious could produce a range of horrors, but it had never constructed anything like that circus and its hall of mirrors. "Are you saying none of that was real?" In the warped sense that illusions were.

"Nope," she replied, no popped P.

"Then what is this?"

The girl rose on her toes to speak in his ear, milky tresses eddying around him. "You're dreaming again." She smoothed the front of his waistcoat. "The difference is that this is your dream."

"It wasn't before?"

One of her hands slid around his shoulder, the other trailing featherlight up the slope of his neck. In the background, a piano played, and leisurely, she began to sway. "Mm-mm. *He* put you there."

Iori blinked at her in confusion. "He?"

"You don't remember?"

He shook his head, oddly at peace in her doppelganger arms. Her tenderness, the way she pulled him along to the entrancing melody, that haunting plink of the keys . . . if he didn't look, he could almost believe she were the real thing. If he didn't think too hard, maybe he could stay—here, in this place, this fantasy. With her.

She wouldn't let him.

"Allow me." Pressing the dip where his skull met his spine, she siphoned off that deluge of blissful unknowing, and it all came rushing back: the jingling bells, his run-in with the Sundered Star, the portal. The Void invading his body.

"Do you understand now?" she asked as he swayed against her. "The *you* out there hasn't been you for some time."

"I need to go." Distress whisked his statement into an airy plea. "How do I get out of here?"

"Come find me."

Her, she meant. The real Ellen. "How?"

"Circ sent you deep, hoping you would drown. But this is your mind, isn't it? Your subconscious. There's a place in here you can go where he can't reach." The piano's melody darkened, the girl's pace increasing with the rise in tempo. "So," she said, "dream deeper."

The dreamscape. He'd only ever accessed it from the physical plane, but if he could travel there from here, even if he couldn't reclaim his body, he should be able to contact the others.

Taking his left hand, the porcelain girl placed his right on her waist. "Close your eyes," she instructed, and he let the music take him. Let her pull him into her delirious dance.

"Allow yourself to fall from this plane into the next, and when you surface, I'll be waiting."

The tempo increased, a frenetic beat plucking at the fibers of Iori's soul as fevered steps carried them across the floor. It reminded him of their dance on the river, their waltz at the ball—only now, she was leading him. Guiding him back to her side in the real world.

I told myself I wouldn't run, and I did.

Around and around they whirled, a spinning top set loose.

But I'm coming back, and this time, I mean it. No more running.

Existence became a blur of music and motion, the fervid strike of the keys a fist hammering at the locked door of that other realm.

Faster.

Louder.

The melody rising until—

Iori pitched forward in his throne, eyes flying open to a world of dreary color as the final notes of the song trickled out of his brain. The porcelain girl and night-dark world had evaporated; however, the dreamscape he arrived in wasn't as he'd left it. This was the dreamscape that plagued his sleep.

Except now, it was real.

The trees leaked a sickly black sap, more oozing from the cracks in the stone floor. Already the Club and Diamond gates were partially submerged in it, the ground sunken beneath them and their light a colorful ripple on the surface, but the Heart—the Heart stood free, tides encroaching though not yet at its bars.

And in the depths of its crystal, a glow.

Iori sprung from his crumbling throne and sprinted across the clearing, ink sucking at his boots. A lethal pit of tar. Halfway there, he lost his footing and splashed into it on all fours, and that was when he spotted them—the inky rivers coursing beneath his skin, broken vessels spawning horrid bruises down the length of both arms.

Blight.

Just like the Club, the Spade was losing its fight. The corruption had begun to erode him from the inside out, and it would only be a matter of time before he succumbed to it.

But with Ellen, with the Heart, he had a chance.

He pushed onward, viscous strings snapping off his limbs and tail, the puddle threatening to pull him in again. Breaking free of its hold, he threw himself at the Heart's towering gate and slapped wet palms onto the gem's facets.

"Ellen," he begged, throat clenching her name like a lifeline. No vibration emanated from the ruby, no connection. Just a faint glimmer within—that tiny spark of light his last hope.

Which would break first: the Heart or the Spade?

Grasping the bars, Iori sank to his knees. "Please, please, please, please . . ." His desperation bubbled up into a cry. *"ELLEN!"*

CHAPTER FORTY-SEVEN
JANUARY 5 | HILDEGRAND, UPPER DISTRICT

Sirens and car horns blared distantly as Ellen and Iori picked their way through a sparsely wooded strip of the upper district. Between martial law and the Void outbreak sweeping through the lower district, Hildegrand had been thrown into panic. And what was Ellen doing?

Wandering aimlessly around the city.

The blended shades of twilight made it impossible to discern their exact location. Or their approximate location. All she could tell was that they were nearing the boundary fence. Past the trees and the few brittle leaves stubbornly clinging to their branches, she could see the bulbs blinking along its rim.

"Iori," she puffed, a burn in her calves and a stitch in her side. "Where are we going?"

He'd finally stopped on an overgrown bike trail, several strides ahead of her the whole trek. She'd assumed they would hunker down at one of his old hideouts, but he didn't seem to be leading her anywhere specific.

He also didn't seem to be *listening* to her.

She paused for a breather against the mossy trunk of a tree. "We need a place to hide. We're going to get caught." His back remained turned, ears forward. "Please tell me you have a plan and you're not just making this up as we go."

Still, he didn't answer.

Exhaustion and frustration and the effort to ignore her own anxiety-induced thoughts pushed her close to tears. She wasn't asking for much. "*Iori.*"

"Alright, alright. I think we've wasted sufficient time." He shoved something back into his pocket, his front dimming. A light going out. Had he been on his phone after Elizabeth explicitly told them to keep their devices *off* to prevent tracking? "I did have a place in mind. We've been there before." He gazed at her from the top of the hill. "Or, well . . . *you* have."

He snapped his fingers.

Cold gusted from below, and Ellen didn't have a chance to react before a bellowing blackness enveloped her. Icy talons slashed at the protective shell of her magic, that same ravenous malice she'd sensed at the Cavity, magnified tenfold, and the death throes of the underworld rattled in her skull even after it spat her out.

She crumbled onto a concrete floor, head spinning like she'd stepped off a moving carousel. Those sirens and horns wailed suddenly louder, intermixed now with shouts and gunfire. And Iori—

"Your kind's level of naiveté is impressive. Put on a pretty face, and you're sold."

No, that wasn't Iori's tone. Not the tempered Amethistian that rumbled playfully in his chest when he teased her. Not his dampened chill. This was sharp, frighteningly so, akin to the talons of the Void that gripped her moments ago.

She didn't have the knowledge to explain it earlier. Something else had been lurking behind the eyes that once tempted her to fall in, and when he discarded his eyepatch, there was no doubt. Both irises ignited blue, a ring around his regular pupil and the spade-shaped one engulfed.

The rhythmic soul who spoke her name like poetry had been pushed aside to make room for another.

The Sundered Star.

Shakily, Ellen got to her feet, hair lashing at her face in the blustering winds. The taller she rose, the further the ground sank, the river and roads a steep drop below. He'd teleported them all the way downtown to Herongate Bridge, to the very spot she'd taken her first—somewhat unwilling—leap of faith with Iori.

"Do you trust me?" he'd asked her then with that stupid Cheshire grin.

She would have given anything to see that smile now.

Was he still in there, locked up inside, or had Circ crafted a replica and buried the real Iori elsewhere? As quickly as it occurred to her, Ellen jettisoned the thought and steeled herself against Circ's knifing chill. "What have you done with him?"

He tapped his head. "Don't worry, he's tucked away safely. For now."

So it was Iori's body. "How is that even—"

"—possible? Easy." Circ hooked a finger in his turtleneck's circular zipper. "I had a way in."

He tugged the zipper down, and Ellen's heart skipped a nauseating beat when he unveiled the pulsating black mass on his chest—a parasite latched onto the inkwell, spewing poison into Iori's veins as it gorged on his life force.

"You're blighting him . . ." And with each passing second, those ghastly marks grew. "If you don't let him go, he'll die!"

Circ chuckled in a voice so achingly familiar yet alien in inflection that it brought fresh goosebumps to Ellen's skin. "That's the idea, princess." He zipped his shirt closed. "And with this mind and this Suit so encumbered by misery, it won't take long. Fortunately for you, I'm willing to make a deal.

"One way or another, the Heart's seal is going to break. It should happen naturally when the Waning reaches its peak, but your beau doesn't have that much time. Thus, my terms are these: Meet me at the Wiseman Estate at midnight. If you call the Heart of your own accord, I'll vacate this mortal form, and you'll have the power you need to save it."

"And if I don't?" Ellen dared ask.

His eyelids settled low over those gleaming irises. "Then you will lose him and doom the rest."

Something wasn't adding up. Why not extinguish Iori and the Spade now and wait for the Heart to awaken as intended? He would be eliminating a key opponent, and he'd get what he desired. By allowing her to call the Heart herself, wouldn't he be giving her an advantage?

Midnight, he'd said. He was on a deadline.

What did he stand to lose if he missed it?

That's not an option. He'd given her a deadline, too, and one she couldn't miss. But could he be trusted to hold up his end of the bargain? She could awaken the Heart, only for him to execute Iori immediately after.

Circ released a high little sigh. "You need to weigh your options. I understand." He retrieved Iori's phone from his jacket. "We have a few hours to go, and I've preparations to make. A troupe to coordinate, menageries to set free. When you've made up your mind, a chaperone will be waiting for you at your headquarters." He tossed the phone off the bridge, into the river below. "Stroke of midnight," he reminded her. "Don't be late."

With another snap of his fingers, a new portal opened, and the devil masquerading as her friend vanished into it. As soon as it closed, she collapsed back to her knees, knuckles pressed to stinging eyes.

Iori . . . I'm so sorry.

That night at the festival, a switch had flipped in him, and she hadn't even thought to check the circuits. She'd chalked it up to a blown emotional fuse, no clue that he'd been rewired by a wicked entity. If she had confronted him sooner, been more assertive, gone after him when—

Pull yourself together.

Circ had arranged for someone to take her to the estate from headquarters. She had to go and check that everyone was alright, and then she'd figure out how to deal with Circ.

The only problem would be getting *into* headquarters.

Ellen peered over the perimeter wall. Through the cherry tree grove, she counted six soldiers patrolling the yard, and the pair on the mansion's front porch didn't belong to Cardplay. These guys wore fancier outfits and carried bigger guns—automatic rifles in place of tasers and batons. Some even carried the full set.

How many weapons did they need?

She hadn't checked the rear entrance yet, but chances were they'd have every access point covered, and she wasn't equipped to go toe-to-toe with armed guards. Maybe she could climb the drainage pipes.

It couldn't be too difficult. People were always doing it on TV.

Gripping the top of the wall, Ellen hopped up and tried to lug herself over. She strained and strained, making no progress. How was she supposed to scale a building when she didn't even have the strength to mount a wall her height? Didn't help that she was already exhausted from the trek back uptown.

Her buckled shoes scraped at the concrete. If she could just hook an elbow over the—

A flash like lightning from behind lit up the trees ahead of her. Before she could turn around, someone hooked her by the middle and smothered her cry with a hand. She kicked off the wall, throwing them off balance, and they toppled backwards with her in their arms. The impact from the ground below and the flailing girl on top forced a pained grunt out of them, but they still didn't let go.

"Hold on a second! Would you stop—"

Ellen clamped her teeth onto the fingers covering her mouth, and with a yelp, they released her. Smacking her skull into their nose for good measure, she scampered clear, summoning her scythe in a hasty breath.

Her attacker rolled atop the browned winter grass, cradling their bitten hand. Tufts of tangerine flicked from under their beret. Freckles peppered the possibly-broken bridge of their bloodied nose, mingling with the ruddiness of their cheeks.

This man wasn't the soldier he was dressed up to be.

"You fecking *bit* me."

"You *grabbed* me." Ellen brandished her scythe, and Cardan McConnell tossed his hands, bitten and unbitten, in the air. Though *Scarlet Gem* posed no real harm to mundane beings, a small girl with a very large blade made for an imposing image. Technically, it could be as lethal as any other blunt weapon, but she wasn't about to bludgeon the guy. "What are you doing here?"

On the surface, it made sense. Wiseman was in town, so his goons would be skulking about too. In disguise, no less. Really, she wanted to know why he was sneaking around peeling fugitive girls off walls by hand when he had a stun gun in his belt and a pistol strapped to his thigh.

"I'm not here to hurt you," he claimed. "I'm a friend. Well, not a friend. An ally, if you'll have me. I was meant to be your escort to the estate." He sniffled, eyes watering as blood trickled from his nostrils. Served him right. "If you're here, does that mean you've agreed to—"

"No, I . . . I-I haven't decided yet." Her heart nudged her in one direction, her head another. "I came to make sure you people hadn't done anything else to hurt my family. Or my friends." She jerked toward him, and again he flinched away.

"We haven't, they're safe." Slowly, as not to startle her, Cardan wiped his nose and pinched it shut. "They've been confined to the arena, and you and me are going to break them out."

Had she heard that right? "Why would you want to do that?"

"*Why?*" Like the answer was stamped on his forehead. "Because I'm done being pushed around and having wool pulled over my eyes. I joined this godforsaken cause for the betterment of humanity. The end should have justified the means, but I can see no end that would justify what we're doing now. Circ's hellhounds are turning the downtown core into a bloody inkbath. We need Empowered on the field ASAP."

Ellen loosened her grip on her scythe.

"Please," Cardan pressed. "I want to help."

CHAPTER FORTY-EIGHT
JANUARY 5 | CARDPLAY HEADQUARTERS

WISEMAN'S TECHNOLOGY HAD BEEN INSTALLED in the arena to preserve structural integrity by deflecting and absorbing the impact of magics tested inside it. Alexander never imagined it would be used to turn it into a kennel.

The National Guard had corralled every known magically-inclined Cardplay affiliate into the pit, including medical staff and even contract workers. Pavati Varma had joined Tatiana and Soren in their glum corner, and Mira Hodge mingled with Cellier and Fornell.

Still comatose as far as new management was concerned, Hikaru had been left in the care of the unempowered nurses.

Alexander and his friends had parked themselves smack dab in the middle, the closest they could get to a vantage point. Not that anyone other than Alexander was utilizing it. Kyani hugged her knees in plaintive submission. Aryel, beaten down without any actual beating, had flopped onto his back. And Naomi's halfhearted interest was invested in her brother, who tampered with his collar while Alexander stared daggers at the guards.

They minded the pit from the safety of the upper level—a pair by the bleachers, one manning the door. Taking into account the distance, their anti-magic gear and armaments, and these damn collars, any attempt at escape would be futile. They wouldn't make it halfway before getting zapped, a jolt Ikkei was about to experience firsthand if he didn't—

BZZZT!

Ikkei went rigid, veins popping in his neck. The shock trapped a groan in his throat, and when the volts finally stopped, he doubled over. *"Motherfucker."*

"Prime example of the species, baby brother," muttered Naomi, chin in hand. She'd warned him about the tamper-proofing. Several times.

He shook out his arms, and Alexander could feel the phantom aftershocks in his own. "Please, a nine month gap does not make me the baby. We're practically twins."

"Thank god we're not. If I had to share a womb with you, we'd both be brain cell-deficient."

"Right, like your demonic bitch ass wouldn't have just absorbed me."

Too wrapped up in his dismal thoughts to pay any mind to them, Aryel mumbled to no one in particular. "I had plans, you know. Ambitions. Hopes. Dreams. My whole future was ahead of me. Now it's all crumbled into dust."

Naomi stroked his cheek with a metallic nail. "Sweetie, I'm gonna have to ask you to quit talking like we're dead. It's really depressing."

"This situation is depressing," Ikkei said. "They've got us locked in our own house like a bunch of wild animals." He hollered up to the guards, "You guys realize how messed up this is, right?"

They glowered but didn't waste energy on a rejoinder.

"Don't bother, Ikkei," muttered Alexander. "They're all bought and paid for." Wiseman would've cherry-picked the greediest, neediest magic-haters he could dig out of the woodwork. Rationale and empathy could not sway them.

The path Alexander had worn in the sand brought him to Kyani. She'd burrowed her black-scaled toes into the gritty granules. "How are you holding up?"

She hunched her shoulders, wings draped over the floor. "I thought my days in captivity were over. Guess I let myself dream a little too big." Her brow wrinkled, and Alexander gently nudged her with a knee. He could see where her mentality was drifting, felt his veering for that same perilous path, but he had no intention of giving in.

"We're going to get out of this," he said. *We have to.*

The mechanical whirr of the heavy doors silenced everyone in the pit, drawing their attention to the upper level. Kyani stood, her gaze locked on something as of yet unseen to the rest of them.

"Oh no . . ."

A second later, two people moved into view—that bastard Cardan guiding Ellen down the ramp by her elbow. Across the arena, Tatiana gasped and Soren's mouth hung open. But more than shock or worry or even anger, confusion had overtaken Alexander. The Sundered Star had lured Ellen out of the building himself. Why wasn't she still with him?

Her expression gave nothing away.

Cardan delivered her straight to the middle of the arena, to her brother, and Alexander couldn't help noticing his inflamed nose. "Looks like you got what you deserved, you filthy prick." Soon as Ellen was within reach, he pulled her into the security of his friends' circle. "Was it worth it?"

Hands up, Cardan retreated. "It will be," he said rather ominously, then vanished in a flash of pastel blue.

Alexander checked his sister over for injuries. "Are you hurt? What happened?"

She clasped his hands. "I'm fine. Just play along."

"Play along with—"

A scream ricocheted from above and wound down to a gurgle. Shouting in dismay, the guard pair by the bleachers whipped out their stun guns. Another flash, and Cardan rematerialized between them. With three cracks of his baton, he knocked one out and the other down, and an additional whack ensured the second stayed there.

He removed their radios, tethered them to the bleachers using their own cuffs. Then, overlooking the crowd of confounded Empowered from the top of the ramp, he held up the remote control for the collars. "I'll cut to the chase," he said. "You know who I am and who I've worked for, but I don't work for them anymore. I should've left when they put the hit out on Mayor Hargrove. I should've left when Charles Wiseman murdered Valerie Renard in prison."

Murdered? A weight Alexander didn't realize he'd been carrying lightened at the news. That hawk of a woman was dead—gone to the same hell as Kane Kros, he hoped.

Cardan wetted his lips. "There are a hundred and one reasons why I should've jumped ship earlier, and I don't expect forgiveness for the suffering I've caused. All I am asking is that you don't blow my head off."

He clicked the remote.

Beeps sounded throughout the arena, and Alexander could feel his magic flowing unrestrained again. Almost in disbelief, Kyani removed her collar. Ikkei and Naomi dropped theirs onto the ground. Aryel slipped more carefully out of his, as if afraid it might shock him.

Alexander peeled his own off and hucked it into the dirt. "Could you please explain what the hell is going on? Where's Circ?" he asked Ellen, then shot another shrapnel-filled glare at the alleged former Player descending the ramp. "And what the fuck are *you* playing at?"

Ellen positioned herself between him and Cardan. "It's okay, he's here to help. I wouldn't have gotten in without him."

"Are we supposed to believe he just had an epiphany and switched sides?"

"As I said, this has gone too far." Cardan slotted his baton into its holder. "Nay . . . we crossed that line a long time ago." He looked to Kyani, posture sagging. "I could write you a novel of should-haves, and it wouldn't change that I kept choosing to stay. But I'd rather go out trying to do something right than die fighting for something wrong."

Understanding glimmered in Kyani's lavender eyes. She strayed beyond the moral lines she had drawn as well, and Cardan had shown her kindness in the putrid bowels of that complex. Alexander still needed more. "One good deed won't earn our trust. Blackjack was a choice *you* made."

"And I'm not going to make excuses for myself. What I can do is be useful." Cardan passed the remote to Alexander. "We nabbed that from the office on our way in. Sergeant Moss has been taken care of and your battlemaster's safe, but Wiseman's guards still have the rest of the building under their control. You've got about thirty soldiers out there loaded with anti-magic prototypes."

Oskar flung his suppressor device into the growing pile on the floor. The collars weren't built for the girth of his neck, so they'd had to put an ankle bracelet on him instead. "What kinda prototypes are we talking?"

"Magic-piercing rounds. Stun grenades."

"How are we going to get past them?" fretted Soren.

"They're not invincible," Alexander said. All armor had a breaking point, and they didn't necessarily need to break anything in order to subdue the guards. "Repellent gear is only effective against certain types of magic. Their bullets also shouldn't be able to pierce non-magical barriers."

Whereas conjured matter would be a hit or a miss, manipulated mundane matter would make an effective weapon or shield, and the gear couldn't ward off non-offensive powers.

Xiaolin's mind was on the right track. "My clouds can decrease visibility. They can't hit targets they can't see!"

"I could disrupt their communications," Dax offered. With xyr hacking abilities, they could maintain the element of surprise.

Benji and Aziz volunteered as distractions; their molecular dispersion and lightning speed would make them difficult to track. The Hein Twins were also raring to fling themselves into the fray, but Alexander urged them to cool their jets. A mutiny wasn't an optimal scenario for a pair of yoyo-wielding rascals to shine.

They had a plan.

Now they had to hope it would work.

CHAPTER FORTY-NINE
JANUARY 5 | CARDPLAY HEADQUARTERS

THE GUARDS HADN'T BEEN PREPARED for their prisoners to revolt. Even with their shielding threads and anti-magic munitions, they were no match for a small army of highly-trained Empowered ready to prove their mettle. In a frenzy of kinetic energy, they divided, bound, and subdued every last one.

The mansion itself had suffered the brunt of the beating. Bullet holes peppered walls, chunks of drywall littered the halls, and some of the windows in the foyer and cafeteria had been blown out. But it was theirs again. They had the bruises to show for it. And as soon as it was secure, all guards locked in the purification chamber, Ellen rushed to the infirmary with her brother, the battlemaster, and Kyani in tow.

She reached Hikaru's room ahead of the others and took a moment to observe him—conscious, off the ventilator, lips cracked but no longer blackened—before throwing her arms around him. He stroked her hair as she sobbed apologies into his shoulder.

"Child, whatever are you sorry for?"

"I should've known. If I'd figured it out sooner—"

"*Hush.* Don't take this burden on yourself. You couldn't have guessed any sooner than I did."

Swift heels clacked upon the linoleum floor. Elizabeth strode over, Alexander and Dr. Fornell unhurried in her wake. "You are going to give me a heart attack one of these days, you know that?"

What would have sounded like venom to anyone else, the headmaster appeared to drink in like a sweet tonic. Her storm the herald of much-needed rain. "I'm sorry I worried you." He swept Ellen's snowy locks aside, the pulse oximeter on his finger gliding over her ear. "Where is the Sundered Star now?"

"He made me an offer—Iori for the Heart." She forced the rest out past an aching lump in her throat. "The exchange is set for midnight. At the Wiseman Estate. If I don't take the deal, Iori dies. But if I do, I'll be giving Circ the advantage. I don't know what to do."

Hikaru nodded, the contemplative groove in his brow solidifying into a resolute one. "Elizabeth, gather everyone in the foyer. It's time I shared something with you all."

Jokers and Keepers alike gathered beneath the crystal globe chandelier. Even Cardan McConnell hung at the fringes, welcomed only as his attendance came at Hikaru's behest. And when their headmaster emerged from the infirmary, preceded as always by the tap of his cane, they greeted him with dulcet applause.

This would be the first some had seen of him since the incident—charcoal ridges woven into his skin, ropes of scar tissue left where the blight had receded. Still weak on his feet, Elizabeth assisted him to the center of the room, where he beheld the crowd around him.

"As your headmaster," he began, vocal cords still rattling hoarsely, "I have asked for you to put your faith in me. To trust in my leadership and look to me for guidance. However, I must confess that my role required a great deal of secrecy, and there were many things I myself did not know until now. But in my absence, fate has dealt us a new hand, and with it, a wealth of knowledge."

Hikaru held out an upturned palm, and Ellen's breath stilled when a buoyant, dazzling object materialized above it. Its warm glow, refracted within a multitude of crystalline panes, glanced off the rim of Hikaru's fractured glasses.

"There is a balance in all things. In life and death, and in darkness and light. Once upon a time," he said, "the Domain and the Void operated in tandem with our world to maintain this balance."

The object exploded into a web of gleaming threads, evoking gasps from the crowd and bathing the foyer in gold. They spun an image of two adolescent figures in fetal positions, heads bowed together and fingers entwined—one feminine with long silk tresses, the other more masculine with an untamed plume of hair on his head.

"In the beginning, two Stars presided over the realms. Radiant and Lambent. As Warden of the Domain, Her Radiance held a sacred duty to usher departed souls unto the Aether. Similarly, as Warden of the Void, His Lambent Grace was charged with the condemnation of the wicked to the underworld."

The image morphed, the twins now standing back to back. The girl craned her neck, the threads of her face gleaming brightly as though basking in the sun.

"Her Radiance was loved by the masses, a receptacle for praise and prayers. But Lambent . . ." The boy's head hung low in his sister's shadow, and Hikaru's tone dropped to a grave depth. "Lambent became the antagonist of cautionary tales and bearer of woebegotten wishes. This grievance bred resentment, and that resentment created a crack."

The boy's hands snapped to his scalp as it split down the middle, his luminance fading as something dark and sinister poured in. Both figures dissolved into a vortex—a star, plummeting through the atmosphere. It struck an unmade surface, the horizon erupting in a mass of claws and teeth at the point of impact.

"In a bout of rage, Lambent unleashed the Void on our world by tearing the barrier that separates us from it asunder. For these heinous crimes against humankind, he was subsequently divested of title and duty, named Sundered, and exiled to the Cavity by his sister."

Threads scattered, a dulling glow. Ellen took her brother's hand, for the rift that once divided them had only recently been mended.

Hikaru went on. "But trouble did not cease with his imprisonment. The Sundered Star's actions caused irrevocable damage to the barrier, and without a warden to temper the Void, it continued to wreak havoc on the mundane world. To remedy this, the Suits were born."

The strings wove each symbol in turn until all four hovered in a circular formation below the chandelier.

"The Heart would aid the Radiant Star in cleansing the blighted so that they could replenish the Aether. Meanwhile, the Diamond and Club would serve as auxiliaries to the Domain and the Void, slaying wicked souls in the mundane world. And the Spade," he said, "would preside over the Void in the warden's stead."

A pang shot through Ellen when that hollow wire frame took shape in front of her, pointed at the top and widening into two angular arcs atop a narrow stem.

"The Radiant Star bestowed these powers upon her four chosen champions, and for a time, peace was restored." The Suits reformed, thinning into humanoid figures with the symbols stamped on their chests. "But just as the Stars were not infallible, neither were the Keepers." One by one, the figures unraveled. Spade, Club, Diamond, Heart. "Using his wiles against them, the Sundered Star broke free from his prison . . . and extinguished his sister's light."

Strands retracted, rewound into their spool—that tiny object floating above the headmaster's palm. "She died," he said, the foyer dimming, "and the mundane world plunged into chaos."

"The Cataclysm," Kyani surmised quietly.

Hikaru dipped his chin in sobering affirmation. "In order to end the Sundered Star's rampage, the Keepers used their own life force to seal the realms, thereby severing his connection to magic and trapping him in Elysian Tower. They made this sacrifice knowing that, one day, the Radiant Star would be reborn, and when that time was nigh, their Suits would seek out new champions to unite her contingency fragment—*this* fragment—with the protostar in the Domain. Without it, the protostar will evolve into a young and vulnerable warden with no memory of her previous iteration or the mistakes she made.

"My purpose as the Guiding Light was to bring the four of you together so that you could see this process through. She entrusted a piece of herself to me, and now I entrust it to you." Hikaru held the object out to Ellen.

She recoiled. "M-me?"

"I assure you, my dear, there is no one better suited to the task. With the Heart and your soul combined, you have a resistance to the Void like no other. Even if the Sundered Star realizes it has switched hands, he cannot take it from you unless you surrender it by choice." He offered it to her again. "Do you accept?"

Ellen watched those panes shiver and shrill. Then, at an encouraging touch from her brother, she nodded. If this was what it would take to win, she couldn't decline.

Tucking his cane under his arm, Hikaru transferred the object to her. A brilliant light engulfed her as he closed her fingers around it, the fragment weaving itself into the fabric of her Suit. And when it was done, she felt markedly unchanged.

Hikaru squeezed her hands, beaming in his subtle way with pride. "My duty is done. The rest falls to you." He looked over the three Keepers. "You must deliver this fragment to the Astral Pool by first light on the seventh, at the height of the Waning."

Kyani's wings straightened. "What do we do about Circ?"

"He must be vanquished before the rebirth, or else we risk losing the fragment and the protostar both." Hikaru rested on his cane. "There is an instrument in the Domain with the power to disrupt the Sundered Star's link to the Void—the *Lustral Organ*—but only one can play it."

"The Spade," Elizabeth clarified.

"The *pure* Spade," Hikaru corrected.

"Who's currently being held hostage outside the city." Alexander huffed. "How do we get him back?"

Ellen had a solution. "By giving Circ exactly what he asked for."

Predictably, her brother wasn't fond of it.

"We are not doing that, it's too dangerous." For once, his worries weren't unfounded. She'd be throwing herself directly into the line of fire and praying she wouldn't get hit. "If the seals have been keeping the Void contained all this time, there's no telling what hell we'll unleash by breaking the last one."

Regardless of what they did, that hell would soon come for them. "It's going to break by itself anyway. Isn't it better if we do it on our own terms?" Her brother had no immediate counterargument, so she pressed on. "We have to get this fragment to the Domain. To do that, we need the Heart, and to stop Circ, we need Iori."

Alexander worked his jaw. "Say you do this. Say you agree to this deal. Never mind how risky that is, how do you intend to get to the estate when we're under lockdown?"

Wary under the Jokers' scrutiny, Cardan entered the discussion, beret gripped to his chest. "That's where I come in. I can bypass fence security and teleport her there in half the time it would take to drive. And for the record," he said, "she's more of a threat to Circ than he is to her. He and Wiseman can't get near her without putting themselves in danger, hence the human shield."

Iori. That explained why he'd insisted on keeping his distance from her since the festival. Circ had been trying to preserve not only his cover, but his safety.

A skeptical Ikkei looped his arms. "What's Wiseman's deal?"

"He's some brand of Void-touched. Circ has this influence over him, and the imp himself's made from ink. To them, her magic is holy water, which is why he wants to meet at the estate. There are leylines connecting magical wells all across the globe, Hildegrand being the largest and most plentiful at the nexus. The further you travel from it, the weaker your power gets."

Ellen's brow scrunched. "Circ knew I wouldn't have the power to save Iori there even if I woke the Heart . . ."

"Aye. Of course, he also didn't account for you being in possession of his sister's fragment." Cardan pointed his beret at her. "According to Circ, that thing is what saved us from being thrown into an apocalypse when the Spade's seal broke. It's the reason we have magic in the mundane world today. With that, not only could you save your friend, you might even be able to do a number on Circ."

An *ooh* from Tatiana. "It's like a video game buff!"

Sabine Brozak ushered in a concern. "If she takes it out of the city, are we going to be weaker here?"

"Marginally, maybe. Might burn out faster, but Elysian Tower's energy output should sustain you."

Every route entailed sacrifice; it was just a matter of which sacrifices they were willing to make and which risks they were prepared to take. Ellen had made her mind up. "I'm going."

"Then I'm going with you," Alexander declared.

"You're not," said Cardan. "I can't move more than one person at a time." Not to mention, her brother tagging along would be cause for trouble.

"That's fucking convenient. So how are you going to bring them both back? Or were you planning to strand them out there?"

Cardan lifted a finger to retort, then curled it. "I haven't gotten that far. But not every step needs to be set in stone. The most important step is step one, and we're on a deadline to put it in motion."

Ire smoldered in Alexander's eyes. "And how do you expect me to trust a goddamn word out of your mouth after you people abducted, caged, and beat the shit out of me?"

An uneasiness settled over the room, then Kyani stepped in to cool the coals Blackjack had set alight. "I'll vouch for him," she told Alexander, to Cardan's apparent shock. "You learned to trust me, right? He was there for me at the complex when nobody else was, and we need him. Give him a chance to prove his loyalty."

"While we do what?"

"Our jobs," said Elizabeth. She swept her gaze over the Jokers. "All hands, meet me in the command centre in ten. If Charles Wiseman thinks he can quash us that easily, he's got another thing coming."

CHAPTER FIFTY
JANUARY 5 | CARDPLAY HEADQUARTERS

To await departure after the meeting, Ellen had gone to dorm 3A. Iori's dormitory. This was where their bond had truly begun to form, in this room with the filigree trellis wallpaper he hated and the plush bedspreads they'd lounge on in their downtime. Though devoid of actual decor, memories hung like photographs on the walls.

Here, he'd sent her that first goofy text.

Here, she'd spilled her secret to him.

By that wardrobe, he transformed from a charmingly bedraggled thief into a damn-near dapper gentleman. And in that bathroom, she'd held him as his body threatened to shake apart in the quakes of his rattled heart.

This distance between them had torn a hole in hers. A spade-shaped one aching to be filled by the boy she'd carved it out for. It scared her to think it might never be full again.

Her motionless feet pressed shoeprints into the carpet as her mind wandered the beaten path of worst-case scenarios: if she failed, if her Suit didn't wake, if the fragment didn't give her sufficient power to save Iori. If she lost him without ever getting to—

The creak of a door interrupted her spiraling thoughts as Alexander entered the dorm.

"Is it time?" she asked. If she had to wait much longer, she would wring her hands to the bone.

"Almost." He scratched his head, the metallic beads of his hair ribbon clattering lightly. Ellen had given hers an extra tug for good luck, and hoped his would bring him the same. They would need every bit they could get. "Ellen, are you sure about this?"

What she didn't need was her brother piling his doubts on top of her already mountainous heap. "I thought we cleared this up."

"We did—"

"Then what are you asking for?" She couldn't have him reprising his overprotective big brother role when she was about to take a leap with somebody who until very, very recently had been swinging for the opposing team. "We don't have any other options. Yes, it's dangerous, and Cardan could be playing us, but if we don't at least try, Iori is going to *die*."

"And I get that—"

"Then why can't you just let me do this?"

"Because I'm fucking scared, okay?"

The crack and splinter of her brother's voice stunned her. His chest heaved, the confession a long-held breath, and with its ardent release, the steely suit of bravery he wore fell away, leaving naked terror in its place.

"I am terrified that if you leave, I won't see you again. For fuck's sake, Ellen, you are *one person* against a several thousand-year-old Star. How are you so confident you can get Iori back from him?"

She held his gaze in solemn resolve. "I'm the only one who can."

Alexander's shoulders dropped—in defeat or reluctant acceptance, Ellen couldn't be sure. But she was sure of this.

She strode forward into his arms, a fortress like her father's, and bolstered it with the newfound scrapings of her own courage. "Hildegrand needs you. Go be the hero your fans always fawned over, and I'll be home before you know it."

"I'll do my best." He planted a kiss upon her hair and withdrew as the going away party arrived.

Tatiana and Soren crashed in, sweeping Ellen up in a hug. After nearly squeezing the life out of her, they filled her up again with well wishes, which she gratefully returned. They would be in good care, assisting Oskar and Sabaa in the evacuation efforts.

They couldn't shelter an entire city's worth of people in Cardplay Headquarters, but they would take in as many vulnerable people as possible from the high-risk zones and direct others to hospitals, banks, schools—anywhere that could protect them from or elevate them above the spreading Void outbreak. The farther uptown they could get, the better.

Cardan, Kyani, and the masters trailed in next.

"All set?" asked Hikaru.

Despite being a quaky bundle of nerves, Ellen nodded.

Elizabeth straightened the lapels of her peacoat, her Joker medallion hidden beneath it. "When you get to Fort Worth, ask for Marshal Kulisch. Tell them I sent you." The military installation was a stone's throw from the Wiseman Estate. If everything went according to plan, they would travel there afterwards and return to Hildegrand with the cavalry in tow.

The outside world was oblivious to the chaos unfolding within the fence. Blackjack had knocked the city off the grid. Internet, telephones, power—all down. They couldn't call for reinforcements or organize a proper evacuation. This would be their chance to blow the whistle.

"Questions or concerns?" asked Cardan.

"One," said Ellen, though in truth she had oodles more. "How many jumps will it take to get there?" Her only teleportation experience thus far had been via Void portal, and if this ride were similar, she wanted to know how long it would be until she could get off.

"Em, well, I haven't made the full trip by teleportation before. Accounting for the distance, the additional mass, and fluctuating magical output . . . A few."

Helpful, thought Ellen with mild sarcasm.

Kyani must've sensed her apprehension. "It's not too different from the transition between the physical world and the dreamscapes. It might be disconcerting initially, but you should get used to it on the journey."

Infinitely more reassuring.

Alexander went to issue one last warning as Cardan stepped in beside Ellen, readjusting his beret. "If you don't bring her back . . ."

"You'll roast me like a lamb on a spit. I know." Cardan placed a hand on Ellen's shoulder, confirmed she was ready, and as he started his version of a countdown, she burned the image of her friends and family into her brain. "Alright, here we go. Just a hop, skip, and a—"

Jump.

CHAPTER FIFTY-ONE
JANUARY 5 | HILDEGRAND, LOWER DISTRICT

THE ISSUE WITH CURFEWS WAS THAT FEW CARED to abide by them whilst their city was being invaded by monsters. Those not content to rely on the safety of their homes or workplaces fled instead to their cars or the streets, thinking if enough people piled up at the gates, they would be extricated from the city.

Nobody had been allowed to leave during the Reemergence lockdown either, and Alexander doubted the man in league with the corrupted ex-warden of the underworld would make an exception. If he had to guess, neither intended to let anyone out at all.

Wiseman wanted carnage—the bloodier, the better. Another disaster of his own making, meant not to garner reverence but obedience. He'd won their hearts with valor, and would seize their souls with fear.

"I think we've glossed over a problem," Aryel piped up as they barreled down Main Street in Ikkei's SUV. "Everyone knows we're under a cease and desist order. This is the opposite of ceasing and desisting."

He and Naomi were buckled into the middle row, the four of them en route to meet the National Guard's local unit. With communications out, they followed the chaos in the hopes it would lead them to where they'd set up shop and prayed Elizabeth could hail them over the ham radio first.

"If Elizabeth makes contact, they should welcome us with open arms," Alexander said. Their leader, General Eze, was a longtime ally and had her own reservations about Charles Wiseman before being brought into the loop for the raid. They could rely on her support. "Worst case, they arrest us."

"Or they could shoot us on sight," Naomi added flatly. "'*Dealt with appropriately*' has some pretty fatal connotations."

Navigating the obstacle course of abandoned vehicles clogging the roadway, Ikkei grumbled, "Trust you to chime in with the inspiring battlefield sentiments."

She reached into the front to flick his ear.

"Ow, hey! No flicking the driver!"

Alexander glared at them from the passenger seat. "Would you two knock it off?" This wasn't the time for petty squabbling. Kyani and the others were depending on them to keep enemy forces at bay in the lower district so they could safely evacuate mid.

They had to focus.

"Take a right on Queen," he directed Ikkei. "That's where they set up their encampments for the—"

The scent hit him—sharp, metallic, like pennies on his tongue—and as they swung around the bend, the street ahead exploded into roiling smoke and flame. Ikkei slammed on the brakes, bringing the SUV to a screeching halt. Soldiers fled from the blast, two diving behind an abandoned car, firing skyward.

Alexander squinted into the smoke. "What are they . . ." He trailed off as the acrid cloud cleared, unveiling an Inkblot unlike any he'd ever seen: giraffe-like in stature with a sloping body that tapered into a whip of a tail at one end, and a three-meter neck at the other. Eyes bulged along the length of it, covering its head and torso too—dozens in varying shapes and sizes, gleaming blue like the veins pulsing on its flanks.

"That's new," said Naomi.

The soldiers kept firing, and the Inkblot kept soaking up bullets like a sponge. If they were dealing any damage, it didn't show. It pounced almost playfully at three soldiers who ran into a corner shop, thrusting spindly limbs through the doors after them.

Ikkei put the SUV in park. "Suppose if we save their lives, they'll realize how much they need us and forgive the cease and desist violation?"

"I don't think they're gonna need much convincing." Alexander threw off his seatbelt and the four Jokers exited the vehicle. Wind funneled hot and cold through the street. Ikkei, Naomi, and Aryel summoned their kits—whips, chains, and staff, twin ensembles of belted vinyl, and a hooded fur-lined cloak fit for the season.

"Come, *Magnelink!*"

"Come, *Dynamo.*"

"Come, *Frostweaver!*"

Alexander lagged behind. They never made it to the fully-kitted sparring stage of their Keeper 101 sessions, and the last time he wore his Suit, Valerie had forced him into it. He hadn't summoned it himself since its initial awakening.

Buying himself a moment to work up the nerve, he dealt out orders to his teammates. "It can't fight all of us at once. Ikkei, Naomi—get in behind it." They dashed into an alley, and he pointed to the sidewalk. "Aryel, see that hydrant? Catch it from the side if you can." He set his sights on the target. "I'll take it head-on."

Aryel split as Alexander marched forward. Every strike of rubber soles on the asphalt ricocheted through his legs, grounding him.

Alright. Let's show them what we're made of.

"Awaken," he said, and like a strike of the flint, he ignited it: *"Blazing Diamond!"*

Embers washed over him in a reverse burning effect, enrobing him in a crisp white poet shirt, breeches, and a tailed vest of black leather. Jacket cuffs became gold-studded vambraces, gloves became gauntlets. He wrapped both around the hilt of his sword and sucked the smoke-laden air in through his teeth, Void particulates like magnesium in his windpipe.

A pained shout drew the Inkblot's attention to the overturned car and the soldiers sheltering there. It gave up on the three in the store and started towards them. Easy prey.

Drawing his blade from its scabbard, Alexander held the weapon vertical and brought two fingers to the fuller. As he ran them up the groove, heat trailed in their path, turning it a lethal orange. The diamond set in its pommel glowed.

Aryel was in position, hidden from the Inkblot's view.

Cover blown, the uninjured soldier hefted his rifle and sprayed. Unfazed by the torrent of lead, the Inkblot planted a reptilian paw on the side of the car and reared back its head, preparing to strike.

Enkindle, the command sparked in Alexander's mind.

And with an upward sweep of his gauntlet, he set the air ablaze. Flames erupted up the creature's front in a firecracker stream, and globs of burning ink rained over the bewildered soldiers below.

"Get inside!" Alexander hollered, drawing up to the crumpled car. The uninjured soldier gaped at him, then gathered his comrade and made for the nearest door. "Aryel, now!"

Slipping out from his hiding place, Aryel cracked open the hydrant. Pressurized water burst from its valve, flooding the ground beneath the Inkblot while errant jets scored its underbelly. It yowled in surprise, unbalanced, and collided with a row of buildings flanking the road.

Aryel's crystal-tipped staff brightened as he poured his cryogenic magic into it. He tapped it on the ground, cast his freezing spell upon the water. The liquid popped and hissed and solidified, trapping the creature's feet in ice. Frost swirled up its legs and body, icing over its numerous eyeballs.

It didn't hold.

The Inkblot wrenched free, snapping frozen limbs clean off and sprouting new ones in their place. A kick from its rear stump sent Aryel careening into toppled waste bins, and before Alexander could deliver another strike, it swept him into a van with a great swing of its head.

Aluminum dented, the impact knocking the wind out of him, and he hit the asphalt with a different copper tang on his tongue. Six months off the field had left him rusty.

"That's cheating!" shouted Aryel, fogging the creature's hindquarters with more frost. His magic alone wouldn't be enough to stop it.

It lunged for Alexander while he was down, liquid jaws and vitrified fangs snagging him by the boot. It hauled him through debris and water and ice, and then those teeth chomped down on his middle—over and over and over. If not for the natural barrier of magic shielding him from its bite, it would have gored him.

Rusty or not, he wouldn't be made a sparkling Void giraffe's chew toy. When its jaws opened next, he slashed it across the maw, cutting through ink-wet cheeks. It dropped its catch and recoiled, chewing on a mouthful of embers instead.

Relentless and angry, the creature came at him again. Still on the ground, Alexander blasted it with a cone of fire. Searing yellow enveloped black and blue—interrupted by a flash of silver.

Ikkei's magnetically-controlled chains looped around the Inkblot's hind legs and yanked them out from under it, sending it crashing to the street. Its jaws snapped shut a foot from Alexander, and he raised his arm against the wafted cloud of ash and grit. Past the hump of the Inkblot's shoulders, he spotted Ikkei, muscles bunched from the effort.

Even he couldn't keep it down.

Despite the chains and the crust of ice clinging to its hindquarters, the creature dragged itself up on its forelegs, pulling Ikkei with it. Alexander pushed to his feet, preparing another attack.

Where had Naomi disappeared to?

Right on cue, she appeared—a bolt of lightning striking down between her brother's chains. Magic arced around her in jagged lines, fully charged, and she grasped the bulky metal links in her white-knuckled grip.

"*Chain . . .*" began Ikkei.

"*. . . Reaction!*" Naomi finished.

Their latest technique.

Volts shot through iron, fed directly into the Inkblot. It let loose an ear-splitting shriek, paws scrabbling at the pavement. Eyeballs squinted, bulged, and burst, streamers of luminous fluid flung about as it tossed its head. When at last it succumbed to the torturous currents, the creature slopped into a puddle of liquid and slush, its starlight fading.

Steam coiled off Alexander's cooling blade, and Naomi went to check on her rattled boyfriend as Ikkei's chains retracted into their holder on his back.

"See?" he said. "They're not so tough."

Three Jokers and a Keeper to take down one Inkblot wasn't what Alexander would define as an easy kill. Smaller forms could be overwhelming in packs, but individuals only posed a real threat to mundane folks. Run-ins with them never left him feeling like a tenderized cut of meat.

Sheathing his sword, he crossed the street to the jewelry store the two soldiers had ducked into. Broken glass crunched under his boots. Colorful gemstones and accessories lay strewn, their cases shattered.

The soldiers had hunkered down by the cash counter, a makeshift tourniquet that may once have been a cashier's lanyard tied around the injured one's leg. Both looked up as the Jokers walked in, presenting a mixture of emotions on soot-mucked faces. Awe, fright. Shock, mostly.

"I'm Alexander Jane. These are my teammates. I don't know what you've been told about Cardplay, but we're here to help." The bloodstain on the injured soldier's thigh was expanding by the second. "I'd like to start by cauterizing that wound, if you'll let me."

No currency more valuable than aid.

Ignoring his comrade's shaking head, the uninjured soldier accepted the offer on his behalf. "Do it. Please."

Alexander crouched by them, clenching and unclenching his fist to stimulate his pyric energy. "Was he bitten?"

"No, shrapnel. Ripped right through."

Good, thought Alexander. His powers wouldn't have had any effect on blight, and with his sister away, the man would've been a goner. Palm heated to an orange-red glow, he directed the injured soldier to remove his hands from the wound. The man uttered *mercy* under his breath, and Aryel swiftly exited the building.

"I'm out. I'm out, I'm out, I'm out."

"You might wanna hold him down," Alexander advised the other soldier, and he did so despite his comrade's whimpered pleas. "It's either this or you bleed out, and I'm willing to bet you're not ready to die."

"No. No, no. No, no, no, no, no . . ."

It could have been an answer, or the only word his panicked mouth could form. Whatever it was, it transformed into a shriek when Alexander pressed his hand to the wound. And as nauseating as the sizzle of flesh under his gauntlet was, it couldn't compare to the smell. Sulfurous singed hair, the hot metallic stench of coagulating blood. Something akin to charred steak coated the back of Alexander's throat.

The man passed out partway through, his plea for mercy granted. Unable to stomach it any longer, Ikkei checked out next. His sister stayed, perhaps out of morbid curiosity.

After another few seconds, Alexander removed his hand and was relieved to see the bleeding had stopped. Never having used magic to cauterize a wound before, he wasn't certain it would work. "What are your names?" he asked, flapping his hand to banish the heat.

"This here is Franco," the uninjured soldier said, folding his unconscious comrade's arms in his lap. "I'm Mabini."

"Are you with General Eze's unit?"

A sharp nod.

"Take us to her."

CHAPTER FIFTY-TWO
JANUARY 5 | FOLKLAN CLIFFS

DISCONCERTING DIDN'T EVEN BEGIN TO COVER the first leg of Ellen's fabric-of-space-splitting journey with Cardan. Thankfully, by the time they reached the Folklan Cliffs, Kyani's prediction had proven correct, and Ellen had grown accustomed to being yanked through wormholes.

Mostly, anyway.

"Whoa, steady. Steady." Cardan caught her when she teetered sideways, pine needles crackling under her buckled shoes. Their cloying fragrance laced the cliffside air, thinner and brisker here than in the city far away and miles below.

Ellen hadn't been this far from home in years.

"Well, here we are," Cardan announced grimly. "The Wiseman Estate."

The building stood at the top of a paved driveway, brittle ivy creeping along its creamy stucco walls and darkened windows. A rustic Ammolitian shell with a rotten core, wherein countless skeletons lay in closets of unfathomable depths.

"C'mon then. Best not keep the Warden waiting." Cardan took Ellen by the elbow and led her indoors, through the tiled entry hall and up a creaky flight of carpeted stairs. Every square inch of the place was infused with scents of aging wood and paint and, most notably, pine.

No wonder Iori couldn't tolerate the smell.

Two months he'd spent here, a prisoner of the devil's advocate, and here he was again—a captive of the devil himself, whose mere presence dragged the air temperature to a chilling low. The corruption rolled over Ellen like a spilled gust from a refrigerator, raising the hairs on her neck when she saw him.

Their meeting place had been arranged to resemble a throne room. A narrow rug spanned the hardwood floor, leading from the entrance to an antique chair, where Circ reclined in his stolen suit of flesh. Moonlight streamed in from a large bay window, silvery rays catching the edge of that parasitic mass on his chest—shirt unzipped to put it on full display.

The blackness curling outward from the scar now licked up his neck, squiggly lines reaching for his right eye and flowing down both arms. Polluted rivers charting the wasteland of his body, at the core of which Ellen hoped to find an oasis.

Gazing upon that ragged landscape, she couldn't hide her fear that there wasn't one.

Let him see, she thought. Let him see the fear, and believe what so many others did: that she was weak, no more than a piteous mortal girl he could bend to his whims. A delicate flower whose petals would bruise at the slightest pinch.

But every rose had its thorns.

So she allowed the tears to well, wore her sorrow on her sleeves. Tonight, her heart would be her sword and shield, and if she had fortune's favor, its enduring beat would be her victory song.

Cardan stooped respectfully. Ellen did not.

A fang glinted in the curl of Circ's smile, his gaze affixed on her. His prize. "Hello, doll." His focus then slid to Cardan. "You can go."

Go? That wasn't part of the plan.

Ellen resisted the urge to glance at her chaperone. If she gave any indication that they were allied, she could jeopardize his position. Jeopardize this whole mission. Perhaps he thought the same, because he didn't look at her either.

With the faintest note of well-masked hesitation, he asked, "Where to?" Unless he was putting on an act for her, he hadn't foreseen this snag any better than she had.

"Business. In the city," Circ stated ambiguously.

"I just got here."

"And now you're leaving." No patience for his subordinate's whinging, Circ gave a dismissive wave. "Hop along. Wouldn't want you to miss the pre-show."

Cardan was a pawn, an expendable piece. If he did not bow, he would be broken. And bow once more he did before he blinked out of existence, leaving Ellen stranded without a life raft. Should he fail to turn up where he was supposed to be, his double agent days would be over.

Alone in the moonlit room, Circ's frigid existence loomed larger than ever. He gestured to the pitcher and two crystal glasses on the table to his right, one of which had already been filled halfway. "Might I interest the lady in a beverage?"

Would it have occurred to him to spike it? "No, thank you," she replied stiffly, not willing to gamble on refreshments.

Circ scrutinized her, running a black-nailed finger around the rim of the partially-filled glass. "Your lack of reciprocation gave me the impression that the romance was unrequited this time. After all, it would have been cheap for fate to play that card twice in a row. But originality be damned, you have fallen for him, haven't you?"

Her refusal to respond proved adequate to him.

"Thought so. It's written all over your face. Ophelia wore the same expression when I turned Vy against her. Inseparable, those two. Doomed from the moment they laid eyes on one another." He picked up his drink, giving it a swirl. "This love of yours is a disease, but if you deign to pursue it, who am I to deny you the nail in your coffin?"

"Why are you doing this?"

"Why does anyone do anything?" He sipped at the sparkling liquid.

Because they want something, thought Ellen. "Okay," she said, and posed the very same question that had been nagging at her for weeks: "What do you want?"

"What do I want?" She flinched at the slam of his glass. "*What do I want?*" He laughed a wild laugh and pushed up from his chair. "Oh, I don't know, a little *recognition* might be nice."

Pain lanced through his voice—a whip-like crack and a flare of damp, sorrowful cold. Somewhere inside him, the sores of a millenniums-old loneliness wept.

He cast his gaze to the window, caught a moonbeam in his palm. "*Star light, star bright, first star I see tonight* . . . Funny how the only star anyone ever saw was my sister. And what a beacon she was—a ray of hope for the wretched and damned. But the thing about bright lights is that they can cast harsh shadows." The beam played between his fingers. "At least . . . until they go out."

He closed a fist.

"It didn't have to come to this." Ellen chanced a step toward him. If the Sundered Star had been corrupted by the Void, maybe it wasn't too late for him to detach from it. "You can still make this right. Protect this world like you were meant to—don't destroy it!"

"Destroy it? You've got it wrong, little doe. I'm not going to destroy it. I plan to make it anew." There was a wicked glint in his eye. "The realms have always been separate. Divided. I intend to unite them. No more above, no more below. No more prayers or blessings or less than, more than. One realm, one people, and one Star to rule. I just need *one* more thing."

The grandfather clock in the corner chimed.

Midnight.

Circ tugged his shirt open further. "The Heart, if you will."

If Ellen were to attempt a purification, she needed him closer. Needed him stationary. She studied the undulating mass attached to the inkwell, which he'd claimed to be his way in.

Could it also be used to flush him out?

"Okay," she agreed. "But we're doing this my way." Fury flashed across Circ's face when she called a name that did not belong to the fabled Suit. "Come, *Scarlet Gem!*"

Before her kit had finished forming, she cast forth a cleansing wave with a swing of her scythe. It crashed into Circ, into Iori, and he howled in agony as smoke peeled off his skin, pinpricks of ruby skittering over the blackened parts of his body.

Holy water.

It didn't stun him long enough to execute her next move.

"You *bitch*." Circ shot across the room at an alarming speed, slamming her against a bookcase. Books shook loose, and she dropped her scythe when those nimble musician's fingers clamped onto her neck. "The deal's changed," he spat. "Awaken the Heart, or I will make sure he knows it was his hands that ended your pathetic life!" He hoisted her off the floor, thumbs crushing her windpipe. "Right before I end his."

Fresh blight slithered under Iori's skin, quick as the adrenaline shooting through Ellen. Circ had accelerated the process, but in his outburst, he'd made a mistake. He'd crossed his own boundary and put himself within her reach.

She met his wild eyes, vision spotty. "Deal."

Channeling her magic into her right arm, she plunged her hand into the inkwell—punching straight through the parasitic mass and eliciting a yelp from Circ. His grip faltered, tightened, and his tone turned shrill.

"What are you doing?!"

"I'm giving you what you wanted," Ellen choked out, "but I'm taking Iori back." Regardless of how they did it, there was one thing the other Suits' awakenings had in common besides being weakened by the Rending Machine: Each had come to their Keepers in a moment of need.

The Spade to Iori's rescue.

The Club to Kyani's aid.

The Diamond to Alexander's defense.

This was her moment.

Please. She screwed her eyes shut. *I need you.*

Drip.

A drop of onyx splashed into the shallow waves sloshing against Iori's legs. First came the ache, a dull throb behind his retina, and then the tears, unbidden, dotted his lashes. How much longer, he wondered, till he melded with the rising tides?

Drip.

His hands had gone numb on the gate's iron bars, his pleas a hush from tired lips. He didn't dare look back for fear that all that lay behind him was an ocean of black. Kept his head bowed between his elbows, mining whatever pale semblance of bliss he could from purposeful unknowing.

The blight was getting harder to ignore.

Drip.

Drip.

The drops ran a little quicker, a little thicker, as he grew colder. Emptier. This was inevitable, Iori knew. An infection could remain latent only for so long before it festered and spread.

Drip.

Drip.

Drip.

Lacking the strength to fight it anymore, Iori surrendered to the fatigue that had been weighing on his eyelids. The Void's drone drowned out the sickly lap of the waves, a steady undulation in his skull that, for once, almost sounded peaceful. White noise, lulling him into an incurable slumber.

And maybe

giving in

wouldn't

be

so—

Ting.

A new noise cut through the din. Iori's ears pricked to the loudening clangor of wind chimes, and relief flooded warm through his extremities. He would recognize that magical frequency anywhere.

Ellen.

He craned his neck to the ruby above him. Light fluctuated within, brighter and stronger with every pulse, and the listless thump behind his ribs rose to match it. Splaying trembling fingers over its facets, he detected the faintest vibration.

The beat of the waking Heart.

In a blink, Ellen had been transported from the salon at the estate to a throne of fibrous ivory. Bleached white trees, crimson leaves aquiver, bordered the snow-dusted clearing in front of her—at the margins of which stood three gates.

Diamond to the left, its gemstone ablaze.

Club to the right, emerald glowing a fervent green.

And dead ahead lay the Spade, its amethyst dimming.

This had to be the Heart's dreamscape. She made it, and it wasn't the desolate graveyard she'd worried it might be!

She left the dais, hastened footsteps ringing hollow over a floor of the same fibrous matter, and brought both hands to the Spade gate's gem. Darkness swirled within like ink dripped into a vial of liquid violet, but beyond its fading vibrations, she heard music—that poignant song plucking at the strings of her heart again.

A melody composed for her. An SOS.

You were calling out to me all this time, and I didn't understand. But I hear you now.

I hear you!

And I'm not leaving without you.

She closed her eyes in the dreamscape and reopened them in the real world, the bane of Circ's existence primed on her tongue.

"Awaken," she said, his face falling in horror, *"Bleeding Heart!"*

A whirlwind of scarlet whipped up around her, her Joker uniform melting into light. Buckled shoes morphed into cloven sandals. A layered skirt of white bloomed at her hips, bodice, sleeves, and leggings clinging frostlike to her figure. Sanguine threads mapped out the Suit's iconic shape on her bust, reminiscent of the veins thrumming with newfound power inside her.

And every ounce, she funneled into Iori.

She pressed deeper, black liquid spilling cold and wet around her wrist. It leaked from his tear ducts, wicking vaporous off his ears. Circ hacked up a mouthful of malice, and as her purifying infusion spread, the archive of Iori's life unfolded before her mind's eye.

First the tarnished pieces, every bit of misery the Void had implanted itself in.

The anguish caused by Wiseman.

By the Spade.

By Noah, and by Alexander.

By those pangs of loss Ellen knew too well.

She felt it all, felt it raw, and persevered through the darkness and the corruption toward that tiny fleck of light still shining at his core. And just as she'd experienced with Kyani, when she delved into that last sheet of fog, she sensed something else.

Someone else.

Vague recollections of the Spade's former Keeper flickered like washed-out reels of film. An imprint made by guilt and remorse and a profound, mournful yearning. But breaking out the other side, Ellen was met by a sea of euphoria.

The highlights of Iori's few yet tumultuous years.

Evenings of catching fireflies and sharing meals with family, blissful hours spent at the piano. She glimpsed his mother's face, how her nose crinkled the same as his when she laughed.

These were the events that molded him, the people who made him who he was. And among them, Ellen saw herself. Felt the love he held close in the moments they shared—by the fountain, on the river, when they danced at the ball, and sang the morning after. Brimming on his birthday, and bursting at the festival.

Thinking back, a part of her always suspected those affections were there, but she had denied them. Denied the signs, denied what she knew to be true—that his heart longed for her, and that hers longed for him too. Distance hadn't only made it grow fonder; being away from him, almost losing him, had given her the clarity she needed.

She knew what she wanted, and she wasn't going to let a Star, fallen or otherwise, cross it out.

Again, Circ's grip wavered. Violent tremors coursed through his commandeered body as he fought to stay in it, but the blight was receding and he was rapidly losing ground. The blackened sclera of his right eye blistered and oozed, warping iris and pupil into a smear of crimson and scintillating blue.

A slick cord slithered past Ellen's submerged hand—the parasite, squirming in a shrinking pocket of Void with nowhere to run. She clamped her hand around it and *pulled*.

A dual-toned scream tore from his throat, Iori's and Circ's voices overlapping. Wet tendrils lashed for purchase, desperate to hold on.

Ellen gritted her teeth, the spots in her vision close to blotting it out, and with one final effort, she ripped the blue-black blob from the inkwell.

No longer tethered by the Warden's wires, Iori's fingers slid from her neck. She fell to her knees, gasping for air, as he staggered backward and collapsed with a dull thud on the rug. The sentient blob of Circ wriggled free of her grasp, escaping into the seams between the floorboards.

Hopefully that had bought them some time. Right now, Ellen had a more immediate concern knocked out on the floor.

She watched Iori intently, waiting for him to draw breath as the oxygen-starved heaves of her own lungs slowed.

Praying he was alive, that her power had been enough. That she wasn't too late, and he hadn't slipped past the point of no return.

Breathe, Iori, she urged. *Breathe.*

And he did.

A sharp inhalation spurred Ellen into action. She scrabbled to his side as coughs wracked his frame. "Iori?" She cupped his ink-stained face, patted his cheek. "Iori, can you hear me?"

His throat bobbed, the pained lines of his expression easing. "We really have to stop meeting like this," he croaked, peering at her through slitted eyes. And he *smiled*. Fresh off the brink of death, and the idiot was smiling.

Swept up in a wave of emotion, Ellen dove into a kiss, crushing her lips to his in a clumsy, unpracticed way. She was fairly certain kisses weren't supposed to hurt, but in that instant, she didn't care. Not about the ache or the bitter taste of ink.

When she peeled away, silvery tresses a moonlit curtain around them, Iori stared at her in beet-red disbelief. Laughter bubbled from her mouth. She could hardly believe she'd done it herself.

She bent her forehead to his, tears sparkling along the bridge of her nose. "The feeling is mutual," she whispered, her confession magnified in the quiet space between them.

Maybe it was fate. Maybe their story had been written in the constellations above. What mattered was, after so much doubt and confusion, she could finally say she loved him. She loved him, she loved him, she loved him. Whether predestined or a roll of the dice, she loved him, and she wouldn't change it for the world.

So, screw it. If we're meant to be, we'll be.

She sank down on top of him, chin nestled in the crook of his neck as his hand came to rest at the small of her back. They stayed there a moment, a comfort in the swell of his ribcage against hers and the unspoiled warmth that radiated from him. No corruption, no chill.

This was how he was meant to feel.

"Thank you for coming for me," he said. "Thought I was a goner for a minute there."

"Sorry it took me so long."

He shrugged. "Worth the wait."

Much as Ellen wished to hold him like this forever, she couldn't ignore the looming anvil of responsibility and the vital payload she carried. She shifted into a kneel and Iori slouched forward, grinding the heel of his palm into his temple.

"What hurts?" she asked, tucking her hair behind her ears.

"Only everything." He examined himself, the scar on his chest. The Void mark had been erased, leaving behind soft pink tissue—made tender by the trauma, judging by how he hissed when he touched it. Ellen wasn't sure who to blame for that: the vicious parasite, or herself for sticking her whole hand in it.

Both, she decided. *Definitely both.*

Iori dabbed at his right eye, blinking rapidly.

"Let me see that." Holding his chin steady, Ellen leaned in for a closer look. His sclera had been restored to a pearly though not entirely healthy white. Daubed in blood, more pooling in his cornea, and the crimson fibers of his iris now spilled into the pupil like a stirred pail of paint. "Can you see out this side?"

"Sort of. It's hazy."

With any luck, his healing factor would kick in and repair the damage. Ellen couldn't treat a hyphema out here by herself, let alone mend a torn iris. "We'll have Dr. Fornell look at it when we get back. Keep your head elevated and try to rest it in the meantime."

A dopy smirk crossed his lips. "Good thing you're a sight for sore eyes."

One tiny dose of reciprocation and suddenly he had all the confidence in the world. "Yeah, you're gonna be fine." Ellen gave him a gentle shove and he chuckled deliriously, riding the adrenaline high.

"Nice rack, by the way." He flicked something above her head that sent a tremor *into her scalp*.

She reached up, stiffening when she found two bony protrusions growing there. Not just a couple of nubs, either. These twin beams swept back and branched off into tapered tines. "It gave me horns?!"

"Antlers, technically."

"Do I look like I care about technicality?" She had forgotten about this part—the animal traits. She got up and spun around, checking that she hadn't sprouted a tail as well. The rest of her appeared normal, as far as her range of view allowed her to see.

"It's nothing to freak out about," Iori said. "They suit you."

She was about to berate him for the insensitive if gallingly appropriate pun, but he'd already turned to scan the room with his undamaged eye. His ears twisted downward, unsettled. "Are we . . .?"

"At the Wiseman Estate," Ellen confirmed.

"How did you get here?"

"It's a long story. I'll tell you on the way." They didn't have time to hang around, and he was probably itching to leave. On the bright side, the trek from here to Fort Worth would give them ample opportunity to catch up. She offered him her hand. "Up for a walk?"

CHAPTER FIFTY-THREE
JANUARY 6 | HILDEGRAND, LOWER DISTRICT

AT THE WEST END OF THE LOWER DISTRICT, as far from honorable society as you could get within city limits, stood a big ugly concrete box: the Hildegrand Correctional Institution for Empowered. The place was a house of horrors for those inside, and a warning to magic users who weren't.

Tonight, that would stop. They'd come to recruit the prisoners for their cause, freedom at the price of allegiance. The way Cardan saw it, they would be releasing them from one horror show into another. They were just waiting on Circ to join them for the casting call.

If the Jane girl succeeded, he may not be.

Wiseman hadn't moved from his post on the curb. He seemed oddly unbothered by Cardplay's violation of his cease and desist order. Tickled, even, by their efforts. Perhaps he thought they'd lost their chance to turn the tables.

Perhaps they had.

Cardan did abandon their one good shot at the estate. Should any harm come to her, that loss would be on him, and her brother would burn him to a crisp sooner than he could explain. At least while his cover remained intact, he could keep tabs on his former associates.

"Keep clenching your jaw and you're gonna give yourself TMJ," Sybil said from one of the benches along the paved footpath. She was spying at Cardan through the scope of her sniper rifle, laser sight trained on the tip of his nose.

"Can you not point that thing at me?"

"Chill out, carrot cake. I'm not gonna shoot you." She removed her eye from the scope. "Unless you give me a reason to."

Clearly neither of them suspected he'd been involved in the liberation of Cardplay, or Wiseman would've had her lodge a bullet in his cranium by now. *Nay, knowing this lot, they'd skin me and hang me by my entrails.*

Or by the scrotum, if Sybil had any say in it.

A slash of light split the pavement, sputtering like a downed power line. Wiseman finally turned as it expanded into a pentagram, a portal whorling open, and from its oily depths crawled a burbling, cussing blob of ink. It hauled itself from the ground in a flurry of wet, slapping limbs.

Sybil lowered her rifle to snigger at the sorry creature. "The fuck happened to you?"

The gelatinous blob contorted and grew, cursing between its—bubbles? Cardan couldn't see any teeth—about *that brat, that bitch, that damnable Keeper.* Did that mean she was alive?

"You underestimated her, didn't you?" he asked flatly, trying to mask his concern for the girl.

Circ warped into something person-adjacent, two eyes bulging from a fat globule of a head. *Now* it had teeth, a mishmash of sharp points in a crooked cleave of a mouth. "We are not talking about this."

Wiseman's shined shoes halted at the edge of the puddle. "Is it done?"

"The Heart is awake. The seal should dissipate shortly."

"And the Spade?"

"Dealt with."

The same way you dealt with the Guiding Light? Circ's spitting of the answer implied that Ellen and the Spade's

Keeper had been left in better shape than intended—a prospect that relieved Cardan as much as it appeared to disturb Wiseman. He'd started rubbing that right arm of his again.

Sometimes, Cardan wondered if it was fear that kept the man from visiting Hildegrand. Fear of the boy who got away.

Circ congealed into his regular gray-skinned shape, adorned in silver and billowing blue. "Let us proceed."

As mayor, Wiseman would have no trouble getting into the institution, and Cardan and Sybil would clear the security checkpoint in their disguises. Circ, on the other hand . . .

"We won't get through with you looking like that," said Cardan. "You blend in 'bout as well as a chimp in a trench coat."

Actually, a trench coat might do the trick. But Circ had a different idea.

"Why blend in"—he raised his arms as they strode through the automatic doors—"when you can *stand out*."

The guards manning the front desk didn't even have the chance to scream. They bent and blackened, engulfed in vaporous shadow, then splashed to the floor, reduced to puddles in a manner of seconds.

Bowled over by the sight, the suddenness, Cardan caught himself on the frame of a walk-through metal detector. "What the fucking shite did you do that for?"

Circ curled his nails into the pads of his palms. "I needed a boost." He tilted his head in Cardan's direction, a flare of ravishment in his eyes. "No sweeter indulgence than libation."

What libation? They hadn't offered him a drop. He'd taken their lives, their dust, by force—harvested every ounce without so much as a greeting.

Wiseman and Circ carried on past the front desk. Merry as ever, Sybil pulled the fire alarm on her way. An automated voice accompanied the bells, directing inmates to the outdoor recreation area. Cardan didn't follow until Sybil hollered for him, snapping him out of his daze.

They cut through the building to the walled-in yard, emerging on a ledge that overlooked it. A handful of prison guards lined the perimeter, monitoring the two hundred-and-some collared inmates in the grassy middle, all of them rubbernecking in search of the fire.

Jasper Van Buren's mountainous form was a landmark among them, Felix "Flick" Taggert a crooked toothpick next to him. On the opposite side of the yard, Camille Langdon's pink ringlets bounced in a throng from the juvenile ward, running with a crowd of her own. She never did fit in with the other Players.

Camille's hunger for vengeance had made her a useful tool in hunting the Keeper of the Spade, but her reluctance to get dirty blunted her edge. She and Kyani were similar in that sense. The only dirt Kyani enjoyed working in was the soil in her garden.

Cardan wished he'd joined her there more often.

"My fellow citizens, do not panic. There is no emergency here." All eyes landed on Wiseman, then darted more quickly to Circ. Confusion rolled through the masses, the three Players outliers in their relief. Wiseman gestured to the open roof, to the city beyond the mesh-lined walls. "The real emergency is out there, and as the gifted few, I invite you to partake in our righteous cause to quell it."

Guards exchanged uneasy glances. The inmates buzzed in excitement, aroused by the smell of jailbreak.

Wiseman's inspiring sales pitch continued. "Our world has entered a state of change. We stand at the dawn of a new era, and those of you touched by the heavens have been chosen to walk alongside our divine Lord Warden."

Cardan doubted any cared to walk alongside an alien-looking fellow they'd barely met. They simply wanted out, and he had them chomping at the bit.

"I offer ascension in exchange for a humble contribution of power." Wiseman hoisted a remote in the air. A master control for the inmates' suppression devices, like the one Cardan used to liberate the Jokers. "Are any among you willing to devote your power to our cause?"

His proposition was met with resounding accord.

"Would you give yourselves unto the Sundered Star?" He motioned to Circ, basking in the limelight, and spurred an uproar. Camille pumped her fist, desperate for freedom. Flick whistled, eager for payback. Jasper stood firm, consenting in his silence. The rest had no idea what they were signing up for.

And as Wiseman clicked the remote and the Warden took to his ominous cloud of a throne, lifting those sinewy arms once more, Cardan realized with a sinking notion that he too was none the wiser.

"Then sing your prayers," said Circ. "And say goodnight."

Shrieks erupted as plumes of Void consumed the crowd. Bodies broke and mouths spewed ink, malice and misery streaming down warped faces. Jasper, Flick, Camille—none were spared, not even the guards. Though protected from the noxious emissions, their gear couldn't save them from the *teeth*.

Bleeding eyes flared luminous blue. Horns curled from scalps, claws sprung from nail beds, and maws filled with shards of polished jet. They swarmed the guards, ripped into them like crows to a cadaver, and when the screaming stopped, a chorus of moans followed.

Thirst sated, the Inkwraiths swayed in position, awaiting their Warden's order. In that tiny fraction of a second between their collars deactivating and their magic flooding in, he'd stripped them of their humanity and made vacancies for monsters.

Cardan didn't understand. They were Empowered. Unless bitten or wicked at their core, they should've been resistant to the blight, and surely not all had darkness in their hearts. Was it because they wished it? Consented without realizing what they were consenting to?

As Circ drank in the aftermath of his massacre, Sybil crouched at the edge of the ledge. She cocked her head at an Inkwraith, and it cocked its head back at her in curious mimicry. She scoffed. "Some ascension."

"We have done them a kindness," explained Wiseman, impossibly serene. "They were suffering, and now their suffering has ended. They can be more now in death than they ever were in life. Theirs is a worthy sacrifice."

Kindness? Sacrifice? Cardan wanted to snap. *You lied to them. You tricked two hundred people to their deaths.* This wasn't a sacrifice, it was a slaughter!

Beneath his feet, the ground began to quake.

"Ah, there it is." Circ pointed skyward. "Our window is opening." He rotated to his three underlings as the Inkwraith horde shambled toward the exits. "Wiseman and I shall make way for Elysian Tower. You two—keep an eye on Cardplay and those pestilent Keepers, but make no move on them without my order. We need them alive."

CHAPTER FIFTY-FOUR
JANUARY 6 | HILDEGRAND, MID DISTRICT

"ATTENTION RESIDENTS. ATTENTION RESIDENTS. Curfew is in effect. Please shelter in place until lockdown has lifted. I repeat: Curfew is in effect. Please shelter in place until lockdown has lifted."

The robotic modulation of the emergency broadcast system echoed throughout the mid district, punctuated by the drumbeat of artillery. It would seem the soldiers Wiseman had deployed to enforce his lockdown had their hands full with the outbreak downtown. The Void didn't care which side they belonged to.

From her perch atop the front overhang of Woodridge Long Term Care Facility, their latest stop, Kyani watched smoke columns rise in the distance. Her ability to detect magical auras made her the perfect candidate to stand sentinel while Iris, Yusuf, and Miriam evacuated the facility.

They were too close to the hot zone, and the building wouldn't keep out emissions or monsters for long. If they listened to the broadcast and stayed, they risked being swept away in the flood.

The lower district was already under water, so to speak. For those who hadn't fled earlier, sheltering in place would be their best bet.

Alexander was currently wading through those tides. A true Diamond in the rough.

Last she heard, he and his team had reached General Eze's encampment. They'd been able to maintain contact using earpieces Elizabeth distributed among the Jokers. The short-range devices hadn't been tested in the field and were intended for inter-team communications, but with cell towers and internet offline, they had to rely on these to stay in touch.

Kyani perked at the anxious purl of her father's voice. With a flap of her wings, she hopped down from the overhang, landing barefoot in front of him as his nurse rolled him out in a wheelchair.

"Oh my," gasped the nurse.

Jabari stopped babbling to gaze at his daughter in awe, fully clad in *Verdant Club*'s feathered attire. Though, those weren't the feathers that had caught his attention.

Iris and Miriam emerged from the sliding glass doors behind them, followed by a slew of nurses and patients. Wheels bumped over the curb, mobility aids and dollies carrying supplies. Yusuf was still getting the previous group settled on one of the care home's minibuses.

"Is this the last of them?" Kyani asked, getting an affirmative from Iris. Wings folded, she crouched and took her father's hands. "I know this is a lot for you, Baba, but have faith. They're going to take you to Cardplay Headquarters. You'll be safe there."

He fumbled with her fingers, squeezed them as if to keep her from slipping away. "You're not coming?"

"I'll be there soon. We have a couple more stops to make." They'd passed a double-decker bus on their way here. Dax had gone to hijack it so they could round up more civilians before heading back. Kyani glanced at the nurse's nametag. "Helly here will keep you company until then, okay?"

Clearly shaken, the nurse nodded in agreement, and so did Jabari despite his reluctance. Kyani then released his hands and sent them off. She had hoped to show him around her workplace under lighter circumstances, during a pleasant day trip rather than the stressful haste of evacuation.

Can't always pick your moments.

While the nursing staff loaded the last of the patients onto the bus, the Jokers reconvened in the parking lot. Yusuf ruffled the hickory coils upon his head. "I just received an update from Oskar. HQ is almost at capacity."

"Already?" exclaimed Miriam, peaches and cream in her frilly Joker kit.

"Between our drop-offs and walk-ins off the street, yeah."

"We've got a population six digits long," Iris pointed out in her bouncing accent. "It was bound to fill up quickly."

With its complement of Jokers and mesh-lined arena, Cardplay Headquarters made an effective fallout shelter, but it could only accommodate a fraction of the city's residents.

"Let's pray Alexander can convince General Eze to open the gates," said Yusuf, "otherwise, we're going to have—"

The group collectively jumped at the chirp of a nearby car alarm. Another started shrieking next to it. Then another, and another, until every vehicle in the area was blaring—triggered by a growing tremor Kyani had assumed was a faraway explosion.

Pebbles clattered on pavement, power lines swayed. Miriam put her arms out for balance. "Earthquake?"

This didn't feel like an ordinary quake.

Another flap of Kyani's wings propelled her into the air, and she didn't need to look far to locate the source. Even from this distance, she could see the wisps of blue-white aura peeling off Elysian Tower. The obelisk's natural glow had brightened too.

She pinched her earpiece. "Alex?"

"I'm here." He sounded jostled. The tremors would be more intense downtown. *"What is it?"*

"Elysian Tower just lit up like a beacon."

There was a pause on the other end of the line as the meaning of that sunk in: that his sister's Suit had awakened and its seal had broken. Before he could reply, a racket picked up in the background. Things breaking, people shouting. *"Shit—Ikkei, barricades!"*

"What's wrong?" pressed Kyani. "Alex, what's going on?"

He didn't need to explain. She could see the bleak aura billowing out of the tower's base from here. With the final seal removed, the crack in the dam separating the Void from the mundane world had been split wide open. Black spokes shot outward in all directions like pyroclastic flows, one tearing through Alexander's approximate location and another racing in Kyani's direction.

"Go!" she shouted to the Jokers below. "Get them out of here!"

Miriam sprinted for the bus, tapping her own earpiece to alert Dax as Yusuf and Iris dashed for her car. No sooner had the doors thudded shut than the ground split open like an egg, releasing a brood of Inkblots into their midst. They seeped from the widening crack by the dozens, several taking on forms much larger than Kyani was used to seeing.

She drew her bow and let her arrows fly, piercing their liquid forms and snaring them in bursts of spawned bramble. More kept coming, too many for her to hold.

At Yusuf's command, the road curled into a barrier between the minibus and the fissure, the earth-mover's foot stuck out the passenger side of Iris' car to establish contact with the ground. And as the bus sped away from the parking lot, burning rubber, Alexander's voice broke over Kyani's earpiece again.

"Fall back! Fall back to headquarters!"

ACT IV

BRING DOWN HEAVEN

CHAPTER FIFTY-FIVE
JANUARY 6 | FOLKLAN CLIFFS

FORTY KILOMETERS OF ROCKY WOODLAND spanned the gap from the Wiseman Estate to Fort Worth—an arduous trek that would have been shorter as the crow flew, but Ellen wasn't about to risk getting lost in the woods. So winding cliffside roads it was until they could hitch a ride.

This early and this deep in the cliffs, though, that seemed unlikely.

If I can just catch a signal . . .

She held her phone to the cloud-barren sky, encouraging the bars to fill. Reception wouldn't afford her a call home if communications were still down, but it could be their only hope of getting where they needed to be. Drained in every sense of the word, she and Iori couldn't even reenter their dreamscapes. Pretty soon, their legs would give out too.

Maybe sooner than she thought.

Iori's feet dragged on the asphalt, his arms cinched around his middle to suppress bone-rattling shivers. Both of his eyes were shut. Ellen only advised resting the one.

She slipped her hand into the crook of his elbow. "Iori?"

He mumbled in hazy acknowledgment. Didn't open them.

"Are you feeling okay?"

"I've been better," he replied, lucid enough to quip. "I've also been worse, but I'd call clammy, shaky floatiness a solid *fine*."

Clammy, shaky, floaty. "When did you eat last?"

"Unless Circ remembered to refuel the human vehicle he stole while preoccupied with world domination . . . probably the festival."

He couldn't have been running on empty this long; he would've collapsed by now. Still, he was crashing, and they had miles to go before they reached their destination. In hindsight, it would've been wise to raid the cupboards at the estate, but they'd come too far to go back for supplies.

Please show us some form of civilization soon.

As if in response to her plea, a diesel engine coughed in the not too far-flung distance. Ellen peered over the ridge, Hildegrand a blacked-out tract of land bordering the sea beyond, and immediately below: a convoy. Four large trucks with canvas canopies, barreling south.

Iori squinted at them. "Military vehicles?"

"They must be headed for the city . . ." Could that mean Elizabeth had gotten word out? "That's our ride. Come on!" Ellen took a shortcut down the steep slope, shredding grass in her wake. Iori skidded more clumsily after her, and she sprinted ahead to cut the trucks off at the fork in the road, putting on her best wacky inflatable tube guy impression.

High beams struck her blind. Brakes squealed, engines dropping to an idle rumble. The lead vehicle's doors creaked open and out stepped driver and passenger, equipped with a couple of scary-looking automatic rifles. Somehow, Ellen had always found those more intimidating than magic.

"What are you doing out here . . . dressed like *that*?" The driver ogled Ellen suspiciously. She'd forgotten about the antlers. Although she'd disengaged *Bleeding Heart* and reverted to her regular attire, the antlers had stayed—same as her brother's scales, Kyani's wings, and Iori's ears and tail.

Even out of uniform, they must've looked like wandering convention attendees.

Those details weren't necessary. They had places to be and someone very important to see. "My friend and I are trying to get to Fort Worth. We were sent by—"

"Halt!" A shout from the passenger cut her explanation short. Weapons snapped to Iori when he caught up and stepped into the light. He put his hands up, Ellen sliding in front of him as if her minute frame would actually make an effective shield against a volley of lead.

"Don't shoot! We're—"

"Is he infected?"

She stammered confusedly at the driver's interruption. Alerted by the commotion, other soldiers exited their vehicles and stalked over, firearms raised. Ellen hadn't come all this way, wrestled with a fallen Star, and freed Iori from the clutches of evil just to wind up shot over a misunderstanding.

"Could it have spread this far already?" uttered the passenger. Ignoring him, the driver jerked her rifle at Iori and repeated her own question.

"Your friend. Is he infected?"

Ellen tossed a glance at Iori, his ears pointed back, tail fluffed, and . . . face smeared in ink. "N-no! He's clean." She had stains as well, hidden beneath her gloves—the nullified residue her magic couldn't erase. Harmless in this state. They had no reason to worry unless . . . "Wait. What do you mean, *spread*?"

The driver didn't answer. "That's not what I'd call clean. Were you two attacked?"

"No—I mean—"

"We work for Cardplay," Iori offered when Ellen couldn't rally her vocabulary. At that, the soldiers lowered their weapons ever so slightly.

The driver squinted at him. "In what capacity?"

Slowly, under the lethal focus of their rifles, Ellen opened her jacket to reveal the medallion pinned to her sweater. Its banner and windrose glinted in the headlights. "My name is Ellen Amelia Jane. I'm a Joker, Second Class. And this is Iori Ryone. He's a student."

"You're Empowered?"

For a moment, Ellen thought they may have won the soldiers over. Proven they weren't a threat. For a moment, she thought they'd hit a home run and wouldn't have to fight for a part of this plan to go accordingly. Then the driver blew out her optimistic flame.

"Arrest them."

"Wait! We haven't done anything wrong!"

Several soldiers approached, whipping out cuffs whose inner bands shone copper.

"Empowered persons are prohibited from traveling outside of Hildegrand. You broke that law when you left the isolation zone."

Iori spat a curse as they wrenched his arms behind his back, Ellen wincing when they snapped a matching set of silver bracelets onto her wrists. A metallic click, and a light went out inside her—the Heart stuffed into a jar. If the suppression tech had smothered the fragment too, she couldn't tell. She hadn't been able to feel it from the start.

Part of her, yet separate. Its own entity.

"You wanted to go to Fort Worth, didn't you?" the driver asked smugly as the soldiers ushered them past. "That's where you're going."

CHAPTER FIFTY-SIX
JANUARY 6 | CARDPLAY HEADQUARTERS

IT WAS A MIRACLE THEY MADE IT BACK TO HQ with General Eze's unit in no fewer pieces than Alexander had found them in. Their numbers had been slashed in half, many missing or killed in action, and more could soon follow.

A few of the survivors had been admitted to the infirmary with flesh wounds and blight, the latter's fates in limbo—dependent on Ellen's return. But they were alive, and that was the most anyone could ask for.

How long they would be safe here was another matter.

The arena, while fortified, could only hold so many. People were already overflowing into the halls, the cafeteria, the dorms. If the Void emissions pouring out of the fissures downtown reached the upper district, they would have to rely on Sabine's force field for protection, and she couldn't sustain it forever. All batteries eventually ran dry—even magical ones.

Which was precisely why they needed to evacuate the city.

Alexander had escorted General Eze straight to the masters, hoping they could convince her to open the gates, but her beliefs hinged on tangibility, on sight, and her struggle to grasp the boatload of fantasy Hikaru had ferried into her port was clear. Quiet filled the office as she processed his tales of Stars and Keepers and unseen realms, and Cardplay's plan to circumvent a bona fide apocalypse.

Even a repeat of the event that made myth of the magical era in the first place wasn't a sufficient threat to force her hand. "Regardless of whether what you're saying is true, opening the gates would be a breach of containment. That fence could be the one thing standing between us and a global outbreak."

"The fence?" Alexander flung the word back at her. "After everything we just told you, you'd rather put your faith in the fucking fence?"

Elizabeth drew up from her weary lean on the headmaster's desk and started to rebuke him, but he refused to bite his tongue when Cardan McConnell himself had debunked the security of the fence.

"Ignoring that Wiseman built it for the express purpose of confining us, the Void doesn't give two shits about structural boundaries. It is traveling *underground*. It's airborne. And the more souls it consumes, the stronger it gets. The only way we're going to slow it down is by getting as many people as far away from here as possible."

General Eze scrutinized him. It must've sounded like hogwash, and Alexander knew how deeply outbreak protocol had been drilled into the military. Eze wanted to take what she believed to be the best course of action to protect her country, but protocol would not save its people.

"Your forces can barely keep it at bay. We can make a dent, but magic isn't an unlimited resource either." He'd already exhausted his reserves carving out an escape route. Oskar, Sabaa, and half a dozen others were on the same bench. "If you don't open that gate, you will be signing a death warrant—and not just for one person. Not just for a hundred. We are talking about an extinction level event." Alexander's desperation weighed on every word. "Please think very carefully about which call you want to make."

The General's chest sank with a long exhalation as she chewed over her options. Brave the streets with jumpy civilians, or bunker down at the risk of being trapped indefinitely by the encroaching Void. Neither was ideal, but Alexander would sooner take a chance out there than be a sitting duck in here.

Cacophonous dialogue filtered in from the foyer when the door opened, and it was as if Kyani had lifted the lid off a pressure cooker. "Oh—sorry." Her wings snapped to her sides like a startled finch. "I didn't mean to interrupt."

The headmaster's leather chair released a sigh as he reclined, looking rougher now than he sounded. "It's quite alright. How is your father settling in?"

"Well. He's settling in well. He's in the lounge playing checkers." Kyani hung in the doorway, her feathers as ruffled as Alexander felt. He'd intended to check on her but hadn't had the opportunity. From the frying pan into the fire, and back into that cast iron purgatory to sputter around helplessly.

General Eze gave Kyani an evaluating look. "I take it this is another one?"

Confusion clouded her expression. "Another . . . ?"

"Keeper," Alexander clarified. "This is General Eze, commanding officer of the National Guard's local unit. We just brought her up to speed."

After an almost dazed delay, Kyani introduced herself. "Kyani Oto. It's nice to meet you."

"Likewise," Eze replied, any genuine pleasure lost to the graveness of their predicament.

"Alexander, why don't you take Miss Oto to the cafeteria?" Hikaru suggested. "Get some food, and get some rest. We need you both at full strength."

Eating was at the very bottom of Alexander's to-do list, which was a sure sign it should be at the top. Even when the world wasn't falling apart, his studies and duties often took precedence over sustenance, hydration, and sleep—to the point where, in their training days, Ikkei had become his relentless personal reminder.

In the interest of hastening his magic's recharge, he bowed out of the office with Kyani. They hugged the wall as Heather Doherty sped by, an infant bawling in her arm and triplets toddling at her heels. Making use of her babysitting experience by watching over the evacuee children.

"How did it go in there?" Kyani asked.

"Eze is sticking to her guns. We're still trying to persuade her." Alexander wiped his brow, dry as a desert. Oxygen levels could be managed with breathing techniques; he couldn't keep sucking down water to stay hydrated on the battlefield. If he kept pushing, burnout was inevitable. They needed his sister to pull through. "We should've heard something from Ellen by now . . ."

The Heart seal broke over an hour ago, and every minute that ticked by without an update clipped his fuses shorter. If any harm came to his sister, he wouldn't be able to forgive himself for letting her go. Not that staying would've ensured her safety.

"Have you tried contacting her yourself?"

"Not yet." He'd been hesitant to try in case he couldn't reach her, or in case he failed to enter the dreamscape unassisted. That part had proven more challenging than he wanted to admit, connecting to his *inner self*. Kyani had been the victim of many a frustrated earful regarding that.

She touched his arm. "We'll try together."

CHAPTER FIFTY-SEVEN
JANUARY 6 | FORT WORTH

IF ELIZABETH HOWARD'S NAME HELD MERIT, nobody cared.

Arriving at Fort Worth, Ellen and Iori were frisked and separated for interrogation. No one would tell her where he'd been taken or how he was, wouldn't entertain her request for an audience with Marshal Kulisch. Unless she was answering questions, they didn't want to hear a word out of her. But with less than twenty-four hours to deliver the fragment to the Astral Pool in the Domain, she couldn't give in.

So, she persisted until they did.

Two soldiers breathed down her neck while Kulisch read over the interrogation transcript on their tablet. Behind them, flagpoles flanked a world map that spanned the width of the wall. Amethis' purple and white hung next to Amberlye's coat of arms on the left, and the multicolored continental flag of Ammolitia kept the National Guard's insignia company on the right.

Kulisch's mouth twisted beneath their hooked nose, but there was a note of deliberation in their throaty purr of a voice that gave Ellen hope. "There's a hole in your story. Several, in fact. For one, Hildegrand is in lockdown. How did you exit when the gates are closed?"

"Um . . . magic?"

The Marshal didn't take kindly to Ellen's vague reply. "You're listed in the database as a pyric type, and your comrade as umbric. Pyrotechnics and shadowplay would not get you past the gatekeepers without engaging them in combat, which I don't believe you did. This would suggest you had help, yet you made no mention of a third party." Kulisch wobbled the tablet, Ellen's prior account stored within. "Empowerment is also not known to result in mutation. So if you're wondering why I'm having trouble putting the pieces together, perhaps it is because you have not provided me all of them."

In her effort to avoid selling a far-fetched tale or accidentally incriminating herself, Ellen had come off as a liar and driven herself into a corner, and continuing to withhold information when Kulisch had sniffed it out would only cause more problems.

Surreptitiousness had gotten them this far, but the time had come to lay all their cards on the table.

"We had help," she said. "From a teleporter—Cardan McConnell." She could practically see the red flag waving. All high-ranking officials in the area knew him by name. "I realize how that sounds, but he doesn't work for Blackjack anymore! He deserted them to help us. He got me past the fence."

"McConnell wasn't with you when you were found."

"He had to go."

One of the soldiers behind her grunted incredulously.

Kulisch shot the soldier a look. "Why would Sergeant Howard send a student and a low-ranking Joker rather than spare us this headache and make the journey herself?"

"It had to be me. Getting reinforcements was the second part of the plan; the first part was a rescue mission. Iori, the boy I was traveling with—Blackjack took him hostage in the cliffs. I came to get him back." It seemed simpler to omit

Wiseman and the Sundered Star from the equation. They were all part of the same league of villains anyway.

"And what," asked Kulisch, "makes a seventeen-year-old Second Class Joker the best candidate for such a task?"

Here goes.

"I'm a Keeper," Ellen confessed. "There are four of us in total. Iori is one, my brother Alexander is another. The fourth is Kyani Oto, the girl we rescued from Camrand Island. Our magic is different from most. In my case, different from anyone's." She fidgeted in her cuffs, chain links jangling as a bubble of skepticism inflated around her. "The soldiers we met on the road thought my friend had been blighted, and they were right. He had been. But my powers allowed me to purify him so Blackjack couldn't use him as leverage."

Kulisch's arms slid from their knot. "You reversed his blight?"

She nodded.

"Come with me."

The Marshal and the soldier pair escorted Ellen through the building's sparsely populated halls. She'd expected a lot more personnel on-site. And where were they holding Iori? Was he hidden behind one of these closed doors, or had they carted him off to the jails?

Maybe that was where they were taking her, too—down to the brig to pay for sullying mundane soil with her magical feet.

To her relief, and to the shock of her anxiety, they didn't toss her into any steel-barred cells. Instead, they led her to the infirmary, where four patients in medically-induced comas had been quarantined with varying stages of blight. A bite on a forearm, a scratched and blackened leg, murky veins trailing from a shoulder wound. The torso on the worst of them looked like a well-used punching bag.

"Where did they come from?" Ellen asked, though she had a terrible inkling. *Spread*, the soldier from earlier had said.

"Inglehurst," Kulisch told her. A community just outside of Hildegrand. "They're what's left of the unit we had stationed there. Got caught in the quakes, the quakes opened fissures, and the fissures spawned Inkblots. With communications down, they couldn't call for aid, so they came to warn us. Most of my troops have already been deployed to outlying municipalities to assist in the evacuation, and along the provincial border to enforce travel restrictions."

"The whole province is going into lockdown?"

"The Prime Minister called the state of emergency a couple of hours ago." Solemnity further squared Kulisch's angular jaw. "I'm no fool. I know we cannot win this fight. Our forces don't have the power necessary. But, there may be hope." Kulisch motioned to one of the soldiers for their keys, then released Ellen from her cuffs and let her magic flow free—a buzzing warmth through every capillary. "Prove that you can do what you say, and I'll get you the reinforcements you need."

They sent her into the quarantined room, an airtight space made up mostly of windows. Ellen went to the patient most urgently in need, the man whose blight bled outward from within. His were the kind of marks you got from Void emissions, inhaled and absorbed through the skin.

She lay her hands on the man's chest, felt the shallow rise and fall of his breath. The cold swirling inside. With any luck, the Radiant Star's fragment would give her the boost she needed to cleanse him.

Her magic leached into the sickly flesh, saturating muscle and organ with a ruby gleam. Flecks of light began to peel off his skin, taking the darkness with them, more and more until his complexion had been restored to a rich olive tone. His vital signs stabilized, the disease cured.

Outside, her spectators had gone slack-jawed.

And if that weren't sufficient, Ellen proved her worth again and again and again with the other three patients—but she didn't do it for Kulisch or the National Guard. She did it for these soldiers, for all the people in Hildegrand who were depending on her. She did it for this flawed world she loved so dearly, because it was the one world she had, and she would go to any length to defend it.

As a show of gratitude and cooperation, Kulisch took her to the holding room they'd moved Iori to. Ellen could hear him slinging sarcasm at his tight-lipped minder from out in the hall. He stopped when he saw her, brightening momentarily before a shadow she couldn't decipher fell over him.

"How are you feeling?" she asked as he stood.

"I'm . . . better," he told her unconvincingly. The shakes had passed, at least, and a pad had been applied to his injured eye. "They fed me, so. That's one problem solved."

"Our other problem might be solved, too." Hopefully some positive news would lift his spirits. "I told Marshal Kulisch about the plan. They're going to send reinforcements to Hildegrand, and we've been given permission to contact Alexander and Kyani through the dreamscape."

Nervousness flitted across his expression. "Now?"

"Is now not a good time?" The sooner the better, she would've thought.

"No—no, it's fine." Iori took her hands, his cold and damp around hers. "Why don't you take us there? Yours is the only dreamscape I haven't seen, and you haven't taken another person for the trip yet. I'm also not sure I have the, uh, reserves for it."

Was that all? "That's okay, I can try." Admittedly, her own confidence was lacking, but if Iori couldn't scrape together the magic to do it, she would have to. She'd watched him commence the journey numerous times, and witnessed her brother and Kyani do the same. With him, with each other, with her. It couldn't be too difficult.

Closing her eyes, Ellen tried to ignore the audience of soldiers and turned her focus inward.

Iori's gentle encouragement helped. "You can do it. Remember what I said: it's all about will and intent. Wish for it, and it'll happen. You just have to wish hard enough."

Her brow wrinkled in concentration.

"Maybe not that hard." His thumbs stroked her knuckles, working the tension out of them. "Focus on the Heart. You went to its dreamscape when you awakened it, right?"

"I did . . ."

"Take a breath and picture it."

She inhaled deeply, calling to mind the visceral scenery. Bone-white birch with blood cell leaves rooted in a landmass of fibrous bone, and all blanketed in the pleasant cool of winter bordering on spring.

Every detail formed crystal clear in her head, every scent and sensation. But how was she to send her consciousness over the barrier between reality and dream?

"I don't think it's working," she said. "I don't know how to—" She paused mid-sentence when she opened her eyes. The holding room at Fort Worth had been replaced by the frozen landscape she'd envisioned. A whirl of a breeze welcomed her back to her throne, weaving humid threads between empty fingers.

Iori was nowhere to be seen. She must have failed to form the link correctly.

At least, that seemed like the logical explanation until she started in the direction of her brother's gate and noted an absence of color where there should've been vibrant amethyst.

The Spade's gate had gone dark. Not dim or clouded by the shadows of corruption, just completely devoid of light—duller even than her ruby prior to the Heart's awakening.

Her chest tightened. What could that mean?

A fretful falter in her steps, she carried on to that shining yellow diamond and pressed her palm to it. And she waited. And waited. This went much more quickly when they were in the same room anticipating each other's calls. Right now, Alexander could be anywhere.

In a meeting.

On the battlefield.

Knocked unconscious.

Under the knife.

He wasn't dead, that she could tell. The Diamond's light would have gone out with his, right?

Vibrations continued throbbing through her arm, her request unanswered or unheard. She was about to give Kyani's a try when he finally picked up.

Ellen's immaterial form disintegrated into sugar-fine particles and reformed amidst the wheat and summer heat of the Diamond's dreamscape. And there she saw her brother, waiting outside her gate.

"Thank god." His shoulders slouched with relief and he reached out to grab hers, testing the solidity of her. "I've been trying to reach you."

The suppression cuffs she'd been wearing until recently had blocked the signal. Like her cellphone, she'd been without reception. "Sorry, we ran into some trouble. The National Guard picked us up." She decided to spare him the details of their arrest. "But we made it to Fort Worth! We're safe."

"'We' being . . .?"

"Me and Iori," she said. "The purification was successful."

Her brother's eyes drifted to the lightless gem behind him, a dirty mauve in the flaxen hue of this atmosphere.

Ellen kneaded the pads of her palm. "I did try to bring him." Iori had claimed his reserves were too low to initiate the trip. It was conceivable they were too low for him to even enter the dreamscape, but that didn't explain the inactive gate.

Did she want the explanation for the inactive gate?

Apparently not keen to mull over the implications himself, Alexander changed the subject. "What about Circ and Cardan?"

"Cardan was sent away after we got to the estate, and—"

"He *left* you?"

"It was that or blow his cover." Alexander didn't appear satisfied with that excuse. "As for Circ, he's gone. Not gone-gone, but the purification did a number on him, and he took off."

"That makes sense."

"How do you mean?"

Alexander's hands rested on his hips, exhaustion weighing on every part of him. "We expected the Void to pursue us when we retreated to headquarters. It didn't. So far all we've got uptown are emissions, because Circ's army has congregated around Elysian Tower. He must be there; that's why they're guarding it."

The mention of a retreat elevated Ellen's worry. Seeing as he made no indication that anyone at home had been mortally wounded, she tried to placate it. There was another detail she had to share. "I think I figured out what he's planning. He was talking about bringing the realms together as one under him, and it didn't sound like his vision included free will."

The Void was a hivemind given voice by the Sundered Star. Every creature it spat out was connected to the same malevolent body, and if Ellen was right and Circ prevailed, every living thing on the planet could be absorbed into it.

Alexander let out a long, drawn-out curse, then attempted to put his game face on. "When do you think you'll be back?"

"I'm not sure. Marshal Kulisch agreed to help, but it's going to take time."

"We don't have time."

"They're moving as fast as they can. Communications are out for miles, and they're having to call in reinforcements from the border. The government's putting the province under quarantine."

"The *entire* prov—why?"

The trepidation in his eyes, churning like the smoke of a smothered flame, told Ellen he'd already guessed. "The blight is spreading, Alexander. They've started evacuating the regions around Hildegrand." He exhaled, and the wind seemed to sigh with him. "Have you gotten the gates open yet?"

"No. This might be enough to sway General Eze, though."

So his team had tracked down the local unit. That was a positive. "I should let you go and tend to that." He had a general to persuade, and she still had secrets to divulge so their reinforcements would know exactly what they were up against. "I'll contact you when I have an update."

"Alright. Sounds good."

Neither brother nor sister made an immediate move to leave, reluctant to, part again. But the longer they stayed, the more power they burned. Power they couldn't afford to waste. Ultimately, Ellen was the guest in his mental landscape. She had to exit first, or else be forcibly expelled.

She requested that he pass on a message of luck, then departed from the waking dream.

CHAPTER FIFTY-EIGHT
JANUARY 6 | FORT WORTH

IORI'S EARS HAD BEEN RINGING since he reclaimed his body, almost as if someone had struck a tuning fork between them. A result of the physical trauma involved in retaking one's corporeal meat suit, he'd thought.

Then the suppression cuffs went on, and he felt nothing.

Checked his eye, and saw nothing. No sign of healing.

And when Ellen went where he could no longer follow, it became clear that what he'd been hearing . . .

Was nothing.

In the beginning, he had begged for silence. He didn't know just how *loud* the world could be until he got these ears. Traffic and people and animals, the hustle and bustle of life alongside machinery and magic—every sound had been magnified to the point where stabbing out his eardrums became a real temptation.

Eventually, he'd grown used to it. Learned how to use this enhanced sense to his advantage by tuning out insignificant sounds and honing in on others. With his hearing now restored to the regular human range, however, this silence was almost as deafening as the noise had been.

Parked on a borrowed cot in the empty barracks, his fingers slid back and forth over the shallow slope of his sternum, traversing the slash of scar tissue on his chest. It was smoother without the Void matter woven into it. The marks encircling his feline appendages had vanished too, and with them, the Spade—his Suit as much a Schrödinger's cat to him as he was to the outside world.

Alive or dead, who could say?

"Iori?"

He snapped around to see an antlered silhouette in the doorway. Ellen—no chime to alert him to her approach, and steps so light he hadn't heard her coming. Prickles of embarrassment crept along his neck. "Finally got the jump on me, huh?"

The concern she wore deepened. Wry wit didn't make an effective mask when she could see right through it. When Iori spoke again, he spoke low, his own voice too loud in the echo chamber of his skull. "Were you able to talk to your brother?"

"Yeah. Everyone's holding up okay. They're working on evacuating the city." She joined him on the cot, springs squeaking softly beneath her. Whatever mingled in the air between them, it wasn't magic.

"It's dark, isn't it?" he asked.

Out the corner of his vision, a faint bob of her head.

He'd had a feeling—or rather, a lack thereof. When Kyani failed to summon the Club following her purification, she'd still been able to sense it, and he'd heard it humming then as well. The Spade, it seemed, had packed up and gone without even leaving a note. Just this grisly scar.

He curled his fingers over it, a sting in the path of his nails. "I wanted it gone for so long, I never imagined I'd miss it. Suppose when demons are the only company you have, you're bound to form attachments. You know which part I miss most, though?" He glanced at Ellen, and the release her gaze invited almost stole his voice away. "Your chime," he said. "I didn't realize how much I'd come to rely on that sound to ground me. Without it, I feel sort of adrift."

It was the tether that kept him from spiraling into the abyss, the reason he slept better when she was near. She must've thought him silly and ungrateful for mourning the loss of the monster she'd freed him from. And perhaps he was, and perhaps she should tell him to suck it up and direct his eyes to the silver linings she painted so generously.

But she told him none of those things, and her brush stayed in its pot. What she did instead was coax him closer and guide him gently downward, bringing his ear to her chest and a mild rouge to his cheeks. "Listen," she said. "This is my sound, too."

Her heart drowned out the ringing in his head. *Ba-dum, ba-dum, ba-dum*—quick and steady like a mini bass drum.

Iori melted against her, arms looped around her waist, and let her rhythm filter out the din of his plights while she played with his hair. And when her fingers found the velvety fur at the base of his ear, his weak spot, every last bit of tension bled out of his body.

Frankly, any spot she touched was liable to become weak.

He didn't need someone to twist his frame of mind into a more appealing, more confident shape. In this moment, in this limbo, all he needed was room to wallow, and she had provided that space amply.

CHAPTER FIFTY-NINE
JANUARY 6 | EN ROUTE TO HILDEGRAND

REINFORCEMENTS ROLLED IN AT DUSK, a convoy of armored trucks belching diesel fumes from their exhaust pipes. After checking in with Alexander and Kyani, Iori and Ellen were loaded into one of the troop transports and sent off by Marshal Kulisch.

The soldiers crammed into the passenger cabin with them appeared no more pleased to be in the presence of Empowered than Iori felt in theirs. They peered through their visors, twitchy fingers glued to their firearms. Granted, they could also have been apprehensive about driving virtually unprotected into what may as well have been a radioactive war zone.

The Wiseman Corporation hadn't the material to mass produce anti-magic tech; only the leftovers from the founder's vile contraptions went to fortifying the local authorities and a few select structures in the city. All these soldiers had to rely on was basic body armor and the airtight shell of the vehicles that carried them. Their gas masks would provide some resistance. The fewer openings, the less exposed skin, the harder it would be for the Void to get in.

And if they succeeded in their mission, all afflicted would be cleansed before they could succumb.

If they didn't, no one could stop it.

Ghost towns slid past the window slats, their residents having fled hours ago. Cardplay would be in the process of evacuating Hildegrand as well; General Eze finally caved when she learned containment had already been breached. Strange, though, that they hadn't encountered more traffic by now. They were on the main highway.

There was a knock on the partition window. A soldier in the front cab notified them that they'd passed kilometer marker twenty-five. ETA: fifteen minutes to Hildegrand.

Not sixty seconds later, Ellen tensed beside Iori.

"What is it?"

She hiked up her sleeve to reveal the goosebumps on her forearm. "Void," she reported, the word alone enough to set the troops on edge. The village of Inglehurst was within ten kilometers of Hildegrand. For her to sense it this far out . . . that couldn't be good.

She grew increasingly restless as they neared the city, rubbing her arms and shooting glances out the window.

A transmission crackled over the soldiers' short-range communication devices: *"All units, be advised: we're approaching the boundary fence."*

The bulbs lining the gate posts bathed the truck's rear cabin in stripes of red as they chugged through the checkpoint, unimpeded by people or other vehicles—save for those that had been abandoned on the road.

Congealing puddles of ink sloshed thickly under the convoy's tires. Iori glimpsed them through the slats. Various footprints dotted the streets and sidewalks, shoes and feet and paws. And there were corpses. Bloodied and blackened, half-melted and mangled, blending together in the ominous hue of the Void-tinged atmosphere.

Ellen paled at the sight and Iori's stomach clenched, flashing back to the aftermath of the Reemergence. Hildegrand gutted of its inhabitants, armored vehicles roaring down the streets, bodies smeared in inky black and dingy red, and monsters slinking in the shadows. The air had smelled of metal and decay, and pealed with devastation.

Tonight, an unnerving stillness had settled in the absence of fighting, as if the city were waiting with bated breath for a bigger calamity to strike.

In due course, the convoy crawled up the incline to Cardplay Headquarters, and an unexpected wave of emotion swept through Iori when he saw the grove wisped in smog.

Although his stay in Circ's mental prison seemed short, the days he'd missed in the waking world were catching up to him. Almost a week had passed since he last stood here, freezing his tail off whilst panicking over the choreography of a kiss. Which angle would be most effective, which placement and style would convey his feelings in the clearest, most concise manner?

Funny how quick that had become the least of his worries. It worked out in the end, though. Dare he believe a miracle could be worked here, or had their defunct Ace of Spades turned their winning hand to rags?

The convoy rolled to a halt, cooling pops resounding through steel hulls. Doors groaned open and boots thundered across the cabin floor as soldiers piled out. They ushered Ellen and Iori out last, and the barrels didn't need to be pressed to Iori's spine for him to feel as though he were at gunpoint.

When they dropped onto the driveway, gravel clacking under their shoes, the first thing Iori noticed was the iridescence encapsulating the mansion. A cubic scaffolding of light adhered to the structure's geometry, shimmering over shingles and windows and all its many angles.

A kinetic barrier to ward against the Void.

The front doors lashed open and out rushed Alexander, Kyani and Elizabeth trailing behind. The battlemaster, furbished in a new set of threads, stopped to speak with

Lieutenant Gou—the Fort Worth unit's commanding officer—as the two Keepers carried on ahead.

Siblings collided in a binding embrace, the same force that nearly bowled them over keeping them on their feet. Past them, Iori caught Kyani's eye, and as if the diesel fumes stagnating in the winter air weren't enough, the condolence on her face sickened him further, because that indicated he had lost something. His aura.

How painfully ordinary he must look.

Brother and sister parted. Alexander hummed and hawed, still struggling to find that level terrain between him and Iori. "We're lucky to have you back," he said at last.

And Iori had to go and throw spikes under his tires. "Are you?"

The instant the snide reply was out, he wished he could retract it. For once, Alexander was being genial, but self-pity and self-doubt had turned Iori into a bristly, miserable thing. Don't look, don't touch, don't speak to it, or else you were bound to get pricked.

Equipment clattered with Elizabeth's stride, her and Lieutenant Gou's advance relieving them from the awkwardness. "I'd love to give you a minute to catch up, but we don't really have one to spare." She tossed her head toward the mansion and led them to the oaken doors.

Iori wasn't prepared for the sea of people on the other side. He hadn't seen this many bodies crammed into one room since the charity ball. Unlike the sparkling splendor of wealth that had his thief's fingers itching then, however, this was a sorry crowd to behold. All scuffs and tatters, swathed in blankets instead of ball gowns, their faces smeared in grime and tears—no glitter.

"I thought you were evacuating," said Ellen.

"We tried," Alexander replied as they waded through the throng. "By the time we got the gates open and got these people moving, the emissions had gotten too strong. Most are too scared to leave."

They started up the left side of the double staircase, the right too clogged to climb. Kyani's wings skimmed the railing. "You can't blame them. They're protected here."

That, and some may prefer a swifter demise within the blast zone to the slow decay brought on by the fallout.

Iori kept that morose perspective to himself.

Cresting the staircase, he spotted Sabine Brozak on the balcony—back straight, chin tucked, legs folded underneath her. The shield-maiden was deep in a meditative state, focus dedicated to her barrier. The fortitude of the senior Jokers was something of a marvel. How long had she maintained it already?

How long until she can't any more?

Iori couldn't even win the skirmishes against his own mentality, every faintly positive thought challenged by disdain. But his internal strife jarred to a standstill when they entered the headmaster's office and his good eye bypassed Chief Gardner and General Eze to land on Hikaru.

Ellen said Circ had attacked him. She didn't say how.

Pink tissue and Void matter spliced the man's cheek like veins of onyx in a craggy cliff face, vaguely in the shape of a handprint, and guilt spilled into the pot of emotions souring inside Iori. The magic responsible for the damage may have been Circ's, but that print belonged to him. His palm, his fingers. It was his corrupted Suit that took the man's leg, too.

Yet, Hikaru regarded him warmly. Still smiled in spite of the pain those scars must've caused when they dimpled and creased—because he forgave too easily, and he cared too much. No matter the trouble, no matter the hour, if someone needed help, he would always endeavor to lighten the load.

"Ryone," he said, relief smoothing his weathered voice. "It's good to see you."

And here Iori had come to burden him again.

CHAPTER SIXTY
JANUARY 6 | CARDPLAY HEADQUARTERS

THEIR PATH TO VICTORY HAD BEEN SET: enter the Domain, defeat Circ, deliver the fragment, save the world. However, unless the Spade reawakened, step two was a no-go. Apparently it was the key to the *Lustral Organ,* some sacred instrument that could decouple Circ from the Void. And without a bleeding hint of magic in his veins, Iori doubted he even had the divine authorization to complete step one.

Heart, Diamond, and Club would pass through the silver gates, and he would be left on the stoop—a beaten, broken stray.

They'd hoped his stores would recharge on the return trip, or that proximity to the magical well would stir the Spade once more. Instead, its continued silence had rendered him the center of disappointed attention.

"This just keeps getting better and better," grumbled Chief Gardner, he and Elizabeth tinted green by the desk lamp's glass shade.

Similarly disgruntled, General Eze slung a sidelong glance at the headmaster. "Weren't expecting that spanner in your works, were you?"

Hikaru stared over his interlaced fingers, either deep in thought or at an utter loss because Iori returned with nothing useful to contribute. *"It's not your fault,"* he'd insisted, and he could repeat that until he was blue in the face, but it wouldn't change how Iori felt. His fault or not, he failed to bring them what they needed.

"We knew this was a risk," said Ellen, beside Iori on the sofa with her hands tucked between her knees. "I thought the boost from the fragment would be enough, but . . ."

"It can't just be gone," Kyani put in, poised on the sofa's arm. "If the Club wasn't always *Withered*, it's possible the Spade wasn't always *Bloody*. Maybe it needs to be called by a new name."

"You think I haven't tried that?" Iori bit back. The flinching curl of Kyani's toes didn't dissuade him from the ensuing rant. "I can't make a connection. If the Spade is there, it's not listening to me. And if it was, you should be able to see it. *I* should be able to hear it."

Alexander looked down on him from the middle of the room—in the literal sense rather than figurative given his upright stance, but it felt more the latter. "She's only trying to help."

I know that. Iori raked his nails over his scalp, mentally checking out when the group started digging into their heap of theories for a solution. He'd paced the barracks for hours, fumbling around inside himself for the Spade's reboot switch. What could they come up with that he hadn't tried already?

He wanted to believe it was still there, undergoing a metamorphosis within the cocoon of his soul, soon to emerge bold and powerful and pure. Of course, that didn't guarantee it would emerge in time. If only there were some way to—

He released his claw-like grip from his head. "That's it."

The others stopped flipping through their ream of speculations.

"What's *what?*" asked Elizabeth.

"We could force it out." Iori sprung up from the sofa. How had it not occurred to him earlier? "If the Spade regressed into a pre-Reemergence stasis, its magical signature could be too faint to detect, which would also explain why I can't summon it. It's not ready yet. But that didn't stop Wiseman from waking it the first time."

"Wiseman used a *torture device*," Alexander reminded him.

Kyani spoke quieter now, probably afraid of offending Iori again. He hadn't intended to snap at her. "Even if we did consider his methods, we don't have access to a machine. The two he built were destroyed and dismantled, and it took years to engineer them."

"I'm not—I'm not talking about the machine." That said, if they had one at their disposal, he would've braved it as a last resort. "It's a partnership, right? Our Suits have a responsibility to defend us, and the Spade has always jumped in to protect me when my life's been under threat. Most recently, by *him*." He pointed at Alexander, drawing uneasy looks from around the room—from Lieutenant Gou in particular, who wasn't aware of their complicated history.

"What precisely are you suggesting?" Concern laced the headmaster's tone.

Wasn't that obvious? Gesturing to himself, Iori closed the gap between him and Alexander. "Fight me like you did on *Duels Day*, no holding back. If you pose a genuine threat to my wellbeing, the Spade will have to intervene."

Alexander recoiled. "Have you lost your mind?"

"It worked before."

"Yeah, because the Spade was *corrupted*."

"The Diamond's pure. It saved you."

"The Diamond's resolve had already been weakened by the machine. If I come at you and the Spade doesn't take action, you could get hurt."

"If it doesn't take action, I'm as good as dead anyway." A twinge shot through Iori at Ellen's hushed exclamation of his name. Why was everyone acting like he'd thrown his wits to the wind? "There is no place for me or you or any of us in a world where the Sundered Star wins, and we need the Spade in order to defeat him. Without it, this whole mission falls apart. So unless you have a brighter idea, *fight me.*"

"No."

"*Fight. Me.*" Iori planted his fingertips on Alexander's chest, crisp shirt dimpling beneath them, and pushed.

That got a reaction out of him—a flare of nostrils, a jerk of the shoulder. "Keep your hands off me."

How many strikes to light the kindling?

Iori pushed him again, harder. He wasn't the sort to pick a fight, certainly not with a guy who'd decked him on more than one occasion, but if their lives depended on it, he was prepared to do anything. Wasn't Alexander?

"You had no trouble coming at me in the arena. Where's that fire now, huh? Where's the fury?" Another slam to the chest knocked him off-kilter, causing the others to rise and raise their voices, but that didn't stop Iori. "Why won't you help me?"

What finally did stop him was Alexander snagging him by the wrists, thus reminding Iori just how weak he had become. His arms shook against the unbending hold, no better than a tuneless instrument.

"This isn't the way," Alexander said, each word carefully measured. Where did he get off speaking to him so gently? "If the Spade's gone into stasis, it may reawaken at the height of the Waning—like the Heart was supposed to. Your idea could get you killed before we even have the chance to find out."

Iori sagged, humiliation filtering in as the fight left him.

"I'm going to let go now. Hit me again, and I'll cuff you to the radiator."

Perfect opportunity for a witty comeback, and Iori didn't even have strength in him for that. After Alexander released his wrists, he kept his head down, avoiding contact with eyes that bore judgment and scorn. Pitching a fit in front of the people reliant on you to save the world—what a look.

The fate of humanity rests in the hands of an emotionally unstable teenage boy. How was that for an inspiring pitch?

As the tension in the room lifted, Hikaru reached a decision. "We shall proceed as previously discussed." He rose from his desk and took up his cane. "Lieutenant Gou, General Eze—if you would please assemble your forces in the command centre, we will take you through the operation plan."

CHAPTER SIXTY-ONE
JANUARY 7 | ELYSIAN TOWER

FROM THE MANMADE POD ATOP ELYSIAN TOWER, Circ could
see all of Hildegrand. The tumultuous sea to the south, all but
one of its islands lost to the tides; the peaks and dips of the
northern cliffs, shielding the magical well from the outside
world; and nestled between them, a metropolis gashed to its
earthly bones, weeping splendid decay.

Once a stretch of sacred ground, now marred by the
blemishes of humanity's heedless expansion, their history
buried beneath iron and concrete and filth. No wonder they
forgot. But the past couldn't so easily be scrubbed into
oblivion. By tomorrow, these streets would run ebony with
ire, their sins come back to haunt them, and the remains of
this blasted era would serve as the foundation for another.

More, more, more, more, more.

Hungry howls sibilated through him as booms
ricocheted across the city. The Void emissions were pluming
thicker below, insidious claws ripping the fabric of reality
apart inch by precious inch.

Patience, he counseled. The further the dimensional
barrier waned and the further the Void crept through, the
stronger he became, and the closer their prize grew. Soon it
would have its feast, and he his throne. He angled his face
skyward, to the imperceptible plane where the protostar had

entered its final stage of evolution—evident by the obelisk's mounting glow.

The next time we meet, sister, it shall be the last.

Footsteps clapped on the luminous marble floor behind him. "My Lord Warden," said Wiseman. "I've received word from Engstrom."

Their loyal and far from noble sentry, posted in the mid district with Cardan McConnell to keep watch. "What does she have to say?"

"Cardplay is on the move. It would appear they've enlisted the help of the National Guard." Making a last ditch effort, were they? Excellent, thought Circ, more lambs to the slaughter. Then Wiseman added in a disgruntled mutter, "A unit from *outside* the city."

Outside? Wiseman had ensured no aid would come from beyond the boundaries. Hildegrand was under lockdown, no one in or out. Not even the military. Their communications had been stifled, cut off, the city's vocal chords effectively crushed. They would have no reason to enter unless—

The girl.

Circ's nails bit into his palms, hard enough to draw blood if he had any. This Heart was proving to be a sharper thorn in his side than her predecessor, a weak-willed harlot right up until she and the others gave their wretched lives to imprison him. Would these novices have the audacity to make such a sacrifice?

"What are your orders?" prompted Wiseman, a faint crackle accompanying the twitches in his right hand. The living matter of malice that filled his body's cavities was growing restless, wanting but forbidden to feed on its host. Perhaps a Keeper or two would sate its thirst.

Even if they had the audacity to pull off their predecessors' stunt, they wouldn't have the power. Circ had kept them alive this long for fear that slaying them would raise the seals once more, but the barrier had torn too far for the Suits to patch it closed. The dam had burst, and their only hope of stopping the flood now would be to push the waters back.

He didn't need them anymore.

Circ uncurled his fingers. "Kill them."

CHAPTER SIXTY-TWO
JANUARY 7 | HILDEGRAND, LOWER DISTRICT

WILDFLOWER AURAS DOTTED THE BATTLEFIELD. White-hot daisies of thermic energy, telluric bursts of daylily orange mingling with materic butterbur, and a dozen more blooms east and west of her team's position, fighting against the onslaught of blight.

A blue-black projectile blazed towards Kyani, trailing streamers of smoke. She snapped her wings inward and dove out of its path like a plunging shuttlecock, fanning them again to catch herself after it skimmed by and struck a building.

She scanned the field for the Void entity that hurled it at her. It had to be one of those newer gargantuan forms. There were more of them now, all starlight-infused ink, ranging from long-bodied reptilian shapes to multi-limbed insectoids and crustaceanesque shells. And amidst the waves of smaller Inkblots, she spotted a giant black scorpion, its bulbous stinger ballooning with liquid and light in preparation to launch another mortar.

Kyani armed her wooden bow, three arrows forming between her fingers, and loosed them at the creature. The wind whistled through their leafy fletchings as they speared the night, two striking their target with a wet crack while the third bounced off its armored shell.

The creature screeched and scuttled off, leaking fluid, and Kyani swooped after it. She couldn't afford to lose it. Essentially living tanks, these big ones dealt too much damage. They had to be eliminated on sight.

She tracked the glowing bulb at the tip of its tail through the smog. It bobbled down the street like an angler fish's lure, round the corner, into an alleyway, and then it winked out. There and gone in the bat of an eye, the creature's aura indistinguishable from the toxic emissions clouding the air.

That thing was the size of a car. Where could it have gone?

Wings beating, Kyani pored over the area, instincts flashing a warning sign in her mind. She'd strayed deeper into enemy territory, her allies a block or two behind her. While her skills were sharper than ever, she was too inexperienced to be this far from support.

As she turned to go back, a shimmer caught her eye. The Void scorpion's stinger, poking up over the lip of a building.

There you are. It must've crawled in through a window.

She flew around for a better angle, nocked an arrow, and—

BANG.

Blood and feathers exploded in Kyani's peripheral vision. She fell from the sky as the shot rang out, floundering to catch the wind. The only thing she caught was concrete. She crash-landed on a rooftop, mask coming free and skidding away in a disintegrating cloud of green. Agony burned through her cheek and shoulder and hip, sharpest in her wing.

Her aura flared around the wrist of her feathered limb, magic rushing to seal the hole—circular, straight through—until another force repelled it like a drop of soap to water.

Anti-magic tech.

Marshal Kulisch's reinforcements were bringing up the rear. Did she get hit with a stray bullet? Except . . . hadn't all of the prototype weapons been given to General Eze's group?

"How's it going, tweety bird?"

A twinge of alarm gripped Kyani. Across the rooftop, between the boxy ventilation units and whirling turbines, stood Sybil Engstrom in her military disguise. Jacket billowing open, sleeves hiked up to display blade-edged tattoos. Her sunset aura dimmed to an idle glow. She must've been using her thermal vision to track Kyani's flight.

Kyani had been too intent on the scorpion to notice her.

At the yank of the bolt handle, her sniper rifle's ejected casing clinked onto the rooftop. From the day they met, this girl had it out for Kyani. There hadn't been a right foot for them to get off on. But all of her badmouthing and harassment had been a game with no end, as per Wiseman's order.

Now it was clear: all bets were off.

"I've been waiting for this for a long time." Sybil brought her iron sights to rest on Kyani, plump lips quirking into a sneer. "Let's dance."

"Naomi, on your left." Ikkei said—his voice clear next to Alexander in the shelter of a metal-made barricade, and a crackly echo in his earpiece. Lightning scored the intersection, hitting nothing but asphalt, and he added, "Your *other* left."

"*I only have one left,*" his sister snapped back.

"Then use it!"

A growl of frustration preceded another burst of electricity, which lanced through a swarm of Inkblots, popping them like water balloons. As swiftly as she exterminated them, more poured in from up ahead.

Naomi and Aryel had positioned themselves in an adjoining street with Oskar, shielded by a barrier of ice. Nightshift was to the east, the rest of the dayshift with Kyani, and Elizabeth had hung back with Kulisch's support unit. Their conventional weaponry might as well be peashooters against Void entities, but peashooters could slow them down, and magic-suppressant stun cartridges had an—albeit brief—effect on them. Their efforts still mattered.

But would this be enough?

"We won't make it to the tower until tomorrow at this pace," Tatiana bewailed. She rested on the elaborate curve of a scissor blade's handle, winded after exercising her *Gale Force* technique on a pack of Inkblots that tried to ambush them from a side street.

They were tangled in the fringes of the enemy's vanguard, a sizeable stretch of the lower district still between them and Elysian Tower, and enemy forces were only growing thicker, increasing the risk of being surrounded. They didn't have the numbers to encompass Circ's army. They had to cut *through*, which at this point was akin to tunneling through gravel. Dig out one shovelful, and more would tumble into the hole.

Baby steps when they needed strides to carve a path for General Eze to move up with Ellen and Iori. They had been sticking to the shadows of the Jokers' frontline, Iori too vulnerable to fight and Ellen a secret weapon waiting for its moment to be drawn. And every minute that weapon remained sheathed, another Inkblot spawned. Another Inkwraith was born. Another soul became blighted.

Alexander could cut a sizeable chunk out of the enemy's forces, but it would be costly, and the Keepers had been advised to preserve the bulk of their energy for Circ. None of them had fought him in his true form or at full strength yet.

There's gotta be something more I can do.

He scanned Void swarms filling the intersection.

Scanned the area, full of wreckage.

Scanned the Jokers and found Soren clutching his scepter, a ball of captured sunshine in its spokes. Soren was a photic type who could bend light. With the sun down and the city blacked out, he would be running low on ammunition. But pyrics could create light, and if Soren piggybacked off Alexander's flames, they could clear the area at a fraction of the cost to the Diamond's stores.

"Kabr," he called, and the boy's attention snapped to him, a sheen of nervousness on his face. No better place to nurture his potential than in live combat. "If I give you enough fire, can you light up this intersection?"

"Maybe?" At a prodding stare from Alexander, he amended his reply to a somewhat more confident, "I-I mean, yes! Probably!"

"Good. Stay here and wait for my signal."

"What's the signal?"

"You'll know when you see it."

As Alexander peeled out from cover, Ikkei hollered after him, "Where do you think you're going?"

"To make a dent." Pumping magic into his sword, its pommel shining and blade searing orange, Alexander marched into the intersection. A pair of Inkwraiths caught sight of him and broke formation, loosing banshee screams as they charged.

Are you watching, Circ?

He slashed the first across the belly, downed it with a kick.

You'd better be.

Embers sparked in his gauntlet.

Because I want you to bear witness as we raze your army to the ground.

He seized the second Inkwraith by the face, fingers sinking into the skeletal dips of its skull, and drove his blade up into its chest cavity. It screeched and batted at his arm as pyric energy unfurled within, and was engulfed a second later in a roiling column of flame.

The heat haze wavered, the column's fierce radiance accumulating into spherules of light. They expanded and brightened, and like a hundred sunbeams focused through a magnifying glass array, they raked the intersection, scorching great swaths of the enemy horde.

Crystallized ink turned to ash, black liquid sputtered.

The metallic taste in the air intensified, and with the Inkwraith almost burnt to a crisp in his grasp, Alexander glanced over his shoulder at Soren. He stood in the middle of the street, eyes aglow and scepter held forth, magic gleaming along the spokes of its wheel as his cape flapped behind him.

This had to be the most power he'd exerted at once.

And such exertion was bound to take a toll.

His irises dimmed, legs wobbling. Ikkei rushed to catch him when he fainted, and the street darkened again—Alexander's column of flame shrinking as the Inkwraith crumbled from his gauntlet. Ember and ash flitted on the breeze, the only remaining howls those of the wind.

For a moment, at least, the area was secure.

Calling for the Jokers to advance, Alexander strode over to Soren and Ikkei. Tatiana rushed to check on her friend as well, the boy's body sagging in the larger man's arms.

"Did I do it?" Soren asked drowsily.

Ikkei chuckled. "You sure did, kiddo."

Alexander patted Soren's shoulder. "Thanks for your help," he said, then ushered them along to the next block. The next space on the board. He reached for his earpiece to inform Elizabeth that she and Lieutenant Gou could move up, but before he could push the button, a warping sound thumped against his eardrums.

Cardan flashed into being behind him, a question tumbling out of his mouth. "Where's Kyani?"

Anger surging, Alexander wrenched the man forward by his lapels. "Where the fuck have you been?"

"That's not important! Just tell me where—"

"You abandon my sister, disappear without explanation, and you honestly think you have a right to pop out of nowhere making demands? Give me one good reason why I should tell you a damn thing."

"How about 'you just lost your plot armor?'" Cardan wrenched free and dusted the ash off his jacket, ruddy complexion whitened by panic. "Circ issued a kill order. He sent me after you, and Sybil after Kyani, and you need to warn your sister too."

Alexander's heart plummeted. "Why?"

"Because he sicced Wiseman on her."

When Ellen and Alexander moved home after the Reemergence, most of the city's wounds had been masked in a guise of renewal. Roads obliterated by artillery had been repaved, and crumbling storefronts were concealed by scaffolding and housewrap. Detour signs had guided traffic away from the worst of it.

This must've been how it looked before the dressings were applied.

Wreckage and ruin lay beyond the second story windows of the decrepit office building Ellen and Iori had hunkered down in. Overturned vehicles, burnt and abandoned, lay in the streets. Black puddles that used to be people dotted the ground. Fires and floods, buildings toppled into unrecognizable heaps.

It almost felt as if she were on a movie set, the bodies being dummies and actors in gruesome makeup. Debris purposely strewn, smoke produced by a machine. And the monsters—well, those would have been animatronics. Practical effects at their finest.

If only this bone-deep chill were nothing more than winter.

Her focus slid to Iori, whose undamaged eye stared out the next window over. Since his meltdown earlier, he hadn't spoken more than necessary. An affirmative here, a murmured inquiry or concern there, and she imagined more had piled up behind his teeth. The effort of holding them in sharpened his brow and squared his jaw, morphing all his smooth contours into fierce lines.

To take his mind off them, Ellen decided to fill the lull with an easy kind of talk: small. "When this is over, where's the first place you wanna go?"

He let out a lackadaisical scoff. "Assuming we're all alive and there are still habitable places to go?"

"Pretend with me."

He ruminated on it for a moment. "Anywhere?"

"Anywhere," she said.

He cast his gaze to the street below, where a couple of General Eze's soldiers had stepped out to check the perimeter. The copper barrels of their prototype rifles gleamed a dull orange in the night. "I'd go someplace with a view that doesn't contain the city, maybe to some hill or valley far from civilization." He shaped his reverie in half-mumbled syllables. "There's a girl I'd like to take with me, too, so I can tell her all the things I wish I'd had the courage to before."

Me, Ellen realized. *He's talking about me.* In his weirdly charming roundabout way. She rested her head against the rough concrete wall and prompted him for more. "What would you say to her?"

His jaw relaxed, brow softening. "I'd tell her . . . she made me better. That I admire her will and her propensity to dream, and that she deserves more credit than she gives herself." He picked at the remaining flecks of polish on his nails. "And I would tell her how falling in love with her was the easiest thing I've ever done . . . and the hardest. But I decided if I were to give my heart to anyone again, it had to be you."

Ellen blinked. She read it in his texts to her best friend, felt it in his kiss, and even waded into the pool of emotion in his memories, but hearing it directly from him—in words intended for her and her alone—it sounded sweeter.

A smile flickered over his face. "You don't have to keep it if you don't want to. Just don't drop it, okay?"

"Don't worry," she said. "Your heart is safe with me."

Although impossible to tell where this would go, she could rest knowing that theirs was a forever kind of love. Even if it didn't last in this form, they would be eternally bound—as partners, as friends, as mates of the soul. In duty and life, wherever it may take them. At this point, it would take divine intervention to part them.

"What about you?" Iori tossed the proposition back to her. "Where would you go?"

To the west, Sabaa's thunderclap boomed. When all was said and done, there was only one place Ellen would rather be.

"Home," she told him. "I want to go home."

Noise sputtered over her earpiece, popping her tiny bubble of a fantasy. Her brother's voice slid in and out of the heavy static. *"El—n? . . . —len do you read?"*

His group must have cleared the next block. Ellen pinched her earpiece to reply. "I can hear you." *Sort of.* "Are we clear to move?"

"You ha— . . . —there—!"

There was a spike in his tone. Panic? She plugged her other ear. "Can you repeat that? You're breaking up."

Probably detecting the apprehension in her own tone, Iori gave her an inquiring look. She hunched her shoulders at him, unable to decipher Alexander's transmission.

Then came the shouting from outside, followed by gunfire and a sound like a wrecking ball crashing through wall after wall after wall. Getting closer, getting louder.

Bitter cold slammed into Ellen.

And the building caved in on top of them.

CHAPTER SIXTY-THREE
JANUARY 7 | HILDEGRAND, LOWER DISTRICT

Coughs rattled in Iori's chest, his throat and nose thick with dust as the whisper of shifting rubble roused him to wakefulness. He dragged himself onto all fours, grazes stinging knees and knuckles and jaw. His eye pad dangled uselessly from his cheek by a strip of tape.

So much for protection.

He made several attempts to grab it before pulling it off in a struggle to properly coordinate his limbs. "Ellen?" he queried the haze, blinking the blear from his vision. Dead static hissed over a radio, emanating from a gaping hole where the other half of the second floor—and Ellen—used to be.

Rising on jellified legs, Iori picked his way down the slope of loosely-held-together debris and called out again. He could hear movement deeper in the building, grumbles and muffled shouts. None of them belonged to Ellen.

Then, weakly: "Over here."

He weaved through what had once been the lobby, flinching when a piece of the floor above moved and released a trickle of grit, and found Ellen peering from a gap too small for either of them to fit through. Their hands met in that cramped window of a space, separated by a mishmash of office building innards.

"You're hurt," said Iori, relieved to see her standing but shaken by the ribbon of blood flowing from her hairline.

She dabbed her brow, sticky and red. "I'm okay, I think." Of course, her accelerated healing would've kicked in already and started mending her injuries. "Are you?"

"I'm in one piece." By some mercy. With his healing downgraded to the sluggish rate of a regular human, bumps he previously would've shrugged off could be life-threatening again.

More clacks of crumbling infrastructure, another rasp of dust—the structure's warning for them to get out, or else be buried alive. Ellen urged Iori onward. "See if you can find an exit; I'll meet you outside."

He hesitated, fingers tensely twined with hers.

"I'll be alright," she said. "Go."

Unsure which scared him more—leaving her, or fending for himself unempowered—he ducked and clambered through the battered building until a cool draft led him to a break in the wall. Gingerly, as not to displace the wrong chunk and bring more toppling down, he cleared the rubble from his path and squeezed out into the smoke-choked atmosphere.

The damage extended past their hideout. A whole strip of buildings had been leveled, and those still standing had slashes carved in them as though raked by laser beam claws. Had something exploded? Puddles of flame dappled the surrounding area in orange and yellow, licking up every piece of flammable material in reach.

And through the heat haze, Iori sighted a figure.

Too upright for an Inkblot, strides too even for Blighted. Iori almost called out, thinking it must be a soldier or Joker from one of the other teams . . . and then the spikes jutting from its scalp came into focus, a jagged half crown of onyx. An Inkwraith, strayed from its—

No. Dread curdled in Iori's stomach.

He knew that posture.

Those even strides.

That ivory suit.

He knew this monster, now as monstrous on the outside as it had always been at its core.

The man had shed his wealthy veneer, his overcoat and his jacket, and rolled his sleeves to reveal one arm of unmarred flesh and one of onyx. Blackness crept from the collar of his shirt, veining across jaw and brow into ravening eyes, submerging wisteria irises into a night-dark sea.

Iori had wondered which version of himself would prevail if and when he confronted Wiseman. The kid, the beast, or the justice-seeker. But the beast from which he'd drawn his bold-faced courage had been slain, the justice-seeker downtrodden and magicless, which left only the petrified kid.

Taloned fingers lengthened, liquefied.

Run.

A devious twist of thin lips unveiled fangs disguised as perfect alabaster rows—the viper rearing back its head, ready to strike. "Hello . . . *Master Ryone.*"

RUN.

Wiseman cast forth his flogger of an arm, barbed tails ripping through the asphalt towards Iori. He dove out of the way, and they raked the front of the office building as he slipped behind one of the cylindrical columns supporting the entrance's overhang.

He panted, on the verge of hyperventilating, cold sweats dampening his skin. Every muscle, every instinct, every cell in his body shrieked at him to run—but he wouldn't.

Not this time.

Barbs clattered over pavement, tresses retracting. "Hiding, are we?" Wiseman's voice drizzled in like acid rain. "Here I expected a challenge from the infamous Keeper of the Spade who left my Players shaking in their boots, yet you won't even face me. Did you lose that fighting spirit along with your magic?"

Shit. He knew.

Iori gulped a breath to stave off the panic. He had to fight. Somehow. *How?* He had no weapons, no protection. Even if he were skilled in melee, mundane fists wouldn't be any match for the monstrosity Wiseman had evolved into.

"This power was squandered in your hands." He stalked nearer. "You could have had this city groveling at your feet, and instead, you chose isolation. Imagine what a force you could have been if you had embraced it." Footsteps scraped through grit, startlingly close now. "Then again, it takes an iron will to harness the malice of the Void, and you always were just a scared little boy."

Too close.

Flogger fingers struck the column. Iori scurried clear of the falling concrete, only to be caught by the ankle, whipped up and around, and thrown into a pile of rubble.

The world spun, full of stars.

Before he could pick himself up, Wiseman lent an unwelcome hand, grabbing him by the shirt and lifting him off the ground. While his onyx arm had reverted to a mostly human shape, black veins now coursed the length of his left, pumping inhuman strength into it as he hoisted Iori higher, legs cycling beneath him.

Every semblance of manufactured warmth had been erased from the man's eyes. They pierced Iori with ruthless cold, the kicking and clawing doing nothing to faze him. In this condition, tail lashing, Iori was no more a threat than a feral kitten. "I'm impressed. You have some fight left in you after all. You never did know when to quit, did you?"

"Go to hell!" Iori spat, fear and anger vying for dominance in his voice.

Wiseman cooed mockingly. "Rest assured, Master Ryone, there will be hell on this earth, but I will not be the one toiling in its trenches. I will rule as its king, and had you picked your allies more wisely, you could have served at my side. But you ran . . ." Behind him, a bounding flash of white and red. ". . . and I will not have cowards in my—"

"Hey!"

Ellen!

Gleaming like a snowdrop in the dead of a desolate winter's night, a blood-dipped blade arching over her head. Its crystalline edge glowed the same vibrant scarlet as her eyes, an image of lethality swathed in disarming elegance.

Her breath misted in the air. "Leave. Him. *Alone.*"

Wiseman scowled at her. "My Lord Warden may fear your abilities, girl, but know that I do not share that fear."

"Maybe you should."

He evaluated his enemy, a thoughtful hum in his chest. "Children shouldn't play with knives."

At the flourish of his right hand, the inky splatters on the pavement nearest Ellen began to ripple, began to rise. She wrapped both hands around the snath of her scythe and retreated several unsteady paces as they drew up into humanoid forms on invisible strings.

"Knights of the Void are entitled to a portion of their creator's power, just as the Keepers possess a share of the Radiant Star's." Wiseman splayed his taloned fingers and his puppets bent towards Ellen. "And with this, I intend to make an example."

The street detonated into a whirlwind of claws and choppy cleansing waves. Puppets dipped and dived and lashed out at Ellen. Her swings were onerous, feet unbalanced—a result of the injuries she'd sustained in the collapse. It wouldn't matter how full her reserves were if her body didn't have the strength to channel them. It'd be like trying to fire a rusted gun, and every missed shot was a vital round of magic spent.

Wiseman knew this, too. "A tool is only as powerful as its wielder, and it would appear the Heart's Keeper is not up to par."

Red sickle slashes cleaved the night, his puppets evading every one. They weren't going for the kill, not yet. Wiseman was using them to drain and distract her so she wouldn't be able to defend herself when he did strike.

"She is only human. Fatigue makes humans prone to mistakes." The puppets danced tauntingly at the languid wave of Wiseman's fingers, holding her attention while he summoned another from a puddle behind her. It stumbled forward, dragging something long and metal and grating. A broken piece of rebar. "And mistakes . . ."

Terror hammered through Iori. "No, wait—"

". . . can be fatal."

"Ellen, behind you!"

With a sickening crack, steel skewered back and organ and sternum. Ellen stiffened, her scythe vanishing in a puff of shining particles, and the rest of the puppets froze in position. Shock lanced through Iori's chest as hers juddered with gasps, her darkening eyes on the clouds.

It's alright, thought Iori. *She can heal.*

She'll be okay.

She has to be okay.

She didn't look okay.

Wiseman gazed almost pityingly at her. "There is a caveat to the Heart," he said. "Magic, as I'm sure you're aware, is fueled by the energy of its user. When the primary glycogen fuel source has been depleted, it will begin to siphon energy from other sources, much in the same way that starvation triggers autophagy. This can lead to dehydration in aquatics, hypoxia in pyrics, and even hypothermia in cryogenic types. The Heart, however, must feed off the life force of its Keeper. How long do you reckon it can keep her alive until it bleeds her dry?"

At the twitch of a digit, his puppet gave the rebar a sharp twist, wringing another gasp out of her—followed by a mouthful of blood.

"STOP!" Iori keened, stunned silence giving way to raucous desperation. "Stop, stop, stop, please, stop! Don't hurt her, please . . . Ellen!" But no matter how he blubbered and begged, Wiseman would not concede.

The crunching twist slowed, metal grinding against flesh and bone. Ellen's arms went limp, her body sagging onto that slick metal rod. Her eyelids fluttered, crimson rivulets streaming down her front.

"Life begets life, and hers is wearing thin." Wiseman's focus slid back to the boy still squirming in his grasp. The crescents Iori had carved into his forearm had no effect. "So much fuss for such a pitiful girl." He tilted his head, fragments of firelight flitting in soulless eyes. "Did you honestly think you could save her . . . when you couldn't even save your own mother?"

That low blow struck a chord.

In a bout of rage and defiance, unable to do anything else, Iori spat in Wiseman's face. And like every bout of defiance that came before, it was only after he acted out, only as the man's expression cooled to impassable stone, that the consequences occurred to him.

Iori's snarl went slack as Wiseman's onyx hand morphed into a stake-like point.

"*Manners*," he growled, and punched straight through Iori's torso as if he were made of tissue paper. The rapid extension of that ghastly right arm yanked him from the grip of the left and nailed him to a vertical slab of concrete, the impact forcing a spurt of blood from his mouth.

It was all he could taste, all he could smell—pouring off his chin in shimmering strands when he looked to the elongated limb. It disappeared into his abdomen at an upward angle, shock dulling the pain to a nauseating throb. His blood ran down the length of it, soiling the cuff of Wiseman's pristine shirt.

Wiseman wiped the spittle from his face with a handkerchief. "I commend your efforts, but when push comes to shove, the strong will always triumph, for our spines have not been burdened by the plights of the impoverished. This is where your weakness lies: in your compassion. Your need to help those who cannot help themselves. To think if young Miss Jane had prioritized her own life over yours, she might have lived."

Another visceral crunch signaled the loss of more blood, more magic, and with every drop, Ellen's life force waned. And as she withered, so too did Iori. Time and again, she had mended his wounds, both of flesh and feeling, but when she needed him most, he couldn't return the favor.

Don't let her die, he pleaded to any power that would listen. *This world needs her more than it needs me. Take me instead. Please.*

"Humanity is on a path to extinction. In order to ascend to a higher level of being and secure our survival," Wiseman counseled, "the weak must be extinguished. There can be no place for faint hearts in the new era."

Faint—her heart was anything but. It took great strength to hope, to care, to take a chance on those who had already forsaken themselves like she had with Iori. She saw potential that he never knew he had and worked tirelessly to ensure he could fulfill it, even when he tried to push her away.

She was his strength.

His courage.

His reason.

Something stirred within him, warm and airy and achingly familiar. Ellen didn't give up on him, and he wasn't about to give up on her.

An inhalation gurgled in Iori's throat. "You're wrong."

"I beg your pardon?"

"Compassion . . . is what makes us human." Iori braced himself on the limb impaling him, the soles of his boots scraping the slab at his back. "It's the thing that binds us . . . that gives us the will to keep pushing forward. Without it, we're no better than monsters."

A rhythm thrummed in his eardrums, rising from the deepest parts of him until that pipe organ was singing through his marrow again, untarnished by the Void's harrowing drone.

"I am here . . . because of the kindness others have shown me. They made me realize I was still worth something. They gave me family." He met Wiseman's eyes, widened in dismay at the flare of violet in Iori's. "And I am not going to let you take them from me."

He dug his nails into Wiseman's blackened arm, infusing it with music. With *magic*. Wiseman tried to pull it free, but couldn't. The frequency of the sound waves vibrating through it had turned his ink-made skin to glass, solidifying more and more of it the further they traveled.

Here on this hill of ruin, Iori would sing him the song of his undoing.

"Awaken, *Melodic Spade!*"

Light plumed, pure and bright, unraveling the threads he wore and rewinding them into an iconic shape. Tall black boots and fingerless gloves, jeans of stone-washed gray, a cropped leather jacket embossed with the dark purple mark of his suit, and a patch over his warped right eye.

With sound as his weapon, he harnessed the crackle of fire, the roar of the Void in the atmosphere, and the mounting timbre of his own voice, and fed every chord into Wiseman. They resonated within the glass prism of his arm, pitch increasing until they reached the socket and—

Shattered it.

With force enough to send the man careening down the street. His puppets followed suit, ripping the rebar from

Ellen's chest as they crashed into smithereens around her. Iori dropped next onto wavering feet, a dismembered portion of Wiseman's onyx arm still lodged inside him.

Ellen didn't rise immediately. With the rod out, the Heart should be able to take care of her until Iori could, but this game wasn't over yet.

Short a limb and missing several points of his crown, Wiseman crawled on his knees. Platinum strands curtained his face, and the tattered holes in his shirt and vest had left his mangled body exposed. Every part the Spade had gouged out in its initial awakening, the Void had rebuilt in knotted fibers of malice. But malice alone couldn't maintain this form whilst preserving whatever sorry excuse of humanity remained in it.

If Knights of the Void were equivalent to Keepers, he would be tethered to Circ the same as they were to the Radiant Star. Without her, without her fragment, they were powerless.

Cradling the stake in his abdomen, Iori hobbled down the debris pile. For years, he had lived in fear of the ghost of this man. Now, broken and disheveled and kneeling in the grime, he wasn't so intimidating. Hardly more than a puppet himself.

"Boy," he fumed, "I should flay you where you stand!"

Empty threats wouldn't serve him here. "You lost your chance. You can't hurt me anymore." Iori raised his hand, he the conductor and the world his orchestra. Those were star-strung cords holding Wiseman together; all he needed to do was override the commanding frequencies that coursed through them. The Void would do the rest.

From the pandemonium, Iori drew his notes, seizing Wiseman once more. It didn't take much to release the Void from its master's control. His spine arched, pain rupturing his fury as the black veins spread—every crime, every sin, rapidly staining his skin. "How . . . can you . . ."

"You might be a servant of the Void, but the Spade was created as a proxy for its warden. That means my power trumps yours, and your stint as king is over." Iori lifted his arm high, middle and forefinger pointed skyward. Decibels climbed, vitrifying the corrupt atoms of Wiseman's soul.

Horror flashed over the blackened angles of his face.

"Checkmate."

Fractures shot through his torso, his neck, and his remaining limbs, all leaking violet light. Iori cranked up the volume, the frequency. Skin chinked and crackled, and then, like his arm, the man exploded into a million pieces. And as his obsidian shards rained down, the demon slain at last, Iori's legs buckled.

Painful spasms gripped his stomach as he wretched dizzying amounts of blood onto the asphalt. More dampened his glove, seeping out from around the chunk of Void matter plugging his wound.

Could the Spade repair a hole this big?

That thought brought his mind swerving back to Ellen, who should've regained consciousness by now. She lay across the street, the petals of her skirt fluttering in the breeze. Deathly still.

"No," the word dripped from Iori's mouth. He half stumbled, half dragged himself over and dropped to her side. "Ellen? Hey, you can hear me, right?" His hand hovered over her, afraid of what a touch might tell him.

Her wound had sealed. It was already beginning to scar, her healing more rapid than his had ever been.

Why wasn't she moving?

He put his ear to her chest, wherein her magic chimed to the beat of a laboring heart. Slower and softer the longer he listened, her sound gradually fading.

"No, no, no, no, no. Ellen. Hey, stay with me." He gathered her in his lap, anguishing at the weight of her—

impossibly heavy for such a willowy thing. Her Suit must've drained too much of her energy.

In trying to save her life, it would be the end of it.

He scanned the area in search of help, shredded what was left of his voice crying out for it. Nobody came. They were all trapped or dead or too wounded themselves, and this required more than first aid. But at the rate Ellen's pulse was dropping, just a flicker now, she wouldn't make it to a hospital or to headquarters.

Even if she did, who would know how to fix this? She wasn't injured. Her magic was consuming her.

What can I do?

He looked over her face, blurred by a wash of tears.

What can I do?

They splashed onto her cheek. "Please," he whispered, wiping them away. "I just got you back. Don't leave me like this." He screwed his eyes shut in refusal of the cruel reality in his arms and bundled her tighter. Her chime had become so faint he could barely hear it.

They were so close. *So close.*

He couldn't lose her here.

A new sound tickled his ears then, a subtle twinkling not unlike her magic's hum, and when Iori lifted his head again, the atmosphere glittered—not with embers, but ruby flakes. The remnants of Wiseman and his fallen puppets were evaporating, the same way blight did during a purifica—

Iori yelped, pain sudden and sharp in his abdomen.

"It would hurt less . . . if you'd stop moving."

At that small croak of a voice, his attention snapped to the girl in his lap, her lacquer black lashes closed but fingertips aglow on the onyx stake protruding from his abdomen. As she whittled the stake down, her chime grew louder, and her heart beat stronger. She was absorbing the Void matter, recycling it into energy for herself while simultaneously using it to boost his healing factor.

This was the power of the Heart. A give and a take.

An exchange.

A sob of a laugh escaped Iori. "Hi." He swept aside the silky threads of hair clinging to her face, her cheek weakly rounding with a smile, and rested his brow between the coronets of her antlers. "I thought I lost you."

"Consider it payback for all the times you've made me worry," Ellen teased quietly. Intensifying pain turned Iori's next laugh into a moan, and she pressed against him. "I know, I know. Focus on me."

His focus was on little else, but it was difficult to ignore the sensation of his internal organs knitting back together. Restored nerve endings sparked like live wires, the regrowth of muscle and tendon a deep ache inside him—worse than the tunnel her brother's bullet had carved there before. But this was a welcome pain.

He had never been so content to hurt.

CHAPTER SIXTY-FOUR
JANUARY 7 | HILDEGRAND, LOWER DISTRICT

ANOTHER SNIPER ROUND PIERCED KYANI'S WING, sending her crashing to the rooftop again. Each time her wounds healed and she attempted to take flight, Sybil would shoot her down like a clay pigeon, every bullet packing a magic-suppressant punch. Not potent enough to knock out her awakening, just enough to render her helpless.

And this time, Sybil had her cornered.

Pinned in the dead end of the HVAC maze, she turned over to face her opponent, scooting back against a ventilation shaft. Sybil limped toward her, an arrow stuck in her thigh—the only one Kyani had been able to sink.

Firing at a living human was a very different thing from firing at a monster, and she didn't know if she had it in her to land a fatal shot. But if she didn't, Sybil would have her way, and as she'd illustrated right down to the goriest detail, her way involved carving Kyani up like a solstice turkey.

Kyani armed her wooden bow, quaking fingers bringing a misshapen arrow like a gnarled twig into existence. An effect of the suppressant shock.

Snapping the stem off the one in her leg, Sybil cackled in disdain. "Go on, take the shot. I dare you." She tossed the broken piece aside and spread her tattooed arms wide. Kyani's aim wavered from chest to head to hip. "You can't do it, can you? Not even to save your own sad little life. What did Mr. Wiseman see in you?"

If these were to be Kyani's last moments, she wouldn't spend them being trampled like a weed. "What did I ever do to you?" she demanded, voice as taut as her bowstring.

Sybil's arms fell back to her sides. "Seriously? We fed you, paid your daddy's health care bills, accommodated you rent-free—in a room that should have been mine, by the way—and you repaid us by stabbing us in the back."

"No." We, us. That didn't sound right. Sybil had never cared for anyone besides herself. "What did I do to *you*? Personally. You've had it out for me since day one. If you're going to kill me, at least have the decency to tell me *why*."

"Have you considered that maybe I just don't like you?"

It had to be more than that. There had to be a reason. Sybil hadn't been fond of Camille either, but she didn't target her with the intensity that she targeted Kyani, and that hatred grew after the Club awakened. Spiked whenever Kyani was invited to dinner. Reached a new height after Wiseman assigned Sybil to be her tutor in marksmanship.

What did Mr. Wiseman see in you?

Her Suit.

What did Mr. Wiseman see in you?

Her potential for ranged combat.

What did Mr. Wiseman see in you?

Her ability to detect magical auras. She never told him she could, but having such extensive knowledge of the Keepers, he must have known. Would he have shared that knowledge with Sybil, who had a visual enhancement of her own?

Their skills overlapped. If he had been able to win Kyani's cooperation and use her keen sight and aim to hunt Keepers . . .

—in a room that should have been mine, by the way—

. . . Sybil would have become expendable.

The girl may not have cared about other people, but she cared about herself very much, and Kyani had unwittingly threatened her position. "You were afraid of losing your seat at the table . . . to me."

Sybil's wide nostrils flared. Kyani had struck a nerve and set her off on a rant. "You should've been at the bottom of the pecking order. I worked my ass off to prove my worth. I *earned* my place. All you had to do was *exist*. You were his shiny new special edition toy, and what did that make me? Chopped fucking liver.

"All my life, I've been tossed aside in favor of pretty, quiet, manipulable doormats like you. I'm sick of it. And I'm sick of looking at your face." Discarding her sniper rifle, Sybil whipped out a pistol and pointed it at Kyani's head. "Wasn't nice knowing you."

If Kyani didn't loose her arrow now, she would die.

She readjusted her aim.

Let go.

Sybil's finger slid onto the trigger.

Let—

A shot rent the air and Kyani flinched, sending her arrow whistling into the night. But the bullet never hit its mark.

Alive, unscathed, she lifted her gaze, and sorrow pierced her heart at the sight of the man before her—standing directly in the bullet's path, his back to her, haloed in pastel blue with a windblown mop of tangerine upon his head.

"*Cardan?*" Ahead of him, Sybil held a smoking gun, her face screwed up in anger. "What the fuck are you doing?"

"Something I should've done a long time ago." He stifled a cough and spat out a gob of bloody saliva. "Put the gun down, Sybil."

Her rage gave way to laughter. Laughter as a former ally, a person she'd worked with and joked with for years, bled in front of her. "I knew that soft spot was gonna be the death of you someday." She jerked her pistol. "Now move so I can put a bullet in this bird's brain."

Rather than step out of her way, he shifted to further obstruct her line of sight to Kyani. "I can't let you do that."

After all the trouble Kyani had caused, going so far as to exploit his benevolence to secure her own freedom, how could he stand there, having taken one bullet for her, and be prepared to take another? In that instant, she had a multitude of things she wanted to ask him, and even more she wanted to scream at him. *Get out of here! Save yourself! Don't do this for me!*

The only words she found were: "Cardan . . . why?"

He cast a look at her over his shoulder, the wind tugging at his coat's lapels. There was a boyish gleam in his lopsided smile, red smudged at the corner. "I owe you one."

The finality of his words rammed into her like a tidal wave. She lurched forward on skinned knees, reaching for him. "Hold on, you don't need to—"

He teleported. Kyani's hand skimmed the emptiness he'd occupied a millisecond earlier, and he reappeared in front of Sybil, clapping his arms around her. A second shot rang out as he bowled her over, her gun sandwiched between them, but before they could hit the ground, a flash of light enveloped them.

And then, Kyani was alone.

Her fingers closed around the vacant air as the rooftop fell still, the din of magic-waged war muffled in the background. The only aura she detected amidst the Void's all-consuming shadow was her own, a shivering green that framed her vision.

No sunset, no forget-me-nots.

They were gone.

Cardan was gone.

And he wasn't coming back.

CHAPTER SIXTY-FIVE
JANUARY 7 | ELYSIAN TOWER

TING, TANG, TONG.

One by one, Circ felt his wires snap under the blade-like bow of the Spade's song. Felt a part of himself perish as the fragment he'd entrusted to the Wiseman family crumbled like a brittle lump of coal, and heard the crown clang to the floor as his faithful Knight drew his last breath.

Icy torrents of rage ripped through Circ. He'd chiseled the Spade to the minutest granulations by the time that whelp of a girl expelled him from its Keeper's body. Pieces so small they shouldn't have been able to produce a single note, let alone a symphony.

Worse, the other three were still alive.

The Heart still beat.

The Diamond's fires still blazed.

The Club still flourished.

And the Void's horde, for all their many eyes were worth, couldn't locate the two Blackjack operatives he'd tasked with eliminating them. Cardan and Sybil's failing he could understand, they were magic users of the lowest calibre, but for Wiseman to fail?

Circ had given him purpose.

Granted him power.

Promised him a crown.

A kingdom.

Sworn *everything* to him short of godhood.

And he let his hubris get the better of him.

Worthless. *Worthless, worthless, worthless, worthless—*

"*WORTHLESS!*" Circ bellowed, whipping away from the sky pod's window. Humans could traverse the mundane plane in ways celestial beings could not, especially in this modern era. They had access to tools and tactics he would have fumbled with, held manipulable relationships he could never forge. But without Stars to guide them these past three millennia, they had forgotten their place.

He should have cut their disobedient, lying, scheming strings himself the instant he was able.

He gave them one job.

One.

But enough of this nonsense. The pinnacle of the Waning was nigh, and these raging torrents within him were brimming now with dark magic—at its strongest yet since his release. He didn't need humans for this next phase, no audience of loyal servants. The vermin of the mundane world would be audience aplenty.

A snap of the fingers transported him to the Cavity, where sounds of battle rumbled through the earth, muted by the dense black matter from which the hollow was formed. The glow from the ramps spiraling into it had become harsher, buzzing at the edge of his senses—not so intense as it was at the tower's peak.

Here, the Void's presence dominated.

Circ could feel it reaching across the city to the towns and forests beyond, thirsting for jungles and deserts and oceans.

More, more.

Everything that lived, everything that breathed . . .

More, more, more.

. . . every human, animal, and insect . . .

MORE, MORE, MORE.

Every crumb of stardust this world had to offer, the Void would devour, and in the throes of their transcendence, as they clung to their mortal existence, humankind would know true suffering . . . before he welcomed them into the sweet release of his embrace, and thus into the Void.

Malice could be a mercy, too. He would show them that together, he and the Void could offer them all that his sister had and so much more.

They'll see. With a thousand eyes, they'll see.

Circ hopped into the pit at the center of the hollow and padded to the nexus of the fissures—the crater made by his fall. A hive of restless souls churned beneath his feet, hungry and eager. They had been waiting for this moment eons longer than he had.

Could the Keepers withstand their wrath?

"Try this on for size," he hissed, and slammed his palms onto the cavern floor. Starlight bolted like lightning into the planet's crust, threading the holes in the barrier, each subsequent strike tearing those holes wider and wider.

The ground shook. Fissures became chasms, shot through with midnight blue, and a fog pitch as a moonless night seeped up from the ancient depths.

Below, something moved.

CHAPTER SIXTY-SIX
JANUARY 7 | LOWER DISTRICT

NEAR-DEATH WASN'T AN EXPERIENCE Ellen had on her bucket list, but she was happy to check it off.

Until tonight, the worst injury she had suffered was a bad bump on the head. She'd been whizzing through the house, no more than five, when she slipped and collided with the coffee table. For ten whole minutes, she blubbered and wailed like tomorrow was gone. Like her world, so small then, was ending.

Three kisses later—one from Dad, one from Mom, and one from her brother—you could barely tell it happened, save for the telltale weal on her scalp and the nicknames that stuck with her after.

Eggy. Eggnog. Egghead.

That was the memory circulating her mind when she awoke in Iori's lap, the battle reduced to a traumatic blur like the car accident and him the only solid thing therein. Now, led by trails of inky carnage, they shambled arm-in-arm towards the rendezvous point alongside General Eze and the battered remnants of her unit.

With radio communications disrupted by interference from the tower, it was no surprise that Alexander nearly fainted when he saw them. He and Kyani peeled away from their post, taking in the damage—the frazzled hair, the dirt and blood, and the fresh welt of a scar on Ellen's chest—and before Alexander could inquire about any of it, Kyani gasped at Iori.

"Your aura!" She cupped her hands over her mouth, enthralled by what must have been a brilliant nimbus of light around him. "And your clothes! The Spade, it's—"

"It came back," he confirmed, still hoarse. "Unfashionably late, too."

Ellen watched her brother's gaze skim the river of hobbling soldiers, all coated in dust and debris. She recalled his static-laden transmission. "Wiseman found us," she said, bringing his focus to her. "That's what you were trying to warn us about, isn't it?"

"Yeah, Cardan gave the heads-up. Apparently we've outstayed our welcome. I was about to come looking for you when we got swarmed again." Alexander surveyed Iori once more. "Is Wiseman . . . ?"

"Dead," Iori stated. "I made sure of it this time." His weight shifted onto Ellen and off again with a wince. If he was leaning too heavily on her, she hadn't noticed—more preoccupied with where that mop of orange hair was in the crowd.

"Where is Cardan? Is he here?" She hadn't thanked him yet for his help.

Kyani went to reply, then she exchanged a look with Alexander, and her hands sank to the club-shaped bust of her dress. "He got shot protecting me from Sybil. I'm not sure where they went—he teleported away with her—but . . . I don't think we have to worry about her coming after us anymore."

A film of solemnity settled over them. How many more allies and innocents would succumb or be killed before the battle's end?

The would-be king was dead, his pawn missing in action.

"That leaves Circ." The ringmaster. "We have what we need, now we have to get up there." Into Elysian Tower, a couple of blocks away, but near and bright enough that it illuminated the Void fog around them. And through the portal at its peak, the Domain, the *Lustral Organ*, and the Astral Pool awaited.

Alexander jerked his head toward the rendezvous point's slapdash fortifications. "We were just getting ready to push ahead. Here, let me give you a hand." Stepping to Iori's other side, he relieved his sister of support duty.

A smirk drifted across Iori's face. "I knew you liked me."

"Don't get any ideas. I'm doing this for her, not you."

"Why for her? I'm the one who's injured."

"She's my sister. You're a *menace*." Alexander tugged Iori's arm over his shoulder, lugging him about like a sack of grain. "I'm giving her a break from carrying your dead fucking weight, and I can drop you just as easily, so *can it*."

Even here, even now, they couldn't help squabbling.

Together with General Eze's unit, they filtered into the commercial intersection the battle group had barricaded themselves into. Alleyways had been clogged by ice and stone, roads fenced off with vines that resembled the metropolitan jungles of post-apocalyptic fiction.

General Eze and her soldiers settled with Lieutenant Gou and his while the Jokers licked their wounds, stealing a moment to recoup their energy. Oskar poured water over Sabaa's blistered palms, then chugged the rest of the bottle. Others scarfed down energy drinks and snack bars to increase their recharge rates.

They couldn't have chosen a better location. First aid, fuel, materials to manipulate—the stores encircling them provided everything they needed for that final push.

Ellen expected *some* fighting, however. "It's so quiet."

"Circ's pulled his forces back to the tower grounds," Alexander explained. "Must be feeling the heat."

"Or he's attempting to lure us in," said Iori.

"Jokes on him if he is. We don't have any direction to go but forward." Alexander led them to the entrance of Main Street, which had been given two vertical rows of scrap metal teeth. Ikkei and Iris' handiwork. He would've held the scraps in position while she welded, cobbling together car hoods and street signs and any other stray alloys they could.

Currently, Iris was utilizing those welding powers to apply an improvised brace to Yusuf's leg. Ikkei, resting with the A-Team, waved to Ellen and Iori when he spotted them. "Hey, look what the cat dragged in!"

"I'd say it's more the cat that's being dragged in," corrected Naomi, rubbing Aryel's back. He sat shivering by a burn barrel to counteract the effects of overexertion. Frost that had begun to swirl over his skin melted now into thin streams as he warmed.

Alexander lowered Iori onto a stout concrete barrier outside the shop they'd fused the scrap shield to. He went down with a grimace, holding his side. Hoping to take the edge off, Ellen went to give him another boost, and he stopped her.

"Don't waste your energy on me."

"It's not a waste if you need it. You can't even stand on your own." Figuring the worry on his brow was for her life force, she added, "I won't use too much. I promise." She could replenish however much she spent provided she had an adequate supply of Void matter, and there was no shortage of the stuff here.

"Just in time." Elizabeth appeared in the doorway, gleaming holes in her magically spun garb, as Iori hiked up his jacket and shirt to reveal the misshapen tissue where his surgical scar used to be. Rapid healing was effective, not pretty. "What in god's name happened to you?"

"Got stabbed."

"By *what?*"

"Let's just say the guy was armed and dangerous. I'd rather not recount the whole ordeal."

Fingertips igniting like matchsticks, Ellen crouched in front of Iori. He flinched at her touch against bare and tender skin, then relaxed as the redness faded, his pain alleviated by another few degrees.

"Holy shit," exclaimed Tatiana, ogling Ellen's work as she and Soren hurried over.

Soren blanched at the grisly wound, becoming less grisly by the second. "You can heal people?"

"It's limited to Keepers, I think. Or at least Empowered." Most somatic abilities depended on a connection to the recipient's magic, and as far as Ellen could tell, this only accelerated Iori's preexisting healing factor. "It's not perfect, but it gets the job done."

Iori's tail flicked. "So modest," he ribbed, tucking his shirt in once she'd finished.

"Better?"

"Much."

Straightening, Ellen turned to the group. "I can also recycle corrupted matter into energy." She'd felt the change when cleansing the soldiers at Fort Worth, like a new valve had opened, but she hadn't been able to identify its purpose until instinct guided her hand to that chunk of Void glass.

It was a receptacle.

Always, since the day her powers manifested, she'd had this hollow inside her that ached when she purified the too-far-gone. Ached because, while they couldn't be saved, there had been a place for them. A chamber within the Heart. Now that it had been unlocked, she could fill it.

With the blighted.

With the wicked.

Turning misery and malice into power.

"This is how we save *everyone*. If I can purify Circ, it should give me enough energy to cleanse the people he's blighted." He was a Star made of Void; if the intensity of his chill were anything to go by, it'd be like siphoning a charge off the world's most powerful battery. And if those afflicted by his magic were linked to him as Wiseman had been to his puppets, she could in theory purify all of them without laying a finger on a single one.

"Do we *want* to purify him?" Aryel's teeth chattered around the question. "He fell once already. What's to stop him from falling again?"

"Purification can't save him," said Ellen. This union he'd forged with the Void had pushed him over the threshold. Only one outcome awaited him. "He'll die."

People had died at her hands in the past, people whose lives she'd failed to save. This, however, would be the first life she had set out purposely to end.

At least this way, his tormented soul could go in peace.

In the distance, thunder rolled. Then it got louder, closer, and bits of debris jumped about on the pavement. Windows rattled and metal fortifications swayed, creaking and groaning and popping at the seams where they'd been fused.

Ikkei cast a magnetic field over the barrier to stabilize it, and Elizabeth steadied herself against the doorframe.

"Another quake?" she wondered.

The next shockwave ushered in an arctic squall, raising goosebumps from Ellen's scalp to her toes. She twisted southwest to confront the wind, Iori's ears swiveling to its howl. Alexander shielded his mouth from the metallic scent it ferried in, and Kyani cast her gaze to the roiling shadows.

All stemming from Elysian Tower.

The breaking of the Heart's seal triggered the last quake. What could this be?

The Keepers climbed the precipice of wreckage sandwiched between the barrier's teeth, rebar and fence posts and other long pointed objects positioned outward to hinder incoming enemy forces. From here, they had a clear line of sight to that glowing edifice, and the undulating mass of Circ's army should have been visible, too, if they hadn't been engulfed by Void emissions.

Up they billowed like ash from a raging volcano. And with an earth-shattering boom, it erupted.

Ink spewed from the earth, black geysers thrashing like the limbs of a living thing—because it was alive, and it was *angry*. Malice pelted Ellen with the ferocity of a hailstorm as tentacles spiraled skyward, dotted not with suckers but a myriad of bulging, starlit eyes. They coiled around the tower, buckling iron and breaking glass, climbing past its teardrop pod to its antenna spire and higher still, stretching for the clouds that whirled overhead.

They stabbed and pierced and ripped the sky open, then reached inside that light-limned pocket and pulled something *down*. The tear widened around a colossal hunk of rock, white as chalk and woven through with hoary vines. Rough like the outer crust of a geode, the bottom of an iceberg.

The underside of a floating landmass.

"Oh, holy fuck," breathed Ikkei.

A breeze ruffled Kyani's feathers. "That's . . ."

"The Domain," Ellen finished.

When Circ told her he planned to unite the realms, she assumed he intended to riddle the mundane world in corruption. Now she understood: he meant to merge them. To bring heaven and hell and earth together as one realm, one plane, one shared dimension. And if that landmass was the Domain, then this inkborn kraken had to be the physical manifestation of the Void.

Their time was nearly up.

With a twirl of her fingers, Ellen summoned her scythe. "Let's finish this."

CHAPTER SIXTY-SEVEN
JANUARY 7 | ELYSIAN TOWER

CARDPLAY CLASHED WITH THE Sundered Star's army in a maelstrom of magic and ink. Lethal torrents, pulled from the water mains by Oskar Trey, swept throngs of Inkwraiths off their feet—to be trapped moments later in Aryel Rizka's flash freeze, which made ice age exhibits of their bodies.

Ravaged by Naomi Toi's volts, Inkblots popped like insects in a bug zapper, and more burst from the sheer concussive force of Sabaa Faizan's thunderous claps.

The prairie twister that was Tatiana Kosta cut down huge swaths at once, winds gusting at the swing of her crystalline scissor blades, and the gore left behind sizzled under the scorching heat of Soren Kabr's sunbeams. They pierced the smog, illuminating the battlefield in brilliant flashes of yellow.

Chain links glinted in the light, whisking through the air to rip mercilessly into other ink forms. If not for the shock of blue on his head and the metallic shimmer of his aura, Kyani might have mistaken Ikkei Toi for one of the monsters. His chiseled physique had been glazed in black, leaving little of the actual man visible.

The conflict unfolded as she soared overhead, Iori and Ellen bounding over rooftops below as Alexander rocketed straight through the horde, racking up a body count but not stopping to log numbers. Their priority was Elysian Tower and the colossus that had overtaken it.

Her fellow Keepers close behind, Kyani landed inside the half-collapsed chain link perimeter of the tower grounds, vacated by the army now surging at the Jokers. Faint signals traveled through the bare soles of her feet, emitted by flora slumbering beneath the multi-tiered concrete plateau.

With the tower inaccessible from the ground, obstructed by the kraken clinging to it, they would need a new path to the peak, and with the assistance of her earthbound acquaintances, Kyani would build one.

She took point, casting her magic and her thoughts underground to coax vegetation to the surface. *Forgive me for interrupting your sleep. I know it's not your season, but the world needs you now.*

Lichen unfurled in her footsteps. Weeds crept out of the cracks in the pavement, curling their leaves against the tainted atmosphere. They weren't impervious to the blight. If they didn't take action, it would come for them as well.

So if you would be kind enough to lend your support . . .

Flowerbeds that had lain barren since the Reemergence flourished anew. Leafless trees budded boldly against winter's bite, their splintered trunks flushing with color.

. . . we'll make this a place you can thrive in again.

Concrete swelled and fractured, an aurora of magic dancing above it. Roots punched up from the soil, growing longer, thicker, and spilling out in ringlets of green and brown. With a sweep of her hands, Kyani directed them to the tower, and she didn't need to give any further instruction.

They lunged for the kraken, seizing its limbs, and strangled and squeezed with the might of a swallowwort. A roar sent shivers through them as the beast strained against their binds, tearing some, but they did not yield, and they would show it that mother nature was a force to be reckoned with.

Whilst the tentacles were restrained, more roots wound around the tower's exterior, building organic bridges to the top.

At the wave of her hand, Kyani's beaked mask reformed over her face. "They won't be able to hold it for long. We have to move!" She drew her bow, and a great flap of her wings hoisted her into the air.

Ellen took off with a spring in her cloven-sandaled step, splashes of ruby punctuating her ascent. Iori blurred past her on his acoustic skates, streaking violet, and Alexander propelled himself to one of the upper root spirals on roaring jets of flame.

Eyeballs ranging in sizes from boulders to houses rotated in liquid sockets, tracking the three Keepers, and multiple tentacles broke formation—a tsunami of ink about to crash into them. Loosing a volley of bramble arrows, Kyani tethered several to the structure.

A cluster of eyes zeroed in on her, pupils narrowing to slits. The beast lashed out at her, its movements deceptively slow from afar, and swatted at her as if she were no more than a pesky mosquito. Dwarfed by its scale, she felt like one too.

She dove to evade it, tentacles corkscrewing after her, and sail upward again when they gained on her.

She was quick, but they were quicker.

One snagged her by the ankle and yanked her back down.

She flapped frantically to maintain altitude, twisted to get a bead on her target, and let another arrow fly. The thorn-sharp tip punctured one of the creature's eyeballs and it promptly recoiled, flinging streamers of gleaming blue fluid in an agonized rage.

Those had to be its weak points.

She nocked three more arrows and took aim.

Charles Wiseman once likened the Diamond to the gemstone of its namesake, and Alexander hated that the commonalities between it and him went beyond those that man had drawn. Diamonds may have been among the hardest materials on the planet, but a strike in the right spot would shatter them like any other rock. Not to mention, the slightest fault could compromise the gem's integrity.

And faults—Alexander had many. More than he wanted to confess to, even before Blackjack scuffed him up. But with laser precision he had been burning those inclusions out, and although physically he was still recovering, he felt stronger and sturdier than ever. Of sound mind and spirit, each attack made with purpose.

For his parents.

For his sister.

For his family, and his comrades.

For the tomorrow they all deserved.

He blazed into a throng of tentacles, plunging his blade in deep and hauling it up the length of one. Red-hot fury split the rubbery membrane encasing the limb and unleashed a shower of black gore from within.

More gave chase, closing in on all sides.

He swung left, igniting one.

Swung right, scattering flames.

Tentacles crisscrossed overhead, knitting a ceiling to block him. Alexander slashed upward and through, bursting out the other side amidst a spray of ember and ink and dewdrops of suspended starlight. And he froze there, hovering like a rocket on reentry, dumbstruck by the vastness of the world around him.

The view from an aeroplane couldn't compare to this.

Hildegrand rambled hundreds of meters beneath his boots, the sky a whorl of clouds and night above. And hanging there in all its pearlescent glory, as if the moon itself were being reeled in from orbit, was the Domain—many times larger than it appeared from the ground.

For a moment, Alexander forgot how to breathe.

Then a wave of vertigo washed over him. He listed sideways, jolting to stabilize himself, and sucked in a lungful of air. It slid over the forked tip of his tongue, crisp with winter and sharpened by corruption.

Sound sang through the tower's iron skeleton—Iori gliding somewhere within, the hum of his skates on the framework causing the kraken to quiver. Not far behind, flashes of scarlet flayed its thrashing limbs, Ellen a bolt of white in the carnage.

Kyani was several meters higher than Alexander, wings flapping. Her roots had successfully pried the Void off the Domain, away from the sky pod, and were almost at the tower's peak.

Fire bursting from his heels, Alexander blasted ahead, landing upon the bridge as it spilled in through the pod's broken window and secured itself to the frame. He held his sword at the ready, magic primed.

But the pod sat empty, the Sundered Star nowhere in sight.

Alexander stepped off the bridge and onto obelisk's glowing marble summit—once flawless, now webbed in cracks. As his gaze settled on the web's nexus, where once his sword had struck, an icicle sensation trickled down his spine from the base of his skull, carrying echoes of Valerie's orders.

"Submit," when she'd taken control.

"Awaken the Diamond," when she wanted to use him.

"We have your first assignment," she'd said in this very spot. *"Eliminate the Keeper of the Spade."*

But eliminating the Spade's Keeper was no easy feat. Iori had fought back, and Valerie wouldn't let Alexander surrender. *"Are you going to let him best you? Hit him again."*

His sister's voice filtered in next, a memory of his blade at her neck. *"Alexander, it's me. I know you're in there. I know you can hear me. Put the sword down, okay?"*

Valerie's overlapped hers.

"What are you doing?"

"Please."

"Don't just stand there. Cut her down!"

"We can take you home."

"Kill her!"

"I need you to come home."

"KILL HER."

Glass chinked behind Alexander, shards toed aside by Kyani. Ellen and Iori had crested the root bridge as well. All three regarded him with a mixture of concern and unease, lingering traces of the flashback caught on his face.

He shook it off, cleared it from his throat. He couldn't allow himself to get lost in the weeds. They had a Star to vanquish and a Star to restore, and if the former wasn't here, he'd be after the latter. "Circ must've entered the Domain already."

Ellen's sandals tapped urgently across the floor. "Then we have no time to waste."

"You opened the portal before," Kyani said to Alexander. "Do you think you can do it again?"

He studied the cracks the Sundered Star had emerged from, working his jaw. Last time, the Diamond carried out the task at Valerie's command after his own consciousness receded, crumpled by the atrocity he'd nearly committed. Regardless, would he even be able to open the portal with the surface smashed like this?

If he couldn't, they'd have to propel themselves the rest of the way—by wing, by sound, by fire, carrying Ellen—and he doubted they had the magical reserves to make that trip.

Alexander walked to the middle of the pod, scraping his mind for instruction. Tapping into instinct, into the Diamond. Copying the haze of a memory it offered, he took his longsword in both gauntlets and angled it downward.

He flexed his fingers around the hilt.

Take us up, he requested, and struck the marble.

A vibration traveled through the blade into his arms, the sound ringing out. Light flared, and he staggered backwards as the portal whirled open, bathing the pod in unearthly splendor.

The Keepers eyed the vortex curiously, warily. They could only guess what lay on the other side. They'd heard the stories, sure, but stories seldom lived up to reality. And how may the Domain have changed in the absence of its warden? In the fallout of the Cataclysm?

More than those unknowns, what stayed Alexander's feet was the realization that once they went in, there was no guarantee they would come out. These could be their last moments in the mundane world. With each other.

"So," said Iori with a slow sweep of his tail, "who's going first?"

Alexander extended a hand to his sister, steady somehow despite the weight resting on all of their shoulders. "We go together."

CHAPTER SIXTY-EIGHT
JANUARY 7 | THE DOMAIN

ELLEN FELT AS THOUGH SHE HAD STEPPED INTO A DREAM.

The Domain was just as the legends described: an expanse of pristine white beneath a dome of cotton wool clouds, ever bright despite existing in a bubble of eternal night. Shallow craters in the floor gave the impression of the moon, only these were perfect and precise, and clusters of them were connected by thin channels. From above, Ellen imagined it would resemble a constellation chart.

If it were, would it depict their celestial sphere or another?

The portal had dropped them outside a grand fortress of marble, milky white and polished to a reflective sheen. Aqueducts branched off from the structure, some looming over the larger craters in the floor as if once to deliver water, but their source had run dry.

The silver trees encircling them didn't seem to mind. Their canopies still rustled, full and shining like flakes of foil. Perhaps they didn't need water to survive.

"I can't believe we're actually here," said Kyani, her hushed voice magnified in the eerie solitude.

When people speculated about the afterlife and the heavens, of what lay beyond death, this was the realm they spoke of. It was here they were born, and here they were meant to return when their mortal clock struck its final hour. Over time, it had taken on different shapes, each retelling of the story straying farther from the truth. Morphing whenever passed over another teller's tongue or onto a fresh piece of parchment, later to be parsed by archeologists and retold and reshaped again.

As such, Ellen hadn't known quite what to expect. This emptiness, though, was one thing she hadn't anticipated.

Her hand shot to her chest, a sparking twinge inside.

"What's the matter?" asked Alexander.

"The fragment . . ." It was buzzing like a caged fairy in her ribs, pushing her in the direction of the fortress. *Trouble, trouble, hurry, hurry, hurry.* "Something's wrong. Come on!"

The four of them sprinted indoors. Following the fragment's pull, Ellen led them past the foundations, into the bowels of the floating island. The temperature dropped, steeper and steeper until they reached the understructure, where they skidded to a halt on a crescent-shaped landing. Moonbeams poured into the sparkling quartz cavern through circular openings in the ceiling and floor, illuminating a reservoir of crystalline water.

The Astral Pool.

This was the sacred hollow where gods were made and remade, and where the protostar should have been resting. Instead, it had been plucked from its spot by the Sundered Star. Water trailed ribbons around his forearm as he studied it, this tiny scintillating promise of life. Then he pinched it between his fingertips and held it over his mouth.

"Wait, don't—"

Before Ellen or any of them could intervene, he dropped the protostar upon his blackened tongue and drank it down like a pill. And as he rolled his head to look at the Keepers, new light pulsed in his irises, power coursing through every raised shaft of hair on his scalp.

He cracked a grin, glitter on his lips. "You're too late. The show has already begun!" Laughter splintered from his throat, that hyena cackle bouncing off the walls as frigid gusts turned the reservoir into a storm-tossed lake.

The kraken was back, moaning a whale's song.

Tentacles exploded from the hole in the middle of the pool, moonbeams blotted out by writhing coils of ink.

Fastening her grip on her scythe, Ellen looked to Iori, who'd assumed a fighting stance. He had somewhere else to be. "We haven't lost yet," she yelled over the mounting noise. They still had the fragment, and they could still defeat Circ. "Go with Alexander and find the *Lustral Organ*. Kyani and I will keep him busy."

The boys doubled back, leaving the girls to face Circ alone. So long as there was blood in their veins and breath in their lungs, they had a chance.

How much space could a couple of Stars need?

The fortress was honeycombed with enormous rooms that served no discernible purpose other than lounging. Strangely, many had been furnished in strikingly human fashion, too. Embroidered drapes, seating, ornaments on display—every piece sewn or painted in varying shades of blue, white, and silver with the occasional glint of goldleaf for flare.

It looked as though it had been built to house hundreds if not thousands of guests. Yet at the same time, it felt utterly inhospitable. Harsh and bright, not made for living beings.

And still no sign of this *Lustral Organ*.

Iori raced up a curved stairwell, hand skimming the inner wall as Alexander's boots clopped close behind. From the title, he gathered the instrument must reside where most vital organs did—safely within the structure's core. Where the core was located was another matter.

"What are we even looking *for?*" he puzzled aloud.

"How should I know?" Alexander snapped, temper stoked by exigency. "You're supposed to be the musical genius. Look for something that can make music."

Oh yeah, that narrows it down. It would've helped if the wealth of knowledge Hikaru received had included physical descriptors. How were they to know how an instrument forged by divine hands differed from humanity's creations? Would it have strings, a bow, a skin to beat with a mallet? What kind of music held the power to thwart a pissed-off demon octo—

Something punched through the glassless arch of a window, slamming Iori against the wall, and he found himself confronted by an orb of bottled cosmos.

The tentacle lurched suddenly, the gelatinous fluid in its eyeball jiggling at the bite of Alexander's blade—like a hot cleaver to a hunk of meat. Ink squealed as he laid into it, hacking mercilessly until the tip dropped off and the weeping stump retreated, leaving Iori plastered to the wall.

Alexander peeled him off and pushed him along. "Keep moving."

They passed several more rooms, each as elegant and vacant as the last. Would the *Lustral Organ* even still be here and be functional after three thousand years? If it wasn't, they'd have to devise an alternate strategy fast. Ellen and Kyani couldn't stall the Sundered Star forever. Both were capable fighters, but both had already had close calls tonight—they all had—and they were facing their most powerful adversary yet.

Adversaries, if you counted the *literal underworld.*

However, Iori also knew that if anyone could go toe to toe with a corrupted god and come out victorious, it would be Ellen Amelia Jane.

Iori and Alexander reached the top of the staircase, slowing their stride as they entered a vaulting cylinder of a room. It filled the width of the fortress' tower, one side yawning to the outdoors. Ornate pillars spanned the gap and a draft howled, but not through them. It funneled up through a circular opening in the middle of the room, surrounded by an assortment of staggered metal pipes.

All of which were connected to a polished white console.

"It's . . . a pipe organ," Alexander observed. "That makes sense."

A very large and daunting pipe organ at that, with a sweeping pedalboard and three manuals of keys whose colors had been reversed from the standard—ebony where ivory should be. This must've been his predecessor's instrument of choice, the origin of Iori's internal rhythm. The Spade's magical hum.

Alexander pored over his features, and it was more than prior blood loss that paled them. "Is that going to be an issue?"

"I have never played a pipe organ in my life." Or touched one, or seen one outside of photographs.

"Can't be that hard. You play piano."

Iori threw Alexander a look bordering on disgust. "They're not the same." That'd be like expecting a violinist to riff flawlessly on a guitar without practice. "I mean, yeah, I know how to work a keyboard, but not with that many keys." Not to mention the overwhelming number of knobs and pistons and pedals. An organ of this scale was a whole other beast.

What was he supposed to do, annoy the Void into submission with some novice racket? Why hadn't the Spade chosen another organist?

A roar shook the atmosphere, yowls ricocheting in the stairwell. Terrific, the big monster spawned a pack of little monsters.

Heat suffused Alexander's sword. "You'd better figure it out. Get playing; I'll cover you."

As he went to confront the swarm, Iori inspected the instrument. It wasn't connected to the pipes by the means that traditional organs were. Rather than sitting atop a wind chest, they led into the marble platform the console had been built up from, which hung perilously over the opening in the floor.

The draft caught his curls, whistling past his ears. A faint glow flickered miles below, multiplied by the faulty curvature of his left eye and made bleary by the damage to his right. Even so, he recognized it as Elysian Tower. The shadows whipping over it had to be the kraken's limbs.

This conduit cut straight through the landmass.

A tuneless caterwaul announced the arrival of the Inkblots. One pounced at Alexander, claws clashing with burnished steel.

Iori took his place on the bench, where the former Keeper of the Spade once sat, and prayed that his Suit would guide his hand as it had before. But the instant his fingers made contact, the instrument changed.

Three sets of keys became two. The pedalboard shrank, splitting into three pedals—soft, sostenuto, and damper—and the pistons and knobs melted into the console, which in turn morphed into the open-lidded body of a grand piano much grander than any he'd played.

The lofty pipes remained, unchanging.

Not quite the arrangement he was used to, but he could make this work. Now, to shake off the pre-show anxiety.

Nothing to worry about, he thought.

Only the defining performance of his career.

Drawing a breath to stabilize his nerves, wrought from adrenaline, Iori dove into the music. And this time, he didn't try to fight the current. He let it carry him into a trance, let soul and melody blend until the hammers and strings felt not as a part of the instrument, but an extension of himself.

Hear this, he willed. *Let my heart resound.*

Blue-black projectiles blitzed across the cavern, narrow misses that exploded into singeing clouds of cold when they struck quartz. Between these and the tentacles, getting close to Circ was impossible. He'd positioned himself over the reservoir, opting to lob starlight-infused ink mortars at Ellen and Kyani from the safety of his tempestuous cloud.

Then again, he couldn't hit them either. Ellen swiftly evaded his attacks in her hoof-toed sandals, and Kyani swooped between tentacles with a sparrow's speed.

They couldn't play keep-away forever, though.

Another tentacle lashed at Ellen. She met its downward arc with *Scarlet Gem*, and the scythe's gem-cut edge sliced clean through it. The flopping dismembered chunk shriveled on the floor as her magic gnawed at it, absorbing its ink and refilling a portion of the power she'd spent. It wasn't a one-for-one exchange, but considering the amount of ink filling this space, she wouldn't run out unless Circ deprived her of her energy source.

Wings flapped to her left. An arrow struck the floor and Kyani pulled Ellen into a protective dome of brambles. Mortars splashed over the top of it, plumes of blue and black permeating the gaps in the thorny vegetation. The two of them stole a moment inside to catch their breath.

"Thanks," panted Ellen.

"Don't mention it." Kyani watched a graze on the plump curve of her shoulder heal and fade. Aside from the hazy smear of shed blood that remained, you couldn't tell she'd been hurt. "I don't know how much longer we can keep this up."

They were depending on Iori and Alexander to come through with the *Lustral Organ*, but they'd been gone an awfully long while. What if they couldn't find it, or what if they'd encountered trouble? Without the instrument, they wouldn't be able to subdue the Void. Wouldn't be able to weaken Circ. Wouldn't be able to purify him.

Not unless they could get him to drop his guard another way.

A tentacle thrashed upon the dome, shaking leaves loose. Kyani huddled closer to Ellen, raven wings fanned around her.

Outside, the Sundered Star raged. He'd been pinballing between rabid fury and glee for the duration of the fight, taunting them until frustration flipped the tantrum switch, then he'd regain whatever semblance of composure unhinged gloating passed for.

Unpredictable, unstable, impulsive.

Would he make the same mistake twice?

"Can you distract the tentacles?" Ellen asked.

"What are you going to do?"

"Talk to him."

Kyani batted her lashes. "That's your plan?"

Another thrash, and another, and the roof began to cave.

"I'm gonna try to throw him off his game. That should give you an opening, and then maybe I can purify him while he's restrained." All she needed was to find a crack, the same way the Void had. If she could pull it off, they wouldn't have to rely on the *Lustral Organ* to defeat him.

The Void would have to be dealt with later.

Before Kyani could agree or disagree, a mortar blew her dome apart and sent both girls flying in a shower of foliage. Thorny brambles slashed at Ellen's skin, snared at her skirt, and she crashed into a wall of jagged quartz crystals with a shout. Immediately, another tentacle was looming over her.

She rolled clear as it brought its full weight down, slamming into the floor where she had lain a second ago. Banishing the gruesome mental image of herself as a human pancake, she scrambled to her feet and fled from a hail of smaller mortars.

Splash, splash, splash—right on her heels, which weren't as nimble as they once were. Somewhere amidst the chaos, she'd twisted an ankle, and blood wound red streamers down her forearm and shin.

Kyani had flown off to stuff the ceiling hole with fresh brambles, blocking the kraken's reach. They didn't know where it led besides up, but that was where Iori and Alexander had gone. She fired several more arrows at the tentacles, then kited them away from the passage and away from Ellen.

"If you think I'm going to let a bunch of second-rate Keepers stop me, think again!" Spittle flew from Circ's lips, his hair an untamed creature of its own. "You are half the warriors your predecessors were. Half the saints, half the blasted human beings. Just die already!"

His cloud stormed under him, each biting gale of malice followed by a dense, damp chill. A layer of pain in every outburst.

Those were the cracks Ellen was looking for.

She deflected the next wave of mortars with a cleansing sweep of her scythe and projected her voice for Circ to hear. "I understand why you're angry, but we're not the ones who wronged you. Not us, or any of the people down there. They don't deserve this!"

"No, they don't. What they deserve is damnation, and I am giving them eternity. This is a mercy, and in return, the masses shall worship me the way they worshipped her!" Circ bent forward, gripping his knees. "There was an imbalance from the start—did you know? The scales tipped in her favor the instant we were born. She obtained her every desire, was always first in line. Brightest, purest, most revered—but Lambent, oh Lambent, that dim speck to the south. Lambent wasn't worthy of devotion. Lambent was the wayward one, devourer of naughty children and punisher of sins. You humans blamed *me* for your wickedness when it was you who bred it. And my sister was content to let their disparaging fabrications run rampant so long as *I* was the brunt of them. So long as I did my duty!" He straightened, cracks closing. "Well, granting wishes always was part of the job. Humankind wanted a monster, so I gave them a monster."

The fragment within Ellen shrank at his resignation. She couldn't lose this opening; she had to get under that star-freckled skin.

Which words would hit their mark?

Which statement would sway him?

What did he want to hear?

No, what did he *need* to hear? Not the Sundered Star, but Lambent, the slighted one who saw no other path but down.

Another volley of resentful magic, another wash of ruby to quell it. Ellen couldn't undo what her ancestors did, couldn't amend the past. However, she did carry their essence in the dust that made her—along with, no less, a piece of the sister who forsook him. Therefore, the best thing she could tell him was the truth.

"You're right!"

Circ recoiled as if struck. "What?"

"You're right, and I'm sorry. They shouldn't have maligned you for doing your job." Ellen planted her scythe in a divot to bolster herself against the buffeting winds, the effects of her injuries catching up faster than her healing factor could mend them. "You were protecting us from ourselves, and we turned you into something you weren't. But you're making those fabrications real by what you're doing now, and none of this is even really you. It's the Void!"

The tentacles slowed, eyeballs rotating inward to study the Warden when he fell silent, his cloud's undulations calming.

Now was Kyani's chance. Gesturing discreetly, she coaxed ashen vines from the cavern walls, and Ellen pressed on. "Don't you see how it's manipulating you? It preyed on you when you were alone and hurting. It's taking advantage of your misery to achieve its own goals. You're only doing its bidding!"

Vines snaked over the pool, the ceiling, closing in.

"It's not too late to fix this," Ellen said. "I can help you."

A low growl rumbled within the kraken, and Circ's frown twisted into a snarl. It was speaking to him. "S-shut up." The movement in the cavern accelerated again. He dug his nails into his scalp, hair spiking like hackles. "Shut up, shut up, *shut up, SHUT UP!*"

Fog and electric starlight exploded outward, vaporizing Kyani's vines in one fell swoop. The wave swept her into the wall, where tentacles pinned her by wing and limb, and Ellen went reeling toward the entrance, her plan going sideways with her.

"Cassi is the one who messed everything up. It's not my responsibility to fix what she broke," Circ spat over Kyani's cries as her wings were bent and twisted and pulled. "I wasted too many years trying to curry favor with her and with the likes of you. I won't go back to living in her shadow! She had her time, now it's my—"

The first notes of a piano tune trickled into the cavern and Circ froze, the tentacles relaxing their grip on Kyani. Across the pool, she and Ellen exchanged a glance.

The *Lustral Organ*—they'd found it!

Mammoth eyes squinted and blinked, pupils contracting and dilating and contracting and dilating. The kraken bellowed in rage, in agony, as the Warden clamped his hands over his ears. "This music . . . make it stop!"

Kyani wriggled out of the kraken's hold, dropping to the ground. The beast had turned its might on the ceiling, desperate to penetrate the bramble barrier and silence the source of the music. And with that rapturous melody filling the hollow, the girls snapped up their weapons and dove back into the fray.

CHAPTER SIXTY-NINE
JANUARY 7 | THE DOMAIN

THE VOID SPILLED INTO THE FORTRESS' TOWER. Tentacles slithered between pillars, grappling for purchase as smaller dog-like forms surged up the staircase in droves. The instant Iori started playing, any sense of self-preservation or calculating ability the creatures had went out the window.

They bowled Alexander over, willingly skewering themselves on his blade to get close to him. Glassen claws and gnashing teeth came within inches of his face, his neck—going for the jugular. Raking across his stomach, tearing into his legs.

A new metallic scent tinged the air, fresh and boiling from his veins. And while the Inkblots busied his sword and his magic, determined to keep his hands entirely too full, the kraken made a move for Iori.

Diverting power into his heel, Alexander booted one of the Inkblots in the chest, engulfing the whole pack in a fireball as tentacles lunged for the piano. With a fling of his arm and another lash of flame, he chased them off, then spun to the stragglers stalking towards him.

His lungs burned, steam wisping from the collar of his shirt—close to his limit.

More Inkblots yowled in the stairwell.

More tentacles plunged through the tower's opening.

The medley switched into a new segment, and they all juddered to a halt. Tentacles kinked and thrashed like over-pressured garden hoses, eyeballs twitching madly. Inkblots tossed their heads, screeching and arching their long bodies as the music coursed through them, causing them to shift from liquid to solid and numerous states in between. Hard spikes jutted from fluid flanks, crystalline jaws dribbled into puddles on the floor.

They couldn't maintain their forms.

The grave tune lured Alexander's focus from the enemy to the piano, where Iori swayed to the dips and rises in tempo. And from the tops of the organ pipes, vivid ribbons of violet flowed. They descended into the hole, cascading through the conduit and the hollow to pour over the mundane world.

His magic, his melody, an army of its own.

"It's working . . ." Alexander uttered in disbelief.

With tremendous effort, the Inkblots and the kraken pushed against the musical onslaught.

Alexander gave a deft twirl of his sword, another dose of pyric energy searing down the blade. "It's working. Keep playing!"

A bead of sweat streaked down Iori's temple, flashes of heat curling at his back—some so close they threatened to singe his tail—but his head remained bowed, fingers intent on the keys, and ears angled toward the instrument.

Concentrate. Don't get distracted.

If his attention drifted to the clash behind him, he'd have bigger problems than charred fur. To lose his rhythm would be to lose ground in the fight, which could cost them the war.

The kraken wrestled him in a battle of wills, each shift in his medley a dizzying blow. The Void leeched on emotion. Anger, fear, and misery made easy pickings, while positive feelings were a hazardous delicacy. Too much or without the proper preparations, and they would become poison—a poison which Iori fed the beast with every decisive keystroke.

He started to lose his footing and flipped into the next segment, hoisting his melody to an invigorating height. Percussive beats shuddered through his bones, fingertips long since numbed. He was growing weary, but his opponent was losing its resolve.

As the darkness heaved one final effort, Iori depressed the damper pedal, drawing ponderous notes long. Determination resonated within, a hammer driving the beast down, down, down. Its roars devolved into somnolent moans as it lost its grip on the Domain, on Elysian Tower, and retreated into the Cavity it had risen from.

Nearly there.

Once certain the kraken was in its cage, a firm strike of the chord threw the door shut, and Iori slammed the lock home by diving into the decrescendo. The music became quieter, became soft. With the beast contained, all that was left was to lull it to sleep and clean up the mess it made.

Adrenaline ebbed, urgency washed away in a cool sluice of relief. Iori's fingers danced lightly over the keys in the treble clef range, notes like raindrops plinking into a shallow pond. He slipped out of his trance, eyelids lifting to the thinning ribbons of his magic.

The chink of a crossguard butting against a scabbard's locket signaled the battle's end, and Alexander's bonfire crackle dropped to a simmer as he drew up to the piano bench. A few months ago, Iori wouldn't have been able to picture them like this—side by side, fighting together. Brothers in arms.

What better way to celebrate the culmination of their triumphs than with an uplifting climax?

The music's pulse soared again, Iori savoring the richness of the sacred instrument's tone. Then, sweeping his nails along the keyboard, he brought the medley to a close with a falling glissando. And as that last chord rang through the lustrous organ pipes, peace settled over the Domain.

Disconnected from the well of his power and without the kraken to protect him, Circ hadn't the means to defend himself. Vines sprung from the cavern walls, binding him in ropes of silver until he could no longer move. All he could do was squirm as his body, ravaged by the waning music, dripped ink into the Astral Pool.

The vines held him suspended above the water while he lobbed obscenities—the only projectiles left in his arsenal—at his captors. The words blended in his mouth, accumulating into a feeble cry before he finally went quiet.

From the landing, Ellen regarded the fallen Star not with pity, but sympathy. "Can you lift me up there?" she asked Kyani, who obligingly summoned more foliage. Ellen dismissed her scythe and climbed onto the escalator of ivy, silver leaves fluttering about her feet in the stir of the Club's magic.

Circ yanked harder against his restraints as she neared, a frightened animal backed into a corner. Nowhere to hide, nowhere to run. "Don't come any closer," he barked. "Get away from me! GET AWAY—"

He stilled when she took his face in her hands, his irises dimming to a cooler blue. The luminance faded from his moon-touched hair, and he gave a couple more tugs as her magic bled into his skin, efforts as frail as the voice that shivered out of him. "Wh—what are you doing?"

She hushed him. "It's okay. You'll feel better soon."

The Warden didn't have a brain for her to sift through. Instead, her magic permeated the chasmic cracks of his soul, which submerged her in a profound loneliness that made her feel as if her own had perished.

No images came to her, his memories already chewed to pieces by his corruption. But the emotions lingered, imprinted on his dust. His anguish, his jealousy, and the resentment it fostered. At the center of it all, the source of his internal strife: *love*. The thing he detested, yet yearned for so deeply that he would go to any length to obtain it—and obtain it he had, in a twisted form, from the Void itself. Love was the lure by which it claimed him, an offer he couldn't refuse.

This loneliness, this hurt, welled along his lash line in big crystalline beads that shimmered against the blacks of his sclera. They wobbled there, a shred of defiance in the twitch of his upper lip as he demanded to know, "Why are you crying?"

Ellen smiled past her own tears. "I can feel your pain."

One of those glistening beads tumbled over. She swept it away and it disintegrated into light, just as his corporeal form was beginning to—evaporating into scarlet with each beat of the Heart pulsing through him.

"I only wanted what she had," he sniveled. "If the roles had been reversed, I wouldn't have let anyone believe she was a monster. And if I couldn't stop them, I wouldn't have abandoned her. She had a *choice*." His brows pinched. "Why didn't she choose me?"

Ellen didn't have an answer for that. Whatever happened between him and his sister, it was history largely untold to her. But if she could live again, maybe someday, he could too. Another version of him in a future many centuries from now. The only consolation she could give this version was release.

"Rest now," she said, stroking his cheek.

His eyelids drifted shut and the vines went slack as the last of him turned to dust, depositing in Ellen's palms the protostar—safe and sound and shining gaily. With its myriad of shining panes, it resembled the fragment Hikaru had given her, only this was pale, pale blue.

Cradling it close, she signaled for Kyani to bring her down, and as she dismounted the ivy coils, her brother and Iori returned, primed for a fight. When met with calm, Alexander's gauntlet slid from the hilt of his sword.

"Is it over?"

"Almost," said Ellen. The group gathered around as she withdrew the Radiant Star's fragment from herself, holding it in one hand and the reclaimed protostar in the other. The remains of a deity once slain, and a developing entity with no plights to its name. Per the headmaster's instruction, she brought the pieces together, and they fused into a larger, brighter, more intricate object.

Ellen crouched at the edge of the pool and set it in the water. It bobbed there for a moment, then liquefied, setting the reservoir alight. And in those rippling waves, the protostar evolved.

Sharp corners smoothed into humanoid curves, glass becoming mottled gray flesh and elongating into night-dipped limbs ringed in silver. A collar encircled her neck, its thin decorative chains adorning her collarbones, and twilight fabric unfurled over her body alongside crimped tresses of silk. They spilled from her scalp, the same lunar white as the lashes beneath her icing sugar brows. Then those lashes fluttered open to reveal two perfect pearls inlaid with discs of moonstone, and the Radiant Star, reborn, sat up.

"Salutations," she said. "My name is Cass."

Automatically, awkwardly, lacking any grace whatsoever, Ellen replied with a baffled and breathless, "Hi." Should she introduce herself? "I'm Ellen. Ellen Amelia Jane."

Nobody else spoke, speechlessly captivated, letting Ellen marinate in her social anxiety alone—equal parts intimidated and awestruck by their divine company.

Cass' chortle was a pacifying force. "I know who you are." She emerged from the pool, wet hair and robes clinging to her lissome frame. She went to each of them in turn, first taking Ellen's and Kyani's hands in her delicate hold. "My *Bleeding Heart*, my *Verdant Club*." Next, she touched Alexander on the arm. "My *Blazing Diamond*." Last, she brought white-nailed fingers to Iori's chin. "My *Melodic Spade*."

He shied away from her.

If she took any offense, she didn't show it. She carried on past them, up the polished steps. "Come," she beckoned. "See the afterglow of your labors."

CHAPTER SEVENTY
JANUARY 7 | THE DOMAIN

OUTSIDE, THE ATMOSPHERE SPARKLED with an effervescence like champagne. Motes of light ascended to the stratosphere by the thousands, their weightless forms instilling a buoyancy in Iori that almost made him forget the floor beneath his feet.

The aqueducts were flowing again. Luminous waterfalls cascaded into the once-empty craters, burbling through the channels connecting them as the Keepers followed Cass out of the fortress. There was a discreet bubbliness to her pivoting steps, her arms outstretched for the heavens.

"There you are, little ones," she cooed at the motes with tempered glee, every action distinctly monitored. Controlled. "Don't be shy. There's plenty of room."

Ellen marveled at the sight, those big round eyes of hers brimming with starlight. "They're so pretty."

A couple of motes had taken an interest in her and her brother, drifting lazily around the pair of them. Alexander stiffened as if they might sting him. "What are they?"

"They are the essence of life," said Cass. "Their return here denotes the end of one cycle, and the beginning of another." She entwined her fingers at her back, neck craned to the sky. "The end of several, I should say. The annual migration ceased three millenniums ago when your predecessors sealed the realms, barring the deceased from passage. A necessary sacrifice, given the circumstances. Now the bridge has been reopened and the streams of the Aether freed, the cycle can begin anew."

Another mote found Iori. It whizzed by his right ear, the gold tassel and beads of his earring jangling when he flicked it. Clearly the mote didn't get the message, because it came straight back.

They didn't seem interested in Kyani.

She gasped softly. "Are you saying they're spirits?"

"Indeed."

Content to play with her spheroid tagalong, Ellen giggled at Iori's attempts to shoo his away. When non-violent methods failed, he resorted to swatting. "Would you mind telling your spirit pets to buzz off?"

A hint of amusement tinged Cass' rebuke. "Don't be rude. She's trying to say goodbye."

He frowned. "She?"

Cass snatched his hand mid-swat and turned it palm-up, then retreated a few paces while Ellen, Kyani, and Alexander observed. The twinkling mote settled like a snowflake on his fingertips, and as the protostar had in the pool, it melted into a new shape. Silvery and translucent, all light. A small but strong hand in his, extending into an arm, a body, and a head framed by layered shoulder-length hair that almost resembled his—

"Mama."

It was a reflex the way the word tumbled from his mouth, pushed forth on a swell of emotion, but when her features formed, painted in effulgent strokes, there was no doubt. Those kind narrow eyes, the patient curve of her lips . . .

Iori would know his mother's face anywhere.

She cupped his cheek and he fell to his knees, her touch warm and solid and impossibly real. By all manner of reasonable logic, she shouldn't have been here. This shouldn't have been possible.

Yet, here she was.

Sinking to the floor in front of him, she held him close, and he clung to her as if his existence depended on it. The tears came fast and free, a bittersweet runoff of rusted guilt and grief combined with pure childlike bliss.

"Aranai," he sobbed into her shoulder—*I'm sorry*—over and over until the words sounded as foreign as the day he learned them. Although she lacked a voice with which to respond, Iori felt her understanding in the circles she traced on his back. Felt forgiveness in every scrunch of his hair.

Remembering the others, he stole a glance at Ellen and Alexander by the fortress. The motes that had been flitting around them had transformed as well, into a pair of figures he recognized from the photos in their house.

Their parents, Adeleine and Percy Jane.

Most of Alexander's face was covered by his hand, a gold-studded mask beneath glazed eyes, and Ellen was about as weepy of a mess as Iori envisioned himself to be. They exchanged a quivering attempt at a smile before Percy smothered his daughter in a bear hug, pulling his son and the ghost of his wife in next. Bundling his family together.

A witness to the reunion, Kyani teetered on the brink of tears herself.

"I'm afraid they cannot stay," Cass informed them gently. Of course, why would a spirit be trying to say goodbye if it intended to hang around? "Their purpose here is no less important than yours. By making this journey, they will ensure that your world and its people can prosper by maintaining the Aether's flow."

Iori had sensed the conclusion coming, but it broke his heart all the same. Still hanging onto his mother's arms, he withdrew to take in every line and angle of her lucent visage, etching her image, this moment, onto his brain.

A memory wasn't enough.

He gulped down a sob. "I don't want you to go." He had so much to tell her, so many stories to share. About Cardplay, about Ellen, and even his and Alexander's vitriolic affairs. And there were things he wished to hear from her, too. Things about her life, things she'd promised to tell him when he was older.

Well, he was older now, and having spent almost as many years with her as without, he wasn't ready for her to leave.

Oh, sweet boy, he almost heard her say. She tapped her chest, sending ripples over her ghostly form, then rubbed that same spot on his. *I'll always be with you. In here.*

Just when he thought his tear ducts had run dry, more salty rivers leaked out. Squishing his face, his mother leaned in nose to nose and nuzzled him like she always did when he was upset, stopping only once she'd gotten a laugh out of him. Then she pulled him to his feet, dusted off his jacket, and fixed his mussed-up curls.

Time to go.

Iori, Ellen, and Alexander bid farewell to their loved ones, sharing one or two or maybe three "final" embraces before the spirits relinquished their humanoid forms. They reverted back to simple motes of light, and like fireflies, they rose into the air and winked out amidst the Aether's frothy clouds.

A breeze cooled the damp trails on Iori's skin, running from his cheeks to the collar of his shirt. Of all the things he imagined a trip to the Domain might bring, he never predicted this.

The Jane siblings held each other near, Alexander squeezing his sister's shoulder—trying to collect both himself and her at once.

Kyani folded her wings. "What happens now?"

Cass considered the four of them. "My greatest desire is to send you off to live the rest of your lives in peace, but I must ask you to uphold your duty as Keepers. Due to the damages caused by the Sundered Star's revolt, the products of malice will continue to invade your world. These influxes must be managed to preserve the balance, which also requires the Spade to revisit the Domain once a cycle to temper the Void."

Her moonstone eyes drifted from Iori to Ellen, then to the ground. "I must confess, my brother alone is not responsible for the calamity that befell the realms. I chose human souls to bear my Suits—not merely for lack of viable candidates, but for your sense of loyalty and ambition. Your will. And most prominently, your capacity to care. Despite this, I tried to dictate how much you gave to whom, and in doing so, I made a fatal error. Henceforth, I shall not meddle in your relations."

Ellen parted from her brother and fixed Cass with an unexpected ferocity that appeared to take even the Warden of the Domain by surprise. "I have a request."

"Whatever you wish."

"Whether Circ is reborn or a new Star replaces him, promise me you'll be there for them. Let them know they're loved," she said. "Don't let history repeat itself."

Cass studied her, this small human girl with heart enough to save the whole world, and nodded. "Your wish has been heard. Now, I release you to your realm. The four of you are welcome to visit whenever you please, but your comrades must be anticipating your return." Her emotional restraints loosened a notch, allowing her smile to broaden. "Do give my thanks to your headmaster for his faithful service."

With a wave, she reopened the portal, its light much less blinding here than it had been under the cover of mundane night. And the Keepers left the way they came. Spade, Heart,

Diamond, and Club stepped into the vortex hand-in-hand, and emerged into the sky pod.

Roots still clung to the tower, sagging now without copious amounts of ink to contain, and the points of glass sticking out of the window frame glinted as dawn peered over the horizon. Yellow rays stretched into periwinkle and indigo, a field of stars above and a sea of ruby below.

Hildegrand was in the midst of a mass cleansing. Particles churned in the splintered streets, from the tower grounds to the farthest limits of the boundary fence. Every surviving soul afflicted by Circ's blight—purified by Ellen's power.

Iori could compose a hundred songs, write a thousand poems attempting to capture the beauty of her magic, and all would pale in comparison to sight of it through naked eyes.

Alexander leaned out the window. "What a mess . . ."

"We'll worry about the cleanup later," said Kyani. "There are still people down there who need us." There would be casualties, civilians trapped and injured. Not to mention, thousands displaced. Careful not to tread on broken glass, she started towards the exit. Alexander followed, clambering onto the root bridge.

Ellen's hand slid into Iori's, and he squeezed her fingers assuringly. "Let's go home."

ACT V

FOUR OF A KIND

CHAPTER SEVENTY-ONE

WORDS COULDN'T PROPERLY DESCRIBE what they experienced that night. Or the entire first week of 2028, for that matter. Cardplay had set out to ring in the new year, and ended up ringing in a bold new era instead.

By spring, the city was thrumming with construction—a cooperative effort between crews both mundane and magical. Iori tried to appreciate the constant racket of jackhammers, dozers, and fluctuating kinetic hums as its own kind of music. The strident tune of recovery, of life persevering.

An acquired taste, maybe.

On the bright side, if they continued at their current pace, they'd be through the thick of it by winter. Hildegrand would always bear its scars, but as Tatiana liked to remind him, scars added character. It was just a shame that these had come at such a heavy cost.

And when the eighth anniversary of the Reemergence rolled around, even Queen Tamyl of Amberlye came to pay her respects—the greatest respect of all, perhaps, being her decision to liquidate the Wiseman Corporation and dismantle the boundary fence.

Hell itself pulling the heavens from the sky had worked wonders in changing the public's perspective on magic.

Good thing, too, since it was about to become an undeniable part of the world. With the streams of the Aether reinvigorating leylines across the globe, other wells had begun to refill, and already new Empowered were popping up in neighboring countries. As such, Cardplay had plans to expand.

There would be pushback, but Iori chose to believe with a little push from Ellen that society would adapt.

And if they didn't have enough crammed into May between her birthday, Reemergence Day, and an excruciatingly public graduation, they were capping the month off with a wedding, because *somebody* had popped a certain question on the battlefield. Not that Iori could complain when the bride-to-be herself had granted him the best seat in the house: the piano bench. A seat not without its risks, mind you. While the stakes riding on this performance weren't as high as his last, Naomi had promised him a few volts if he mucked it up.

It was her wedding, after all.

His fingers glided over the grand piano's familiar keys as she and Aryel joined hands on the altar in Jeidish and Berulsian attire, his notes the soundtrack to their happily-ever-after. Once vows had been sworn and rings exchanged, they moved to the courtyard for the reception, after which the wedding party absconded for a photo shoot. The vivacious Toi family and the Rizkas' more humble but abundant flock departed with them, leaving the other guests to mingle under the crystal ball lights.

Sipping a mocktail, Iori teetered in his chair, an arm draped over the back of Ellen's. He'd donned his special occasions outfit and left the shirt partially unbuttoned as advised, allowing the breeze to alleviate some of the humidity that had encapsulated him.

Ellen's blush pink florals complemented his darker ensemble. As did her white locks, her softly rouged cheeks, the regrowing nubs of her recently-shed antlers. Her everything, really. He'd hardly been able to take his eye off her.

Oh, to admire her with two. Sadly, he never did regain full sight in his right. His healing factor had kicked in too late to reverse the damage, so one would have to suffice.

They were seated at what had lovingly been dubbed the *cool kids'* table by Tatiana, who'd thrown on a flouncy halter top dress and let her twintails loose. "Think they'll give us free passes to that museum when it opens?" she asked, munching on a slice of lime.

"They don't really have any incentive to give us special treatment," said Soren, beside her in a tan vest and pants.

"Are you kidding? They wouldn't even *have* a collection if not for us. That's the incentive!"

The proposed *Museum of Magic History* would boast a selection of artifacts from the magical era, retrieved from the archives at the Wiseman Estate. Turned out they'd amassed quite a hoard. Art, literature, and maps to dig sites where more could be unearthed. They even had charts detailing where the leylines ran.

"Maybe I can convince Hikaru to give us an early peek." Ellen dangled the prospect like a carrot on a stick. The headmaster was already involved in the processing of the artifacts due to his intimate knowledge of magic history.

Soren fiddled with his cufflinks. "I wouldn't mind seeing stuff before it's behind glass and velvet ropes. Either way, it'll be cool to learn more about where our powers came from."

"Not as cool as getting to visit a literal goddess in her sky castle." Envy dripped from Tatiana's complaint, sour as the fruit she sucked on. "It's not fair you guys can beam yourselves up whenever you want. Next time you go, take pictures!"

Through the rails of his chair, Iori's tail flicked. "Somehow I doubt photography is permitted, if even possible." Could mundane technology transcend worldly barriers? "You'll see it yourself eventually. Kick the bucket before me and I'll send you off personally."

"Deal, but I'm still planning to outlive you."

They raised their glasses in a toast, and Iori took another swig from his, the fruity splash leaving an oddly satisfying bitterness at the back of his throat. Soren and Ellen regarded the pair of them with mild discontent.

"That's so morbid," Ellen said.

Iori shrugged. "Can't avoid the inevitable."

"You could do less to *encourage* it."

"So, are you two stuck in Hildegrand because of your Keeper duties?" Soren asked. "Or will you be able to travel once the ban's lifted?"

"If blightings keep trending downwards, I can go," replied Ellen. Cases had dropped to a couple per month, but increases could be expected at the end of each year. "Iori only needs to be here for the Waning. Neither of us have plans to move, though. I like this city. This is where I grew up, and everyone I know lives here. For now, anyway . . ." She wilted, and the absent patterns Iori had been drawing on her shoulder changed to soothing caresses. "Alexander might be going abroad."

Tatiana whipped the mutilated lime from her mouth. "Seriously? Where?"

"Ammolitia. The National Guard offered him a scholarship to Ulridge Academy."

"After they rejected him? The audacity!"

"He's considering it. Not to enlist in the army, but to become a magic instructor." At Cardplay's Ammolitian branch, set to open about the time he'd complete his courses. Ellen had been trying to keep her mind off it, so, naturally, it was all she'd been talking about. "But," she said with a decisive pat of her lap, "I'll be fine. I'll have company."

She tossed a glance at Iori, and he took the opportunity to steal a kiss. Then he planted another on her cheek, and generously applied several more along her jawline, rousing a giggle from her.

"Okay, cut it out. You're making me lovesick," Tatiana harrumphed, a month post-breakup and still feeling the pangs. Victory had pushed her to ask out Sabine Brozak. Unfortunately, they didn't last.

"Forgive me," Iori purred against Ellen's lips. "Just making up for lost time." He nabbed one final kiss before straightening in his seat. It wasn't as if they'd have any shortage of time together moving forward. They couldn't say whether their future would involve any official tying-of-the-knot, but for as far as they could see, they would be by each other's sides, and he wanted to make every moment count.

Every day, every hour, every heartbeat.

And if Iori were to grow old with anyone, it would be his privilege to grow old with her.

A deluge of magical hums announced the return of the wedding party. The bride, groom, Ikkei, Alexander, and Kyani—who'd been stolen for the shoot even though not in the party—picked their way over to the alleged cool kids' table.

Ikkei tugged at his tie, jacket discarded elsewhere. "What're you nerds yakking about?"

"Things and stuff," said Tatiana.

Ellen twisted to her brother in his gray suit. Its yellow pocket square accentuated the looping gold chain of his father's timepiece, freed from its display case. "I was just telling them about Ulridge."

"Ah, that."

"Yes, *that*." Ikkei flung an arm around Alexander. "Don't be a stranger if you go gallivanting off to Malachat, alright? I expect video calls. Daily."

"I will call you when I can call you. I doubt I'll have much time for socializing at the start." The certitude in his response implied he'd made up his mind, and apparently others had plans to flee the country too.

"Seems everyone's taking off the second they're able." Aryel nudged Naomi with his elbow. "We'll be honeymooning in Perlay, Oskar's going cruising in the Obsidi Isles. Even our formerly-caged canary is about to spread her wings."

That was news to Iori. "Where are you off to?"

"Peridita, to the town where my father grew up." Kyani readjusted the strap of her jacquard mini dress, acacia designs woven into the material. More patterns adorned her hands, frills and florals in red-brown henna. "I always promised I'd take him to see it again someday. It'd be nice to visit Saphir as well, if he's up for it. My mother never told me much about my heritage. I'd like to learn where my roots lead."

"Are you booking with an airline or flying private?"

She almost answered in earnest, almost fell for it. "Oh, you're joking."

"Yeah, he's kind of insufferable, actually," murmured Ellen with a touch of sympathy, to which Iori feigned hurt.

"Darling, you wound me."

The pocket watch's ticking grew louder when Alexander popped open the lid. "I was about to head out. Did you two want a ride, or are you making your own way home?"

The night had begun to wear on Iori, and Ellen's social batteries couldn't have much charge left either. "I'll go where you go," he said when she shot him an inquiring look, prompting her to accept her brother's offer. And the second Iori rose from his chair, the humidity that had been clinging to him rushed to his head.

He stumbled, Naomi catching him. "Whoa. You okay?"

A tipsy chortle rose from his throat. "Fine, fine. Just a bit lightheaded." He scrutinized the garnet liquid sloshing in his glass, then slanted a mischievous gaze over his shoulder. "Or maybe someone forgot to take the cock out of the mocktail."

He went to slug back the last mouthful, no sense wasting it, but Ellen pried the drink out of his grip before another drop could hit his tongue. "You've had enough."

Still holding him vertical, Naomi asked in her trademark Mom Friend voice, "Is this your first time?"

"Drinking? Yes. Operating under an influence? No."

Naomi instantly switched from Mom Friend to disgruntled bride and passed Iori to Ellen like an unwanted pet. "Take him before he causes trouble."

He tutted. "You have no appreciation for comedy."

Ellen linked arms with him. "We'll see how funny you are if you wake up hung-over tomorrow."

CHAPTER SEVENTY-TWO
JULY 16, 2028 | QASKIR, PERIDITA

"Morning. Or . . . afternoon to you, I guess."

Mirth fluffed Kyani's feathers. On her phone screen, Alexander situated himself at his dining table—an ocean away, but under the same sun. It shone warmly into the kitchen of her private Peridi homestay while weaker rays in Hildegrand bled through a summer shower, casting streaky flecks of light and shadow onto him. She'd propped him up on the sill while she pruned herbs in the window box.

He squinted into the camera. *"What do you have there?"*

"A few things." She plucked a selection of leaves from the mix. A pinewoody sprig that could almost be mistaken for an evergreen clipping, a cluster of sweet and fuzzy oval leaves, and a more pungent picking of flat lacy ones. "We've got some rosemary, marjoram, and I'll be using this cilantro for supper."

Alexander made a face at the latter, genetically incapable of experiencing its full range of flavor. All he tasted was soap.

Lastly, Kyani held up a long stem with lanceolate leaflets. "And this here is licorice." One of the country's most popular exports. "I'm going to use it to make tea."

The hosts allowed guests to harvest their herbs in moderation for cooking. By no means did Kyani consider herself a cook, but she'd taken a few pointers from Ikkei, and her attempts had yielded satisfactory meals thus far. Granted, she hadn't tried anything too adventurous yet.

"Can't keep the green thumb out of the garden, can you?" Alexander teased. The smell of fresh soil, the language of plants . . . she couldn't resist the way nature called to her. *"Is that difficult—making the tea?"*

"It'll be one of the easier recipes I've made. The hardest part will be digging out the roots." Retrieving her clippers, she snipped off a dying stalk of rosemary, its thin pointed leaves brittle and brown. "I could've bought some at the market, but I wanted to make it myself. For Baba. It used to be our once-a-month splurge, and he always swore homegrown was better."

"You'll have to let me know how it goes. How is your dad handling everything?"

Kyani glanced into the living room. Jabari had parked his wheelchair in the sunshine pooling inside the arched patio exit. It lapped at his legs, his arms upturned to soak it all up. Outside, palm fronds rustled in the gale rolling off the sea.

She smiled softly. "He's right at home."

Three days into their stay, and he looked as if he'd lived here his whole life. He would probably be content to live out the rest of it here, too. Having seen Peridita for herself at last, Kyani understood why he'd yearned to come back, and why he wished he'd never left. The desert blooms were more brilliant than cameras could capture, the community more vibrant than stories could tell. She also understood the heat she'd once fibbed about over brunch. Bontago's arid embrace.

"This place is good for him. Being out of the care home in general is, I think. I wish we could stay longer." As not to overwhelm him on his first trip since the stroke, she'd trimmed her initially ambitious trip of five weeks across two countries to a couple in Peridita.

Saphir could wait. This was more important.

So before too long, they would be homebound to Hildegrand—Kyani to her dorm at Cardplay Headquarters, and her father to his room at Woodridge.

"*Y'know,*" mused Alexander, his image fuzzing briefly before sharpening again, "*flights to Peridita are only half as long from Malachat. And about a third of the cost.*"

Kyani paused as she went to clip another stem. Alexander was scratching his head, gaze averted. The rain had almost passed. "Are you implying I should move to Malachat?"

"*Maybe. Eventually. Just thinking how you couldn't wait to get out of here and it doesn't sound like you want to come back. If you don't have any real ties to Hildegrand, you could start fresh somewhere new.*"

Her father wasn't much of a tie. If she moved, so would he. The rest of her family either had no idea she existed or didn't care to acknowledge that she did, and none of them were in Amberlye anyway. Part of her reason for staying was for the friends she'd made, because she didn't fancy starting from scratch in a sea of strangers.

But in Malachat, she would have Alexander, who was arguably her second strongest tie to anywhere.

"What about my Joker duties?"

"*You could transfer to the Ammolitian branch when it opens.*"

"It's so expensive, though." The last thing she needed was to be thrown into financial despair again.

Alexander put his hands together. "*Hear me out,*" he said. "*I'm going to be renting when I first get there, but what if, down the road, we went in on a house together? Like, a duplex or something, so we could still have our own space.*"

Kyani's clippers squeaked shut. "You want me to move with you?"

"Yeah, I like having you around. And if we're housemates, we can split the bills. It'd be cheaper in the long run. I could also drive you and your dad wherever you need to go, and if I'm busy, public transport in Malachat is said to be the best. Gorgeous city, too. Lots of old architecture and green spaces. Shouldn't be hard to find a place with a garden."

Alexander's excitement was a contained and subtle display. Sparks in his eyes and he'd start talking faster, gesticulations becoming smaller and tighter and closer to the chest. Excited or otherwise, he wasn't typically a rash person. A proposition of this magnitude would have required a great deal of thought. About her, their relationship, and how their independent yet entwined lives would mesh. Knowing that warmed her to the idea.

"That sounds nice," she agreed.

"Really?"

"Really."

Alexander beamed. *"Great! Okay. We can talk about it more when you get back."* New voices filtered in. He mouthed something to his sister, then looked to the camera again. *"On that note, we've gotta get to work. Enjoy your evening."*

They exchanged goodbyes, Alexander sliding in one last titter of a "bye" before tapping the button to hang up.

Kyani's eyes drifted to the leaves fluttering in the window box, the brown clippings on the sill. If someone had told her a year ago that this was where her life would lead, she wouldn't have believed it. Sometimes she still couldn't, even now.

This was the beginning of a new story, and she couldn't wait to see where the pages would take her.

CHAPTER SEVENTY-THREE
AUGUST 22, 2028 | OTSWELL, ATTIKA

Weeks ticked by and soon enough, too soon for Ellen's liking, they loaded her brother's belongings into the masters' car and hit the road to Otswell Airport.

After a night of tossing and turning, the pre-dawn wakeup had Iori dozing off shortly after they left. Ellen let him snooze through the outlying towns and cliffs, their rocky faces like choppy pallet knife swipes in the twilight, but roused him as the sun rose. He wouldn't want to miss this.

Gold spilled over the valleys of northwestern Attika, and the smell of sweet country grass poured into the open windows. Iori snaked an arm out, eyes closed as the wind slid between his fingers, savoring his first true taste of freedom since the dismantling of the fence.

Shame the tranquility couldn't last.

After a brief stop to refuel at the halfway mark, Iori became restless, the shrinking distance between him and the airport squashing him like a spring. And an antsy Iori meant hell for Alexander, whose shorter-than-usual fuse hinted at nerves squirreled away. Neither could move or speak without setting the other off until Elizabeth commanded silence and Iori retreated into his headphones.

Open countryside soon yielded to cityscape, rural quiet to crossing alarms and car horns. Untrusting of the GPS,

Hikaru brought out the paper map, and several wrong turns and seemingly endless roundabouts later, they arrived at their destination.

Mossy stone figures guarded the airport's entrance. Ellen had a collection of photos with them, one snapped each time she'd come—for her father's business trips, her mother's conferences, and family vacations. She gathered Iori, her brother, and the masters in for a new addition before unloading the car under the sweltering August sun.

And that wasn't the only thing beating down on them.

"People are looking," Iori murmured uneasily.

"People are always looking." Alexander hefted his suitcase out of the trunk, bedecked in patches from prior travels. He motioned to Iori, himself, and Ellen—eared and tailed, scaled, and antlered. "You stand out, I stand out, she stands out. Forget being a sore thumb, we're a whole fucking hand that got crushed in a drawer."

Not to mention Hikaru's facial scars, only slightly less noticeable without the blackness woven through them.

"You'd better watch that mouth of yours with your instructors," warned Elizabeth, "otherwise you're going to find yourself at the short end of a very sharp stick."

Alexander rolled his eyes. "I know how to turn on a filter."

His wheeled carry-on case clattered as Hikaru set it on the pavement. "Is this really all you need?"

He'd only packed two—one for clothes, one for electronics and bare necessities. "For the hundredth time, *yes*. I'll buy stuff when I need it. Now, would you please stop fussing?"

There was a breathlessness in his plea that implied he was appreciative of their care, even if overwhelmed by it. That didn't stop Ellen from snatching his suitcase away from him, though, and she delighted in the defeated flop of his hand. Denying help from his baby sister would just be cruel.

Elizabeth went to park while the rest of them headed for the check-in counter. Once Alexander had traded his suitcase for a boarding pass, they navigated to the food court. Iori refused everything except mineral water and a stolen bite of Ellen's brownie, which lost its appeal the second she offered it to him. Apparently, the crime tasted sweeter.

By the time Elizabeth rejoined them, they'd finished their lunch, and Alexander was browsing apartments on his phone. Ellen hunched beside him, elbows resting on the little round table as he swiped through the listings.

"Look at this." He gestured sharply at the ultra modern studio apartment on-screen. "Everything in walking distance costs as much as a townhouse here."

"You could get a roommate," said Ellen.

That got a snigger out of Iori. "Your brother's too anal for any old roommate." Before Alexander's glower could escalate, he suggested, "Why don't you just stay on campus until Oto gets there? Saves money and hassle."

"Because student housing is the opposite of appealing and she won't be moving for another year or two." That would depend on how quickly regulations loosened. Emigration was still an issue for Empowered unless they were granted special permissions like Alexander. "Ugh, whatever." He pocketed his phone. "Classes don't start till next month. I'll shop around while I'm getting acclimated."

"I do still have those connections at the academy," reminded Elizabeth, shaking an extra packet of sugar into her coffee. "They could set you up somewhere real nice."

"Listen, I appreciate it, but—"

"—you'd rather do it on your own. I get it. Who knows, you might actually like student housing." She was about to elaborate when a chime sounded over the intercom. They all paused to listen to the announcement resounding through the lofty building.

"Good afternoon. This is the boarding call for flight ten-seventeen to Malachat. Boarding call for flight ten-seventeen. All passengers, please proceed to Gate Two. Thank you."

Other travelers in the food court began to pack up their meals, their drinks, and gather their luggage.

"That would be me." Somewhat hesitantly, Alexander pushed up from the table, the rest of them rising too.

Hikaru and Elizabeth imparted some last-minute wisdom on him, their words lost to Ellen as the reality sunk in that her big brother was actually leaving. After today, he'd be thousands of kilometers away. His room would become unoccupied space, shared meals would be reserved for holidays, and there would be no more background bickering while she tended to her chores.

With that swirling in her mind, she couldn't suppress the waterworks when her turn came to bid farewell.

"Hey," said Alexander with a quaver of amusement. "You told me you weren't going to cry."

"I said I'd try." She latched onto him. All spruced up to meet the officials in Malachat, and here she went staining his pressed white shirt with tears.

She really had tried to hold them in.

"I'll be back for the solstice—that's four months from now. Four months is nothing. Until then, you can call or text whenever you want, even if it's just to say 'hi.' Got it?" Her cheek rubbed his vest in a meek nod and he kissed the top of her head. "I love you."

She sniffled. "Love you, too."

Next in line was Iori, his dark jeans and black dress shirt a contrast to Alexander's lighter shades. He extended his hand for a shake. "Fly safe."

For a moment, it seemed Alexander might snub the gesture. Then, in a move that defied all expectations, he pulled Iori into his firm embrace. For their many clashes to amount to this, it was no wonder Iori had gone rigid.

"Take care of her for me," murmured Alexander.

Whatever ice remained between them melted, the corners of Iori's lips lifting as his ears sank lower. "If she'll let me." His hands settled on Alexander's back, and Ellen thought it funny how flimsy he looked enveloped by her brother's sturdier form.

"And, um. Good luck with your family thing," Alexander added as they parted.

Iori rubbed his neck. "Yeah . . . thanks."

Taking his carry-on from Hikaru, Alexander retreated toward the escalators. One step, two, reluctant to turn. "I'll call you guys when I land," he said, and with a wave, he set off to commence the next chapter of his life, new experiences and new people and new places ahead.

With Alexander out of sight, they moved to the window overlooking the tarmac. Squat tug vehicles buzzed about, towing luggage carts below. Flight 1017 sat a couple of gates down, its tail painted with streamers in Ammolitian colors.

Once all passengers were aboard, the enormous aircraft taxied onto the runway. As it picked up speed, engines roaring, so too did Ellen's heart, quicker and harder, threatening to bust right out of her chest. Then the jet's wheels lifted off the ground, and she let out a breath as it carried her brother skyward.

Onward and upward—not without her, merely apart.

Her brother wasn't the only one taking big steps today. Not long after his departure, a flight from Jeida appeared on the arrivals screen, and Iori nearly bolted then and there. After putting the breathing exercise Dr. Bristol taught him into practice, Ellen managed to coax him downstairs whilst the masters perused the shops.

They waited outside the baggage claim, watching as passengers trickled down the escalator at the far end. A thin veil of a waterfall shimmered upon the stonework wall behind them, OTSWELL spelled out in its inlaid gold letters.

Shortly into the new year, with news of Cardplay dominating basically every media outlet in existence, Hikaru had sent Iori's musical message in a bottle to his family. Their reply came a day later, initiating a back and forth over email with the headmaster acting as an intermediary—the two parties too nervous to speak directly.

Until finally, those emails led to a phone call.

Following that tearful exchange, their communications became more regular, and when both were good and ready, they decided to meet.

They hadn't interacted face-to-face yet, and Iori had declined to exchange photos. He'd been adamant about seeing them in the flesh, fearful that a full virtual reunion might push him to renege on the idea and keep them at arm's length. Ellen didn't totally understand that logic, but whatever made him comfortable, she would support.

Except *comfortable* wasn't how she would describe him now. His ears were pinned to his scalp, tail hugging his thigh, and Ellen's fingers were squished in his grip.

"Hey, Iori . . ."

"Mm?"

"I can't feel my hand."

His gaze darted to his whitened knuckles, her bright pink digits trapped within. Uttering a hasty apology, he released her and wiped his clammy palm on his pantleg.

Ellen retook his hand in her own, his nail polish picked to pieces over the course of the day. "It's going to be fine. You've been talking to them for weeks. What's there to worry about?"

"Them spending an hour with me in person and realizing they made a mistake." His throat bobbed past a hard swallow. "We've been cutting out these bite-sized moments. We haven't even had any deep conversations yet. They're going to see me and realize I'm not the kid they knew. That I've changed. That this space between us where my mother used to be is unfillable and I'm just a painful reminder of what they—"

"Stop." Ellen reached up and pulled his focus from the revolving luggage carousels. "They are going to *love you*. Even if it's only half as much as I do, it'll be plenty."

"What if it's only a third? Or an eighth?"

His attention crept toward the growing crowds and she tugged it straight back to her, their eyes locking buoyant scarlet to deep and tremulous crimson. "A fraction of infinity is still infinity. Look at it this way: you get to meet each other all over again. I think there's something special about that. Don't you?"

Conflict tugged at Iori's mouth, torn between believing her or the cynical goblin squatting in his brain. Thankfully, it didn't have the chance to talk him out of it.

Out the corner of her vision, Ellen noticed a ripple in the stream of passengers. They eddied around a pair of East Coraldan women who'd stalled in the entrance to the baggage claim. Strands of black hair framed the middle-aged one's chary oval face, the rest secured in a bun with flowery pins that matched her blouse. The other was of spindly yet spry demeanor, dressed in a knee-length cardigan and denim capris. Her short salt and pepper 'do couldn't seem to decide where it wanted to go.

Both carried a certain gravity in their posture, emotions turbulent in their umber eyes—a dusty raw shade in the younger, and a burnt reddish hue in the older. And in Iori's, Ellen saw recognition churn at the sight of them.

His aunt Hanako and grandmother Omi.

Ellen gave him an encouraging nudge in their direction. Aunt and nephew met halfway, partner and grandmother hanging back to give them room. They studied one another, Hanako worrying at the strap of her purse as Iori made a visible effort not to further ravage his nails.

"You look so much like her," said Hanako in her level accent, a flicker of a smile on her lips.

Iori's voice thickened around a coy laugh. "So do you."

It was stiff and awkward, neither of them quite sure how to behave. But there was a familiarity and a warmth and a want between them, two halves of a string gradually pulling them closer. The tie Iori had severed.

Head inclined toward Ellen, Omi moved in and made an attempt to allay the tension. "This must be the Amethistian girlfriend you were telling us about."

Excitedly, Ellen shuffled over in her platform flip-flops and gave the women a polite bow. From there, the conversation eased, the frayed ends of that cut tie intertwining as they recounted their journeys and laughed about mishaps along the way. In time, Ellen was confident it would bind them together again—reunited by the same force that once drove them apart.

Magic.

It's hard to believe that, not so long ago, magic was thought to be a myth. The thing about myths, though, is that many are born from truths, and when real magic returned, wreaking havoc in the darkness that followed, it lost its splendor in the eyes of its beholders.

But now the shadows have been chased away, humankind can embrace this power for what it really is. For the miracles it can work, the light it can bring. It's the essence of love and hope, the very fabric of the lives we lead. And perhaps most importantly . . .

Magic is what we're made of.

♠ ♥ THE END ♦ ♣

APPENDIX

MEET THE CAST

IORI RYONE *(ee-o-ree ryo-nay)*
18 | he/him | 5'10" | Jeidish | pansexual | Acoustic Empowered. Keeper of the Spade. Light honey-toned complexion. Crimson irises with black sclera in his right eye. Short, tousled, jet black hair with cat ears and a tail the same color. Can often be found wearing a leather jacket, jeans, and sleeveless turtleneck shirts.

ELLEN AMELIA JANE *(eh-len uh-mee-lee-uh jayn)*
17 | she/her | 5'6" | Thulian-Amethistian | gray-asexual | Psychosomatic Empowered. Joker, Third Class. Has long, wavy white hair, porcelain skin with rosy cheeks, scarlet eyes, and a penchant for skirts and leggings.

ALEXANDER JANE *(a-lek-san-der jayn)*
20 | he/him | 5'11" | Thulian-Amethistian | aromantic bisexual | Pyric Empowered. Joker, First Class. Fair-skinned. Jaw-length wavy white hair with frosty lashes and brows to match. Yellow-brown eyes. Alabaster scales on cheekbones, neck, shoulders, arms, hips, and thighs. Has a scar on his right cheek and tends to dress in business casual attire.

KYANI OTO *(kee-yah-nee oh-to)*
23 | she/her | 5'8" | Peridi-Saphric | demiromantic demisexual | Botanic Empowered. Keeper of the Club. Tawny-beige skin, lavender eyes. Hair styled in a short and feathery black bob. Has a pair of small raven wings and black scales on her shins. Favors dresses and shawls, and prefers to walk barefoot.

NOTABLE SUPPORTING CAST

TATIANA KOSTA (*tah-tee-ah-na kah-stuh*)
19 | she/her | Canilian-Amethistian | lesbian | Pneumatic Empowered. Joker, Third Class. Freckled medium-tan complexion. Dark purple eyes. Spiky, shoulder-length black hair, usually drawn up into twintails. Tatiana is a self-proclaimed love guru and rambunctious best friend to Ellen.

SOREN KABR (*sor-ren kay-burr*)
16 | he/him | Amethistian | transgender | Photic Empowered. Joker, Third Class. Sandy blond hair, pale complexion. Brown eyes with baby blue centers. Timid disposition, steadfastly loyal. Turned the duo of Tatiana and Ellen into a tight-knit trio upon joining Cardplay.

IKKEI TOI (*ee-kay toy*)
26 | he/him | Jeidish | gay | Magnetic Empowered. Joker, First Class. Blue-dyed faux hawk. Brawny. Brown eyes. Tall, muscular build. Ikkei is a close friend and brotherly figure to Alexander, the pair having trained together since Cardplay's first year in operation.

NAOMI TOI (*na-oh-mee toy*)
26 | she/her | Jeidish | polyamorous pansexual | Electric Empowered. Joker, First Class. Athletic build. Long, silky black hair with straight-cut bangs. Golden eyes. Brutally honest, bossy but owns it. Friend and somewhat of an older sister figure to Alexander.

ARYEL RIZKA (*ah-ree-ell reez-kuh*)
25 | he/him | Berulsian | bisexual | Cryogenic Empowered. Joker, First Class. Shaggy yellow-blond hair, blue eyes. Known for his melodramatic tendencies, particularly when it comes to displaying his love for his girlfriend, Naomi Toi.

HIKARU RITSUO *(hee-kah-roo reet-soo-oh)*
44 | he/him | Jeidish-Amethistian | Headmaster of Cardplay, former officer of the Hildegrand Police Department. In a common law marriage with Elizabeth Howard. Hazel eyes, curly copper hair often tied into a low ponytail. Favors old-fashioned attire and wears rectangular glasses.

ELIZABETH HOWARD *(eh-lihz-uh-beth how-werd)*
47 | she/her | Amethistian | Battlemaster, former soldier and drill sergeant of the National Guard, and former officer of the Hildegrand Police Department. Wavy caramel-colored hair, olive eyes. Wears oval glasses.

OSKAR TREY *(oss-kerr tray)*
Late 30s | he/him | Aquatic Empowered. Joker, First Class. Rotund build, brown skin, shaved scalp. Heavily tattooed. Former firefighter who fought in the Reemergence alongside Sabaa Faizan, Yusuf Budak, Iris Makri, and the National Guard. Earned nickname "the Blowfish" from his ability to spew a pressure washer-like stream of water from his mouth.

SIMONE FORNELL *(sih-mohn for-nell)*
Mid 50s | she/her | Somatic Empowered, X-ray vision. Chief physician at Cardplay. Generally mild-mannered but can be snappish. Dark brown skin with long hair styled into bleach-bond twists, rarely seen without her white lab coat.

ARYNNE BRISTOL *(a-rin brih-stuhl)*
Early 60s | she/her | Unempowered. Therapist. A short woman of patient demeanor with close-shorn black hair and cool ebony skin. Typically dresses in business casual attire with large jewelry.

CIRC *(serk)*
Unknown age | he/him | 5'5" | The Sundered Star, former Warden of the Void. Bears the appearance of a slender adolescent boy with mottled gray skin, softly spiked luminous white hair, and bright blue irises against jet black sclera. He wears an assortment of silver jewelry and a pair of harem-style blue-black pants.

CHARLES WISEMAN *(char-uhlz wise-min)*
Mid 50s | he/him | Founder of the Wiseman Corporation. A tall and imposing white man with sharp features, platinum blond hair, and pale violet eyes who primarily wears ivory-colored formal attire.

CARDAN MCCONNELL *(car-din muh-kah-nuhl)*
28 | he/him | Fluorantine | Kinetic Empowered, teleporter. Blackjack Player. A green-eyed redheaded white man of average build with a ruddy, freckled complexion.

SYBIL ENGSTROM *(sih-bul ing-struhm)*
23 | she/her | Metamorphic Empowered, optical enhancement (thermal vision). Blackjack Player, previously expelled from Cardplay. Short and wiry build. Frizzy, dark brown hair dyed with streaks of red. Has several piercings and tattoos.

VALERIE RENARD *(va-ler-ree re-narrd)*
Late 40s | she/her | Unempowered. Former Vice President of the Wiseman Corporation. A tall shapely woman with long, wavy blond hair, plump lips, and deep blue eyes.

GLOSSARY

NOTABLE LOCATIONS

Amberlye: the continent in which the story is set, located entirely in the northern and western hemisphere. The country *Amethis* occupies its westernmost region, wherein the city of Hildegrand resides in a province called *Attika*.

Ammolitia: a continent located primarily in the northern and partially in the eastern hemisphere. The country *Thulia* occupies its northern region, *Berul* the east, and *Canilia* the south. *Malachat*, the country Ulridge Royal Military Academy resides in, occupies the west.

Coralda: a continent located in the eastern hemisphere which includes the country *Jeida* on its eastern coast and *Saphir* in its southeastern region.

Peridita: a transcontinental country that spans between the continents of *Bontago* and *Coralda*.

The Mundane World: Earth. The overworld human beings inhabit, located on a plane between the Domain and the Void.

The Domain: the origin of pure magic, a heavenly realm believed to exist in an unseen plane in the celestial sphere

The Void: the underworld to which wickedness flows, located on a plane of existence beneath the mundane world.

Dreamscape: a mental landscape accessible by Keepers.

MAGIC-RELATED TERMS

Kinetic: a category of magic encompassing abilities related to the manipulation of energy and matter *(i.e., pyric, the manipulation of fire; magnetic, the manipulation of metals; photic, the manipulation of light, etc)*.

Systemic: a category of magic encompassing abilities related to the alteration and manipulation of the body *(i.e., psychologic, the manipulation of mind; psychosomatic, the manipulation of mind and body. Also includes bodily enhancements)*.

Empowered: people who have developed magical abilities

Suit: a unique and powerful form of magic bestowed upon a chosen user that grants abilities above and beyond those of regular Empowered.

Keeper: a person chosen to bear one of the four Suits.

Ink: a product of human malice named for its ink-like color and consistency.

Inkblot: animalistic creatures made of ink and born from malice, generally spawned from a human host.

Blight: A soul-corroding disease contracted either by exposure to toxic Void emissions or via Inkblot bite/scratch

Blighted: people afflicted with blight.

Inkwraith: a human being transformed into a monster, resultant of inborn or forced corruption.

THANKS FOR READING!

Thank you so much for reading *Bleeding Heart*! If you enjoyed this book (or even if you didn't), I hope you'll consider leaving a rating or a review. Word of mouth is an author's best friend, and reviews can help other readers decide whether to invest their time and money in a book. So whether they be favorable or unfavorable, a few words or stars would be hugely appreciated!

ACKNOWLEDGEMENTS

I have never fought with a book as much as I fought with *Bleeding Heart*. From the very first line to the very last, this story challenged me. But as many writers know, the struggle is worth it, because we come out stronger on the other side.

Of course, what made my craft stronger still and made the process all the more enjoyable despite its ups and downs was the friends who joined me for the ride!

So, shout-out to the brave and curious folks who read my 30,000-word chaos summary prior to drafting and assured me the path I was about to head down wouldn't lead to an a trash-tastic disaster.

Huge thanks to my alpha and beta readers (Lexi Biondi, Rebecca Riesberry, E.M. Wright, Cara Nox, Rita A. Rubin, Denise O. Eaton, Monica Gribouski, T.A. Hernandez, Tylor E. Kunkle, Juliana Rose Pagador, Monica Bee, Blake Farron, Rainbowlover25, Mary Lynne Gibbs, Charlotte Hayward, J. Breeden, TK Farias) for helping me whip this baby into shape, and for being an endless source of encouragement and motivation and laughs along the way.

I also want to give credit to Tegan Kilpatrick for Circ's spooky little song. They wrote it for him years ago when the project was still very new, and I'm glad I got to include it!

And as always, heaps of gratitude to everyone who has supported me and my stories. I may write for myself first and foremost, but being able to share my worlds and characters with others is rewarding beyond words, and they wouldn't make it into nearly as many hands without you.

Thank you <3

ABOUT THE AUTHOR

Brittany M. Willows is a queer author and digital artist from Ontario, Canada. Inspired by video games and the stories they told, she began building her own fictional universes at a young age and has no intention of stopping any time soon. When she's not writing about post-apocalyptic wastelands, wild magic, or people gallivanting through the stars, she can be found hunched over a tablet drawing the very same things.

To keep up with the latest news regarding current and future stories, and to find out more about Brittany or delve deeper into the worlds she has created, check out the links below! She can also be contacted directly via these platforms.

A world guide, character guide, playlist, and art gallery for the Cardplay Duology can be found on the author's website.

Twitter: twitter.com/BMWillows
Instagram: instagram.com/brittanymwillows/
Website: brittanymwillows.wordpress.com
Facebook: facebook.com/BrittanyMWillows

Want to support Brittany? Purchase and rate/review her books, drop her a tip on Ko-Fi, or become a patron on Patreon to gain access to some exclusive goodies + a backlog of older content!

Ko-fi: ko-fi.com/brinanners0467
Patreon: patreon.com/BrittanyMWillows
Goodreads: goodreads.com/author/Brittany_M_Willows
Amazon: amazon.com/~/e/B00GLD94RK